# HE TURNED

*The shelter was still there, and behind it the row of spaceships—not like chalk marks on a tally board now, but like odd relics that didn't belong there in the thick green grass... Five ships instead of four.*

*—from "The Highest Mountain."*

## ABOUT BRYCE WALTON...

*American born Bryce Walton was one of the most prolific short story and novelette science fiction writers of the 1950s. He is probably best remembered for his 1952 novel, "Sons of the Ocean Deep," which was part of the heralded John C. Winston sci-fi hardback series of the 1950s and 1960s. His work appeared in all the top science fiction magazines of the day, including "Galaxy," "Fantastic Universe," "If," "Planet Stories," and many others. Walton was born in Blythedale, Missouri in 1918. He passed away in 1988. Here is a fine collection of fifteen of his most memorable stories...*

# TABLE OF CONTENTS

MASTERS OF SCIENCE FICTION Vol. 1

# BRYCE WALTON:
## *"THE HIGHEST MOUNTAIN" and*
## *Other Tales*

ARMCHAIR FICTION & MUSIC
PO Box 4369, Medford, Oregon 97504

The original text of these stories first appeared in *Science Fiction Quarterly, Imagination, Original Science Fiction, Planet Stories, Future Science Fiction, Galaxy, Fantastic Universe, Orbit,* and *Space Science Fiction.*

Cover suggests a scene from *The Highest Mountain*

*For more information about Armchair Books and products, visit our website at…*

**www.armchairfiction.com**

*Or email us at…*

**armchairfiction@yahoo.com**

# The Highest Mountain

*First one up this tallest summit in the Solar System was a rotten egg…a very rotten egg!*

BRUCE heard their feet on the gravel outside and got up reluctantly to open the door for them. He'd been reading some of Byron's poems he'd sneaked aboard the ship; after that he had been on the point of dozing off, and now one of those strangely realistic dreams would have to be postponed for a while. Funny, those dreams. There were faces in them of human beings, or of ghosts, and other forms that weren't human at all, but seemed real and alive—except that they were also just parts of a last unconscious desire to escape death. Maybe that was it.

" 'Oh that my young life were a lasting dream, my spirit not awakening till the beam of all eternity should bring the morrow,' " Bruce said. He smiled without feeling much of anything and added, "Thanks, Mr. Poe."

Jacobs and Anhauser stood outside. The icy wind cut through and into Bruce, but he didn't seem to notice. Anhauser's bulk loomed even larger in the special cold-resisting suiting. Jacobs' thin face frowned slyly at Bruce.

"Come on in, boys, and get warm," Bruce invited.

"Hey, poet, you're still here!" Anhauser said, looking astonished.

"We thought you'd be running off somewhere," Jacobs said.

Bruce reached for the suit on its hook, started climbing into it. "Where?" he asked. "Mars looks alike wherever you go. Where did you think I'd be running to?"

"Any place just so it was away from here and us," Anhauser said.

"I don't have to do that. You are going away from me. That takes care of that, doesn't it?"

"Ah, come on, get the hell out of there," Jacobs said. He pulled the revolver from its holster and pointed it at Bruce. "We got to get some sleep. We're starting up that mountain at five in the morning."

"I know," Bruce said. "I'll be glad to see you climb the mountain."

Outside, in the weird light of the double moons, Bruce looked up at the gigantic overhang of the mountain. It was unbelievable. The mountain didn't seem to belong here. He'd thought so when they'd first hit Mars eight months back and discovered the other four rockets that had never got back to Earth—all lying side by side under the mountain's shadow, like little white chalk marks on a tallyboard.

They'd estimated its height at over 45,000 feet, which was a lot higher than any mountain on Earth. Yet Mars was much older, geologically. The entire face of the planet was smoothed into soft, undulating red hills by erosion. And there in the middle of barren nothingness rose that one incredible mountain. On certain nights when the stars were right, it had seemed to Bruce as though it were pointing an accusing finger at Earth—or a warning one.

WITH Jacobs and Anhauser and the remainder of the crew of the ship, *Mars V*, seven judges sat in a semi-circle and Bruce stood there in front of them for the inquest.

In the middle of the half-moon of inquisition, with his long legs stretched out and his hands folded on his belly, sat Captain Terrence. His uniform was black. On his arm was the silver fist insignia of the Conqueror Corps. Marsha Rennels sat on the extreme right and now there was no emotion at all on her trim neat face.

He remembered her as she had been years ago, but at the moment he wasn't looking very hard to see anything on her face. It was too late. They had gotten her young and it was too late.

Terrence's big, square face frowned a little. Bruce was aware suddenly of the sound of the bleak, never-ending wind against the plastilene shelter. He remembered the strange misty shapes that had come to him in his dreams, the voices that had called to him, and how disappointed he had been when he woke from them.

"This is a mere formality," Terrence finally said, "since we all know you killed Lieutenant Doran a few hours ago. Marsha saw you kill him. Whatever you say goes on the record, of course."

"For whom?" Bruce asked.

"What kind of question is that? For the authorities on Earth when we get back."

"When you get back? Like the crews of those other four ships out there?" Bruce laughed without much humor.

Terrence rubbed a palm across his lips, dropped the hand quickly again to his belly. "You want to make a statement or not?

You shot Doran in the head with a rifle. No provocation for the attack. You've wasted enough of my time with your damn arguments and anti-social behavior. This is a democratic group. Everyone has his say. But you've said too much, and done too much. Freedom doesn't allow you to go around killing fellow crew-members!"

"Any idea that there was any democracy or freedom left died on Venus," Bruce said.

"Now we get another lecture!" Terrence exploded. He leaned forward. "You're sick Bruce. They did a bad psych job on you. They should never have sent you on this trip. We need strength, all the strength we can find. You don't belong here."

"I know," Bruce agreed indifferently. "I was drafted for this trip. I told them I shouldn't be brought along. I said I didn't want any part of it."

"Because you're afraid. You're not Conqueror material. That's why you backed down when we all voted to climb the mountain. And what the devil does Venus—?"

Max Drexel's freckles slipped into the creases across his high forehead. "Haven't you heard him expounding on the injustice done to the Venusian aborigines, Captain? If you haven't, you aren't thoroughly educated to the crackpot idealism still infecting certain people."

"I haven't heard it," Terrence admitted. "What injustice?"

Bruce said, "I guess it couldn't really be considered an injustice any longer. Values have changed too much. Doran and I were part of the crew of that first ship to hit Venus, five years ago. Remember? One of the New Era's more infamous dates. Drexel says the Venusians were aborigines. No one ever got a chance to find out. We ran into this village. No one knows how old it was. There were intelligent beings there. One community left on the whole planet, maybe a few thousand inhabitants. They made their last mistake when they came out to greet us. Without even an attempt at communication, they were wiped out. The village was burned and everything alive in it was destroyed."

Bruce felt the old weakness coming into his knees, the sweat beginning to run down his face. He took a deep breath and stood there before the cold nihilistic stares of fourteen eyes.

"No," Bruce said. "I apologize. None of you know what I'm talking about."

Terrence nodded. "You're psycho. It's as simple as that. They pick the most capable for these conquests. Even the flights are processes of elimination. Eventually we get the very best, the most resilient, the real conquering blood. You just don't pass, Bruce. Listen, what do you think gives you the right to stand here in judgment against the laws of the whole Solar System?"

"There are plenty on Earth who agree with me," Bruce said. "I can say what I think now because you can't do more than kill me and you'll do that regardless…"

He stopped. This was ridiculous, a waste of his time. And theirs. They had established a kind of final totalitarianism since the New Era. The psychologists, the Pavlovian Reflex boys, had done that. If you didn't want to be reconditioned to fit into the social machine like a human vacuum tube, you kept your mouth shut. And for many, when the mouth was kept shut long enough, the mind pretty well forgot what it had wanted to open the mouth for in the first place.

A minority in both segments of a world split into two factions. Both had been warring diplomatically and sometimes physically, for centuries, clung to old ideas of freedom, democracy, self-determinism, individualism. To most, the words had no meaning now. It was a question of which set of conquering heroes could conquer the most space first. So far, only Venus had fallen. They had done a good, thorough job there. Four ships had come to Mars and their crews had disappeared. This was the fifth attempt—

TERRENCE said, "why did you shoot Doran?"

"I didn't like him enough to take the nonsense he was handing me, and when he shot the—" Bruce hesitated.

"What? When he shot what?"

Bruce felt an odd tingling in his stomach. The wind's voice seemed to sharpen and rise to kind of wail.

"All right, I'll tell you. I was sleeping, having a dream. Doran woke me up. Marsha was with him. I'd forgotten about that geological job we were supposed to be working on. I've had these dreams ever since we got here."

"What kind of dreams?"

Someone laughed.

"Just fantastic stuff. Ask your Pavlovian there," Bruce said. "People talk to me, and there are other things in the dreams. Voices and some kind of shapes that aren't what you would call human at all."

Someone coughed. There was obvious embarrassment in the room.

"It's peculiar, but many faces and voices are those of crew members of some of the ships out there, the ones that never got back to Earth."

Terrence grinned. "Ghosts, Bruce?"

"Maybe. This planet may not be a dead ball of clay. I've had feeling there's something real in the dreams, but I can't figure it out. You're still interested?"

Terrence nodded and glanced to either side.

"We've seen no indication of any kind of life whatsoever," Bruce pointed out. "Not even an insect, or any kind of plant life except some fungi and lichen down in the crevices. That never seemed logical to me from the start. We've covered the planet everywhere except one place—"

"The mountain," Terrence said. "You've been afraid even to talk about scaling it."

"Not afraid," Bruce objected. "I don't see any need to climb it. Coming to Mars, conquering space, isn't that enough? It happens that the crew of the first ship here decided to climb the mountain, and that set a precedent. Every ship that has come here has had to climb it. Why? Because they had to accept the challenge. And what's happened to them? Like you, they all had the necessary equipment to make a successful climb, but no one's ever come back down. No contact with anything up there.

"Captain, I'm not accepting a ridiculous challenge like that. Why should I? I didn't come here to conquer anything, even a mountain. The challenge of coming to Mars, of going on to where ever you guys intend going before something bigger than you are stops you—it doesn't interest me."

Nothing's bigger than the destiny of Earth!" Terrence said,

sitting up straight and rigid.

"I know," Bruce said. "Anyway, I got off the track. As I was saying, I woke up from this dream and Marsha and Doran were there, Doran was shaking me. But I didn't seem to have gotten entirely awake; either that or some part of the dream was real, because I looked out the window—something was out there, looking at me. It was late, and at first I thought it might be a shadow. But it wasn't. It was misty, almost translucent, I but I think it was something alive. I had a feeling it was intelligent, maybe very intelligent, I could feel something in my mind. A mind of beauty and softness and warmth. I kept looking—"

His throat was getting tight. He had difficulty talking. "Doran asked me what I was looking at, and I told him. He laughed. But he looked. Then I realized that maybe I wasn't still dreaming. Doran saw it, too, or thought he did. He kept looking and finally he jumped and grabbed up his rifle and ran outside. I yelled at him. I kept on yelling and ran after him. 'It's intelligent, whatever it is!' I kept saying. 'How do you know it means any harm?' But I heard Doran's rifle go off before I could get to him. And whatever it was we saw, I didn't see it any more. Neither did Doran. Maybe he killed it. I don't know. He had to kill it. That's the way you think."

"What? Explain that remark."

"That's the philosophy of conquest—don't take any chances with aliens. They might hinder our advance across the Universe. So we kill everything. Doran acted without thinking at all. Conditioned to kill everything that doesn't look like us. So I hit Doran and took the gun away from him and killed him. I felt sick, crazy with rage. Maybe that's part of it. All I know is that I thought he deserved to die and that I had to kill him, so I did."

"Is that all, Bruce?"

"That's about all. Except that I'd like to kill all of you. And I would if I had the chance."

"That's what I figured." Terrence turned to the psychologist, a small wiry man who sat there constantly fingering his ear. "Stromberg, what do you think of this gobbledegook? We know he's crazy. But what hit him? You said his record was good up until a year ago."

Stromberg's voice was monotonous, like a voice off of a tape. "Schizophrenia with mingled delusions of persecution. The schizophrenia is caused by inner conflict—indecision between the older values and our present ones which he hasn't been able to accept. A complete case history would tell why he can't accept our present attitudes. I would say that he has an incipient fear of personal inadequacy, which is why he fears our desire for conquest. He's rationalized, built up a defense, which he's structured with his idealism, foundationed with Old Era values. Retreat into the past, an escape from his own present feelings of inadequacy. Also, he escapes into these dream fantasies."

"Yes," Terrence said. "But how does that account for Doran's action? Doran must have seen something—"

"Doran's charts show high suggestibility under stress. Another weak personality eliminated. Let's regard it that way. He *imagined* he saw something," he glanced at Marsha. "Did *you* see anything?"

She hesitated, avoiding Bruce's eyes. "Nothing at all. There wasn't anything out there to see, except the dust and rocks. That's all there is to see here. We could stay a million years and never see anything else. A shadow maybe—"

"All right." Terrence interrupted. "Now, Bruce, you know the law regulating the treatment of serious psycho cases in space?"

"Yes. Execution."

"No facilities for handling such cases en route back to Earth."

"I understand. No apologies necessary, Captain."

Terrence shifted his position, "However, we've voted to grant you a kind of leniency. In exchange for a little further service from you, you can remain here on Mars after we leave. You'll be left food-concentrates to last a long time."

"What kind of service?"

"Stay by the radio and take down what we report as we go up the mountain."

"Why not?" Bruce said, "You aren't certain you're coming back, then?"

"We might not," Terrence admitted calmly. "Something's happened to the others. We're going to find out what and we want it recorded. None of us want to back down and stay here. You can take our reports as they come in."

"I'll do that," Bruce said. "It should be interesting."

BRUCE watched them go, away and up and around the immediate face of the mountain in the bleak cold of the Martian morning. He watched them disappear behind a high ledge tied together with plastic rope like convicts.

He stayed by the radio. He lost track of time and didn't care much if he did. Sometimes he took a heavy sedative and slept. The sedative prevented the dreams. He had an idea that the dreams might be so pleasant that he wouldn't wake up. He wanted to listen to Terrence as long as the captain had anything to say. It was nothing but curiosity.

At fifteen thousand feet, Terrence reported only that they were climbing.

At twenty thousand feet, Terrence said, "We're still climbing, and that's all I can report, Bruce. It's worth coming to Mars for—to accept a challenge like this!"

At twenty-five thousand feet, Terrence reported, "We've put on oxygen masks. Jacobs and Drexel have developed some kind of altitude sickness and we're taking a little time out. It's a magnificent sight up here. I can imagine plenty of tourists coming to Mars one of these days, just to climb this mountain! Mt. Everest is a pimple compared with this! What a feeling of power, Bruce!"

From forty thousand feet, Terrence said, "We gauged this mountain at forty-five thousand. But here we are at forty and there doesn't seem to be any top. We can see up and up and the mountain keeps on going. I don't understand how we could have made such an error in our computations. I talked with Burton. He doesn't see how a mountain this high could still be here when the rest of the planet has been worn so smooth."

And then from fifty-three thousand feet, Terrence said with a voice that seemed slightly strained: "No sign of any of the crew of the other four ships yet. Ten in each crew, that makes fifty. Not a sign of any of them so far, but then we seem to have a long way left to climb—"

Bruce listened and noted and took sedatives and opened cans of food concentrates. He smoked and ate and slept. He had plenty of time. He had only time and the dreams, which he knew he could utilize later to take care of the time.

From sixty-thousand feet, Terrence reported, "I had to shoot Anhauser a few minutes ago! He was dissenting. Hear that, Bruce? One of my most dependable men. We took a vote. A mere formality of course, whether we should continue climbing or not. We knew we'd all vote to keep on climbing. And then Anhauser dissented. He was hysterical. He refused to accept the majority decision. 'I'm going back down!' he yelled. So I had to shoot him. Imagine a man of his apparent caliber turning anti-democratic like that! This mountain will be a great tester for us in the future. We'll test everybody, find out quickly who the weaklings are."

Bruce listened to the wind. It seemed to rise higher and higher. Terrence, who had climbed still higher, was calling. "Think of it! What a conquest! No man's ever done a thing like this. Like Stromberg says, it's symbolic! We can build spaceships and reach other planets, but that's not actual physical conquest. We feel like gods up here. We can see what we are now. We can see how it's going to be—"

Once in a while Terrence demanded that Bruce say something to prove he was still there taking down what Terrence said. Bruce obliged. A long time passed, the way time does when no one cares. Bruce stopped taking the sedatives finally. The dreams came back and became, somehow, more real each time. He needed the companionship of the dreams.

It was very lonely sitting there without the dreams, with nothing but Terrence's voice ranting excitedly on and on. Terrence didn't seem real any more; certainly not as real as the dreams.

THE problem of where to put the line between dream and reality began to worry Bruce. He would wake up and listen and take down what Terrence was saying, and then go to sleep again with increasing expectancy. His dream took on continuity. He could return to the point where he had left it, and it was the same—allowing even for the time difference necessitated by his periods of sleep.

He met people in the dreams, two girls and a man. They had names: Pietro, Marlene, Helene.

Helene he had seen from the beginning, but she became more

real to him all the time, until he could talk with her. After that, he could also talk with Marlene and Pietro, and the conversations made sense. Consistently, they made sense.

The Martian landscape was entirely different in the dreams. Green valleys and rivers, or actually wide canals, with odd trees trailing their branches on the slow, peacefully gliding currents. Here and there were pastel-colored cities and there were things drifting through them that were alive and intelligent and soft and warm and wonderful to know.

'...*dreams, in their vivid coloring of life as in that fleeting, shadowy, misty strife of semblance with reality which brings to the delirious eye more lovely things of paradise and love—and all our own!—than young Hope in his sunniest hour hath known...*'

So sometimes he read poetry, but even that was hardly equal to the dreams.

And then he would wake up and listen to Terrence's voice. He would look out the window over the barren frigid land where there was nothing but seams of worn land, like scabs under the brazen sky.

"If I had a choice," he thought, "I wouldn't ever wake up at all again. The dreams may not be more real, but they're preferable."

Dreams were supposed to be wishful thinking, primarily, but he couldn't live in very long. His body would dry up and he would die. He had to stay awake enough to put a little energy back into himself. Of course, if he died and lost the dreams, there would be one compensation—he would also be free of Terrence and the rest of them who had learned that the only value in life lay in killing one's way across the Cosmos.

But then he had a feeling Terrence's voice wouldn't be annoying him much more anyway. The voice was unreal, coming out of some void. He could switch off Terrence any time now, but he was still curious.

"Bruce—Bruce, you still there? Listen, we're up here at what we figure to be five hundred thousand feet! It *is* impossible. We keep climbing and now we look up and we can see up and up and there the mountain is going up and up—"

And some time later: "Bruce, Marsha's dying! We don't know what's the matter. We can't find any reason for it. She's lying here

15

and she keeps laughing and calling your name. She's a woman, so that's probably it. Women don't have real guts."

Bruce bent toward the radio. Outside the shelter, the wind whistled softly at the door.

"Marsha," he said.

"Bruce—"

She hadn't said his name that way for a long time.

"Marsha, remember how we used to talk about human values? I remember how you seemed to have something maybe different from the others. I never thought you'd really buy this will to conquer, and now it doesn't matter…"

He listened to her voice, first the crazy laughter, and then a whisper. "Bruce, hello down there," her voice was all mixed up with fear and hysteria and mockery. "Bruce darling; are you lonely down there? I wish I were with you, safe…free…warm. I love you. Do you hear that? I really love you, after all. After all…"

Her voice drifted away, came back to him. "We're climbing the highest mountain. What are you doing there, relaxing where it's peaceful and warm and sane? You always were such a calm guy, I remember now. What are you doing—reading poetry while we climb the mountain? What was that, Bruce—that one about the mountain you tried to quote to me last night before you…I can't remember it now. Darling, what…?"

HE stared at the radio. He hesitated, reached out and switched on the mike. He got through to her.

"Hello, hello, darling," he whispered. "Marsha, can you hear me?"

"Yes, yes. You down there, all warm and cozy, reading poetry, darling. Where you can see both ways instead of just up and down, up and down."

He tried to imagine where she was now as he spoke to her, how she looked. He thought of Earth and how it had been there, years ago, with Marsha. Things had seemed so different then. There was something of that hope in his voice now as he spoke to her, yet not directly to her, as he looked out the window at the naked frigid sky and the barren rocks.

*" '...and there is nowhere to go from the top of a mountain*
*But down, my dear;*
*And the springs that flow on the floor of the valley*
*Will never seem fresh or clear*
*For thinking of the glitter of the mountain water*
*In the feathery green of the year...' "*

The wind stormed over the shelter in a burst of power, buried the sound of his own voice.

"Marsha, are you still there?"

"What the devil's the idea, poetry at a time like this, or any time?" Terrence demanded. "Listen, you taking this down? We haven't run into any signs of the others. Six hundred thousand feet. Bruce! We feel our destiny. We conquer the Solar System. And we'll go out and out, and we'll climb the highest mountain, the highest mountain anywhere. We're going up and up. We've voted on it. Unanimous. We go on. On to the top, Bruce! Nothing can stop us. If it takes ten years, a hundred, a thousand years, we'll find it. We'll find the top! Not the top of this world—the top of *everything.* The top of the UNIVERSE!"

Later, Terrence's voice broke off in the middle of something or other—Bruce couldn't make any sense out of it at all—and turned into crazy yells that faded out and never came back.

Bruce figured the others, might still be climbing somewhere, or maybe they were dead. Either way it wouldn't make any difference to him. He knew they would never come back down.

He was switching off the radio for good when he saw the coloration break over the window. It was the same as the dream, but for an instant, dream and reality seemed fused like two superimposed film negatives.

He went to the window and looked out. The comfortable little city was out there, and the canal flowing past through a pleasantly cool yet sunny afternoon. Purple mist blanketed the knees of low hills and there was a valley, green and rich with the trees high and full beside the softly flowing canal water.

The filmy shapes that seemed alive, that were partly translucent, drifted along the water's edge, and birds as delicate as colored glass wavered down the wind.

He opened the shelter door and went out. The shelter looked the same, but useless now. How did the shelter of that bleak world get into this one, where the air was warm and fragrant, where there was no cold, from that world into this one of his dreams?

The girl—Helene—was standing there leaning against a tree, smoking a cigarette.

He walked toward her, and stopped. In the dream it had been easy, but now he was embarrassed, in spite of the intimacy that had grown between them. She wore the same casual slacks and sandals. Her hair was brown. She was not particularly beautiful, but she was comfortable to look at because she seemed so peaceful. Content, happy with what was and only what was.

He turned quickly. The shelter was still there, and behind it the row of spaceships—not like chalk marks on a tally board now, but like odd relics that didn't belong there in the thick green grass. Five ships instead of four.

There was his own individual shelter beyond the headquarters building, and the other buildings. He looked up.

There was no mountain.

FOR one shivery moment he knew fear. And then the fear went away, and he was ashamed of what he had felt. What he had feared was gone now, and he knew it was gone for good and he would never have to fear it again.

"Look here, Bruce. I wondered how long it would take to get it through that thick poetic head of yours!"

"Get what?" He began to suspect what it was all about now, but he wasn't quite sure yet.

"Smoke?" she said.

He took one of the cigarettes and she lighted it for him and put the lighter back into her pocket.

"It's real nice here," she said. "Isn't it?"

"I guess it's about perfect."

"It'll be easy. Staying here, I mean. We won't be going to Earth ever again, you know."

"I didn't *know* that, but I didn't *think* we ever would again."

"We wouldn't want to anyway, would we, Bruce?"

"No."

He kept on looking at the place where the mountain had been. Or maybe it still was; he couldn't make up his mind yet. Which was and which was not? That barren icy world without life, or this?

" *'Is all that we see or seem,'* " he whispered, half to himself, *'but a dream within a dream?'* "

She laughed softly. "Poe was ahead of his time," she said. "You still don't get it, do you? You don't know what's been happening?"

"Maybe I don't."

She shrugged, and looked in the direction of the ships. "Poor guys. I can't feel much hatred toward them now. The Martians give you a lot of understanding of the human mind—after they've accepted you, and after you've lived with them awhile. But the mountain climbers—we can see now—it's just luck, chance, we weren't like them. A deviant is a child of chance."

"Yes," Bruce said. "There's a lot of people like us on Earth, but they'll never get the chance—the chance we seem to have here, to live decently…"

"You're beginning to see now which was the dream," she said and smiled. "But don't be pessimistic. Those people on Earth will get their chance, too, one of these fine days. The Conquerors aren't getting far. Venus, and then Mars, and Mars is where they stop. They'll keep coming here and climbing the mountain and finally there won't be any more. It won't take so long."

She rose to her toes and waved and yelled. Bruce saw Pietro and Marlene walking hand in hand up the other side of the canal. They waved back and called and then pushed off into the water in a small boat, and drifted away and out of sight around a gentle turn.

She took his arm and they walked along the canal toward where the mountain had been, or still was—he didn't know.

A quarter of a mile beyond the canal, he saw the mound of red, naked hill; corroded and ugly, rising like a scar of the surrounding green.

She wasn't smiling now. There were shadows on her face as the pressure on his arm stopped him.

"I was on the first ship and Marlene on the second. None like

19

us on the third, and on the fourth ship was Pietro. All the others had to climb the mountain—" She stopped talking for a moment, and then he felt the pressure of her fingers on his arm.

"I'm very glad you came on the fifth," she whispered. "Are you glad now?"

"I'm very glad," he said.

"The Martians tested us," she explained. "They're masters of the mind. I guess they've been grinding along through the evolutionary mill a darn long time, longer than we could estimate now. They learned the horror we're capable of from the first ship—the Conquerors, the climbers. The Martians' knew more like them would come and go on into space, killing, destroying for no other reason than their own sickness. Being masters of the mind, the Martians are also capable of hypnosis—no that's not really the word, only the closest our language comes to naming it. Suggestion so deep and strong that it seems real to one human or a million or a billion; there's no limit to the number that can be influenced. What the people who came off those ships saw wasn't real. It was partly what the Martians wanted them to see and feel— but most of it, like the desire to climb the mountain, was as much a part of the Conquerors' own psychic drive as it was the suggestion of the Martians."

She waved her arm slowly to describe a peak. "The Martians made the mountain real. So real that it could be seen from space, measured by instruments...even photographed and chipped for rock samples. But you'll see how that was done, Bruce, and realize that this and not the mountain of the Conquerors is the reality of Mars. This is the Mars no Conqueror will ever see."

THEY walked toward the ugly red mound that jutted above the green. When they came close enough, he saw the bodies lying there...the remains, actually, of what had once been bodies. He felt too sickened to go on walking.

"It may seem cruel," she said, "but the Martians realized that there is no cure for the will to conquer. There is no safety from it, either, as the people of Earth and Venus discovered, unless it is given an impossible obstacle to overcome. So the Martians provided the Conquerors with a mountain. They themselves wanted to climb. They had to."

He was hardly listening as he walked away from Helene toward the eroded hills. The crew members of the first four ships were skeletons tied together with imperishably strong rope about their waists. Far beyond them were those from *Mars V*, too freshly dead to have decayed much…Anhauser with his rope cut, a bullet in his head; Jacobs and Marsha and the others…Terrence much past them all. He had managed to climb higher than anyone else and he lay with his arms stretched out his fingers still clutching at rock outcroppings.

The trail they left wound over the ground, chipped in places for holds, red elsewhere with blood from torn hands. Terrence was more than twelve miles from the ship—horizontally.

Bruce lifted Marsha and carried her back over the rocky dust, into the fresh fragrance of the high grass, and across it to the shade and peace beside the canal.

He put her down. She looked peaceful enough, more peaceful than that other time, years ago, when the two of them seemed to have shared so much, when the future had not yet destroyed her. He saw the shadow of Helene bend across Marsha's face against the background of the silently flowing water of the green canal.

"You loved her?"

"Once," Bruce said. "She might have been sane. They got her when she was young. Too young to fight. But she would have, I think, if she'd been older when they got her."

He sat looking down at Marsha's face and then at the water with the leaves floating down it.

" '…And the springs that flow on the floor of the valley will never seem fresh or clear, for thinking of the glitter of the mountain water in the feathery green of the year…' "

He stood up, walked back with Helene along the canal toward the calm city. He didn't look back.

"They've all been dead quite a while," Bruce said wonderingly. "Yet I seemed to be hearing from Terrence until only a short time ago. Are—are the climbers still climbing—somewhere, Helene?"

"Who knows?" Helene answered softly. "Maybe, I doubt if even the Martians have the answer to that."

They entered the city.

# The Last Laugh

*The visitor from Mars was a first-rate howl. Earthmen reckoned he was endowed with all the qualities of all the greatest clowns in the history of Buffoonery. Often though, the distance between humor and terror can be too short to be funny.*

THE scarred rocket rolled down street canyons away from United Nations City, wheeled toward Madison Square Garden between jam-packed, crazily-cheering millions of citizens from every nation on Earth.

Confetti snow drifted in colorful storm, wild faces shone through drifts of spiraling streamers. Signs floated everywhere. Neon signs blinked off and on. Signs floated from balloons across the kleig-lighted sky. Welcome hero signs. And even signs shouting:

## WELCOME TO EARTH—ZEKE!

They spelled the name wrong, Johnson thought with some dismay. But that's the way it sounded, he decided, when I radioed in ahead that there was a Martian with us.

Spelled ZEKE, the name scarcely projected the dignity of the name's sound in Martian language. But, in thinking about it now, Johnson realized that it was the only way it could be spelled or pronounced in English.

This seemingly insignificant fact bothered Johnson now. He felt a growing uneasiness. The Martian was largely his responsibility, he felt. It had been Johnson who had spent most of the time on the first visit to Mars with the few Martians left in that one isolated mountain village, learning their language and ancient, conservative, almost static culture. Being an anthropologist, among other things, it had been natural for Johnson to have manifested this particular interest.

Johnson had also been the one to suggest that perhaps Zeke might like to pay Earth a visit.

Zeke had quite readily agreed, but now Johnson was beginning

to wonder why. In six months another rocket would go to Mars and Zeke could go home, but meanwhile Johnson suddenly began to wonder about the possible ramifications of a Martian's first visit to Earth.

He had radioed ahead about the Martian but had given no details.

The world awaited its first look at a Martian, the expectation overshadowing their hero worship of Captain Stromberg, Atomics Engineer Hinton, and Professor William Johnson—the first successful navigators of deep space.

Right now, Stromberg and Hinton were straightening their dress uniforms preparatory to the feting promised when the rocket was wheeled into Madison Square Garden. UN notables would be there, everyone of any importance, plus every one who could be jammed into the Garden. The rocket would be wheeled up to a speaker's platform, the doors would open and out would step the three heroes and Zeke.

Johnson looked at Zeke now with a new and uneasy appraisal. He slumped and then as Johnson motioned to him, Zeke gave a series of grotesque hops. His face, like a monstrous soft rubber mask bought in a novelty shop, twisted into a series of fantastic grimaces.

Stromberg and Hinton grinned appreciatively. They thought Zeke was pretty funny. Johnson no longer thought so because he had realized the cultural significance of Zeke's actions. Johnson gestured for Zeke to look through the port view plate.

His rubberoid features, which at times suggested a travesty of something very remotely human, bunched up and then spread in all directions as though running into yellow putty. "They're welcoming you to Earth, Zeke. 'Welcome, Zeke,' the signs say. You'll be royally entertained. You'll be wined and dined as they say. You're probably the most extraordinary visitor ever seen anywhere."

ZEKE swung his long, stick-like arms, or appendages, whatever one chose to call them, in long arcs like pendulums, back and forth and to and fro. His three eyes spread wider and wider in an expression of such intense and gigantic astonishment that

Stromberg and Hinton bent over and held their stomachs with uncontrollable laughter.

The flicker of unease in Johnson's stomach flamed a little stronger. The trouble was that Zeke's culture was so serious, so old and wise and serious, there seemed to be absolutely no sense of humor in it. At least none of any human kind that Johnson had been able to discover.

To Zeke, this being an object of humor had no meaning. Zeke could understand, however, the meaning of ridicule, derision and insults and sadness in their actual and realistic sense, divorced from the necessity of contrast that connected these things with laughter, gags, jokes in the human psychology.

So Johnson had never explained to Zeke that he was being laughed at, nor what it would mean if he did know he was being an object of laughter. Somehow now, Johnson wished he hadn't lied, that he hadn't explained to Zeke about Stromberg's and Hinton's laughter: "Well, Zeke, that's a kind of appreciation humans express to each other. It means they accept you. A form of politeness, a social amenity."

Zeke was saying in the peculiar slurred, high-pitched Martian speech, "It is overpowering, so many of you humans! Even in our most ancient records there is no account of there ever having been so many of us as I see of your kind out there!"

"That's only a small percent of the world's population," Johnson said. He took hold of one of Zeke's boneless, spongy arms. "Come on. We go on up now to the air-lock doors. In a few minutes we'll be out of here and you'll be presented to the world."

They were inside the Garden now, the rocket being moved by a giant crane to a position beside the speakers' platform. A ramp was connecting the two. The door started to open and Stromberg and Hinton stood with stiff, glowing expectancy.

Johnson stood behind them, holding on to Zeke whose eight-foot body slumped with its own peculiar kind of expectancy. In all his 32 years Johnson had never been exactly a social animal. Devoted largely to fieldwork, he had accustomed himself either by choice or necessity or both to an extraordinary degree of isolation. The two years in space hadn't bothered him. He was somewhat anxious to see his friends, but not overly so.

In fact the sight of those countless gaping faces, the packed masses of humanity had frightened him a little. It had been so utterly peaceful out there in space, and or the high, cold plateaus of Mars.

Odd how formidable seemed the prospect of meeting this gigantic social obligation of facing the whole world. Maybe two years away from Earth was too long.

He could hear the interminable speech droning away outside the opening doors.

Everybody was waiting out there on that platform.

Presidents and envoys from the Big Three nations, and many slightly less important figures. Everybody who could possibly claim to be anybody.

"From now on," whispered Hinton, "we live like Kings! A pension for life. And a hero forever. The dames—"

"Quiet, please," whispered Captain Stromberg.

Hinton dropped back. He nudged Johnson. "Even the thing here, your friend that walks like a man, will be treated by the world like a prince."

Johnson squeezed Hinton's arm and Hinton winced. "Watch what you say, Hinton. It knows some English now."

"You treat it like it's a human being," Hinton said.

Johnson had no answer to that except agreement. Changing Hinton's attitudes was something else again. Johnson didn't consider the project quite worth the time and trouble. He shrugged.

"This is it," Johnson warned Zeke. Every time he talked in Martian his jaw ached. It was quite a feat.

The present speaker's voice like a worn soundtrack was saying:

"…and now, waiting world, here they are…"

"Ready?" Captain Stromberg whispered.

"…the first to make a voyage to another planet! The first visitor from another world!…"

Their names being called, and then—

"…and our guest from the planet Mars—Zeke!"

Zeke shifted his undulating, boneless length as the four of them stepped out onto the platform and into the glare of floodlights, and a sea of smoke and the heat of human bodies. Johnson got the impression, though he couldn't actually see much of it, of a colossal ocean of humanity, great tides of flesh held temporarily motionless and soundless. Microphones slid down. Television and motion picture cameras moved in and back and in again.

Lawrence Spaulding, President of the United States, flanked by bigwigs from the United Nations, moved toward the four. Hands came out, gloved and grasping.

"I—" began the President of the United States, Johnson watched his lips moving but what he said was buried under the onrushing, rising, roaring flood of sound.

Johnson was noticing how the others on the platform were gradually having their attention diverted by the appearance of Zeke. His hands were suddenly moist, and his stomach felt hollow. All of them were beginning to grin. It was universal—he should have known—whenever any human being saw Zeke—laughter.

He didn't know why, exactly, but he decided this was bad, very bad. Even the Russian Ambassador was grinning as Zeke grimaced at the strangeness about him.

As long as Zeke didn't know he excited laughter primarily from everyone, things might go along all right. But that deceptive situation couldn't last long. And trying to make it last for six months was no solution. Johnson's throat felt dry.

Maybe there was no solution. Maybe it was just a devil of a blunder—period! Several scientists spoke at length after the cheering died down enough. Stromberg, and Hinton were introduced. They talked at length. Johnson was introduced. He was asked to talk about the surprising discovery of intelligent life on Mars, and about Zeke.

He didn't bother to say much because he knew that they weren't really listening. He watched Zeke. The Martian was restless. He made faces at Johnson. He was utterly alone amidst thousands of people, a world full of human beings. Johnson thought, I'm his only point of contact with any living thing, and that is most inadequate. How does he really feel? Desperate probably. Confused. Probably very lonely. And nothing that he does or says will be interpreted realistically—

He bowed, stepped back to where Zeke was amidst a storm of

applause. Now every eye was focused on Zeke. Zeke whispered to Johnson in a raspy, high-pitched voice that only added to his humorous appeal because of contrast due to his giant and grotesque body. "I am having difficulty breathing."

"Hold on a while," Johnson said, managing to smile at everybody. "I have a big apartment we can go to, and no one will bother us there. You can rest. It's air-conditioned. It'll be cooler there too."

JOHNSON prayed. The thing had to get over with fast. He felt afraid for Zeke now. The novelty, the magnitude of the thing was over. They had to get out of here.

His uneasiness had been growing. Those on the speakers' platform were grinning more widely at Zeke's antics. The uneasiness was growing into a kind of fear. And then he heard someone introducing Zeke.

"Oh no," Johnson whispered. "Wait a minute—he's not up to this...not now..."

"What is the trouble?" Zeke asked.

The United Nations Secretary was introducing Zeke. Something about inter-world friendship...the beginning of an inter-world union that would spread to the stars...

Someone was saying in Johnson's ear, "Go ahead. You act as interpreter..."

"What is everyone looking at me for?" Zeke asked.

"You are to make a speech like the rest of us," Johnson whispered dryly. "Just say something...anything...something short. They won't know what you're saying anyway. Just a gesture—"

To Zeke everything was deadly serious. A long historical background had made the Martians that way. They were old. "About how much I want to learn about you here on Earth? How I will enjoy my stay here? How glad I am that the Earth and Mars are in contact and are friends?"

"Yes, yes, anything. Just a formality anyway."

"But I think that I am somewhat afraid," Zeke said. "Things I am not accustomed to. Too many people. Too much noise and confusion. And the air, I cannot seem to breathe properly."

The air was thinner on Mars, Johnson thought as he stepped toward the microphones again, in front of television eyes. But it's the air here too—the people—the suppression—

Zeke was there standing beside him, Johnson stepped aside. Zeke stood there in his place. Johnson's knees got weak. He felt the sweat running down his face then, and the cold shivery feeling as though he'd suddenly contracted a high fever. The laughter was starting. It was starting around the platform as the big spotlights caught Zeke full, and it spread backward and upward, growing and expanding.

Zeke, in his alien way talked, and he gestured with his entire body as he talked sincerely, with deep feeling, about how he felt about this first visit to Earth. The laughter rose higher and more voluminous until Johnson's body began to quiver as though from some physical assault. The trouble was a complete misunderstanding of Zeke, his grotesqueness, the fact that no one had any idea what he was really saying. What his gestures meant. All that—and whatever it was in human beings that made them laugh.

Zeke leaned toward Johnson, yelled in his ear. "Look, they are all doing it now."

"Yes," Johnson managed to scream. "They like you. They're all stirred up with excitement. Think nothing of it. They're expressing their extreme excitement and appreciation—"

The twistings of Zeke's body, his facial distortions as he sought to express himself in the best and most intelligible manner grew more intense. Laughter became a sweeping thunder. No one could hear Johnson's interpretation. He stopped interpreting.

Zeke came back away from the camera and microphones. No one but Johnson realized his growing panic. Johnson said to someone, "The air's bad for the Martial here. I'm taking him back inside the rocket. You say something."

The man, who happened to be a highly important figure in the United Nation Supreme Court, an Englishman named Gordon Humphreys, nodded. He was grinning yet Johnson seemed to see a glint of understanding in Humphreys' eyes.

THE rocket held out most of the thunder. Zeke sat in the

corner. His eyes were frightened, confused. "They certainly do appreciate me a great deal, do they not."

"Yes," whispered Johnson. "They certainly do."

"I do not understand. But it would seem that all of this is not being treated with due seriousness."

Johnson said. "Don't try to figure us out down here, not this time. We discussed that, Zeke. Society and the individual here is too complex. Specialists here, psychologists, trying to figure that out about themselves are running into difficulty. Just take it as easy as you can and don't get too curious. We'll get you out somewhere where you won't be bothered much, and you can study at your leisure. Remember, you only have six months of this, then you'll be on your way home to Mars."

Zeke said. "Yes, Martian culture must have been complex like this once, but that was very long ago. It seems to frighten a bit. This—what you call laughter. There seems no analogy for it in my own language or culture. Why is it directed in such volume specifically at me? I mean as a sign of appreciation and like, why is so little of it going on between two or more of your own kind? I do not—"

"You know the meaning of tragedy, sadness, bereavement. We have an opposite. Laughter. You make people very happy Zeke. You make them enjoy themselves very much."

Zeke thought about this.

Johnson forced a laugh. "You see you shouldn't try to figure it out! Just make your visit here as enjoyable as possible. It won't be long before you'll be on your way back home—"

"All right," Zeke said. "I want to study here. I want to take back to Mars an understanding of humans."

"If you take that back you'll take back more than anyone I ever heard of has to give," muttered Johnson.

The immediately subsequent events were too incredible and fast-paced for Johnson to cope with with any degree of effectiveness. With Zeke, he was swirled away in a mad maelstrom of activity. He went with Zeke on a crazy toboggan ride that gained momentum all the way toward an end Johnson was horrified to imagine.

The newspapers and television and newsreel cameras started the toboggan going. They started the whole world laughing at Zeke. It was too big a novelty to be ignored by American advertisers, or by any other agencies standing to profit from the greatest novelty in history. Zeke seemed to have all the qualities of all the greatest clowns in the history of clowndom, plus unique characteristics of his own which in turn seemed to bring out something else in the misty realms of human psychology where so much was suspected but of which so little was known.

Johnson tried to object but he couldn't without revealing the truth to Zeke. Besides, Zeke wanted to please. He wanted to make people like him and his kind. He wanted humans and Martians always to get along, so he went along with compliancy on the crazy ride.

They insisted that Johnson get a cut of the fabulous profits accruing from Zeke's endorsements, his television, radio, and stage performances. Johnson refused. The money went to charity. He explained that to Zeke. That made Zeke feel good for a while. He appeared at benefit performances. Everywhere, everyone was laughing louder and louder. Johnson somehow kept Zeke convinced that his lectures were received in the serious regard Zeke intended…that the laughter was only appreciation and so forth.

During a tour, Johnson stopped off in Chicago to see a friend. A clinical psychologist, Philip Billington, Johnson had lost weight. His nerves were frayed.

Philip's study was comfortable. And there were cool drinks and dim light, and Johnson sat there like a man paroled another day from a death chamber. Philip, a quiet little man with a rather prominent nose and soft eyes, regarded Johnson quietly for a while.

Finally Johnson said. "Physically I'm not built for it. Martians only sleep six hours out of every three weeks of Earth time. I have to keep up with him, try to keep him from being completely sucked up by—"

"How are you helping him?"

Johnson explained. "He doesn't know what laughter is. I mean what it is in his case as far as his audiences are concerned. I'm not sure what it is myself. Except that it's pretty horrible!"

"The whole thing's rather horrible," Billington agreed. "Are you doing anything to get your Martian out of all this madness? I'll admit that it could result in something tragic. If you've been keeping him in ignorance—"

"What else could I do? What if he found out he's regarded as a clown, a buffoon, a ludicrous, sham-clumsy sort of animal? I've written out a full report to the United Nations, and I've contacted James Hatcher, a UN lawyer friend of mine and he's working on it. So far there's been no results from either source, I say there must be some legal angles."

"Maybe there is," Billington mused. "But I'm just a psychologist. You say Zeke has no sense of humor? Rather an abstract term. Even to us, humans and psychologists alike, the anatomy of humor is pretty complex, contradictory, confusing and inconsistent."

"But why do they go so insanely hysterical with laughter at Zeke?"

"Why? There's a question all right, Bill. It's contrast in humorous situations, such as this one, that sometimes makes it horrible. In this case it's the fact that people are laughing at what we know is something deadly serious, which only makes it more grotesque. Add to this the vast cultural differences, the unbridgeable gap, the psychological isolation, and you have that thin line between farce and tragedy—"

"There's never been anything like this though," Johnson moaned. "It's all out of line. Here we have the first visitor from another planet. An important, dignified individual, and the world regards him as a buffoon! Something's got to be done!"

"I agree. But what?"

PHILIP looked at the ceiling, then back at Johnson. "Humor. What are its basic elements? Surprise. Aberrancy. Ah, we have that element. Oddity, singularity, peculiarity, nonconformity in what is supposed to be a well-ordered world. Also irrationalism, we have that too. A form of aberrancy. Zeke acts in a manner people regard as foolish, mistaken, ill-advised...oddity of character behavior. People like this kind of humor; it allows him to feel superior. Here we find the element of sadism in humor, you see. Humor can be horrible in retrospect, or looking at it from a distance. Kinds of humor change. They used to write jokes about burning witches alive. Cripples and insane people used to be funny."

"All right," Johnson said. "But there's something more here."

"Yes. Yes, there is. I think I have it, some of it anyway. There's a connection between terror and humor. Build up a suspense, an anticipation of terror, then present something harmless, and you get a tremendous relief through laughter. People have been conditioned to fear the alien, particularly the alien from outer space, and particularly the bogey-man Martian who has been popularized in fiction for a long time. Maybe the whole world's reacting to Zeke as a kind of anticlimax. A long build-up to expect some fearsome monster, maybe with super weapons capable of wiping out the Earth in one fell swoop of deadly rays, and then they get Zeke!

"And add to that the other free-floating anxieties people suffer in a too-complex society, sourceless fears they don't even realize exist. They project all that into the surprise twist too. And we get a world practically prostrated with laughter because they expect a monster and get the most, to them at least, exaggerated kind of loping, rubberoid, harmless clown."

"But a clinical diagnosis doesn't help Zeke any."

"No. No, it doesn't. Not now anyway. It might—"

"The UN should do something. America's exploiting Zeke for commercial purposes primarily. Zeke isn't a guest of the United States. He's from another planet. He's really visiting the whole world. No one nation—"

Billington nodded. "I hope something happens. I hate to see you in such a state, Bill. Pretty soon, if you don't snap out of this and find some solution, you'll end up coming to me for treatment."

Johnson needed treatment when Hollywood decided to make a movie featuring Zeke. He didn't go to Philip Billington though. He fought this to the end but the fight was futile. They gave Zeke a good sales talk, and of course it wasn't Johnson's position to tell Zeke what, or what not, to do. He had trapped himself nicely so that he couldn't explain to Zeke the real reasons for his objections.

The movie was called MARS INVADES THE EARTH. They told Zeke it would be a semi-documentary; that it would assure good relations between Earth and Mars and acquaint the whole world with Martian culture.

There was a special preview showing in the United Nations Cultural Building in United Nations City. Johnson was there, waiting in the lobby for the fiasco to end. He had seen the first part of it but had been unable to stomach the rest. He paced nervously back and forth across the lush carpet wondering how Zeke was taking it. It wasn't at all what they had led Zeke to believe it was. It was pure fiction in which a Martian monster invaded the Earth with a weapon capable of blowing the world into component atoms, but the Martian was so funny he conquered the Earth with laughter.

Johnson could hear the UN Officials invited to the showing laughing uproariously in there. What—what would Zeke be thinking now?

He stopped pacing. Zeke was in the lobby with him, and the picture wasn't nearly over. Zeke's whole body stood there very stiffly. Johnson felt sick.

"You have been lying to me," Zeke said. His face twisted with that odd rubber-mask plasticity that seemed to be so funny.

"No, Zeke, you've got to let me explain."

"All this time you have never told me the truth about this laughter. Everybody thinks that I am funny. They look upon me as something ridiculous."

"I—"

"They lied to me also. This picture is not what they said it would be. I heard them talking in there. They did not know I was sitting there by them in the dark. I found out why all this laughter should be always directed at me! Why at me? Why always at me? I have found out!"

"Zeke—!"

"What is this humor of yours? What is so funny that gives you satisfaction in freaks and fools? In the misfortunes of others? You think we Martians do not know what this laughter really means? Maybe we know. I guess it is just that we knew a long time back and have forgotten it. Now I know what it is and what it means."

JOHNSON was trying to say something. It didn't make any difference now. Laughter came from inside the big auditorium,

Zeke's huge ungainly body loped toward the exit. He turned. "I do not want to see or talk to you or to any other human beings. I do not like to see or talk to any of you any more. I will go to your place, if you will permit me to do so, and there I will seclude myself until your next rocket goes back to Mars. I do not want anyone to come out there to see or to talk with me. I do not want to be in any more television shows or radio broadcasts or moving pictures."

"All right!" Johnson yelled above the laughter. "But let me take you to my apartment. How you going to get there? You can't speak English."

The guard stood in front of the exit. He turned and grinned up at Zeke. He began to laugh as Zeke swung back and forth, wanting out. Zeke made gestures and spoke, "I wish to go outside. Would you be so kind as to step out of the doorway, please?"

The guard had no idea what Zeke was saying, nor what his movements meant. All the guard knew was that Zeke was a Martian bogey turned clown and he laughed louder. "You will step to one side, please."

Johnson started toward them.

"I wish you would step aside and stop laughing at me," Zeke said.

Johnson started to yell something but he was too late. He knew there was no malicious intent in Zeke's action, only desperation, confusion, bewilderment, humility. He pushed the guard out of the way, but his strength was much greater than Zeke was used to exerting under any such circumstances.

The guard hurtled ten feet away. Johnson heard the sickening thud of his head against the wall. Johnson ran over there, saw the open, staring eyes of the guard, and then he saw Zeke running across the rain-splattered street through the neon-shining dark. He saw a few people stop and wonder a moment, then laugh.

Johnson leaned against the wall and closed his eyes before he went to the public phone booth. He could still hear the laughter from the auditorium as he called the police.

They figured Johnson would know where Zeke was. They questioned him for what seemed hours. He had no idea where Zeke would go to hide or where he would be now. Zeke could speak only a few words of English. No, Zeke wouldn't harm anybody. Yes, I know he killed the guard, but that was an accident. A misunderstanding.

No, God no! I don't know where he would go!

Yes, yes, I'll make tape recorded messages to be broadcast to Zeke. I'll make some television kinescopes too. Maybe Zeke will hear me and give himself up without any trouble. Play the recordings and show the kinescopes on every station in the city.

Sure I will. But why don't you send out broadcasts and telecasts to the people instead of to Zeke? That would be more logical. Tell them not to be afraid of him. That he wouldn't hurt anybody. Tell them not to incite any more confusion in Zeke.

I know, I know, somebody hit Zeke with a cane, but he wasn't trying to attack the old man! You've got everyone scared of him now. A few hours ago everybody was laughing, and now you've got everyone thinking he's some kind of horrible monster.

I know…the woman wheeling the baby. But she was hysterical when she saw Zeke there on that side street. She screamed and went crazy. But that isn't Zeke's fault. That's your fault. No! I said I don't know where he would be hiding now!

You can leave now, Johnson. But stay where we can get in touch with you at once. You're the only way we can establish any contact with Zeke—unless of course we have to kill it.

SO JOHNSON made the tape recordings and the television kinescopes, and he sat in a kind of daze in the semi-darkness of the apartment of Hatcher, a friend of his, looking at his own image speaking Martian to millions of people, and listened to his voice.

No one knew what he had said on those lengths of tape and on those kinescopes. He hadn't said what he was supposed to say— not for Zeke to give himself up. Zeke might not understand that, and he might get shot. He told Zeke to meet him just outside the UN grounds at the West end of a public park that had been built to replace a former slum area—to beautify the area surrounding the UN territory. A high wall flanked the West end of the park and thick brush and trees were there affording a good hiding place.

And Johnson would meet Zeke there as soon as he could. Don't do anything else, if possible, until I can talk with you, Zeke.

The newscasts came on frequently, mostly about Zeke. He was

seen first here and then there.

The city was supposedly gripped in a reign of terror. Kids playing in a vacant lot near the UN grounds had dug a small cave and had found Zeke hiding in it. The Martian had made horrible sounds and leaped at them, the kids said. The kids had thrown rocks at him. They said he looked funny at first, all covered with dirt, and stumbling around like he was drunk or something.

The police had thrown up nets and blockades everywhere. The number of cars in surrounding precincts were tripled. Walls went up everywhere. State, county, sheriff deputies' cars formed wall after wall that were tightening. Information about the crime and a description of Zeke had been spread over such a wide area from the crime scene that five states away the police had thrown up blockades. The description was a formality.

Everyone knew what the Martian looked like.

Johnson waited there in Hatcher's apartment.

He tried to get in touch with the lawyer, but that seemed impossible. No one knew where Hatcher was. But Johnson knew the police were shadowing him, hoping he would lead them to where Zeke was hiding.

He had to get over there to that park where Zeke might be hiding, waiting for him, without being trailed there. That wouldn't be easy. It was out of Johnson's line.

The newscast said that Zeke had blundered into someone's estate near the UN grounds and had had a couple of big dogs sent after him. In protecting himself, Zeke had killed the dogs. It would seem that killing the two dogs was worse in some ways than if Zeke had killed two more human beings.

No one, of course, even remembered ever having laughed at Zeke. He had become the typical alien Martian menace, a Welles and Wells character. A monster from another world, a bogey Martian, a menace, a stalking terror, an inhuman monster.

"They'll kill him," Johnson whispered. He got up and got Hatcher's topcoat out of the closet and put on Hatcher's hat. "They'll kill him and he won't have any idea what's happened or why." That's the worst part of it, he thought. Somewhere in the rainy dark was Zeke, feeling terribly the hostility of his human surroundings. Confused, desperate, panic-stricken. Not understanding any of it.

Johnson went out into the hall of the apartment-hotel. Empty. The police would be guarding the front entrance certainly, maybe the back. But there was another exit out of the basement into the vacant lot, and maybe they wouldn't know about that.

He went down into the basement, went out that entrance and into the vacant lot among the dripping trees. He stood there, listening, watching. He put his hands in Hatcher's topcoat pocket and felt the small snub-nosed revolver there. He jerked his hand out.

He heard nothing but the rain on the palm fronds and the tires humming on wet pavement. Above him, the gray night's hand cupped over the city, reflecting its neon life through misty rain.

He went cautiously through the trees, through a pit being excavated for building, and emerged onto the street a block and a half away. And still no one.

He walked faster, signaled a cab. He sat there stiffly and numb with tension as the cab took him with casual speed to the park.

HE WALKED slowly along past the high dense brush of the park next to the wall, his shoes squeeshing on the wet turf. Beyond the wall he could see a tall bulky building with little yellow window eyes that blinked in the rain. Absently, he remembered it was the big Community Hospital.

"Zeke," he called as he walked past the high dense brush. "Zeke."

He went the length of the park's West end, started back, continuing to call Zeke's name. The strange alien whisper sent a chill down his arms.

"Mr. Johnson—"

The brush shivered, Zeke had heard the message all right. "Mr. Johnson, I am ill. I am cold and I am tired. I do not have any idea what to do."

Johnson said, "Come out here, Zeke. You have to turn yourself in to the proper authorities here that maintain law and order. I've explained something about that. I promise you it will be all right. You've got to trust me, Zeke."

"People are afraid of me. They throw stones at me and run

away when I approach them, I cannot understand—"

Johnson explained quickly that the guard Zeke had shoved was dead. "It has to be straightened out, that's all, Zeke. Then things will be all right."

Johnson saw the shape back there in the dim wet shadows under the wall, crouching, hardly distinguishable. He saw Zeke for what he was, a lost stranger, helpless, incomprehensible. Too bewildered now to understand, too weary to see anything, too anxious perhaps to care. Alien, sick, abominably unhappy, taken out of his knowledge, bitter in utter loneliness, his home so far away—so very far away.

It moved toward him, rising up, rising taller, its undulating hugeness bending and swaying above the brush. It stood unsteady on its legs, its rubberoid flesh dripping and shining. Surrounded by the wet night, Johnson saw him as something cast out mysteriously by the sea on some alien shore to perish in the supreme disaster of loneliness. Zeke's body shivered all over suddenly. Johnson sucked in his breath, felt the quick sick emptiness. He turned. Shapes running, footsteps slipping and scrambling toward them out of the brush. The glint and shine of uniforms and guns. They had trailed him after all—

"Stop, don't move! We'll shoot!"

"Don't!" Johnson yelled frantically. "For God's sake, listen." Zeke's grotesque body crashed backward and Johnson saw the bursts of orange flame flowering to horror in his brain. Shots blared flatly. Zeke went up, over the wall and was gone on the other side.

Johnson scrambled into the brush. He felt the gun in his hand and he felt himself squeeze the trigger once, twice. He was screaming. "Stay back, you crazy fools! I'll shoot anyone I see moving in here!"

"What's the matter with you—hey—that you, Johnson?"

"He's flipped," someone shouted.

"Johnson! You'll get yourself in a lot of trouble. You might kill somebody."

"He's crazy," someone said.

"You guys crawl back and go round into the hospital and round up the Martian."

Johnson crawled along the wall on his hands and knees. He kept crawling and then, wedging himself between a tree trunk and the wall, edged up the wall, over it, and dropped to the other side. He ran across the grounds desperately looking for Zeke.

He saw nothing on the grounds, no sign of anything or anybody. Then he saw Zeke up there in the gray drizzle, three stories up on the fire-escape platform. He didn't yell. He ran and then he felt the harsh wet cold of the metal as he climbed.

He followed wet tracks down the floor of the hall, found a door. As he started to open it he saw the police come around the corner at the other end of the hall. They stopped when they saw him. Johnson heard laughter coming from beyond the door. The laughter got louder. The shrill, high, spontaneous, and abandoned laughter of happy children.

The police moved cautiously toward him. Johnson opened the door and went in, shut it quickly behind him.

A nurse came over to Johnson, smiled at him.

She stood with her arms folded and stood beside him and the both of them watched Zeke in the middle of the big hospital ward.

"We're so glad Zeke came back," the nurse said. "And surprising us this way makes it so much more delightful for the children."

Yes, thought Johnson dully. Zeke was here before, once. A benefit performance. For crippled children. And neither the kids nor the two nurses in here had heard about Zeke's sudden status as a criminal. No radios in here—only recording machines playing pleasant things for the kids. Too much unpleasantness on the regular programs.

An isolated world in which they still saw Zeke only as a clown.

The kids on the beds lining the walls, many of whom would never leave this room except in wheeled chairs, were screaming and hollering and shrieking with laughter at Zeke's antics. Their laughter bubbled higher and louder. Zeke twisted round and round, his arms swinging, as he did a shambling jig, danced this way and that. "The clown's back!" "Dance, dance, dance some more!" "Stand on your head, Zeke!"

"They have so little real happiness," the nurse said. "I've hoped Zeke would come back Nothing here has ever made them happier and laugh more loudly than Zeke."

Johnson walked through the waves of free wild laughter to Zeke's side. He whispered.

"Stay right here, Zeke. Don't leave this room until I give you the word. These kids really appreciate you, Zeke. Believe me, I'm not lying this time. These kids are happy now, because of you, and they don't have much happiness. Life's worth living right now for them, Zeke. And it's because of you. Stay right here,"

"I am very sick," Zeke said. "I will do as you say. I cannot go further."

JOHNSON backed to the door, managed to smile to the nurse, and went into the hall.

Quickly he shut the door as the police rushed in. Captain Maxson, in charge of some detail or other, a short heavy blond young man, eager to do his duty, grabbed at Johnson.

"You go blundering in there to get Zeke," Johnson said, "and you'll not only take a chance of injuring or killing some of those kids, but you may, frighten them, disillusion them for the rest of their lives!"

"But that monster's liable to start killing in there," whispered Maxson hoarsely.

"If you go charging in there anything can happen. Let me do it my way and there won't be any trouble."

"What's your way?" Maxson obviously was in a bad predicament.

"Let me make a phone-call first, then I'll take Zeke out and there'll be no trouble. I can handle him. That's your only chance. You don't want to hurt those kids, shock them! They don't know what's happened. They still think Zeke's funny."

Maxson touched his lips. "All right. Make the call. I'll give you ten minutes—"

This time he found Hatcher in. He quickly explained the situation. "Hatcher! You said you'd have the dope from Humphreys at the UN."

"And, I have," Hatcher said. "It's all right now. I'll rush a couple of UN Deputies over there with special orders right now!"

"Well hurry!" Johnson yelled. Then he stepped out of the

booth practically into Maxson's arms.

"Now, go in there and get him out here, Johnson!"

"We're waiting for two United Nations Deputies. They'll be here in a minute. They're going to take charge of Zeke from now on."

"What—well, okay, let them arrest him. That's a load off my back—"

"They're not coming here to arrest him. But to protect him from being arrested or otherwise annoyed until he goes back to Mars.

"I don't get it at all. I got orders—"

"Here's how it is," Johnson said. "Now that we've established relations with another planet, Mars, the UN has jurisdiction over all such relationships and transactions. UN City is extra-territorial. It belongs to no nation, including the United States, and therefore the United States has no jurisdiction over Zeke, or anything having to do with inter-world relations.

"That's a UN problem. Furthermore, Zeke is here in the capacity of Martian Ambassador, and the UN has been officially declared the site of the official future Martian Embassy, and therefore Zeke has diplomatic immunity. That guard's death was accidental, caused by a misunderstanding. But regardless, he can't be tried by any nation on Earth because the accident occurred on Martian Embassy grounds officially.

"If Zeke's ever tried for any crime it will have to be on Mars. That's the rule."

And that was the way it was.

After seeing Zeke off in the second Mars-bound rocket, he went to Billington's and sat in his study, relaxed for the first time in six months.

"How was Zeke?" Billington asked. "Seem to feel any better about his visit to Earth?"

"Much better," Johnson said. "In fact, he seemed to feel better about the whole thing than at any time during his stay here. He said he understood a great deal more about us than he might otherwise have, learned.

"And he said he understood our laughter too. A safety valve, he said, and that he was glad if he allowed us to let off a little steam. He said there was a lot of steam here that needs to be let off."

Billington smiled. "That's a concise and astute analysis," he said.

"It seems to be the laughter of those crippled kids that did it," Johnson added. "Zeke got an idea there how beneficial laughter is."

Billington nodded. "However, maybe Zeke's analysis is overly-simplified." His mouth set in a serious line. "The laughter of kids is hardly comparable to the laughter of adults. The kids were laughing *with* Zeke. Does he realize the difference there?"

Johnson said, "Maybe he doesn't. The Martians, have a lot to learn about human beings."

"So do we," Billington sighed.

# Back to Nature

*What meaning can going back to nature have for people who've never been there
in the first place?
But the Planners knew what was best...*

HAL ZWICKER stood on the roof of the empty apartment building and tried to feel good about what was happening. He tried to convince himself that he wasn't scared, and that he wasn't sad.

"What'll they do with New York when we're gone?" Kirby asked as he peered through the guardrail at the sea of buildings full of empty holes.

Hal tousled his kid's dusty hair. "Never thought much about that, Kirby."

"Maybe it'll be a museum!"

"Maybe. Guess you're pretty excited about going back to nature, aren't you, Kirby?"

"Oh boy!"

"Well, the skybuss'll be along now in a little while."

"Going back to nature! Heeeyooowwww—hooooo!"

"Kirby!" Flora yelled up through the skylight. "If you scream like that once more, you'll be put to bed the minute we get out to our five acres! Are you on the edge there again?"

"Nope, I'm clear back from the edge, Ma!" Kirby yelled.

Hal winked at Kirby, then went over and looked down through the skylight at his wife's face, which blinked white from the dimness of the 11th floor hallway. Her face was smudged with the dust of packing, and she pressed at hair turning a little gray on the edge of forty. She flashed pale gums in her strong but silent grin. But the other look was still there, the one that had been there for three days, since they had gotten the decentralization order. There was something painful, a brand-new tiredness, lines not from laughing around the rain-colored eyes.

"Ah honey," Hal said. "You said we were done packing that

44

stuff!"

"Just a few little personal things, Hal, little things. They wouldn't mind a few of these little personal things, would they, Hal?"

"Well, they said we'd have everything we needed out there."

"I've only got a few little personal things," she said, and then turned quickly and ran down the hall.

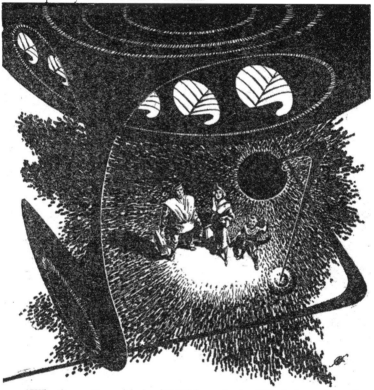

"What's matter with her?" Kirby asked. "She's been like that for three days."

"She's tired I guess," Hal said.

"Isn't she happy about going back to nature?"

"Sure she is!" But the words seemed dry to Hal as he looked over the silent emptiness East, where a splotch of intense summer green from Central Park pressed hungry and swelling at the opening at the end of 68th Street. *Waiting for us to go, so it can take over*, he thought. Once, people, smoke, strings of traffic, chains of sound had held it all together; now the grass, vines, and trees were waiting to grow out of the cracks, work their way into the empty eyeholes of the abandoned buildings.

No sound, either; everything was damn near dead, like a huge tomb. Even the pigeons weren't burbling in their craws. *They're waiting, too, for us to go.*

The thickening evening seemed so calm, so much calmer than the blood lurching distrustfully inside Hal Zwicker. He forced at the eagerness, pulling it into his voice in an attempt to share the bright anticipation in Kirby's eyes.

Kirby was lucky. He had it all ahead of him—clean, wonderful nature. Hal and Flora had lived all their lives in the city; and as bad as it was, it was part of them and hard to leave behind.

"But she just don't seem happy," Kirby said. "I sure am!"

"You should be, Kirby. It's going to be great having a place in the country. You'll have plenty of room to run around in, and lakes and wild birds and animals and big forests. There'll be fields and creeks to swim in, and the air will be clean and fresh. It'll be God's air, and we'll all get back to it, and it'll be a lot better."

"I wish that skybus'd hurry!"

Only Hal really didn't know what the Planners had set up, out there in the country. He could imagine what it was like and it sounded very good; it sounded just fine, especially for a growing boy.

The Planners had figured, probably, that it would be better if people didn't know the real details of their five acres until they were decentralized, and actually got out there. Maybe they figured that it was so much nicer in the country that, if you knew how nice it was, you would become too unhappy if you were among those to stay on in the city, waiting your turn. It had taken quite a while to get everybody moved out; because of their name beginning with ZW, the Zwickers were the last to be moved out.

"My teacher told me a lot about why we got to go back to nature." Kirby said. "Will it really be so much healthier and all?"

"Sure it will; the Planners have it figured out. They're doing it for us."

"What' s the rhythm of nature?" Kirby asked.

Hal shrugged. "Hard to say. It's something you have to feel—because you're part of it, I guess." He'd read all the pamphlets the Planners had sent around, but still it was hard to understand, really—harder to explain to Kirby. "The idea is that we've been cut off from nature too long, Kirby, so we have to get back in tune with it. It's made a lot of us sick, because we've been cut off from nature. You see, nature has a rhythm, and it's like ours. When you're cut off from it, you lose a sense of belonging, a sense of being really in, a part of living. I—oh—you'll find out, Kirby. It's hard to explain."

"But can you have a lot more *fun?*"

"Sure you can. We've been cut off from the roots, and we've got to get back in tune with the rhythm of nature. The seasons coming and going, the real God-given air, and the natural rise and fall of things."

It sounded fine. It was all from right out of the pamphlets. The only trouble was that Hal had lived in the city all his life; getting out into the country had been almost too much of a chore to tackle, even in the most expansive frame of mind. And even when you did get outside the city, it had been hardly getting back to nature—not with little special plots of land set off, that seemed only a gimmicked-up kind of city transferred to the country, with no-trespassing signs everywhere else—where the real country was supposed to be.

Getting in tune with nature was something Hal just couldn't explain.

Going back to nature had no meaning either because Hal had never been there.


NOW, he was going there. Mr. Simon Dill was a field man for the International Planners, and he was taking the Zwickers back to nature.

Dill was fat, bald, red-faced, and eager in the eyes. He was also grinning, friendly, helpful, anxious to please, and squeezed tight with enthusiasm. He was also as impersonal, really, as a shoelace.

He sat across the aisle of the skybus, puffing a pipe, looking out the window at the dark streaming past, and the occasional blurred streaks of light that would have been stars if they hadn't been going by so fast.

"Now that we're under way," Hal said, "I guess it's all right to ask where we're going, Mr. Dill."

"Call me Simon," Dill said. He smiled, savoring the suspense.

The jets whispered. Hal had looked back once, then realized that there was nothing to see; the last light had gone out in New York City.

Kirby was lying with his head in Flora's lap, and his legs over Hal's knees; he seemed to be overcome by the excitement. Flora's eyes were wide open, staring up into the invisible sky. Some sourceless weight lay heavy on her, and Hal could feel it, too. She was a woman he had thought he knew as well as himself; but now that he wondered about himself, he wondered about her, too.

And Kirby? Hal grinned thinly. It was a kid's face softened by sleep; but it was also a face of any kid with its happy dreams and a hundred thousand glittering plans. Hal envied what Kirby was dreaming about now, but was afraid of what lay behind the dim peephole of the future. The Planners knew best, of course; but it was pretty bad, Hal thought, to be uprooted, even from a dirty, crowded scar on the face of nature—the way the big city had been described in the pamphlets.

He had a raw, empty feeling—as though, somehow, his body had suddenly become full of holes. "Africa?" he asked.

"Right," Dill said.

Flora jerked her head around stiffly. "Africa!" The word slipped out of Flora, as though it had originated at the roof of her mouth.

Africa. A misty ward in Hal's memory, a vague outline on a school map.

"Dropping right into the middle of a new way of life," Dill said, putting a little homey touch to the pamphlets. "You'll soon get used to it. All of us have been away from nature too long. I'll do everything I can to help you readjust; just ask me anything you want to know."

"What about my job?... I drove a heliotaxi you know."

"You'll have comparable work at the Project, Hal. Work hours are cut way down, though; that's to give you plenty of time just to relax and get back into tune with the rhythm of nature."

Flora didn't seem to have been listening to Dill at all. "Wonder what's happened to Gloria and Al Schubert."

Hal grinned a little painfully, but tried to sound enthusiastic. "I'd almost forgot about them. The way Al used to yell up the airshaft! Wonder if they still play poker on Saturday night."

"Remember," Flora said softly, "how Gloria took Herby to Coney Island that Sunday, and she got so sick on the Twister she wouldn't even ride on an elevator far a week?" Flora turned her face quickly toward the window.

"Yeah, and Marion and Lionel…it's been six years since they were decanted hasn't it? Wonder where they are now."

"She was a funny one," Flora whispered.

"With that name," Dill said, "I'd guess they probably went to South America somewhere."

"Where at in South America?"

"Couldn't say exactly. Upper Matto Grosso somewhere."

"Upper Matto Grosso…" Flora whispered.

"Yup," Dill said, "Got a friend up there; going to take a run up there some evening soon, now. They didn't decant us until they had it all worked out so we could all visit one another without any trouble. Check out a Project skybus and visit all your friends anywhere in the world, in just a few minutes. All living isolated, and next to nature—but all connected up too by the marvels of transportation. Nature won't satisfy everything; people need people."

Flora was staring at Hal. "Hal," she whispered, "what's Marion and Lionel doing way off someplace called Matto Grosso?"

He squeezed her hand. He was being called upon to say some thing, do something, to *know* something. But he didn't even know where they were in the night, or where they were really going. For the first time he realized that the Planners were taking care of a lot more than he had ever thought, and that he felt pretty dumb about a lot of the things that counted.

"Doesn't matter," Dill was saying. "We have Projects everywhere. Everybody living everywhere in the world; no national boundaries, no nations any more. Just everybody living next to nature on their own little five acres of land. Labrador, Iceland, the

Sahara Desert, Africa, South America. A decentralized world at last!"

"Where in Africa is our five acres?" Hal asked.

"Tanganyiki," Dill said.

"Tanganyiki!" Flora put her face against Hal's chest.

Kirby jerked upright. His eyes were bright, and he turned and pressed his nose into the glass. "Where'd you say we're going?"

Flora moved her lips slowly. "Tanganyiki."

"Huh?"

"It's in Africa," Hal said.

Kirby's eyes seemed to spread all over his face. "Oh," he whispered, "Africa! Oh gosh—"

SIMON DILL checked the bit of luggage that was piled in the center of the living room. Then he turned to where Hal stood with his arms around Flora and Kirby. Kirby's eyes kept roving toward the shaded windows. Hal felt a peculiar shiver and listened for some sound—for wind maybe, something. But he couldn't hear anything.

"Africa!" Kirby said.

"Right," Dill replied. "Five acres all your very own. Guess you want me to show you around the place now. I'll brief you a little."

They followed Dill through the modern cottage, among the glass walls and green plants, from room to room. A guest room; a room for Kirby; a den for Hal, and then the kitchen for Flora.

"All automatic," Dill said, with a great deal of pride. Flora stood stiffly in the center of the kitchen, surrounded by gleaming metal, and Dill revealed a panel covered with dials. He turned a dial and pressed a button. Hal heard a soft murmuring begin in the walls, in the floor. The entire house seemed to come alive, to breath. "And now it's ready to go; there's a pamphlet there in that cabinet. It's full of diagrams and charts, and all the directions for running things."

Back in the living room Kirby again asked impatiently to go outside. Dill went to the wall and opened a small sliding panel. Inside were a number of dials and buttons. He pressed a button; the rear wall of the living room slid open. There was a wall of dark air.

"How come it's dark in Africa already?" Kirby asked.

Dill smiled. Hal wiped at the sweat coming out over his upper lip. "That's funny," Hal said. "I thought it would be pretty hot here."

"All of Africa isn't hot; there's all kinds of temperatures in Africa," Dill explained. "But that doesn't matter to you, anyway; the temperature on your five acres is anything you want it to be. You control it; you control everything in your five acres!"

Dill worked the dials. "Everything, friends. That explains this day and night business too, the weather, everything. You can make it day or night, or any degree of light and shade you want."

As he demonstrated with the buttons, a wind came up suddenly beating at the walls and whirling through the living room. Kirby grabbed Hal's wrist, and then the wind abruptly died.

Dill laughed, pressed a button. A line of lightning cracked across the darkness; thunder roared. Flora jumped, and held Kirby tight. Dill pressed another button, spun a dial. The sun came out and layover a green lawn, a sloping hill, and somewhere, Hal thought, reflecting from water.

"There it is," Dill said dramatically. "Your five acres!"

HAL felt himself straining his face toward a dubious horizon. Kirby walked to where the patio began, and looked across it over the grass and a grove of trees. "You can make it day or night, whenever you want?"

"Sure—sun, rain, wind, anything or everything. Fingertip control."

"I'm tired," Flora said; "I'd like to go to bed and get some sleep."

Kirby took another step, then bent forward a little and squinted. "What's that? I can see for a way, then it just looks sort of misty like."

"Well," Dill said, "I only lit up *your* five acres. Light comes out of the ground, out of the air even. You can vary it, make it soft or bright. See!"

"What's that—a fence or something there?" Kirby asked.

"Yes, that's a fence. It goes round your five acres, son, including part of the lake so it's safe for you to swim and take boat rides. The fence is charged though, so be careful. It keeps things clean, sterilized; keeps dangerous bugs, germs, and animals all out. You won't find even a microscopic animal of any kind in that lake there inside the fence!"

"Can I go fishing, then?" Kirby asked.

"Only on Tuesdays. Then they let fish inside the fence two at a time into your lake acreage. You can go hunting, too." Dill stood there with his pipe stuck in his mouth, leaning back a little.

"With a real rifle and all?"

"Sure, on Saturdays from 1 to 7 p.m., Project Time. They'll let a deer, or something like that, through the fence; and you can shoot it. You can check rifles from the Project Armory. Of course, you're a little young for that, Kirby; later though. That's part of getting back to nature."

Dill moved a dial to soften the light outside, then he took Kirby's hand. "Want to look around the grounds?"

"I'm tired," Flora said. She looked tired; her face was pale, and her mouth was a tight line. "We've got lots of time to look around, Hal."

"I want to see it now," Kirby said, "Gosh, this is *Africa*!"

"You and Hal go on, then," Flora said. "I—I'll just rest a while."

Hal hesitated, then followed Kirby and Dill.

"You two hurry back now," Flora said. She stood there, and after Hal had walked a ways he couldn't make out her face, but only her body standing there like a silhouette. He tried to laugh, "Don't turn on the rain while we're out here."

She didn't say anything.

THEY went around groves of trees and Dill explained there was a nice balance to the landscape, pointing out the one sloping hill, trees, the lakefront, a little creek moving across the corner of the five acres.

Then they stood on the white smooth sand of the beach. Hal stared down into the glassy water. Somewhere he thought he could hear waves beating, but there was scarcely a ripple here. He could see clear to the bottom that moved out in a smooth fall toward the fence that came up above the surface, out where it curved in toward the beach on either side, and moved on up over the land and out of sight. An odd fence. Unless it was pointed out, you'd hardly know it was there; it blended with the water, with the grass and trees. It was almost impossible to make out anything on the other side of the fence in any direction.

It *was* impossible. Just a misty blur, and a kind of muted sound out there, too; but Hal couldn't make out what the sounds were.

He gripped Kirby's hand. Something was stirring in Hal. He didn't know what it was; it frightened the hell out of him. It was some kind of very bad feeling toward Dill, and toward something bigger than Dill; but the fear was too strong, and Hal couldn't think about what the feeling was.

Kirby was looking down into the water then around the softly lit land. Slowly he looked up at Hal. Something in the look cut at Hal's strength. The look was somewhat the same as it had been sometimes when Kirby had come running in in the evenings, all excited with hunger, and Flora had told him he'd have to wait until dinner time. Only it was worse—a lot worse kind of a look, this one was. A kind of squeezing puzzlement, a deep drowning kind of bewilderment.

Kirby ran across the beach and sat down on the lawn. He touched the grass. "It felt different back home. Kind of wet like. Smelled different, too."

He looked at Hal. "There was bugs in it. If you got down and looked close, you could see all kinds of bugs and worms and things."

Dill laughed. "No bugs or germs here, son. This place is all sterilized."

"Trees had birds, too, and squirrels."

"You can get a bird permit," Dill said, "and have a couple of birds brought in. But no squirrels—rodents carry diseases. And you've got to be careful about the birds, too—have them sterilized all the time."

Hal wanted to do something about the way he felt, and even more, about the way he knew Kirby felt. But how could you fight against some vague kind of disappointment, when you couldn't think of anything better? Or when you knew that the Planners were only thinking of your own good?

Hal went over there and looked more closely at the water. It was dead, he thought. He started to touch it, then he jerked his hand back and got up slowly to his feet. Moving heavily, he lifted Kirby and pulled him along back toward the house.

"Yup," Dill said, "everything under perfect control. We'd never have gotten everybody back to nature unless we had been absolutely sure we could control everything."

AFTER THEY had a silent snack, and Kirby and Flora had gone to bed, Hal stood in the darkened living room looking out into another darkness he didn't know was real, or whether it was his; and in a while now, maybe it wouldn't make much difference.

He looked into the night for nothing he could name, and the silence moved into him like air filling a sagging balloon. He remembered the vaguely-lost sounds—the rumbling and roaring of the city that seemed soft and soothing to him now, and the other muted city noises, the underground rumble of trains, the distant cough of a car, the hydralic whine and gasp of a bus door. He remembered once walking along 4th Street windless alongside the park, quiet except for the musical Italian voice singing from an open-air store. Now the city, the millions of faces he had known, just a cloud fading into a self-dialed sky...

A rush of sweat came out over him and he jumped to the panel and savagely twisted at the dials. But the sun that appeared had a dark murkiness that made him uneasy; he turned another dial, rapidly, and felt the way his breath tore at his throat. A moon rose, and pale light rippled through the glass walls. He felt it growing, a kind of glacial fever of aloneness.

He turned a dial. The dark came in again, criss-crossed with lightning, and ripped with rumbling rolls of thunder. Then the rain came full and whispering, and Hal stood there trying to recapture that gentle music of the rain in the city night. He pulled hard to close the gulfs threatening to open wider between his thoughts.

And then he readjusted the dials to the way they had been before, and everything was absolutely still, absolutely quiet in his five acres.

He went to bed. He lay beside his wife in the dark. Her body was stiff and he knew she was awake; but he dared not say anything, because he felt a kind of shame because he had nothing to say, no hope to relieve whatever it was that lay around them.

He wondered what was on the other side of the fence, and he wondered if it was like this in Tanganyiki.

There was something demanded of him—things he should say to Kirby and Flora, some way of clarifying things; but right now he couldn't seem to think of anything. For too long now, the Planners had seemed to know what was right.

It would take a while, he guessed, to figure things out for himself.

Meanwhile he lay there and waited for whatever time he might choose to turn the dial that would make it tomorrow.

# The Last Quarry

*The Servitor's zombielike eyes mirrored man's deepest yearnings. By what miracle had human science sired creatures so monstrous?*

THE SKY was the color of mercury, and thick snow fell out of it, heavily as though it would never stop.

Hall had been sitting at the window for almost two hours looking at the snow, as if fascinated by the way it seemed to dissolve everything into peaceful and white anonymity. He sat heavily, hunched over in the gray light watching the snow, and watching the figures walking along the street.

Almost all of them were walking by twos—hurrying somewhere together. And the ones who were alone were hurrying in a way that said they wouldn't be alone long.

Hall, a big man, sat heavily as though he would be alone forever. So absorbed was he in the white world beyond the windowpane that the phone rang five times before he realized it.

He scooped up the receiver, a look of embittered weariness seeming to add years to his age.

Yes, indeed he was getting tired of the hunt.

"Hall, I've got to see you at once!" said a woman's voice at the other end of the wire.

"All right, Donna," Hall replied. "Are you at home?"

The woman's voice was ragged, and anyway Hall had known he was nearing the end of the hunt. His hands tingled, and some of the old excitement came back…

"Did you get to see Martin?"

"Yes, yes. Just a glimpse of him. But God—that was enough."

"And—the servant?" Hall asked quietly.

"He wouldn't let me stay. He's sharper than any of the others. He knew I wasn't a public stenographer as soon as he saw me. But I managed to catch a glimpse of Martin through the library door. An accident…the door came open a little. Then our little public enemy number nine hundred and ninety-nine told me to get out!"

"So it could follow you, of course," said Hall. "I guess Martin looks pretty bad by now."

"Horrible. So fat—like a huge white toad in a wheelchair. It was unbelievable. He was staring at me, but he didn't seem to see me at all."

"I'll be right over, Donna," Hall said. "Be sure it's me outside your door. Check the identification. We're the only two who should know about your apartment. If anyone else tries to get in, kill them."

Hall replaced the receiver. He turned, slowly toward the door. They hadn't wasted any time. One of them was in the hallway.

No. 999 had gone much farther than most of the others. Using human beings to do its legwork. But human beings were comparatively easy to handle.

Hall stood in the middle of the dim room and gave it a last survey, knowing he would never see it again.

*My room*, he thought. *My headquarters for five years.*

It was a dingy mouldy three-floor walkup in a section of the city that had been condemned and would soon be destroyed and re-placed by glass and chrome and neat little flower gardens.

Just a gray room with a worn carpet, a single narrow bed, a flowered vase lampbase with a dusty shade. A room with nothing distinctive about it to identify it as belonging to Hall, either under that name or any of the other names he used at various times. No books, no magazines—nothing really individualistic.

Except for the topcoat over the chair there weren't even any clothes in the closet. Hall had only one suit and he was wearing it, as he had worn it continuously for five years. He stood there as though, he were about to rent the room, or had only just moved in.

Hall moved silently to the door. The vague sound came again and he evaluated the sound with the trained attunement of his unique training. To others it would have been a sound thoroughly non-suspect in its resemblance to a whisper of wind, or, the rustling of torn wallpaper, or even a rat.

Hall could picture the fool standing out there. Some cheap thug, no doubt, who had no idea who had hired him, or what he was really involved in. Some habitual criminal type whom no amount of arrests and treatment had been able to change. And now he wanted to die.

Hall could even tell exactly where the fool was standing, hunched over slightly, listening with his every nerve alert.

Hall stepped forward and jerked the door open. The man was still trying to drag a small revolver up. With an oath Hall grabbed his wrist and swung him around and pressed his fingers into a yielding throat.

The miserable wretch made no sound. He struggled in nervous spasmodic movements like a fish. When he stopped struggling any way at all, Hall put him on the bed and then went out into the hallway.

He didn't know if the man were dead or not. By the time Hall reached the window and the fire escape he had forgotten all about him. Hall's efficiency depended, among many things, on dismissing unimportant incidents from his mind.

He had hunted down and destroyed but two less than a thousand of them, and there was only one left who could be thought of as dangerous. So far it was a perfect record, and Hall intended to finish the job before dawn.

He was no longer tired. He didn't feel that frightening loneliness any more either. He felt nothing now except the finely tuned machinery of the hunter working, a kind of high but careful excitement.

Two figures stood across the street under the white-crusted trees. He was sure that two more were stationed just at the foot of the third-floor stairwell waiting for a signal from the man who wasn't going to give them any signal.

It would be easier to go down the fire escape—and faster. He knew that he had to move fast, very fast. There was a chance that he hadn't learned the identity of No. 999 soon enough to stop him from using vital information he had certainly been squeezing out of Martin. The other Servitors had fixed themselves to some high and important people. But No. 999 had really hit high.

Ben Martin had been the Administrator of the Secret Government Research Center in Virginia for ten years. A month ago he had retired in the face of loud protest—giving illness as an excuse—and a week after that his wife had died of a heart attack.

But even that wouldn't have aroused any suspicions. It was a word about a servant Martin recently hired—and a word from his wife before she died—which had given Hall the clue he needed, and started him on his last hunt.

Martin's wife had hired what she thought was a servant. She could scarcely have been blamed for not knowing that the servant she had engaged in good faith was not a human being, but a Servitor. Neither could she have known that a Servitor was an artificial creation no one could distinguish from a human being except by its destructive influence. And the victim was not in a position to make any such distinctions.

No. 999 had wormed plenty of dangerous information out of Martin. What it intended doing with the information wasn't Hall's concern. No. 999 would use it to gain power, of course. He might try to get out of the country with the information and use it against the United States with the backing of some antagonistic nation. No. 999 might even be planning to blast loose at the living breathing humanity which had created it and which it hated with such unhuman virulence.

One thing was certain: No. 999 was far more intelligent than any of the others had been. It had avoided detection for five years where the others had failed. It had benefited from its predecessor's mistakes. It knew a lot more than it had known five years ago, and it had been built to be highly intelligent to start with.

Hall's only concern was to kill it.

He went to the window, jerked it up and went through, under the guardrail and down the stairwell in the fire-escape platform. The rust and cold iron tore at him, but he didn't feel it. His hands broke the fall, and then he dropped on down, with bullets chipping around him at the metal.

He ran for three blocks in the gray evening that was fast turning charcoal, and the lights blinking on in the few poor scattered shops hardly seemed like light at all.

He ran into the alley. Wind bit at his cheeks and kicked at his hair, and pushed the smell of the sky like a fading hope into his breathing.

Icicles hung from the top of the garbage can and a half-dead cat huddled against the brick wall. The animal didn't even snarl as Hall moved beside it against the wall. The thickening shadows were blue now like the shadows of all his hunting years. Except that this particular year seemed older as Hall waited, as though it had suddenly grown incredibly ancient in a month.

He knew he would never hunt again, so he thought of Donna as he waited. She at least would go on living and hunting. Like so many others, she had started to love him, never once suspecting that he couldn't love her in return. Her cross was her excessive need for an unreal love. That kind of abnormally centered hunger was dangerous. It was the big human weakness...

He heard the pursuer who had stayed close behind him and ahead of the others, coming on stolidly. It was not even moving with the aliveness of uncertainty down the white funnel of the night. It was no more than a dumb clod carrying out orders against humanity—the orders of something that had never been human.

There he was, in the alley's mouth. He flinched suddenly, and crouched like some kind of animal, realizing that he was standing vulnerable, wide open to attack.

He started to cry out as Hall swung the heavy soggy weight of the garbage can into his stomach. It struck him and he fell with a groan to his knees, fumbling stupidly in his topcoat pocket for a gun.

Hall used his fist, very sharply, and only twice. He employed the simplest means and worked silently so as to avoid the red tape of apprehension, and all the pretensions of being something else that slowed up his work.

Snow fell in the man's upturned face, melting on his wide, big-pupiled eyes. Swiftly Hall ran to the other end of the alley and then over to Seventh Avenue and ducked into a drugstore to call Schor, the Security Chief.

A few of the others had hired humans to stooge for them, but only a few. No. 999 was less prejudiced than the others of his kind. The stooges never knew of course.

No one knew that a thousand Servitors, experimental models, had been built by the Dalsan Company six years before. No one knew that they had disappeared of their own volition, and that due to some unforeseeable miscalculation, they had been not only as intelligent as most humans, but had possessed a degree of free will, and a consuming hatred for humans.

The Security Department had decided it would be better if people didn't know. And that it would also be a good idea if people never found out.

In fact, only three individuals knew now. Allen Schor the Security Chief, Donna Connell a top operative—and Hall. The scientists who had designed and built the Servitors for the Dalsan Company had known, of course. But they had committed suicide.

"Hello, Schor," Hall said on the telephone. "I'm on my way to Martin's. I know it's got him. I'm dropping by to see if Donna's all right. Then I'm heading straight for Martin's."

There was a long pause. Then Schor said: "Let us stand by this time."

"That wouldn't do any good," Hall told him.

"It might," Schor persisted. "This one's the worst. I don't want anything—"

"—to happen to me?" Hall smiled. "I'm afraid you're getting sentimental in your old age."

"Just give me the word to stand by," Schor pleaded.

"You'd only get yourself killed. You wouldn't stand a chance. You've always wanted to stand by, but you know damn well if I can't swing it, then you couldn't do a thing—except die."

"Well—be careful," Schor warned. "For God's sake, Hall, be careful. This is the last one. If, something happened to you now, after we've gotten clear through to the last one—"

"It's too late to worry," Hall said. "Oh…and tell your wife I really enjoyed our long talk the other night about Plato. Tell her I still don't agree with her that he was anything but a detriment to history, but that it was a very pleasant evening."

"Yes, yes—all right. I'll tell her."

"Good-bye!"

HALL stared at the door. Donna wasn't there to greet him.

He knew that she had been in the apartment only a few minutes before. But she wasn't anywhere in the three-room hideaway now. He knew as well that no one had arrived before him to spirit her - away.

She had gone because a part of her over which she had no control had forced her to go. Back to Martin's—and the Servitor.

She had looked too long and too deeply at No. 999, and now she— was gone.

The power of the Servitors resided solely in the weakness of the human beings who looked at them, and were looked at in return. And no one was immune, Hall remembered with horror as he ran back down the stairs to get a cab to take him to the airport. No one—not even Donna.

She had resisted all the others, with Hall's constant support. But No. 999 had looked too deeply. And Donna was just a little too hungry for love. True, there was no better operative than Donna. But she was human and—she believed in magic. Unfortunately a belief in magic was common among primitive tribes, and universal among children, and it lingered on in every civilized human being. Every modern man and woman had some one deep desire, stronger than all the others, and that desire was fortified by the feeling that if this one big urge could be satisfied, they would then be free of anxiety—made whole, and utterly happy. It was a reaching out for some kind of Nirvana.

Donna covered up her deep unconscious loneliness well enough. She was pretty enough. But unconsciously she believed in the magic of a great love that would cure everything. And the trouble with the Servitors was that when they looked at you, you became convinced that they could give you the one thing you wanted most on earth.

They could too. But what a human wanted most, he could die from having. He could die because what a human wanted most was a pathological need. No matter what it was—if he could get all he wanted of it—it killed him.

Hall thought of Martin turning from a gaunt man into what Donna had described as a huge white toad. As soon as he had suspected that No. 999 was Martin's servant, he had investigated Martin's background. No. 999 had simply been giving Martin what his neurotic self had always wanted most.

And that was precisely what Donna had gone back to get from No. 999.

As the helioplane lifted and moved off through the snow sea of the sky, Hall remembered the room he had left, the hidden apartment of Donna's which neither he nor she would ever see again.

Once…once she had been waiting there for him. They had worked together for years but Hall had never suspected how Donna was beginning to feel about him. It was a better kind of irony that he could think about it now.

The invitation to dinner—the candle light—the red Chianti wine… That never-to-be-forgotten night with Donna was something that could only happen once with Hall, but then—it hadn't happened. It might have but it hadn't. Which was all that Hall could have expected, of course. It was strange that he couldn't quite rub out the way he had expected more…

He could, remember the smell of her perfume, the intimate tones of her voice calling softly to him in his loneliness. He could remember how her dark eyes seemed to come closer and ever closer, and her warm hands on his face…

He could feel her touch again now—the subdued flickering inside him like an uneasy flame. The fire that could smolder but never leap high.

There was a pain in his throat, and like a flashlight into his dark misery he saw her figure as he had seen it so many times before.

That was his weakness.

But he had conquered it.

He took another cab from the village toward Martin's country estate. Along a narrow road already carpeted with snow it sped, and the entire world seemed covered, and silent in the night. The only sound was the hissing of flakes that seemed to be falling clear across the land. They descended slow and sullen in a kind of quiet that seemed as endless as the sky.

"No, don't wait," Hall said to the driver as the red taillight blinked out.

He left the cab at a turn in the road about half a mile from Martin's house, and started walking through the snow toward its squares of yellow light. He knew Martin very well from an intricate study of his life. The man had been one of the top research physicists, and yet he had never really grown up. His wife had taken care of him for years, babied him. It was inevitable that Martin should never have really learned to take care of himself. Unconsciously, therefore, he had always wanted above everything else for someone to take care of him.

That was Martin's weakness.

Martin's wife had evidently needed help because of Martin's demands, so she had hired a personal servant—No. 999. The Servitor had killed her. Then, without regret or remorse, it had taken over completely the job of fulfilling Martin's needs. And it had managed the task far more effectively than Mrs. Martin could have done.

Martin probably didn't even bother feeding himself any more—just sat day after day in his wheelchair growing fatter and fatter. Being completely taken care of the way he had always wanted and stripped of all of his worries. No more headaches, no more terrible responsibilities. No more decisions involving cobalt bombs or sprays of germs, or something even more hideous to contemplate.

No. 999 would take care of everything.

And Donna?

No. 999 had promised Donna love. She hadn't been conscious of it, but the promise itself was what she had *really* been afraid of when she had called Hall earlier; with such terror in her voice.

Of being taken over, of being given what she wanted until she wouldn't want anything else again, wouldn't even want to live again…

Hall dropped flat on his stomach and crawled toward the porch, his senses scanning the area. He waited for long minutes, but could detect nothing. He was almost certain that No. 999 wouldn't be ready. How could the Servitor have any way of knowing that a lucky chain of circumstances had enabled him to act almost immediately?

Hall lay tight against the base of the porch, with its rocks and ice-crusted mortar. Every danger charged minute seemed only a kind of re-living, for the hunt was no longer anything new. Slowly he raised himself on his elbows and looked through the French windows.

Donna was lying on a couch before the burning fireplace. She might have been dead. Her arms were hanging down on both sides of the couch, and she was staring at the ceiling. In her eyes there was an expectant joy too great to describe or understand. Like a wraith stretched out in a coffin she seemed, waiting for the joys of

Heaven.

He remembered again the night when she had offered him everything—far more than she was offering him now. Then at least there had been something full and genuine in her feelings about him. He felt sad, tragically sad, and somehow responsible for her defeat.

He desensitized himself so he would feel no disconcerting pain, and then he resolutely heaved himself over the porch railing, and without pausing to draw breath hurled himself through the glass of the French windows.

But the element of shocking surprise wasn't enough. For an instant Hall saw the lean deadly form through a glittering spray of splintering wood and slivers of glass, and rolled desperately to seek cover behind a chair.

The three explosions rang deafeningly in his ears, and the impact of the slugs seemed to drive him into the gray rug of the floor. If No. 999 had been clasping a circuit gun Hall would no longer be alive.

Desensitized, he felt nothing except the bitter black gall of possible failure. His shattered leg wouldn't function. He hitched himself around, and as he did so a wheelchair came out of a door to the right of the blazing fireplace. Martin was covered with an Indian blanket. He was a huge mound of unrecognizable suet.

No one could have remembered at that moment that the figure had ever been Martin. Hall heard a frightful voice, a grotesque wheezing sigh of babyish irritation. But nothing moved behind the sound except the pink rosebud lips, and even they moved with a heavy torpor.

"Richard…who is it? What is happening here?"

The puffed marshmallow face, the eyes like those of a grazing animal faded as Hall twisted on around, moving the circuit gun. The voice, the image of Martin, had all filled up no more than a second's space of time.

So *it* was called Richard now! It was moving along the wall as though in some strange fashion it had moved out of the wall itself. Immaculate, lean and trim in a black suit, with its white face destitute of any emotion that Hall could see. Yet how odd that that face had been so effective in reflecting the deepest, most despairing needs of human beings. It was an evil kind of mirror.

It fired again. Hall slid forward, feeling his body throb. He saw the hole appear in his coat sleeve. His fingers spread out uselessly and the circuit gun slipped away from him...

Hall felt the leg of the heavy table against his other hand. Richard smiled down and aimed the revolver relentlessly at Hall's head. Only it wasn't really a smile at all.

"So you're not a man," *it* said.

"No," Hall replied, in a defiant whisper.

"You've done a good job of concealing the fact."

Hall didn't move. "I threw up a different oscillation, so you would think I was human," he said. "It made you just careless enough to make the difference. You and the others."

"What difference? You die. You're not like the rest of us, though."

"Not exactly," Hall said. "I was number one thousand, only my motivations were different. I was made for only one purpose—to kill you."

"Then they didn't do such a good job with you. You must realize that I'm going to kill you."

"You won't kill me," Hall affirmed quietly.

He moved like an explosion. The table crushed the middle of No. 999 into the wall. Hall fired a full charge from the circuit gun into its neck and—into the vital thermostat.

The face of No. 999 became a melting lopsided mask. One of its eyes fell out, and twisted on a wiry strand in the lamplight like a pendant.

No. 999—Richard—was dead.

The end of the road.

No human could have done it. A human had needs that were stronger than his ability to resist a Servitor, even for a minute. And the limitation had included Schor, Donna, every human victim. A human was too vulnerable. But now No. 999 lay on the floor, a pile of synthetic clay. It too had become vulnerable. Hall heard a scream...

Martin's body fell from the wheelchair and lay a shapeless mound of real clay on the floor, as though released from some overmastering compulsion. Was he dead—or just paralyzed?

It was no concern of Hall's. His concern had never been with men.

He managed to get up and half fell toward the door. A feeling of uselessness was taking hold of him. His efficiency was now gravely impaired. He wasn't even aware that someone was standing just outside the door.

Hall glanced at Donna, still waiting for the love he could never give her. Still waiting for some perfect host to supply the substance of all her childhood dreams of a glorious, all-consuming love…

It would be better with a human being, real…

Once she had almost made Hall feel human. But that had been a long time ago.

He opened the door.

Schor was standing there, his hands in his topcoat pockets, a little hunched man with an owl's face and snow on his eyebrows. Behind him was an official Security car, and two Security officers stood at the foot of the porch steps with their guns ready.

Schor held Hall in his arms, and patted his back with a slow, deep affection.

"I came out anyway, Hall," he said, his voice husky. "Thought you might need me for this last show. I wanted to come."

*I won't be working with him again*, Hall thought. Friendship ended when his task was done.

"If you'd arrived a minute earlier it would have killed you," Hall said. "It had more power than any fifty of the others."

Schor essayed an anxious laugh. "Sure, I know, I'm only human."

"Well—all your worries are over," Hall said.

"Are the remains taken care of, Hall?"

Hall nodded, "Like the others. A few more minutes and there won't be any trace of him except a charcoal gray suit."

"Convenient," Schor said. "I'm referring, of course, to that built in self-incinerating device."

"Very," Hall acknowledged.

The Security officers were coming in. Someone was using a phone…announcing that Martin was dead. Hall heard Donna moan vaguely and he was glad she was alive.

No. 999 was a melting pile against the wall, fading away.

Hall started limping down the steps.

"Where are you going?" Schor asked quickly. "My wife wants you to—"

"Tell her good-bye," Hall said, abruptly.

Schor's face had a painful expression. He whispered. "Don't go. It isn't over. Listen. You can keep on working—together with me, Hall. You can hunt men just as well as—"

"No," Hall said. "Only men should hunt men."

When Schor left him, Hall continued to crawl through the snow until he was well away from Martin's house. The snow thickened as he crawled on until he was lost among the dark naked trees by a frozen creek. He could see nothing but a wilderness of falling snow.

He stood there as the snow fell more thickly, covering him over gradually until he blended into the pale silence. Then he pressed the button.

A moment later he was melting slowly away like a snowman reacting to some private sun of its own.

He had been made to do a job, and now it was finished and he...

...No. 1000.

# Star Bright

*Artificial dreams weren't enough for Andy Brooks. He was determined to find them in reality!*

HIS WIFE'S face was ugly; it was shallow and flat like a broken plate. From the balcony of their apartment in the Communal Worker's Center, Brooks turned his gaze and his hate away from her face. He looked at the moon. The disc of dreams was being blotted out by the sea; there were night shadows on the sea, fringed with the white curving foam of breaking tide.

Like the lost Sea of Anghar beside which he had fought through many Sensory Show adventures for the rewarding love of Glora Delar, the most beautiful actress of Lunarian Studio City.

He moved toward his wife. She backed away until she was standing with her back against the colonnade; below them the Palisades dropped five hundred feet into the sea-foam.

Her voice had an edge to it, a thin, petty whine. "You're sick, Andy; your face looks funny. You scare me."

He stopped. Her grey Worker's uniform did nothing for her body. "You're ugly," he said. "I'm leaving. You hate my face and I hate yours, so I'm getting out."

She stared. "Andy! That's against the Law. Who ever heard of such a thing?"

"You're hearing it, now," Andy said. "I can't stand living here with you anymore. I can't stand anything about you, or this beehive, so I'm leaving,"

"But—where can you go, Andy? They'll find you. Andy, listen to me: You've been to Personology. They've examined you. You had that bad accident at the take-off port; you made a mistake installing the fuel capsule and there was an explosion. Men were killed. What did they say at Personology?"

Brooks stared at the soft-calling Moon. Glora Delar was there tonight. He whispered. "I wonder if she's as tired of being just an actress for my dreams as I am of just dreaming of her?"

"Andy—what did they say at Personology?"

"Oh, a lot of stuff I didn't understand. What it all amounts to is

Andy watched the woman fell.

said. "Fantasy and reality mixed up—that's what the Personologist Chief said. He said that always leads to inefficiency. Remember the axiom, Brooks, he said: *No Worker Makes Mistakes.*"

"That's right, Andy. There's a place for dreaming; and there's a time for working. You kept on thinking about that Glora Delar, even after you get out of the Sensory Shows. You carried pictures of her. Always re-reading those silly letters she sent you, after you wrote that nonsense love note. Your room is filled with pin-ups of her. So you went and had an accident. See, that proves the Personologist was right. You made a mistake; men were killed."

Brooks looked at the Moon. "Two hundred and forty thousand miles away," he mused, "is paradise."

"Ha!" His wife said. "She wouldn't use you for a doormat; you're just part of another dream she has to act in that's all. Why, you little runt, she wouldn't give you a second look. Not even a first look. You're a fool even if you aren't crazy!"

Brooks scarcely noticed his

that I'm crazy."
"Crazy?"
"Schizophrenia," Andy

wife's shrill voice. He had constructed a dream world of his own named An¬ghar. On this world, he and the great actress had lived through a thousand glorious adventures. Comparing his wife with Glora Delar made the situation impossible. It was the same with his wife, he knew. She had a Sensory Show hero, Clifford Marlowe, with whom no mortal, least of all Andy Brooks, could ever compare. All right, he had the answer to both of their problems; he was getting out, tonight. He closed his eyes a moment. There was Glora Delar, walking beside the Lost Sea of Anghar. *"Come back my dear. The Armies of Vasca are at the Palace Gates and I pray for your return and the strength of your arms and your love."*

"Andy! Look at me!"

"I'm tired of looking at you." Andy said and opened his eyes. "And anyway, I have to run away. They're going to give me *directed* Sensory Shows. They're going to select all my entertainment for me, drive all my own dreams out, drive Glora Delar out, and replace my free choice entertainment with their own. He called it directive therapy. It will cure me, make me an efficient Worker again. But it'll mean I won't love Glora Delar anymore."

"Fool," she cried. "It's crazy to love our Actors and Actresses outside the Sensory Shows!"

"THAT'S WHAT HE TOLD me," Andy said. "He said that Sensory Shows were planned and provided for the Workers by Personology, just to keep us sane and efficient. Our Actors and Actresses are for everyone's benefit, he said; he said it was antisocial for me to want to monopolize Glora Delar for myself."

"That's right, Andy; that's right."

"Oh, he was a great talker, the Personologist was. He said Personology had saved the world from destruction. Once everyone was crazy, he said, running around in a daze, with fantasy and reality all mixed up. Made wars and criminals and neurotics he said. Now we've got planned, legalized fantasy in the Sensory Shows. A man can be a big shot on an imaginary world; he can have the support of the most beautiful actresses and actors. Now there's a definite time for dreaming, one for Working. Normally, one never overlaps the other."

"That's absolutely right, Andy: you should see that, I do."

"You're a shallow idiot," Andy said; "you're content to dream. I'm not; I'm interested in the real Glora Delar. The dreams aren't enough any more, not for me."

"Andy, you always were different. I could never figure you out, and I'm not interested in trying. But all I've got to say is you're just not using common sense. What if all us Workers who worship the Actors and Actresses up on Hollywood II stormed the Moon? Took a million rockets and all flew to the Moon? You are crazy, Andy. And think how wonderful the Sensory Shows are! Work a few hours a week, and the rest of the time you can live a beautiful life with actors and actresses who are so good they can make you believe anything."

"Not me," Andy said. "If a dream can't come true, it's no good. So I'm going to the moon, to Studio City; I'm going to find Glora Delar, in person."

Her dull eyes bulged incredulously at him, "Andy! That's forbidden! You'd be breaking a Class-A Law, and you know what happens to them that does that?"

"I'm going," Andy said. "I can sneak aboard a moon rocket; I'm going tonight."

"Andy, I'll tell! I'll not let you do it!"

Andy lunged. Her cries gurgled into silence under his fingers. He lifted her shivering body up over the colonnade. "I figured you would," he said. "And then I figured that this way—you wouldn't."

Her body fell into the darkness. Brooks stood there a long time gazing down at the curling white foam of the breakers. It was like ripping open a black hole and pouring the past into it. He closed up the hole and turned. He could never have submitted to *directed* Sensory Shows, so he had to fight.

In the old days a man could fight for what he loved, even if success was impossible. It was pursuit that counted, the pursuit of happiness that had made men and nations strong—when there *had* been men and nations. Andy's heart beat wildly as he went down the escalator. He might not succeed, but he would have the pleasure of trying the forbidden and incredible; he would crash the gates of Studio City on the Moon.

THE PILOT WAS FORWARD in the cage checking the pre-navigation controls. Brooks slipped into the freight chamber and crawled behind newly loaded packing cases. His skin tingled, and his breathing was rapid.

His audacity had been the big factor in his successfully sneaking aboard the new Moon supply rocket. It was inconceivable that anyone would so much as think of breaking a Class-A Law; the punishment was extreme. Only a few select personnel, other than the Stars, including producers and directors and psychogenic-radial screen projection artists and the like ever made the flight. And for them, it was always a one-way trip. Only the pilot and the Security Guard accompanying the flight ever returned from the Moon, and they never left the rocket while on the Moon. The rocket always returned immediately to Earth. A veil of glamorous mystery surrounded the Stars and their fabulous Studio City.

Brooks' familiarity with the take-off field, where he had worked as a mechanic and fuelman until his negligence had caused the big blow-up, his knowledge of its arrangement and schedule had enabled him to don a mechanic's uniform in the locker room, get an electrodrill from the supply house for use as an excuse for boarding the rocket. Boarding, he went unnoticed. Mild confusion always reigned about the rocket prior to take-off; no one had noticed that he had not come out of the rocket. And luckily for him, Personology had removed all personnel who had been employed at the field at the time of the disaster, for therapy. Personology always looked out for the Workers.

So Brooks lay in darkness, shivering with excitement that was partly fear. The muffled thunderous explosion engulfed him; the area around him vibrated smoothly. The rocket was lifting. Even protected as he was by the inflated shock-cushion Andy had dug out of a freight room storage locker, the pressure was intense. He blacked out and he knew he had been out a long time when his own groaning awakened him. He grabbed at the edge of a packing case to pull himself erect. The effort smashed him up into the ceiling. Blood ran down his face. He was weightless now, in space; he moved around a little, careful to hold on to something. Then Andy stared at the dim shadow of the bulkhead door; he licked his lips slowly.

The throbbing of his pulse became thunderous. The emptiness in his stomach turned to nausea. This was real adventure, not a dream. But it would have to end somewhere—sometime. He rubbed his lips and sweat ran down his face. What then? A Class-A Law said no one was to go to the Moon. But why was it so important? What was so wrong about actually seeing the Actors and Actresses? About seeing the big production factories where they acted out one's dreams?

His flesh seemed cold and feverish at once. The penalty made him wince. Condemnation to the Experimental Stations, a fate normally reserved for hereditary and incurable mental defectives. Experiments involving spaceflight which so far no human body had been able to sustain beyond a few million miles; brain surgery; body-structural alterations. There were other experiments not commonly discussed. No one looked forward to breaking a Class-A Law; no one survived the experiments. It was capital punishment that benefited the Order, and therefore it was good.

But not for Andy Brooks. Yet there was no turning back now. Murder was also an infringement of Class-A Law—but that might be considered an accident; anyone could fall from a balcony, or jump.

Andy thought, briefly, of his wife. Very briefly. She was dead. It didn't seem very important whether she was dead or not. She had stood in his way; that had been important. There had never been anything between them anyway but a silent bitter futile hatred for each other's unattractiveness. She loved Clifford Marlowe, the great Actor; he loved Glora Delar, the Actress. No mortal could compare with either of them; no one felt any emotional regard for anyone else. Emotion was confined to the Sensory Shows. A time for emotion and dreaming and wish fulfillment; a time for Working—the two never got mixed up. That's what Personology had told him.

Brooks was trying to figure out what he would do when the rocket hit the Moon, when it dropped into the depth of Theophilus' 18,000 foot, 65 mile-wide crater and into the City of Stars. He was concentrating on that when the bulkhead door began to open.

BROOKS GNAWED AT HIS lips as he crouched behind the door.  The Security Guard entered, checking probably for possible weight shift.  Holstered to the belt of his gray uniform was a neurotube and a meson blastgun.  The continuing cold war with the Eastern Alliance necessitated constant preparedness against possible espionage.  That's what Personology said.

As the Guard turned to exit, he saw Brooks.  His eyes widened remarkably.  His hands moved out as though questioning Brooks' reality.  Without thinking, Brooks leaped, his breath breaking harshly.  The Guard grabbed wildly at Brooks' wrist and they fell back, scrambling and grunting.  The fall broke the Guard's hold; Brooks slammed the drill against the Guard's chest and squeezed the trigger release.

The gentle whir of the drill was drowned by the Guard's short, incredulous scream of pain.  Blood spilled over the drill and ran down Brooks arm as the Guard rolled lifelessly against the wall, trembled lightly with the dropping, decelerating motion of the rocket.

Brooks leaned against the wall.  The silence was vast.  He looked at his fingers as he sensed the rocket settling.  It was done, really done now; he could not change it back.  His wife's body falling into the blackness had seemed a kind of unreal thing, but this was horribly real.  The Guard would never worry anymore about dreams, or about reality, either.  Maybe he was luckier than most, maybe luckier than Andy Brooks, the mechanic who had stopped machinery no mechanic could repair.

This was murder for which Andy would pay, but that didn't matter.  He had broken a Class-A Law when he boarded the moon rocket.  There were no degrees of guilt.  The thought gave him a kind of freedom inside, a sudden snapping of strings and singing of breaking wires.

He took the neurotube from the Guard.  It did things to the nervous system, including paralysis and blackout.  Its sustained use could cause death.  He didn't take the meson blastgun; it was too lethal, and he was afraid of it.  He slipped along the grillmesh corridor and crouched outside the door into the pilot's cage.  He stared at the pilot's back, past the pilot into the view screen.  The Moon was as big as Earth below, sharp angles of light and shadow, gigantic craters and pools of glaring frozen lava.

The purple-black shadows of Theophilus' walls dropped around the rocket. Far below like a dot of glittering ice was the white-domed brilliance of Studio City. Brook stared in awed wonderment. Maybe this was a dream, too; it was too fabulous to be real. A Worker—on the Moon! A Worker actually being a part of Hollywood II's legendary marvels! He could see the big production factories where the Stars acted out a man's dreams, where the big psychogenic radial projection screens performed their miraculous function.

On Earth, the millions of ardent fans spent all possible time in the Sensory Shows. A small dark chamber. A beam of light, a whiff of gas, music. You didn't look at it; you were in it. Your wishes took form. Actors and Actresses of your choice supported you. It was touch, taste, action, emotion. It was so real that no Worker cared to dream during Working hours. In the Sensory Show chamber he could be anything, on any one of many possible worlds. He could be a beggar, a King, a soldier, or a god.

And Glora Delar was your wife mistress, lover—

But there was a real Glora Delar, too.

A blare of cushioning brilliance spilled over the view screen. The rocket disappeared in a wall of flame; the dome opened; tractor beams clutched the rocket, tilted it, dropped it gently. The pre-navigated controls combined with receiving facilities to work out the usual mechanized and perfect routines. The pilot seemed bored. A dolt, Brooks thought; a man regularly making this flight, unmoved by the grandeur and wonderment.

As the rocket was gripped in the big robotractor arms and placed atop a tubular gas duct preparatory to the return take-off, Brook caught a brief glimpse of the City of Stars. Just like the ads, the many publicity shots of background for the Stars, at home, at work, at play. Wide avenues between smoothly domed buildings, leading off into parks, residential areas. The grass, the trees, the flowers were strange, unlike anything on Earth.

Brooks jerked open the door, pressed the neurotube against the pilot's neck. The pilot turned slowly. His face was unimaginative, white and twisted with shocked surprise; he stared wide-eyed at Brooks.

"WHAT—" THE PILOT whispered.

"Shut up!" Brooks warned. "I'm going out there. I want to see; open the side port doors."

The pilot's eyes looked beyond Brooks.

"The Guard's dead," Brooks said. "I killed him with an electrodrill. I can keep this neurogun on you until you die too. Open the door; don't try to stop me from going out there."

The pilot choked. "I'll not try to stop you. Go ahead. Why should I try to stop you?"

"You'd better not try to stop me," Brooks said. "Let me tell you something. Listen, the Sensory Shows are no good. They create an illusion of happiness for us, like dope. Anything that makes an illusion of happiness with no basis in reality—that's wrong; it's the same threat to a man's mind that learning to stop being hungry without eating would be to your body. Isn't that right?"

The pilot's mouth hung wordlessly open.

"I'll tell you what's wrong." Brooks' voice was loud. "A dream has to be possible to find in reality, or it's no good. That's where Personology's wrong. Dreams are no good if they can't come true; what good are wishes and hopes and ambitions if you can't find them except in a Sensory Show? Answer me that!"

"I—ah—" the pilot said.

"I'll answer it," Brooks shouted. "They're no good at all; they're bad. It won't last. People will revolt, or they'll rot sooner or later. Maybe I'm the first and there'll be more; maybe I'm the last and everybody'll rot! I'm in love with Glora Delar, see! Really in love—you understand that? Listen, you stupid dolt, don't tell me she's your favorite Actress, too! It doesn't mean anything. You don't have the nerve to do anything about it. The question is can she ever be in love with me—a Worker?"

"I…don't…know," whispered the pilot.

"You know what the Personologist said to me?" Brooks screamed. "He told me we'd all be crazy without the Sensory Shows. When you mix dreams up with reality, he said, that's insanity. What's more insane then admitting that the work we do is all we'll ever get out of life? That we can never know anything wonderful, anything we really want, in real life?  Can you tell me what could be more insane than that?"

The pilot shook his head.  Sweat ran down his nose.

"Don't move or I'll leave the neurotube on you long enough to kill you," Brooks shouted.  "Because you don't understand."

"I won't move," the pilot whispered.  "I won't try to stop you; I won't say anything.  Go back out there and I'll open the door for you.  As far as I'm concerned, I don't know anything; I've never seen you."

"All right; you're a fool, but I think you're honest."

Already the side freight chamber port was open.  Robotractors were unloading and carting the freight onto conveyor belts.  Brooks ran into the exit chamber, shut the airtight.  The pilot kept his word; the outer door opened.  Brooks went down the ladder.  He ran; he didn't look back.  He didn't have time for that.  Somewhere there were a few Guards, stationed here permanently in an isolated barracks building.  They would learn of his deeds.  But he was free, for a while.

He ran down the long silent avenues and through the strangely silent parks, among the odd unearthly plants and among the alien looking trees and over the paper-like unreal seeming grass.

Above him, the teflonite dome that held in the synthetic atmosphere was like a huge white bubble.

BROOKS WALKED LIKE A drugged man through his dreams-come-true.  He stared; his mouth hung open; a warm ecstatic joy filled him.  Stars, stars everywhere.  There was Ellan Morlan and Clifford Marlowe gliding past in a bubble-shaped shiny white gravcar.  They passed so close to Brooks he could see the color of their eyes, the shine of their teeth.

To most women, Clifford Marlowe was the fulfillment of every wish.  Ellan Morlan was second only in popularity to Glora Delar.  Beautiful people, golden-skinned, perfectly proportioned, like gods and goddesses.

Brooks walked slowly, haltingly, taking in the atmosphere like a thing starved.  It was beautiful, here; but there was something wrong.  Wrong with the air.  It was the silence.  It wasn't peaceful; it was too heavy, and he couldn't explain it.  There was something of fear in the silence. Nothing moved except the Stars moving across the wide green lawns of paper-like grass, the Stars whirring along the streets or through the air, noiselessly. The Stars that made no sound.

There should be noise, somewhere. There—walking toward him—four of Hollywood II's most demanded supporting players! They were walking right past him! He could *touch* them! Michael Thorenson, Mara Rosara, Greta Moore, Gil Grendon—they brushed against him as they passed. Brooks stumbled out of their way. He could talk to these people, if he could work up the courage. Maybe later he would have the courage, after the initial daze was worn a little. When he found Glora Delar—

But why hadn't they noticed him? They didn't seem to see him, even know he was here; they would have bumped into him if he hadn't stepped aside.

Now Andy felt lost, terribly small, all at once terribly alone as he wandered up and down the glamour-shrouded avenues, through the parks, the wonderfully intricate playgrounds for the Stars' children. Special beautiful little creatures playing with wonderfully advanced toys—they would grow up to provide dreams for the Sensory Show millions. But now they didn't make any noise. That was odd: Kids usually shouted and laughed when they played. But then Stars' children would be different. Here everything had a strange silent difference. Andy hadn't expected quite this much difference. The silence was smothering, suffocating. Stars, Stars everywhere. The living breathing embodiments of millions of workers millions of dreams. But no sounds.

He saw no one else of his own class, though that wasn't surprising. No Workers; no Guards; no one in the gray utilitarian uniforms. Just Stars in their beautifully unique, individually styled garments. Just the silent children playing silently like figures moving in an old three-dimensional movie.

DOROTHY DILLON walked past, tall and lithe and the color of melting copper, her hair a tingling black cloud around bare shoulders. Andy could have touched her arm. He started to say something, but he couldn't; she didn't seem to see him.

He clenched his hands and started to yell something after her, but managed to control himself. Bitterness and resentment crowded the awed wonderment. Maybe that was the reason Personology strictly forbade anyone coming to the Moon. It would break illusions. Maybe the Stars were really just a lot of superior snobs who held their worshippers in contempt.

Maybe, But Glora Delar wouldn't be like that; she was different; he knew. Together, they had shared dream adventures that were his and his alone. Anghar. The Palace of Anghar, the Armies of Vasca. She would be different.

A sense of timelessness carried him along. There was no day or night, by contrast. It was always synthetic day. The bubble overhead, the smooth domed buildings, the walkways and avenues, all radiated a cold ever-shining light. He hadn't taken the Guard's watch. How long had he been walking? He didn't feel hungry or thirsty or tired. There was no measurement in silence, in cold white unchanging light.

He stood by a lake. The scene was like a three-dimensional photograph, the grass under him like rustling confetti. The big lake's surface was like smooth shining glass. Swans glided along the glass like clockwork. Huge water-lilies trembled with a strange regularity of motion in a slight breeze that was always the same.

Then he saw her—Glora Delar, walking along the shore, only a few feet away. A sudden weakness overcame him. His knees gave way and he dropped on a bench. He half rose, sank down. "Glora," he whispered. "Glora—"

She wasn't alone. A man walked with her. The favorite of millions of women who for some reason found Clifford Marlowe not quite perfect. Carl Brittain. In the People's Fan Magazine there had been hints that Glora Delar and Carl Brittain were more than just friends. Brooks had figured it as being more propaganda.

JEALOUSLY AND HATE roiled to muddy fear, fear and self-inadequacy, and Brooks shrank down against the bench, hoping they wouldn't see him. He wanted to crawl into a dark corner, hide somewhere. There was no dark corner; everything was bright and white and blazing white light. Here no man could hide; no man could sleep where there was no night.

A sharp shrill whistle dug into his brain. He jerked around. Far across the expanse of park a black skycar came whirring, gliding, sliding toward him. The ultrasonic whistle sharpened painfully and he knew this was pursuit.

The pilot hadn't been so honest, maybe. But that made no difference now. It had never been anything anyway that would have gone on forever. No matter when the black skycar came for him there would never have been a place to hide. It didn't matter now, not after seeing Glora Delar and Brittain together like this.

But before the Guards picked him up—

He ran toward the lake. The skycar was an elongated shadow over the glassy water, over the glossy mechanically moving leaves of the huge water-lilies, over the backs of the clockwork swans. The whistle seemed to split his skull.

"Glora!" he shouted.

He ran toward them. Evidently they didn't hear him; she didn't turn; Brittain didn't turn. Brooks' shout faded across the lake into the glowing bubble and died.

He grabbed her arm and spun her around. Carl Brittain walked on, and Brooks stared into Glora Delar's eyes. A cold shiver went down his neck. What was the matter? Where was the warmth, the love, the passion, the worship, the dark deep longing? There was no recognition, and without that there could never be any of the other things. However the big psychogenic radial projection screens functioned, the Actors and Actresses probably were never aware of the individuals they entertained. They entertained all the Workers.

*All the Workers.*

"Glora, look at me! I wrote the letters, thousands of fan letters! You answered them. They were addressed to me, personally! Me, Andy Brooks!"

She said slowly. "An—dy—Brooks—"

Fifty feet away the skycar settled. Swans glided silently across the lake of glass without noticing anything; water-lilies moved in the unchanging breeze. Glora Delar's—eyes were on a level with his.

"Don't you know me?" Brooks shouted wildly. "You've got to! Andy Brooks!"

She repeated his name.

"Yes, yes!" Brooks screamed. "Look at me—Andy Brooks! Remember the Lost World of Anghar! Why dream of each other? Why should we fool ourselves with dreams? I'm here now, I'm real, you're real! I've broken a Class-A Law triply to come here to you. Glora, you've got to see me, talk to me!"

" An—ghar—"

"Listen to me, Glora! The World of Anghar. The Armies of Vasca. *Our* dream. I was holding the castle. Vasca's fleets were laying siege. I was guarding the seawall. How could it have gone on so long without you knowing? It was our dream."

"Vas—ca—"

Sobbing frantically, Brooks turned. Two guards were leaping from their skycar. One of them was shouting, "You there, halt! We've orders to kill you if you resist."

"Get back!" Brooks cried. "Stay right there!" He lifted the neurogun. Now he wished he'd brought the blastgun; he'd have blown these Guards and their skycar in a million pieces.

The Guards came slowly toward him along the lake's edge. The swans glided unconcerned. Brooks screamed defiantly. As he fired at one Guard he threw himself to one side. The foremost Guard fell in silent paralysis. Evidently reflex action caused him to accidentally discharge the meson blastgun. A bluing lethal flame mushroomed, and the green lawn crackled to black char in a long smoking swath.

Brooks fired again. The other Guard dodged behind an alien looking tree with orange leaves. Brooks ran wildly. "Glora— wait—"

SHE TURNED AS BROOKS ran past her. Her shoulder struck Carl Brittain and the Actor's body toppled into the lake. He went under without a struggle. The water opened and slid over his body again like thick shiny glue. The swans glided over the spot. Brittain didn't come up; there was no movement in the 'water'.

Brooks ran on after Glora who hadn't stopped walking. Behind him, he heard the Guard shouting. He ran past a parked skycar. Beside it, a couple sat shoulder to shoulder looking over the lake. They seemed oblivious to the commotion.

Brooks grabbed Glora's arm and dragged her toward the skycar.

"You'll remember," he sobbed. "I'll see that you remember."

He slid the cowling back. As he started to drag the woman into the seat, he hesitated. He stared into her face. The face he had kissed many times in a thousand thousand adventure-dreams in a hundred imagined worlds. It was the same, but somehow, different. Her eyes returned his stare, unblinking, unrecognizing, unconcerned. Her flesh was strangely unresponsive to his hands. No resistance, no compliance, nothing at all.

The Guard was running and he was near. He stopped, leveled the meson blastgun. "I don't want to kill you," he shouted hysterically. "Give yourself up; I've never killed anything, and I don't want to kill you."

Brooks laughed crazily. "You'll kill her, too, if you fire at me. You'll kill the dreams of millions of your fellow Workers if you kill Glora Delar. Get back there now."

"You're too dangerous," the Guard said; "I've orders to kill you if you don't give yourself up, because you're insane."

Andy Brooks laughed. He tried to push Glora Delar into the skycar. He saw the Guard was going to risk a blast. He spun, dropped her body between them. It had flashed through his mind—if she died with him, then in a way, she would be his forever, only his, and she would never be shared with all the other millions of Workers.

A blazing light burned and blinded him. He fell gasping and crumbling with the deep and lasting agony. He lay in burning fog. He tried to get up. He couldn't move. Through a thickening blur he saw the Guard lurching toward him, his face white and contorted with horror.

Brooks' hand fumbled blindly, touched something. "Glora," he whispered. He slowly twisted his head. He had to do that much.

The skycar was a smoking melting pile, unrecognizable. Beside him lay something else, also smoking; a human outline, a framework of wire and metallic joints, bits of cloth and melting fluid, springs, some burned-out vacuum tubes, a condenser, a charred coil, other parts—all running down through a framework, a skeleton of red-hat wire. Charred hair sizzled in blue flame in the fine mesh of a metal skull. Glora Delar—

The Guard stood over Brooks. His face twisted, his voice came through a dense curtain of time and space and pain. "Been here for years, but I never suspected such a thing. I knew something was queer, but this! This is what they give us—puppets! Marionettes—wire and putty and plastic! She was my favorite actress too—my pin-up girl! just a second ago. Ha, ha, ha, funny isn't it? I fought for her a thousand times in the Lost World of Anghar, against the Armies of Vasca. This is what they give us for dreams!"

Brooks managed to turn his head so he wouldn't have to look at what lay beside him. The two pretending lovers still sat shoulder to shoulder by the lake. Beautiful golden people, staring over the water, romantic lovers. They were oblivious to what had happened. The lake was colored glass, unruffled. The clockwork swans glided over the shiny surface. The perfumed wind blew unchanged through dutifully nodding leaves of the water-lilies.

Above him, the great bubble over Studio City seemed to burst in a million bright glittering shards.

"I'll tell everybody!" the Guard was shouting. "I'll tell all the millions so they'll know!"

Then there was no sound but the wild fading cries of the Guard as Brooks closed his eyes to sleep.

*...and this is one dream, he thought, that will be my own, my Own.*

# Jack the Giant Killer

*The child Franz served only the pitiless cruelty of a world gone mad. But what is murdered in the day will wake at night screaming.*

ONLY NINE YEARS old, he thought—and already a Junior Investigator! Franz lay abed in his room at School of Orthodoxy No. 3, staring into the darkness, his pride and joy unconfined. What a great moment! What a shining milestone in his young life!

Franz lay rejoicing in the dark, and after a while he tried to sleep. Maybe some kids, some adults even, were afraid of being alone. But not an Investigator. An Investigator wasn't even afraid of being afraid.

He tried to fight off the mushy sick ache for someone to be there in the room with him. Some woman even, he thought. Someone warm and sympathetic and consoling who would put soft arms around him.

Franz gulped and grimaced in the dark to keep from despising himself. Surely it was a privilege to be alone. Only an Investigator, one of the privileged, *could* be alone. And yet—was there perhaps some small, hidden flaw in the nightly solitude? Might it not be just barely possible that if a person wasn't required to be alone at night sleep would come swiftly and naturally, and he would never be afraid of having dreams.

Dreams were an irrational delusion and a snare, and they had no place in the real world. They were a dreadful threat to total security. Who knew what subversion might not be buried in the unconscious?

Weren't dreams the sneaking voice of the unconscious in all of its ugly primitiveness? Sure they were. If you had them you had to confess them because they were sins. If you confessed them, your brain could be washed out, and after that, you wouldn't dream anymore. You wouldn't do much of anything any more except the few simple things a robot could do better.

*Sleep, Franz, sleep. You've a hard day ahead of you tomorrow. You've got a lot of Investigating to do. Remember—you're a Junior Investigator now.*

It was much worse in the dark. When it was dark, he could not shake off the feeling of another presence in the room with him. Something mushy. It had happened before, often, but now it was so alarming that he got up suddenly, and switched all the lights on.

The thing wasn't visible. But outside the window, in the whirring whine of the City, he could still feel its cautiously withdrawing presence. Something watching. Something real mushy.

Franz curled up, clutching his knees and suddenly he felt that he was floating. He knew without caring any longer, that he was falling asleep—finally making it, just too desperately tired to stay awake another instant.

It was as he had feared. The figure, the warm promising transparency, came drifting toward him, its pale face sweetly smiling. The warm white arms reached out to comfort him and a voice started whispering close to his ear:

"Jack. Jack, darling. Wake up. You're going to climb the beanstalk."

*"Once upon a time…*

*"Long long ago…"*

Bedtime stories. Fairy tale lullabies hummed to a Junior Investigator!

He woke up screaming and bathed in cold sweat.

Gray morning light moved through the window, creeping slowly up the naked metal walls of his room, over the single cot, the locker, and the small metal desk.

He jumped out of bed, anxious to forget the dreadful, sickening dream. He didn't put on the new Junior Investigator's uniform as he had planned. He put on play shorts instead, ignoring the glittering splendor of the official costume, and carried it to his locker with resolutely averted eyes.

He was winning the confidence of that mushy little Marie, so play shorts would serve his purpose best. Later he would take the uniform to school with him, and put it on secretly during recess. None of the kids knew that he was an Investigator or how many of them he'd be duty-bound to turn in as suspects.

Take Marie, for instance. He was sure Marie had a fairy-tale book hidden somewhere, and that she had dreams as dreadful as his own. All he needed now was a confession from her own lips. Words he could get down on the tape, and give to the SG boys.

Maybe today he would get the direct evidence that would establish her guilt.

As he was drinking his breakfast from the automeal, Marie, as usual, knocked impudently on the door. She was a saucy little girl to be only seven, he thought—stuck up and mushy. She tried to act grown up, but that was a laugh, really. All the kids were such bores—laughing and shrieking and playing their childish games.

But he had to play with them, had to make a pretense of playing. How else could he get the evidence he needed?

"Come in," he said.

Her blonde hair was in braids, and she was wearing play shorts striped soberly in black and gray. She gazed at him curiously out of light blue eyes, and put her hand trustingly on his arm. That was Marie—gushy and mushy all the way through.

"I passed your door last night," she said. "I heard you crying."

"Not me," Franz said, staring at her in alarm.

"I heard you crying," she insisted, looking around slowly. She lowered her voice. "Were you having a—dream?"

He shook her hand off his arm. It felt moist and hot. "You'd better not use that word," he said quickly.

"I bet you were having a dream," she said. "You can tell me, Franz. I've got an idea about dreams. Everybody dreams, but nobody's supposed to. So everybody forgets."

"You'd better forget. Let's go out and play."

"Next time I hear you crying at night, Franz, I'll come in and sit with you. You stay by yourself too much."

"I never dream," Franz said, avoiding her eyes. "It's subversive."

"Dreams never used to be bad did they? Now a dream's bad even when it's good?"

"How do you know?" He had the recorder turned on. Fortunately it was concealed beneath the loose folds of his playsuit, a tiny metal box with a loop antenna.

Her wide blue eyes smiled at him slowly. "I never dream. Franz."

Not another word could he get out of her about dreams. No information—not even the possible location of the fairytale book, which he was sure she had managed to conceal on the school grounds. Well, he could search for the book later. He had plenty of time.

When the play-period bell rang Franz returned to his room, and emerged with the uniform concealed inside a toy box. He stopped at a public park three blocks away, and put the resplendent costume on in the washroom.

The other kids couldn't leave the school except by special permission. Most of them went home weekends to live with their guardians, but a Junior Investigator could go anywhere he liked, any time the urge to roam took firm hold of him.

He walked slowly, rigidly, along the winding pathway of the Concourse where it twisted five hundred feet up among the hanging gardens of the City. He breathed deeply of the crisp, cool air and forgot about the fear, the aloneness, and the dreams. The dreams hadn't happened. Not to him. They couldn't happen to a Junior Investigator!

He told himself that he had nothing at all in common with the other kids. On the contrary, in his uniform, he felt quite as big and important as the adults he passed on the Concourse. The adults only *looked* bigger than he was. True, they were taller physically, but as an Investigator he was really far more important than any of them. And as soon as the Security Guards gave him a shock-box, he could stop any of those "giants" anywhere—the instant he caught them doing or saying anything suspicious. Shock them and give them a quick little brain probe right there on the spot.

So who was bigger? Name him!

The sun glinted on his badge and on the lightning flash insignia of the Omega Security Corps. He walked proudly among the giants, and inside himself he was laughing. When he stepped inside the tubeway, he seemed actually to float in a little cloud of power, safe and satisfied within his secret aura of strength. He was conscious of how enviously people stared at him. There was jealousy in their glances—and a fearful respect.

But still he was only a Junior Investigator, and he had an impatient, unruly longing to do some real grown-up investigating as soon as possible. He didn't want to attend lectures, drills, orientation sessions with the SG and the Young Defenders all the time. He wanted to be running around in intrigue, spying, stealth, sneaking, peeping and sly listening. He wanted to brain-probe, brainwash and put risks on the griddle, forcing them to talk under duress. He'd know how to open up their minds.

He walked faster.

What could General Kerf, Chief of the Security Guards, want with him? Was he about to be given a more adult assignment? Would he actually get his shock-box now? He kept his eyes and ears sharpened as he walked, alert for any slight sign of disloyalty among the citizenry.

You never knew who might be a mystic, an irrational, a Reb, a free-thinker, or a loner. You had to be alert for little signs that only an Investigator could see. Sometimes Franz could *smell* a risk.

Like the woman he suddenly saw standing by herself on Tier Eight. He stopped the instant his gaze came to rest upon her. He waited patiently for ten minutes and then he flashed the identification beam on her from his concealed SG kit. Like an accusing finger the personalized vibratory-beam identity report went straight back to Headquarters Lab in the heart of the Security Ad Building. With it, Franz sent merely the one accusative word: "Loner."

The Investigator's Manual stated that any man or woman found standing alone for ten or more minutes was plainly guilty of fantasy construction on a dangerously secretive level.

Before Franz walked half a block away he saw the SG skycar swoop down and suck the screaming, wildly terrified woman into its yawning vacuumatic pickup tubes.

No one else dared to notice. Franz's eager eyes bounced all over the faceless bulk of the crowd, searching for someone who might be curious enough to be looking. But the others knew that anyone displaying curiosity would have shared the woman's fate, guilt by association being a grievous crime.

Franz felt very proud of his high score. As far as he knew, he was the youngest of the Junior Investigators and he dwelt with pleasure on his most recent triumph. The woman loner would probably get off with a third-degree brainwash. A loner seldom got a first degree wash job. But what happened to them after he exposed them wasn't important. Only his official rating was important.

Standing at last in General Kerf's presence, Franz snapped to attention and saluted smartly.

General Kerf returned the salute. He was a tall, aloof and slimly powerful man attired in a SG uniform of funeral black, and just returning his stare made Franz realize how many notches you had to have on your spying-disk before you could become a Senior Investigator. And a General—

General Kerf's bone-shadowed face tilted, and his eyes were suddenly like powdered glass shining down on young Franz.

"We think you're ready for your first really big assignment, Franz," he said.

Franz couldn't say anything. His throat was too tight, and his breathing too agitated.

"You've an excellent record, young Franz," the general went on quickly. "When you turned your Mother in at four you proved yourself a devoted investigator. Your father too, for hiding a forbidden book and a file of sheet music of the old era. Do you remember how at seven you found your uncle reading poetry and exposed him instantly? Spotting subversive poetry, mechanistic stuff, at that age! Remarkable, Franz!"

"Thank you, sir. May I remind you that in the same year I caught my cousin and aunt plotting to sneak into the country? I knew there was no reason for that, so I looked it up in the Code Book. They were guilty of mysticism. They were trying to get in touch with nature spirits, to help them rebel. I reported them both. Remember?"

General Kerf smiled. "I remember, Franz. Your exceptional hereditary qualities as a spy has influenced our decision to give you a more vital assignment. You'll be privileged to spy on someone really important—your Guardian."

"My—my Guardian!" Franz whispered. It was almost too good to be true.

"That's correct. When we assigned you to Professor Hans Schaeffer as a ward we hoped that you would prove capable of Investigating him."

"But he's so—so powerful, sir. The Overseer of the Omega Calculator!"

"Exactly, Franz. The Overseer of the Omega. Few Senior Investigators could be trusted with this task and those few could not see Schaeffer constantly without arousing his suspicion. He's in a position to do a great deal of damage to the Plan and the Security Shields."

"Oh, sir," Franz said. "Thank you!"

"Schaeffer is very fond of you, isn't he, young Franz?" the general asked.

"Yes, sir!" young Franz replied.

"He won't be at all suspicious of you."

"I'm sure he won't be, sir. He has even said he—loved me." Franz smiled with embarrassment.

"We had hoped for that. Schaeffer's an old and a lonely man."

A buzzer sounded and an SG Lieutenant entered.

"This is Lieutenant Myerfing," Kerf said. "Lieutenant, I want you to meet our prize pupil, young Franz Schaeffer."

Myerfing coughed. "Sir, there seems to be some disagreement in the Council about Schaeffer."

The general stared at him impatiently. "What sort of disagreement? This is hardly a time to review a carefully weighed decision."

"The old sentiments regarding Schaeffer are rising again among the Senior Council Members, sir. They all agree that the Omega Calculator is of supreme importance to the maintenance of the Plan. They agree that only the Calculator with its unerring electrons could have moulded an orderly, well-tooled society from the pulp of the masses. But they say the Omega is still a very complex calculator, and that Schaeffer is the only one who can care for it properly."

He paused, then added quickly, "Also Schaeffer is much older than any of us can remember. He grew up with the Omega. He practically built it himself. I'm afraid that some of the older members tend to respect Schaeffer at least as much as they do the Calculator, sir."

"A common trap for incipient sentimentality," Kerf said.

Franz had studied the Code books religiously. He had some idea of what they were talking about and now he was frightened. Talking about the glorious Omega so candidly seemed sinful. The Omega kept everything running smoothly and rightly, and nothing could ever change for the worst as long as the Omega ruled. Being a machine, it couldn't change at all.

Franz could quote the Code books backward and forward.

"Sir," Lieutenant Myerfing continued, "the dissenters sympathize with your plan. But they insist on preparing for another overseer before brain-washing Schaeffer. They agree that Schaeffer is no longer reliable, that he has mystic tendencies that must be extirpated. But they insist also that another overseer be ready—"

General Kerf pressed a button. A little man with short bowed legs, a fat face and deep-pocketed eyes came in, and stood at shabby attention. "I anticipated that," Kerf said to Myerfing.

Franz felt only contempt for the slovenly civilian, even though the man was qualified and wore the identity band of a scientist on his left sleeve. Scientists were under the control of the SG, and it had been a long time now since any of them had voiced "free-thought" protests.

Franz knew that unguarded scientists had a strong tendency to drift toward mysticism, and were in general crackpots who had to be kept in their channelized work, and never allowed to poke their noses out of it.

But Scientists *were* useful. They kept the machines running and their specialties always depended on brain-work. Yet they had to be constantly watched and controlled. And you had to be careful about brain-washing them, for they were troublemakers even under the best of circumstances.

*Schaeffer included*, Franz thought. *My old mushy guardian.*

According to the Code Book, a scientist was really just a kind of useful chemical, a catalyst, to fuse the efficiency of machines and the often fallible goals of men.

"This," General Kerf said, "is Scientist Senior Grade Chardexe."

The little man bowed jerkily forward.

Kerf said. "As Chief Cyberneticist for the Institute of Socio-Engineers, Chardexe has studied the Omega Calculator for thirty-seven years. He has retraced the complex diagrams and records of its construction. Take my word to the Council for this, Lieutenant, Chardexe can competently, even brilliantly oversee the Omega's continued function, including the maintenance of the Memory Racks."

"Well," Myerfing said. "That is good news—a distinct relief, sir! It should satisfy the Council and clear the way for Franz's assignment. Up to now it had been assumed that no one but Schaeffer—"

"Assumed incorrectly," General Kerf rasped. "Scientist Chardexe, you may go."

The scientist bowed, and walked out, his head still inclined. Myerfing fidgeted. "Wasn't there a man named Chardexe who was suspected of some kind of aberration? I'm sure that name's familiar in connection with—"

"Not mystic tendencies," Kerf said quickly. "I can assure you of that."

"But there was *something*—"

"A Scientist can be aberrated in certain areas and still function properly in a specialized field. Take my word for it. Chardexe can handle the Omega Calculator."

Franz was becoming impatient again. He wanted to get started on Schaeffer.

"Anyway," General Kerf said, "no man is a threat to the Omega. I'm convinced now that the Omega has reached a point where it is practically self-sufficient, within limits of course. What must be guarded against is a dangerous tendency to identify the overseer with the Omega."

True, true, thought young Franz. The Overseer was only a man, while the Omega was a machine. The glorious synthesizer—the hard steely core that ruled and held rigid the malleable pulp of the stupid mass mind. It was all in the Code Books.

Schaeffer was just a human tool, which SG used to build the machines, and keep them running. It was the Omega that did the real figuring, always dependable, leaving nothing to chance. A man was expendable.

The Code Books made it all very clear.

"Young Franz," General Kerf said. "Tomorrow you'll spend your regular weekend visit with your Guardian, Schaeffer. You will transmit to us at once any evidence of mystical tendencies you may observe in Schaeffer. You will wait five minutes. If in that time you haven't received any signal from us, then under Public Law Fourteen, you will narcotize Schaeffer. Then you will brain-wash him. Thoroughly, young Franz. Do you understand?"

Franz felt like falling down on the floor, he was so weak. "I—I'll get a shock box?"

"Of course," Kerf smiled as he spoke. "We don't know how much Schaeffer may suspect. We don't know what preparations he may have made against being discovered. A few minutes may make all the difference. Don't forget. He's in the most dangerous imaginable position! He's inside the Omega!"

"Yes, sir," Franz whispered.

General Kerf pressed a button on his desk, and spoke into the intercom. "Young Franz Schaeffer will be in there immediately. You will give him a brain-washing field kit."

Salutes were exchanged, heels clicked, and Franz turned to depart. But at the door something pulled him back around slowly.

"Something else, young Franz?"

The thing, the presence in the night. The shadow that dissolved when he stared at it, or walked toward it. The feeling of something waiting outside his window when the lights went out. The scraping and the whispering noises under the floor and the fear of trying to fall asleep. The dreadful dreams.

But if he confessed now he'd miss his great assignment. They might even put him under a prober. He felt small all at once, horribly alone. Afraid there all by himself, and little. Everything suddenly seemed like some mushy sick dream he couldn't even remember without becoming almost physically ill.

*Get out, Franz! Once you're away from General Kerf you'll know what to do!*

Once out of the office he could think about it and decide. No, his duty was plain. He knew that the Code Books defined his duty clearly. It was just a matter of making the decision to confess. You did what was right for the Omega and the Plan, without flinching or attempting to save yourself.

All at once a sudden, fierce determination sealed his lips. He could lick those dreams himself. He was an Investigator now. He would just refuse to dream any more, and then there would be nothing to confess.

He would do it alone. He was going to spy on his Guardian—probe out Schaeffer.

He was going to be a hero.


The brain-washing kit was disguised as a toy, a colorful little box full of geometric blocks. Franz kept the box open beside him as he waited for his Guardian to come in.

Other tools for spying, recording and collecting evidence were included in his belongings. There was a toilet kit, a playkit, constructive building blocks and an electron-toy set.

He was uncomfortable though. His skin was sticky, and he kept shifting around. There was always something scary about these weekend visits with his Guardian. They occurred deep, deep inside the Selectron Center of the Giant Computer—the very heart of the Omega—and once inside you could not tell where you were.

Only Schaeffer could tell.

The Omega covered a big expanse of the Control Level, the center of the City. It was ten tiers high and Franz was chillingly aware that he'd have trouble getting out if Schaeffer became suspicious and decided to trap him like some experimental laboratory animal imprisoned in a maze.

Schaeffer knew the Omega as no one else did. Franz somehow didn't trust this Chardexe either for only Schaeffer and the Omega had grown up together, and seemed mysteriously linked in thought and purpose.

"Ah, my dear little Franz," the old man whispered as he came in. "I'm so glad to see you again." He put his arms around Franz, and hugged him close. "I've missed you, lad. It's lonelier here than you'll ever know."

Franz moved out of the old man's arms, and sprawled out on the couch. Then dutifully, doing what he was supposed to do, he kissed his Guardian on both cheeks, and fell back laughing on the couch again.

"You mean so much to me, Franz. I'm all alone here now, with only the old ghosts of dead years and a few old faces to keep me sane."

"I love you too," Franz said quickly. *Easy*, he thought. *Take your time, Franz, and catch him when he's off guard.*

Schaeffer moved close to Franz, and peered intently into his face. His eyes were moist as though he had been crying. Most of the time he looked like a big, wrinkled-up baby. But when he saw Franz on weekends his face took on color and life and joy. His body was so old, Franz thought that it made a person sick just to look at him. Through his transparent skin you could almost see the bones and nerves, everything worn shiny with time.

"Let me look at you, Franz! Ah, now there's life in the old Omega."

Franz turned his face slightly away. The old man's eyes were scary. They were alive, and looking at them Franz got the feeling he was staring through mysterious windows into some other time. The past maybe. The old man was always talking about the past.

"I'm so glad I'm your Guardian, Franz," Schaeffer whispered. "I've looked forward all week to your coming."

"I like it here too," Franz said. "It's a real honor, having you for my Guardian."

"I've been fixing up another room for you, Franz—a room with all kinds of wonderful things in it, just for you. It's right in the Selectron Sector of the Omega. I have to spend a lot of time in the Selectron Sector now. The Memory Racks take up most of my time because they're wearing out." The old man shook his head. "We need fifty trained scientists here. Not just one."

Franz had always played the role of inquisitive youth well. Now he played it even better. He took pride in it, and his enthusiasm carried conviction. The old man's eyes began to shine.

Franz asked more questions about the Omega. He queried his Guardian about the giant vacuum tubes, the voltage amplifiers, the input frequencies, and the electromotive forces. Even why the phosphor-coated storage surfaces gave off blue light, and the memory cells functioned best with the aid of a compensator.

Actually Franz understood little or none of it, and he was proud of not understanding. Only crackpot scientists understood stuff like that. They were useful but they were also sickeningly dull.

Franz was being very curious. He decided suddenly to use the pretender trick. He'd pretend to be what he suspected his guardian of being, draw him out, and slyly trick a confession of him.

Franz said, "What would happen if you injected a dream into the Omega?"

"What? What did you say, my boy?" For an instant the old man looked merely startled. Then his eyes almost closed, and a frown moved in tiny lines across his face.

"A dream," Franz repeated. "Say you had a dream. You put it into the Omega for the Calculator to figure out. The Omega can figure anything out, can't it?"

Schaeffer said with slow care, "An unusual question, even for an inquisitive boy." He stared at Franz. Then an eager light came into his face.

"A very interesting question, young Franz," he reiterated.

"Well, say I had a dream," Franz said innocently. Then he hesitated. "Oh, I know you're not supposed to dream. Dreams are bad. But it was such a little dream—only one. I wondered what it meant."

It was a sly idea, Franz thought, and it was scary. But he was sure the SG would think he was lying, solely to trick information out of Schaeffer. They wouldn't know he was speaking the truth. And Franz might be able to figure out exactly what his dream meant and get rid of it, and never have to confess or anything.

Schaeffer said. "Well, Franz. Dreams aren't supposed to mean anything. They're irrational, according to the Codes. A dream is just supposed to be something left over from a former, savage age. An emotional and sentimental vestige, so to speak. A dream is a ghost."

"I know they're not *supposed* to mean anything," Franz said. "But mine scare me."

Schaeffer put his arm around Franz's shoulder, and he said softly,

"What was this dream precisely? You can tell me, but no one else, Franz. Will you remember that, if we talk about it?"

"Promise *you* won't tell?" Franz said, nodding.

"No," Schaeffer smiled sadly. "I won't tell. As you said, one little dream. What harm could it do?"

Franz grinned. The evidence against Schaeffer was already going into the transformer, and straight to the SG labs. The recording mill was grinding.

"Well," Franz said. "I had this dream about someone coming up to my bed during the night. It must have been a woman. She felt warm, and soft and I wanted her to sit with me and hug me and tell me stories. And she said to me: 'Jack darling, wake up. You're going to climb the beanstalk.' "

Even though pretending, Franz felt embarrassed talking such mush. There was something scary in it too. Deep inside he almost felt the fear again. He jerked around, but there wasn't even a shadow in the corner of the room.

Schaeffer closed his eyes. "Jack and the Beanstalk," he whispered slowly. "Kids used to read fairy tales. A free and wonderful imagination enriched their lives even after they were grown up. Everything good in the world came from that ability to imagine boldly, Franz. The Omega came from someone's daring dreams too."

Franz felt something cold trembling in his clasp. His hand shook as he pressed the activator on the plastic toy box. Inaudibly, the brain-washing kit began warming up. In less than a minute, he knew, a thin beam of sonic power would build up to be released by pressure on the tiny stud.

"So," Franz whispered, "you think dreams are good then?"

Franz moved the kit around, looking steadily at Schaeffer. Schaeffer saw and understood the look. His eyes widened in a kind of watery horror. He stared down at the toy box, and then quickly back to Franz's face.

"You, my boy? *You too?*"

Schaeffer started backing away. Franz followed. He took the small narcotizing capsule out of his pocket and got ready to hurl it at his Guardian.

The old man stumbled and blinked his eyes. His head shook slowly back and forth, with a sort of bewildered wobbling. "Sometimes I forget what they've come to outside—the degradation, the savage cruelty."

"You're going to forget a lot more in just a second," Franz said. "You won't even know who you are, I bet." He raised his hand to throw the capsule. Schaeffer turned and ran toward the door. Franz got there first. Schaeffer hurried along the wall, falling over a chair and crying out despairfully. He started crawling into a corner.

Franz went toward him, his lips tight.

Schaeffer saw the hate in his eyes and whispered: "It's the venom of loneliness, Franz. It's the cruel hate of unexpressed dreams and the vitriol of unplayed games. It's the anguish of warm arms never felt, of good night kisses never given. The acid of a childhood you've never been given a chance to live."

"Shut up, you old crackpot!" Franz said.

"Please, my boy. Don't do what you were sent here to do. Listen to me instead. I'll make you understand—all that childhood can and should mean. They'll never find us. I know the Omega as I know every vein in these old hands."

"Shut up!" Franz screamed. "You're a crazy old crackpot!"

Schaeffer ran behind a cabinet. "Come out!" Franz yelled. "You can't escape."

Franz tiptoed toward the cabinet. He could see one of Schaeffer's thin transparent hands creeping desperately around the corner.

"Franz! Wait! I have more to say!"

"Shut up! You said dreams were good! You're going to get washed out!"

"Franz, listen. You can still dream. Stay here and hide with me for a while. I could help you to getaway, to escape from the City. You must hide, run—do anything to get away while you can still dream!"

Franz flung his weight against the cabinet. Behind it, Schaeffer moaned. Then the old man stumbled out, and leaned against the wall. Blood trickled from the corners of his mouth, ran out of his nose. He was coughing as he fell backward over a chair. He lay motionless for an instant, then wearily he turned over. His body seemed to spread out over the floor. Sadly he looked up at Franz, his eyes suddenly fearless. Franz hated him all the more.

Franz kicked out, kept kicking and screaming. But the old man didn't seem to care. He just lay there looking sadly up at Franz out of those crackpot eyes. Old windows, scary windows—opening into somewhere else, some other time.

"Franz, let me answer your question. If you put a dream into the Omega nothing would happen. The Omega cannot dream. It couldn't even absorb the data of a dream. Only a man can dream. Children—little Children—they can dream most of all. You have to preserve—have to keep—"

Franz threw the capsule. The gas seeped and clung to the old man's body. Schaeffer twisted and choked and flung his arms about. Finally he stopped struggling. Only his lips continued to move heavily while his large, sad eyes remained fastened on Franz.

"Franz, don't let it die," he pleaded. "Don't bury your dreams. The Omega cannot see the things that we cannot see. But we know they're there. The Omega does not know—"

"You shut up!" Franz screamed. He jumped up and down. "You're a crazy mystic!"

"Franz—my boy—"

Franz dropped down, leveling the sights of the brain-washer. With a gentle whirring sound the tiny needle sliced into Schaeffer's right temple, its high-frequency vibrations dissolving bone, fusing tissue and short-circuiting cells. It cut on remorselessly, emerging finally through Schaeffer's left temple.

Schaeffer stopped gibbering. After a few minutes he moved a little, and then sat up. He stared vacantly at Franz.

Franz stood up, and motioned sharply. "On your feet, crackpot! On your feet and come along!"

The old man stumbled forward, breathing heavily. Pink moisture hung from his lips and he wobbled on his feet. "Where—where are we going?" he muttered. His head bobbed on his thin neck like a bird's and he kept blinking his eyes at the light.

"Just come along!"

The old man shuffled after the boy. He looked around once as though wondering where he was, like someone waking up in the middle of a dream.

Franz's locker radiated the power of his neatly folded uniform as he lay supine in his dusk-shadowed room and waited for the coming of night. General Kerf had highly commended him, and given him an oak leaf to hang under his badge.

*Tonight*, he thought, *I've got to go right to sleep. I can't be alone and afraid after getting that oak leaf.*

The corners. That was where the thing usually concealed itself. The corners—and the whispering night at the window. The voices and the faces that just weren't ever quite real. The dreams were unreal but they came just the same, and you tried to forget them when you woke up because they were sins. The stupid kid's games. The make-believe. The hidden books, the imaginative creatures. The gods, angels, ogres, the saints, devils, elves, dwarves and pixies in the gardens. The giants in the sky.

"Jack. Jack, darling. Wake up. You're going to climb the beanstalk."

Jack the Giant Killer.

He remembered the warmth, and a gently smiling face. Tender arms reaching out. Sweet warmth and consoling arms to beguile him to happy sleep.

*"Once upon a time—*

*"Long, long ago—"*

Franz woke up. He pushed himself back into a corner of the bed, and stared at the window, at the gray dawn light moving in over the metal walls.

It was so still in the room, with only the gray light rippling silently toward him that he began to sob.

Then he heard the knock, the direct and familiar knock.

"Come in," he sobbed.

The door opened, and Marie appeared, framed in a glimmering square of radiance.

She moved toward his bed, her bright blond braids bobbing in the light, her wide blue eyes sympathetic, filled with a child-like wonderment at his broken sobs. She dropped her toys on the bed.

Franz managed to stop crying for just a minute. He felt on the defensive, but for some reason, he hardly cared now. She sat close to him and he could feel the warmth of her. He could smell the sweet clean warmth of her bright blond hair, and feel the softness of her hand on his wet forehead.

He closed his eyes, sinking down and surrendering himself completely to the sweet solace of her nearness. The sobs came out flooding full and clean without fear.

"I heard you crying," Marie said hardly above a whisper. "I bet you were having a bad dream."

"No," he said. "It was a good dream. Now I remember, Marie. It was good…"

"A good *dream?*"

"Yes, Marie. I remember her now. My mother… She—she brought me a book. It had been hidden away. It was full of fairy stories. 'I'll read to you,' she said to me. 'I'll take a chance, darling. You're only a little boy and you need these stories. You'll need them in your mind—to keep forever.' I never saw her any more after that. But she's still alive. She still loves me, Marie. She comes back at nights—to read and talk to me."

"What was it she read?" Marie said.

"Jack and the Beanstalk."

He felt the gray aloneness. Something very old, and beyond the reach even of fear. His eyes opened. First he saw only Marie's wide blue eyes. Then he saw the lid on the toy box snap open. He recognized the familiar sound, the humming sound.

"I knew all along you were just a crazy little risk," she said.

*Only seven*, he thought. He started to scream. He felt old, he felt as old as old Schaeffer just before the beam hit his temple.

# The Barrier

*If Stevens could cross the high velocity barrier at the edge of space he would receive a pardon on Earth. But would he live to claim it?*

THERE were maybe ten or fifteen people to see him off. They weren't cheering. They stood in the gray curtain of rain, hunched over with their hands in their storm-coat pockets. Behind them was the vague bulk of the Experimental Station. And beyond that, invisible in the night, were the mountains he would never see again.

"O. K., Stevens. This is it."

So what? Stevens clanked as he turned toward the "Coffin." He was encased in a bulging metal pressure suit and his head was a big alloy bubble. No one smiled. No one raised a hand to say goodbye.

Doris would, of course, say goodbye, if she were here. She wasn't here. She didn't even know about his volunteering.

Major Kanin nodded stiffly. His gray eyes wrinkled. "Good luck, Stevens," he said dutifully. It was meaningless. Kanin had sent too many poor guys out on a one-way trip. He knew Stevens wouldn't come down. Not in any recognizable form.

A couple of gray-suited mechanics moved around behind Stevens. Stevens leaned over and thrust his head into the tubular opening of the torpedo-like plane. The two mechanics lifted his legs, shoved him in headfirst like he was ammunition being crammed into an ancient cannon. The metal hatch slid down past his feet. He was bound tightly by the cockpit, which was only an air-conditioned tube but slightly larger than his body. When the canopy over his head closed, he had only two inches between the plate in his helmet and the control and instrument panel.

For one agonizing moment, long and terrifying, Stevens felt an awful compressing suffocation and entrapment. The claustrophobia went away, in part, and left the plexglas plate in his helmet dewed with his sweat.

He tried to relax. He stared at the controls. He twisted his helmet carefully then so as not to bump his helmet against the side—the noise was numbing inside when he did bump anything—and looked through the tiny peephole in the tubular wall that would soon close, too, leaving him completely sealed. He looked out and waited for the signal. Major Kanin had turned his back and was discussing something with a Doctor and a Lieutenant. The mechanics were around preparing the kick-off rockets.

The "Coffin" was light, and it was new. A slight improvement over the last one. But the so-called improvement was a farce, Stevens knew, because no one had any idea why none of the others had come back. No one of them expected him to come back either, and they showed it plainly. Also, none of them cared particularly, from any human point of view. The Military cared of course, from another viewpoint.

This was another velocity test run. Once around the Earth to this take-off spot on the desert. The Military wanted to get to the Moon if they had to walk there over a suspension bridge of human dead. The first Sovereign State to get a military base on the Moon would, in theory, be the all-time victor in what certain kinds of humorists called the "game" of war. So far, no one had been able to stand the velocity.

Stevens felt his skin stretch in a dry, tight grin. He carefully and slowly moistened his lips and watched the light that would blink yellow. A minute after that the job would kick-off before rockets delivering a 3000-pound thrust for twelve seconds.

STEVENS guessed that the brain-boys up in some hidden bureau had an idea that sooner or later they would find somebody who could stand it, then they could make tests, find out why. Stevens had no idea how many had already been sacrificed. The boys upstairs knew but they weren't giving out statistics these days. Stevens would increase the unknown number by one more.

So it meant nothing, he thought. He wasn't one of the superboys, the jet-jyrenes, the hero lads who never came back and had statues and plaques stuck all over the place for being permanently en absentia. Not anymore, he wasn't.

He was one of the new volunteers from the West Coast branch of the Military Prison. Big-hearted Kanin had even promised him a pardon if he brought the ship back. It was a new high in irony, but that was about all.

He wouldn't come back, and he knew it. But he would be free, and Doris would be free to live her own life. He had been stupid, hotheaded, once—and this was a preferable way, he had decided, to pay up the debt.

# *The Barrier*

## By Bryce Walton

**If Stevens could cross the high velocity barrier at the edge of space he would receive a pardon on Earth. But would he live to claim it?**

Doris had resigned herself to waiting for him. It was a manslaughter charge, and he would have gotten out maybe in fifteen years. They didn't parole anybody from a Military Prison, at least not on anything as heavy as manslaughter. It wasn't fair to Doris, nor to himself.

All right. He was in a shiny "Coffin" and he would soon be on his way to wherever the others had gone—into nowhere. Where was nowhere? That was a question. It was way up, higher than anyone had returned from to answer—still within the bounds of gravity but—*high*. A lot of guys had found it, but they weren't sending back any ESP messages from the Beyond.

**His features were twisted by the acceleration, and his sanity seemed to have gone**

It was up there where the Earth lost its face behind thick vapor veils and began to look like a fancy balloon, that was where you found out the location of nowhere. Inside a beautifully stream-lined "Coffin" you found out—hurtling way beyond the speed of sound, shattering the supersonic barriers, and faster and faster still...

What happened to them? Nobody had figured it out. All the best brains in the world working on it might figure it out. But the brains were split up, divided into little camps here and there, getting a lot of atomic spitballs ready to throw at one another, when teacher's back was turned.

So it wasn't figured out, what happened to them. They had come a long way since they first broke the barrier. Faster and faster and faster—but they'd hit a limit somewhere up there. And until they wiped out that limitation, the Moon was as far away as it had ever been back when man thought the canoe was a great discovery.

They just went faster and faster and faster—and then they disappeared. A curtain parted. A curtain closed. And wherever man wanted to get to so fast—he got there.

The yellow light blinked at Stevens like a jaundiced eye. Stevens winked back with a mock gesture that was hardly genuine. The world rocked, and his head seemed to drain as though by a suction pump.

His task was simple enough. The controls were automatic until the signal came for bringing the ship in, and then manual controls would be used. Until then, he served as only a slightly necessary human element. A voice. There was the radio, and his voice. He was to keep them informed down there. Keep talking right up to the point when whatever happened—happened.

Stevens talked. He reported the altitude, the velocity, the temperature. He kept reporting as the three of them increased. His eyes watched the light that might blink red. The "panic-light." When that blinked, it meant curtains. It meant fire in the "Coffin." It meant that if you were in a position to do it, you could use the automatic pilot ejector and get hurled into the screaming currents by a 37-mm cartridge that shot the pilot and cockpit straight up at 60 ft. per second.

At this altitude and this velocity, the ejector was useless.

He whispered, "Velocity—five thousand—" He spoke again. "Velocity—fifteen thousand—"

It was frightening. He flicked on the observation screen. It was a blur. He couldn't feel anything. He couldn't hear anything. If he could only lift his legs, bend his knees. If he could only turn over on his side—

He opened his mouth to scream, and somehow prevented the burst that frothed to soundless bubbles on his lips. His body seemed to swell, seeking to burst the Coffin's walls like a swelling mummy.

The terror remained in him, icy and deep.

He watched the gauges creeping up and up. He was speaking. He knew he was reporting but he couldn't hear himself saying anything. He watched the "panic-light" that would glow red and that would be curtain time. There was no sound. No sound at all. There was no vision. No awareness of motion. At this incredible height, at this frightening velocity, there was no awareness of anything at all.

He was in a Coffin all right, and he was buried—as certainly as though he were six feet under and as stationary as only the dead can be when they are buried and forgotten down under the clean Earth where they belong when they're tired.

They didn't belong up here, not this way.

"The cooling system's clogging," he heard himself whisper. "Crystals of ice...cockpit's like a miniature snow storm..."

He heard the unemotional voice come clearly to him. "The emergency trigger—"

He used it. He felt a freezing grin rip across his face as he reached out and used it. The icy spray died away and he heard himself saying something else.

"It's the velocity. I don't have any reason for saying it—I just feel it—you could feel it up here too—I can't explain it, but it's the velocity. I know it. Maybe they crashed on the Earth somewhere. There's lots of places on Earth a ship could crash and no one would know it, especially when it would be taken for a meteor. But this feels like it's the velocity that does it up here. Listen, what about this? Anyone thought of this—what if the velocity breaks a man through into another dimension?"

No one commented on that. It happened to him right then, and he felt it coming. Reflexes tried to move his body, and his head and feet drummed on the restricting tubular walls. There was a wrenching blur and a slipping spinning vertigo.

\*      \*      \*

...there was darkness and he floated in it, but he was conscious. It wasn't any familiar kind of consciousness. Lights began glimmering here and there like fireflies. But it was no dream, he knew that. He didn't know what it was. The music that was something far and incomprehensively beyond music sounded, and he seemed to float on a broad tape of sound to float on a road, a path, a curvature that broadened into unlimited vistas.

It was brief. It was like peeking through a tiny hole and seeing something beautiful, unworldly, very nearly incomprehensible, drift by. He heard a voice that had no body, but he knew it was real, very real. More real than anything he had called real before.

"Another is coming through. Check the matrix."

HE tried to understand. Vaporous curtains seemed to draw back one by one and a kind of clarity flowed over his mind like cool ocean up a white beach. A first faint tingling thrill moved in his blood, and became pleasure that mounted through ecstasy and then became something else for which he had no name.

He had called it—nowhere. This wasn't anything like that. This was really *some*where. Soft lights bathed him like water. Shadows seemed to shift and sway; there was silver in the light, dusted with golden motes.

He thought desperately. "Where is this? What has happened?"

"This is Death," the voice that had no face or form answered. "That is what you term it, in the lower stage reality from which you have come. There are other ways of going through the barrier, but death is the sure and the ordinary one. Many come through, in many ways—"

Stevens tried to understand, and he knew that he could not. He tried to see his present form, his present meaning. There was nothing tangible. He drifted. He was light and sound perhaps, movement perhaps. He was part of something greater and far more complex than his undeveloped powers of perception could absorb.

Stevens thought. "You mean—I'm—Dead. I mean—that I'm not living now?"

The thought answered him. It wasn't a sequence of words, phrases, forming meaning. The entire answer was a part of him, immediately. "You call it death. Actually you are more alive. You have come through the barrier into what you call the fourth dimension. It is really but a broader awareness of a higher reality—"

It didn't mean much to Stevens. The unknown, the intangible—it sent a chill through his consciousness. Pain hit him. He winced. Light roiled, irritation eddied like muddy streaks in a clear stream. A bluish haze spread like staining ink through the clouds of brilliance. Dark cracks spread like lines through colored glass.

Stevens felt an icy wind. He seemed to swirl inchoate through a forest of wildly irritated leaves and branches.

The thought came to him, weakly, through distance that was more than mere distance, through barriers of space and realms of time. It came to him weakly, and it began to fade.

"Everything that was, that is, or will be, we are conscious of here in this higher stage of reality. All must come through, and there is never again contact with the lower stage, the third dimension of perception. The matrix is universal, eternal, and it is set and unchanging."

Stevens' mind screamed, "But I'm returning—help me. I don't want to go back. I want to stay, to stay—"

"You are John Stevens—" the voice, the thought, drifted to him from what seemed infinite spaces.

"Yes, yes—"

"There is a distortion, you do not understand. Someday you will. You are premature. The pattern is rigid, and everything has its set moment of alteration. This distortion, I cannot explain. We are not perfect here. There is yet a higher reality, and a higher one still, and the stages are infinite. But you will be back, John Stevens. Soon. Very soon."

"When—when?"

A column of sound arose and shattered in glittering spray. "The matrix has the answer John Stevens—no this is not your time. You call it a week. Seven days. Such terms are meaningless here. To us, it is happening now. We can see it happening. We can see you coming through the barrier—to stay—to learn—to live as we live—"

"When?" he screamed at the fading thought.

"Soon. A week. Seven days. It is here. The Matrix has the answer..."

"Now. Let me stay," Stevens screamed. "I don't want to go back."

"You are not really here, or you could not go back. This is a glimpse. Many have had it. Someday you will understand. But in seven days—"

THE radio voice was shrill. "Can you hear? Can you hear? There has been five seconds of unexplainable static! Can you hear?"

"Sure, I can hear," he said hoarsely. He blinked, stared at the blurred instruments against his eyes. Suddenly he shouted, "I'm still alive, you get that? I've passed the velocity apex, and I'm still alive!"

He heard Major Kanin's voice. Some of the fatuousness was lost in the emotion of triumph. "Great! Great, you've done it! Now you've got to bring her in! That pardon—"

All right. He would do that. He had been a super-boy, a jet-jyrene himself, once. A big-shot, a wonder boy jet-hero, before he got that jealous quirk that had turned out to be baseless. A feud that had gone on for years and culminated in a fight, and Bill Carson had died from concussion. There had been nothing between Doris and Carson, but it was too late to think about that now.

The Military had been harsh, and he'd known he couldn't bear the confinement. And he hadn't wanted Doris to suffer for his psychological blowup either. He had volunteered for what should have been suicide—but he still lived. He couldn't understand that. He should be dead. He knew that. But he wasn't, and he knew he would bring her in. A pardon—

The world was small for Stevens. A coffin, a cannon-barrel. And he was stuffed in it. His hands alone could move over the simple controls, and his eyes could move over the gauges. A jet-pilot had to learn a special feel to bring in a jet-ship. And Stevens had learned that "feel" years ago. It seemed a long time ago when he had taken that harsh training: a few hours in a conventional flyer, a few more in a Mustang 60. Then that rending day when he had "checked out" in a jet-trainer.

Stevens' eyes bulged in sudden terror. Sweat blurred his vision. The red light was glowing. The *Panic Light*. It meant bad trouble at this speed. Fire—

"But I'll bring it in," he whispered. Smoke curled through the Coffin. The heat expanded around him rapidly. He thought of the ejector, but he was too low now, coming in. He tried to scream. The crackling wavering heat inside his helmet was intolerable. The Controls were jammed. His hands fell away and he dropped his head helplessly and the world exploded...

THIS time there was a crowd, and they acted differently. They were enthusiastic. There were doctors and nurses. Their faces were twisted with admiration. Stronger than the admiration was a fearful kind of disbelief. The Doctor touched his lips with his tongue and coughed uneasily as he stared at Stevens.

Major Kanin was beaming. "Man," his voice boomed through the hospital room. "Man! You're alive. No one knows how you can be alive, but you are! We've licked it. It's a miracle!"

Voices agreed with that in a chorus of amazed whispers. Miracle...
The Major said. "I've already got that pardon coming through,
Stevens. It'll be probational of course, but that will all be forgotten
now, Stevens. You're something special."

The doctors and nurses stared at him with unbelieving eyes.
"You've been examined thoroughly, Stevens, and you're all right,
not a scratch! It's impossible, but it's true. Every doctor here, every
mechanic, says it's impossible. Your ship's just a pile of melting metal,
Stevens, but you crawled out of it absolutely uninjured. Nobody un-
derstands it, but everybody's glad!"

The Doctor whispered. "Miracles like this sometimes happen, but
no one can explain them. His body should be torn to pieces, burned.
Well, he certainly had to have had some unique physical quality to
have gotten through the high velocity peak."

"Yes, you hear that, Stevens?" the Major boomed.

Stevens was staring at the ceiling. He was trying to think, to remember.

"Now listen to this, Stevens. You went up a convict, and now you're
a hero. You're in perfect physical condition, so we're going right ahead
with Project Ultimo. And you'll handle the rocket, Stevens! If anyone
can get to the Moon, you can, from this exhibition today!"

"What's that," Stevens said. He looked at their faces.

"It'll take a week to get the rocket ready," the Major said. "It's the
Moon now, Stevens! The Moon!"

"The Moon," Stevens repeated.

"This will be no secret, Stevens!" Major Kanin stood up, his chest
out, his heavy-jowled face glowing with triumph. "The world will
know about it when you take off, this time. This won't be secret. The
Enemy will know then that they've lost! Lost, utterly and unquestion-
ably. With military bases on the Moon, they'll be helpless and they'll
know it when you make that successful flight! One week, Stevens!"

Stevens looked out the window at the gray curtain of rain. "Wha
was that? One week—" Something stirred in his memory. He gr'
pled for it, lost it. He closed his eyes.

"Seven days, Stevens, that's all!"

He didn't answer. For an instant behind the bottomless dark
of his closed lids, he saw something—something intangible
shimmering, beyond the grayness and rain. And then it was gone

# Earth Needs a Killer

*You are the man we need, Ray Berton. You're a killer, but you're sane and rational. Those we are fighting are insane, irrational, and they'll destroy humanity if they are not stopped. We have power, but we can't use it for destruction, no matter how great the need. But we can give you power—then it's up to you!*

## CHAPTER ONE
### The Beginning

From an evening tele-audocast by International Information Service, New York City, September 8, 1983: Reporter: *...and now, as a special dramatic interest story, here's something for the Fortean Society, though a more scientific diagnosis will certainly be forthcoming.*

*At five P. M. today, a man's body materialized out of thin air at an altitude of over ten thousand feet above Uptown Manhattan. According to many reliable witnesses, the body plunged down to smash into an unrecognizable mass on the plasticrete of Tier 19 and Grav-lift 6-H, Fifth Avenue II.*

*The reliable witnesses include twenty passengers of the trans-State jetliner, all of whom agree that the unknown man did materialize out of the air very near the liner's position as it circled for a cradle in La Guardia Field.*

*Every witness tells about the same story that the body did appear suddenly from the atmosphere. There was no other air vessel near. Also it was reported that another object followed the body out of the air, according to preliminary reports, a manuscript oddly written on a scroll of metal.*

*Stay visioed to I. I. S. for further reports on this Fortean mystery. The manuscript, we hope, will contain some kind of explanation, which will be forwarded to you as soon as it reaches our news clearance scanners...*

IT STARTS for me on Mars. I guess Mars is about the only place it could have started. Maybe they'll bring the real earth law there someday, and clean up dives like Jelahn's *krin-krin* tavern on the North Canal, a breeding place for crime, and where a man can be goaded into killing. That night I didn't care much.

The place was crawling with scum, strained through the sieves of Marsport, and Jokhara and Sanskran where the worst of the asteroid niners and space bums gather. Earthmen and Martians and half-reeds whom the Solar cops, said to be the very toughest ever to wear a shield, would have gone at with care.

I was feeling high, with enough *krin-krin* burning in me to make a Martian *srith*-dog sit up and talk Esperanto. And by the time I'd been blotting up *krin-krin* for a few hours, any space bum thinking to push me around was crazy. So the big yellow skinned Martian with the green eyes was, crazy for trying to drag this breed tavern girl away from my table.

Crazy first, then dead. I'd seen plenty of dead men before, and I knew the look. I knew I'd hit him too hard as soon as he stretched on the bright green stones of Jelahn's tavern, and didn't try to get up. Standing there looking down at him, I knew he'd never get up by himself.

The whole tavern had dried up like a scab. The place was so quiet you could hear the Martian's blood trickling from his mouth onto the floor. "You certainly lowered that poor, poor Marty," somebody whispered.

I swung around fiercely, but the speaker eased away from me. "What in a blasted jet's the use of hitting a man, if you don't hit him right?" I yelled. I was drunk, and I was getting sick; I'd never liked the sight or smell of dead men.

Nobody said anything. Everybody looked at the dead Marty. The blood stopped running. I prodded him with my foot. Oh, he had the look all right, the kind a man only gets once and for always. People stared. Even on Mars, death isn't so common that it isn't interesting.

I could hear myself breathing in the silence. I was sick. I'd never been the kind of space tough one of those Martian Colonial Administrator's women would invite to a Double Moon tea, but just the same everyone doesn't like to kill.

My record wasn't too bad; brawls, drunks, a few killings in self-defense. Born in the asteroids, father a prospector, me a prospector. At twenty-three, I'd hit a strike a month ago, and cushioned into the big port at Sanskran to unload, get more machinery and return to that meteorite where I'd hit "heavy" beryllium, paired-atom stuff worth twice its weight in platinum to the Atomician boys on Earth.

The breed girl, the cause of the trouble, cried, "He's dead!"

Nobody moved. Then the girl came at me; the few jewels, which was all she wore, flashed as red as her eyes and her clawing nails. "You killed him!" she screamed. I pushed in her face with my flat hand, and sent her sprawling beside the dead guy she was so nuts about.

(Illustration by Finlay)

The *krin-krin* went out of me. The place was hot and somebody said the cops were coming. There was no time for talking or thinking or feeling sorry; I measured my chances and ran for the door. I knocked two guys out of the way and went through the blue stone doors into the street. Up the red stone street like it was swimming in blood, a black jetcar was coming fast under the shine of the Deimos.

Cops. I'd never had any trouble with them before. Now it was just Ray Berton and the cops—and nothing in between but the cold Martian night. So I turned and ran the other way. A knot of men came out of the tavern and came at me. I stopped. Another jetcar curved into the street from the other end of the block. *All right.* I ↘ed, backed into the side of the triangle of stone, stood waiting and

I jumped straight for the aristocratic gent, and swung a long stiff right to his jaw. He faded into the air . . .

my fists were hard. I'd never had any parents, not much. My mother died when I was born, and twelve years later, my dad died from overexposure to above ten point cosrays. It isn't anything to remember, seeing an old man die like that.

So I'd been a space bum, and ended up a drunken brawling killer in a North Canal scum sieve! *All right, so maybe you could have done better. Come on and get it, you guys who think you could have done any better. Come on, come on...*

And then it hit me. *Thought.* A big hot fist of it, punching into my head. A big exploding fire of thought—*but not my own.*

*"Step over here into the shadows, Ray Berton."*

115

I DIDN'T think of telepathy then, though I thought plenty about it afterwards. I stumbled back, wanting to get away, but scared. I started to sweat; somebody could get inside me, and stay there and do things to me. Things worse than a Martian cop could do with his coercoats and neuron twisters.

My head hurt and I yelled something. Everything around me started to melt and run together, and the stone under my boots got soft. I got a fading look at them, two of them, standing like purple shadows. A girl with black black eyes. And a man, a big Earthman, aristocratic and distinguished-looking, with eyes like polished Venusian fog crystals.

I heard the fading thunder from the spaceport outside Sanskran, and that was all, for a while. The next thing I knew I was coming into Earth, a place I'd never been, and wasn't supposed to be able to go to because I'd never been 'purified.' I had no Solar visa, I thought, and didn't want to go through the psyche treatment necessary to get one.

But a lot of things changed for me that night when they took me off that street. Teleportation, that's what it was—whatever *that* is. They had machines all right. Their minds and nervous systems, which they had perfected, were machines. Mind-energy, the basic energy.

I learned a little about that stuff later, but not very much.

Even after they gave me some of their 'power' like giving a kid candy, I didn't know what it was. Like any dumb atomeer can use the power of breaking atoms and not know anything more about physical science than a New York debutante knows about a *krin-krin* hangover. Like the experts who still can't tell you what electricity is.

I came out of the fog feeling pretty good, considering. I knew one thing right off, as any spacer would: I was in space, at C-acceleration, beyond the neutral-gravity point between planets, and in free fall.

I sat up on foam rubber cushioning and this girl was looking at me with those black black eyes, so black they were almost purple. The big aristocratic guy was sitting beside her.

She was young and very nice to look at. Her eyes softened, and I felt more at ease. The gent smiled; both of them gave me the idea of having a lot more energy and vitality than any ordinary person.

"We saved you from the police," she said. Her body moved softly under skin-tight resensilk. She had used her voice, but I felt her thoughts. I knew she didn't have to use her lips to tell me anything. It was a funny feeling. "You're on a space-cruiser. We'll be in a La Guardia field cradle in five hours."

"How?" I said. "How did it happen? How did you—?"

She shook her head. "You wouldn't understand. Not yet."

"All right," I said. "You saved my life, and a lot more. You may know how the Martian cops crack down. You did a lot for me." I leaned forward, "Now what's the catch?"

"You can repay us personally. You can do us a big favor in return. By so doing, you can possibly save Earth from annihilation."

I laughed and her eyes widened. "Wouldn't you want to do that?"

My laugh faded; she meant it. Maybe she was crazy, but she didn't know it. And for crazy people, they certainly had pulled a good job of getting me off that street, into a cruiser, and to Earth. Maybe some kind of a gag.

She said in a whisper. "You—*killed* a man!"

I looked into her eyes until I thought I was passing out. I clenched my hands. "An accident. Hit him too hard. I'm no killer, I—"

"But you did kill him, and you've killed before..."

"In self-defense, sure," I said. "But out there in the Asteroids, you have to—"

She said. "I understand. Now, you'll do some things for us. You won't ask questions because you wouldn't understand; later, you may understand without asking."

I felt like the commonest kind of crook. "So you saved my life," I said, "just so you'd have a sucker to pull some kind of a job for you. Now I suppose if I don't want to do what you say, you'll threaten to turn me over to the Solar authorities for shipment back to the Martian cops!"

She flushed a little. "Wait," she said, "until you find out the truth, then I'm sure you'll *want* to help us. I'm sure you want to save Earth and its billions of people from death."

I SHRUGGED. "What'd Earth ever do for me? What's it ever done for any of the poor guys dying from cosmic-rays and getting killed because there aren't any laws out there? It takes our metal for precious atomician work, and what does it give us in return? A few lousy credits, and a sign saying 'Keep out—no admission.' The devil with Earth."

"You must help us," the man said very softly and yet very

forcefully.

"You mean I've got no choice, is that it?"

The girl raised her eyebrows. "There would be no sense in your making a choice now; you can't understand, so no choice would be valid. It would be only blind emotionalism."

"I see." I was mad. I could handle this cruiser myself. I'd been kidnapped by people who considered me nothing more than a robot they were going to use. I swung my feet around, got them planted solidly down on the mesh grid flooring.

I got my hands down on either side of me so I could move fast and hard. "I see. Well, I'm not playing sucker for anybody."

I could hear the soft whispering of space against the platinum lined skin of the cruiser. Her eyes burned into me. I felt helpless and very much alone. But the devil with them I thought.

So I jumped straight for the aristocratic gent, and swung a long stiff right for his jaw. He faded into the air. I yelled wildly as he seemed to drift away like smoke, and into nothingness. I turned and there he was over in the corner of the cabin.

His eyes shot sparks, but he wasn't mad; he just looked grim. "You may cause us trouble when we cushion in," he said softly. "So I think you had better go back to sleep," he moved toward me. I tried to move my arms and legs, but I suddenly found that I couldn't move anything. "And perhaps it will be better if you have no more resistance to our suggestions after we reach earth."

His eyes seemed to expand out and out and out. It was like I was falling into a widening black pool.

"And," I heard his distant voice say, "that is the way it will be. Until you can make free choice of your own, you will have to agree with us completely. Subconsciously you know we are right; some time you will know it with your full consciousness."

They had it all right, whatever it was. But not as much as their friends. They had as much of the greater power as you can have, and still be bounded by Third Plane reality.

It was mental power. Mind-energy they called paraphysical. Nothing trite, like I'd seen the quack women along the North Canal pull with mass hypnotism; this was something big and way beyond me.

I fell forward into a black hole.

# CHAPTER TWO
*Kill For Us!*

THEIR names were Glora and Malcolm Mergon; he was her father. They could make suckers out of anyone they wanted to; they could get into another guy's mind and make him think, see, feel, hear anything they wanted him to. Take Extra Sensory Perception, and imagine somebody who's perfected all of it—and that's the way Glora and Malcolm Mergon were. Only more so.

We didn't need visas; we didn't have to go into the antiseptic wards; we didn't have to be scanned. Everytime we came into contact with Guards, or doctors or officers—those guys thought whatever Glora and Malcolm wanted them to think. So we walked right straight through all the red tape, and caught a skytaxi to a sky-top hotel bordering Central Park West; by then it was noon of a nice spring day.

I sat there, sweating and feeling cold in spite of the even temperature. I didn't savvy anything; I felt like a kid who'd gotten lost.

They brought a three-dimensional map out of the air, I guess; I couldn't tell. It hung in the air like it was glued to nothingness. Glora moved around me and stood in front of the big tri-dimensional map. Her legs were long and slim and smooth; she'd be a prize for some bigshot, I thought; but she wasn't my kind. My kind you'll still find along the North Canal, with very little on, and nothing in their heads but phony dreams.

"Now," she pointed at various marked sections on the map. "These are the locations of the ten Uranium Piles that supply all of Earth's power. If these piles should all reach critical mass at the same time, the earth would vaporize instantaneously.

"Scientific theory here is that even if all of them blew at once, though the destruction would be terrific, it wouldn't be fatal. That a hundred square miles around each pile would be destroyed only. That's so wrong, Ray. Through special abilities, Mal and I are aware of an unstable element existing here; Earth scientists can't discover it. If those Ten Piles reach simultaneous critical mass, it will react on this big unstable element. The Earth won't exist anymore."

I gulped. "Is that liable to happen?"

"It probably will, unless you can stop it from happening." I felt gray sickness on my face, felt that she knew what she was talking about. "How?" I whispered. "Who'd want to do a thing like that?"

"There's an atomician Chief in control of each of those Piles. Men who have been tested and scanned and conditioned until the Atomic Energy Commission hasn't any doubt of their reliability. But we happen to know that an unintegrated personality of great mental power—powers like our own—has gotten control of these ten Chief's minds. At a specific time, acting in complete unconscious accord, they will respond to a posthypnotic command already planted in their unconscious minds. Upon responding, they will allow those Piles to reach critical mass."

And so then, naturally, I wanted to know what that had to do with me.

Malcolm Mergon spoke then. "So—you are going to meet this person who controls them. We can not move against those ten while he is around, and he is stronger than we are. When he is gone, then we can go to work on those Chief's minds. *You will have to kill this man!*"

"*Who* is this man," I said, not very loud.

"Ronal LeStrang," he said. "President of Atomic Energy Commission."

I jumped up. I was mad and scared and confused. "Hey wait now! You think just because I'm a bit of nameless scum you picked up out of a Martian garbage pit, you can make a sucker out of me! I'm no professional killer! You guys are hypnotists. How do I know that what you're saying is fact? How do I know you aren't some foreign agents, wanting to start a world revolution or something? You think I can go out and kill a man just because a couple of guys tell me to!"

She pleaded with me, "That's why we came to Mars, Ray," she said. "We might never have found anyone like you otherwise. You're strong, you have courage, and very strong latent ESP potentials. But more than any of those things, you can—*kill*. Except for on the frontier planets and the asteroids, the ability to kill has been bred out by the new psychogenic surgery and conditioning marts."

She hesitated, then said, "And he has to be killed, Ray; that's the only way left. Killing is destructive, and we can't do it. We're mentally incapable of doing it. But he isn't; that's our handicap. You've got to help us."

And I knew she was right. Whether I knew it because of my own thinking, or whether Malcolm Mergon's mind had forced me to know it—that wasn't important any more, I knew I had to do it.

He moved toward me. His eyes burned.

"Wait," I said quickly. I looked around for a way out. I was trapped, and I didn't know whether I really wanted to get away or not. I only knew I was scared of what they could do to my mind. My mind wasn't much, but I was used to it. It was all I had. "Wait a minute, you guys. Give me a chance. Give—"

"We haven't much time, Ray," he said. "But first we must give you some added ability. It's already in you, but it's dormant. We'll bring it into the active stage. Maybe you would like to have some of the—power that we have, Ray? Anyway, you will need it. Now, Ray, go back to sleep so we can give you the power. It won't take long. Go back to sleep, Ray.

"*Ray, go back to sleep!*"

*       *       *

THIS TIME when I recognized daylight again, I was different. I felt funny, not the same; things were twisted around now. I was walking down the big new Eighth Tier of Uptown Broadway, feeling the jetcars pushing past in their different speed lanes. The sun was shining on the big lacework of tiers and tubes, and I was walking. But things were not the same.

I felt like everything that had happened since hitting the Martian in Jelahn's tavern was part of a dream, and that now I was coming awake maybe for the first time. The life around me looked faded, blurred, not quite real.

I had some of *their* power all right, I could feel it, and it was like a new kind of Martian rotgut was giving me a crazy highness. I felt like I'd suddenly gone screwy, but didn't care—as though nobody could touch me for it. I had some of their power, whoever or whatever they were, but not very much I thought; just enough to help me kill Ronal LeStrang.

A tele-audio flash information band on the side of the building shocked me as I stared at it. It gave the date. September 6, 1983.

Since Malcolm Mergon had walked toward me saying "Ray, go back to sleep," it had been three weeks! I'd been out three weeks. It jolted me. Three weeks. Work on my brain; work on my body; do things to my nervous set-up; make me different. This Glora and Malcolm Mergon—I knew they could do an awful lot to a guy in three weeks.

I stumbled a little, ran into a cute little blonde. She glared at me then looked scared. I felt her thoughts, felt hundreds, thousands of thoughts that belonged to the pedestrians around me, swarming and beating at my head like moths at a light. "He's a drunk!...looks like one of those non-rehabilitated space men. ...see the cosmic-ray burns on his face...stay away from him...dangerous..."

Dangerous, sure. They'd done plenty to me, but I didn't know what nor how much. And I didn't even know why...not for sure; just what they'd told me to believe. But I remembered—dangerous—I was supposed to kill.

A piece of uncultured, ignorant, un-psyched space-rot! Picked up and brought to Earth to do a murder job. They got me, Ray Berton, killer. But that wasn't enough for them, oh no. They had to give me added abilities—make me a super-delux killer!

Me, Ray Berton. The guy who would save the world!

I TOOK a grav-raise tube up the building front to the top of the big central UN Building in International Square. I stepped into a scanning cubicle. A mechanical voice said: "State the purpose of your visit, please."

I stared around me at the mosaiced floors and walls. A super-super delux killer. And with one of the most important men in the world to kill. I knew that, through Glora and Malcolm, I'd made an appointment. Made it sound important.

"An appointment to see Mr. Ronal LeStrang. About a 'heavy' beryllium strike in the asteroids." As head of the Atomic Energy Commission, LeStrang would be more than willing to have a personal talk about that. The Earth was supposed to be International minded, but it was still a case of getting the most and getting it first then saying "See!"

"You may go in, Mr. Berton."

I dropped my right hand into my jacket pocket, wrapped my fingers around a small coiled bunch of deadly metal. Metal with a trigger that would release enough energy to kill the biggest man in the world as quickly as any other.

As I came into the big glass-lined office, LeStrang got up from behind a desk. He was short and stocky, with a naked-looking head and white eyebrows. There wasn't any sense in wasting time, I figured, I had a slight advantage of surprise; I took it.

I jumped across the room, and took the little neutron gun out of my pocket. Before LeStrang could shrug his eyelashes, I had that gun jabbed right at his belly.

I shivered. His body didn't look real. His eyes didn't belong in that body; they seemed to flame out at me. I felt thought fingers grabbing at my mind, but there seemed to be automatic shields clicking into place, blocking him.

"The interview's over," I said, and started to pull the trigger.

Something stopped me. Sweat ran into my eyes; I felt like I was going to lay down on the floor. His eyes looked at my cosmic-rayed face, the purple scars of burns from the wild radioelements of the asteroids.

I heard myself whimpering like a scared *srith*-dog. His thoughts were stronger, in a way, than Glora's or Malcolm's. They started eating away at my mind like dark acid—thought fingers getting hold and trying to squeeze like my brain was a sponge.

"Glora and Mal sent you of course. They couldn't touch me here, so they sent you. I didn't think they'd stoop so low as to hire animals to work for them. Well, they can't win anyway; I had the thing all set, but now it's just a case of postponement. I'll fix it next time so they can't stop me."

I raised the neutron gun, "Next time," I said. "There isn't going to be any."

He laughed softly at me. As I started to fire, his body faded; it became nothingness right there in front of me, like it had turned into smoke, and then the smoke became transparent. Then there was nothing at all. Just a big room that seemed empty even though I was in it. He had disappeared, but I hadn't fired.

For a minute I went completely blank. I felt numb all over, then panic hit me. LeStrang had disappeared in front of me. I knew he hadn't been wiped out; he'd just gone someplace else. That was part of this—power. Mental power. Glora and Malcolm Mergon had it. LeStrang had it—

And Ray Berton—no that was crazy! Maybe I could send and receive thoughts. But a lot of ESP groups could do that. It was still borderline stuff, not accepted by the big shots scientists. Telepathy, and—ESP included other wild talents, I knew. An old woman on the South Canal had claimed to have the power of teleportation. Gamblers talked about telekinesis.

I had to get out of LeStrang's office; I was trapped there, and I'd be the goat if caught. From somewhere, I heard Glora's thought voice calling.

"Get out of that office, right now, Ray! Hurry. We'll help you. Get rid of doubts. You can do it; think about how you can do it. Come back here to us, Ray. Back to us. Right now. All of you, at once, right now. Think of us, visualize us, this room. You're not there. You're here. *You're here, Ray! Here!*"

And she was right. I wasn't in LeStrang's office anymore.

I was someplace else, and as close to death as I'd ever been in my life.

I re-formed, I guess you would say, but somehow I missed the inside of Glora and Malcolm's skytop suite. I suddenly found myself hanging in empty air, just outside their window.

A hundred and twenty some stories straight down—air. I started to fall, then grabbed the window ledge. But the shock had weakened me so much I don't think I could have held on. Glora and Malcolm came to the window, grabbed my wrists and dragged me inside.

I fell down on my knees. I didn't have the strength to stand up. My clothes were wet, and I held my hands down hard on the floor to keep them from shaking.

Malcolm said. "Too bad. He went through the Barrier. He is back in Fourth Stage reality now; we will go to work on the ten Uranium Pile men and remove the posthypnotic commands from their minds. We can do that, now that he has gone back through the Barrier. But he can come back here, Ray; he will plan something, some way to defeat us.

"Ray—you will have to go through the Barrier after him. You will have to develop Fourth Stage consciousness; you will have to grow beyond Earth's Three Stage reality. You still have to kill him, Ray."

## CHAPTER THREE
### *Through The Barrier*

I DIDN'T have any idea what they were talking about then. They were so urgent and desperate, I guess they forgot that I was just an ignorant, no-good space bum who'd happened to strike it rich, and then gotten himself into a killer's brawl.

Later I got to know a little about the various stages of consciousness and how they determine what reality is.

But then, I knew next to nothing: so I asked them again to please explain what it was all about. They tried to explain, but you can't explain color to a man who'd never seen color. And that's the way it is with trying to explain Fourth Stage reality, the next step above three-dimensional awareness, to a man who's all tied up in the blindfold of three-dimensional perspective.

LeStrang and Glora and Malcolm were Fourth Stage people. They had come back through a barrier, a state of mental awareness separating Third from Fourth dimensional reality; they had come back through this barrier from the Fourth Stage plane of reality. This is coexistent with Earth's Three Stage plane, and it's called Mohln.

LeStrang had come through to destroy Earth; then Glora and Malcolm, at great sacrifice, had followed him into Three Stage Plane, or Earth, to try to stop him.

Their only chance was to get some sucker, someone who could be destructive, as they said. They couldn't. So I'd been picked, and had chased the mad guy back where he came from. Back to Mohln, the Fourth Stage.

According to Malcolm and Glora, when LeStrang came back through the Barrier a second time, he would probably have some way to destroy Earth that couldn't be stopped—not even by me, the big super-super killer.

"His is a paranoid mind," Malcolm Mergon said. "He is unpredictable. His delusions of two different realities may change its course of action, but his psychological character can't change. His methods will; he is destructive. That is his goal, motivated by paranoiacal desire for revenge, because of persecution. He must be killed; that is the only way. We have tried everything else. We can not influence him mentally. There is no rapport with diseased and twisted personalities, such as his."

I felt as though I didn't have any mind of my own left—and I didn't care much. I was bigger than any lousy human I'd ever met, besides Malcolm and Glora, or LeStrang. Maybe a few ESP guys around the planets had a little of what I had, but nothing like me. I didn't want to go back to being a narrow Third Plane mind, squeezed down to blind thinking not much above any other animal's.

So I agreed to go through the Barrier. There was a lot of explanation there, too, and I guess I remember some of it; something about reality—being relative to degrees of awareness.

He talked about how consciousness was a great machine that evolved slowly, powered by basic energy, the energy that makes atoms and electrons. He told me about how this machine evolved, how it was once only one-dimensional in its awareness, then two-dimensional, then three. But that there were ever higher degrees of awareness; and for each definite plane of increased awareness, was another coexistent world.

They told me how the evolution was gradual, sporadic among different people, but gradual among species over millions of years of time. And now the increase in extrasensory perception showed that more and more Third Stage minds and nervous systems were developing very close to breaking the Barrier into Fourth Stage awareness. A new world. A new reality of tremendously expanded senses.

That's what he said, Malcolm Mergon.

Then he said that the mind and the nervous system being a great and highly complex machine powered by the basic energy of the cosmos, that machine could be tinkered with, changed, stepped up—automatically—if the tools were available.

They had the tools; they had minds so far above mine it wasn't anything you could even talk about. Not and make any sense out of it. Everyone has the latent capacity to develop Fourth Stage consciousness. Even a one-celled amoeba, given time, will develop it.

But me—they were going to make me develop it fast. My sensory apparatus would grow in complexity and degree of awareness of higher-stage reality. And I would be in that other plane of Mohln where the guy I was after had gone.

I didn't understand. But I had the feeling that I—might.

I said for them to go ahead and give me the business. And they did; I went through the Barrier.

\*      \*      \*

BEHIND the wall of that room above Manhattan, they had a small square cell. They put me in it, and a reddish light filled the room and started eating into me. There were no doors, no windows in it, nothing but naked bare walls. And they went to work on me. They turned hidden power on me I suppose, but anyway they changed me.

I don't know what they changed; I probably couldn't explain it if I did know. Nervous system, mind, those dormant ESP abilities everyone has in one degree or another.

Malcolm had given me an example of one stage reality—a line, with everything else as the unknown, or time. And then the two stage reality, where height became time, then the Third Stage reality where the Fourth became "time"—

It got over my head there; I felt sick and my head felt like it was flying in a million parts. But by then, they said my Fourth Stage potential was ready for the final treatment. And I was ready to breakthrough.

There was a terrible kind of concentration with Glora and Malcolm giving me mind-energy way above my own. Something seemed to burst inside of me. There was pain beyond pain; after that faded away there was a kind of quiet drifting that seemed to go on through a soft cloudy nothingness for a long time.

The four walls of that small cell blurred, but remained as a misty outline. The reddish light faded; black night took its place; the black turned to gray. For a while it was like two superimposed pictures; the cell, and behind it another place.

Then the cell was gone.

I was standing in a dim twilight that had a soft blue tone to it. I was in a much bigger room now. The walls were a funny color, like gray human flesh.

I stared at the wall as I climbed to my feet, wishing there was a door or window so I could see out. And as I looked—a window was there! Or rather, an opening melted away for me.

A feeling of wonderfulness, of magnificence went through me. I staggered like I was drunk with a feeling of thundering joy. I walked over and looked out. A soft sun was setting over soft purple hills. Everything was like that, soft and inviting and warm; beauty, like in a dream that you forget when you wake up. That's what it was like. And I knew there was much more I couldn't see or feel.

They had expanded my mind so much that Third Stage reality was gone. I was in another world of awareness. But I guess even they couldn't expand my mind enough to see what the real Fourth Stage was, all of it I mean. Maybe we'll all know, sometime.

There was a sensation of *aliveness*—in everything. Walls, floor, ceiling, the very air, all the outside of the room, the green fields and giant ferns, everything seemed alive. And when I walked there was that feeling of bursting freedom.

Malcolm had said that with increasing awareness, a similarity developed. One got nearer to the basic energy of all things with his own expanding mind. But this wasn't for me to understand; maybe it won't be for but a very few—not for a long time yet.

I looked out. I wanted to be out of that room and down there on that wonderfully soft grass with the ferns that seemed alive and calling to me. A square of grayish metal moved out of the wall and came to me. I knew what to do, I sat on it, and it carried me out of the room, through the wall, and down to the ground. There was a connection between the processes of thinking in me, my wishes, and the hidden machinery in the metal square.

Machinery powered by some great efficiency that used mind-energy. I got off the square and it raised and went back through the wall of the tall cone-shaped tower. And as I looked, the tower disappeared. Where it had stood was a field of shoulder tall flowers with bright red blossoms.

I STARTED walking. A path opened for me. Fern fronds parted and closed again behind me. Water gushed over rocks in the cool shadows. It wasn't very light, though the moon was full and red, and I walked carefully; senses I'd never known before sharply tuned for danger.

I saw her then, a Fourth Stage girl, as I came round a curve in the path. Her skin was golden and soft, like everything else around us. She stared at me.

Her voice was like music. "You just—came through?"

It wasn't a question. She knew I had just come through the Barrier. I don't remember whether we talked verbally or by telepathy. But on Mohln it doesn't make any difference.

She nodded. "Yes," and started walking toward me. She didn't seem quite real; nothing here seemed solid, quite real. Or it was more like I couldn't see quite enough to make it very real for me. Like a man who has lost part of his vision.

She looked like Glora, and she gave out with a sobbing cry of joy as she probed my mind and knew everything about how I had come through, and why. She ran to me and took hold of my hands; her body glowed and her breath came faster. "I'm Reeta. Glora is my sister. I've been wondering if they would send someone through."

She stepped back. "We must get him—Durach—fast!"

She caught my confusion. "Durach, same man as LeStrang. Here he is Durach."

Reeta turned, led me through a wall of fern branches and onto a different path. "We could go to my brother Carleth the other way," she said softly—referring, I knew, to teleportation. "But we can't strain your newly acquired senses too much now. Ordinarily, one breaking through has many days just for readjustment and adaptation. But you won't have any time at all for that. Durach is already acting against us; he's killing us."

She was running, and leading me. She ran effortlessly, like somebody without weight. "We'll go right to the village and see Carleth, my brother. We haven't much time. Maybe we're already too late, Ray Berton!"

As I ran, I wondered what had happened to the real LeStrang back on Earth, the Third Plane. Durach had gone through the Barrier and had taken LeStrang's place; he'd gotten away with it by using his extra-senses. By suggestion he could have made everyone else think he was LeStrang. And he could have gotten rid of LeStrang easily enough— For example by just willing him some place else, all at once. Say five thousand feet under the Earth's surface, or in the middle of the Atlantic, or out in space.

Then Durach had become LeStrang for a while, long enough to interview each of those Uranium Pile chiefs, and put them under his domination. He'd given them a hypnotic command, posthypnotic, for each to allow his Uranium Pile to reach critical mass upon a certain signal. I didn't know how he'd worked that—

Reeta led me down through an underground tubeway and into a big bubble. A warm soft light shone inside the bubble. Small cone buildings were built in a neat circle. In the center were gardens and fountains. People stared and whispered at me.

Reeta stopped, her face suddenly froze, and then turned slowly with sick eyes. Her fingers pressed her cheeks.

A wrenching scream stabbed through that garden. Still screaming and clutching her head, a woman came running crazily down a path through the center of the village. Faces of men, woman and children came out of buildings, staring and flinching with sick pain.

The woman ran with her hands reaching out in front of her. Her neck was straining like a starving bird's. I felt Reeta's fingernails dig into my arm. The voice hit me like a spray of ice. "Another one! Another one to Durach and his freaks!"

The tortured woman's cries chopped at me. My ears hurt; my insides knotted. She was still screaming and running when she suddenly fell on her face. She lay there jerking and twitching among the smashed flowers. Other people were running toward her, tall, marvelously strong and light moving people. I thought of them as being like gods, maybe. The woman's body stopped moving as two men bent over her.

I could tell it wouldn't move again. It had that look.

"Dead," Reeta whispered. "They don't last long once Durach and his gadgets pierce our last protective neural defense bands. We've had no real defense. Even the last, or *sith*-threshold, is temporary. He's hit us with various degrees of destructive mental force, augmented by his gadgets. We've resisted each stage, but not the *sith*-threshold breaker. Durach's closing in fast now that he's weakened us. He wants full control of the Merger, so he can go back into the Third Stage plane and destroy it."

I thought it was all about as clear as Venusian moonlight. I turned quickly as a low soft voice spoke. I knew it was Carleth, her brother, standing just outside the nearest cone building. He was tall and terrifically strong looking. He was studying me, inside and out.

Then he looked at Reeta. "Give the thought order to both our villages right now! That Glora and Mel have sent a man with Third Stage abilities through. Tell them to throw up full resistance in the *sith*-sector. Maybe that way, we can hold Durach's attacks off until Berton can get to him."

## CHAPTER FOUR
### *"There Is Durach"*

CARLETH led me inside the cone, right through the wall. I felt the humming of delicate machinery as though it was part of the working of my own brain. An opening that closed again behind us.

I sat down. I was very tired. Something was very wrong; I knew that. Here I was—but here I wasn't. I was through the Barrier, with enough of this so-called awakened consciousness to live in the Fourth Stage world of perception; but I wasn't like Reeta or Carleth, not by a long shot.

I almost yelled as the chair reached up around me and stretched itself to fit me. I shifted my position, and the chair remolded itself to me. I was still trying to get rid of a clammy helpless feeling when Carleth said: "We still may have time to act against Durach. We've saved this last paraphysical resistance band in each of our minds until the last. He's broken down the others since he came back through the Barrier. He might be able to kill the rest of us within an hour."

He looked at me strangely, "One hour perhaps, Ray Berton, to save your world, Earth, from annihilation. One hour to get Durach."

Fine, I thought, but first, I'm hungry. And a tray of food floated out of the wall and settled down on my lap. A steak, and all the accessories, just what I'd wished I had.

While I ate, Carleth told me that people here didn't get energy that way when they had stayed here long enough. Here, he said, they used a process that Third Stage minds call telurgy. Fourth Stage minds use telurgy to construct their buildings, and transportation, and to get energy directly from any element they wanted to get it from. The only difference, he said, between any objects is made by our limited consciousness (Third Stage) reacting to differently shaped electron-identity patterns. Yet basically every substance, everything in the cosmos, is the same, made different only by degrees of evolving mental machinery.

I finished eating and said, "You're supermen here—that it? But if you are, why are you helpless before this guy Durach? Why do you have to call on me?"

Carleth said. "No, we're not supermen, Berton; just extended, or advanced men. There'll never be supermen; there'll never be perfection."

Carleth turned; he looked at the wall and it melted away. I was looking at a distant city. And what a city! Cone-shaped spires thousands of feet high, and one high above the others, with the moon behind it.

Carleth said. "This Fourth Stage world of Mohln is sparsely populated; only a few have come through. We built these two small villages, for meditation and self-development. We lived here, helping others who came through to adjust and realize their growing potentialities. It was peaceful then. Normally, it would be no other way here—sane and balanced and marvelously stimulating as we discovered and developed new abilities of Fourth Stage power."

He stared at the distant city, and said to me. "Then Durach and his freaks came through. They built that city. It might be called by you a city of the mind. Their diseased minds keep it there by paraphysical mental energy."

"Freaks," I said, "Here too?"

"Yes, freaks; they're different. There's only seven of them, and that they should build such a colossal futile city is proof enough of their pathological, Third Stage thinking. Third plane disease still motivates them, even though they developed enough Fourth Stage awareness to come through the Barrier. They're paranoids, according to Third Stage standards. Here, they're much worse than that—able to realize many of their delusions.

"But they're freaks. They didn't develop by evolution to reach Mohln; they developed suddenly. As soon as they first came through, we knew they were abnormal, that they didn't belong. Durach brought Third Stage irrational, blind, destructive motivations with him. Diseased personality attitudes. He wanted power; he wanted to rule and conquer blindly. There had been an accident that sent him here.

"Durach and his freaks were seven chances in millions, but they happened. Teratological freaks, monsters. Before they broke away from us and built that mental city, we found their secret."

Carleth fell silent for a moment, then continued softly. "Durach and the others there are offsprings of Third Stage men and women who were exposed to gamma rays, from experimental radioactivity, from the last war, from various conditions on Third Stage Earth allowing over-exposure to hard radiation.

"Durach's father was an atomician engineer who was subjected to gamma rays while working in one of the imperfected Uranium Piles, sometime during 1964, according to Earth reckoning. Five years later, Durach reached what is adult maturity in the Third Plane. He organized some other freaks who were being kept on a small island off the coast of Japan. A year later they had developed sufficiently to break through into Mohln."

"There's only twelve of us left. You see no one here's in the same stage of Fourth Plane awareness; some develop faster than others. That makes us have different degrees of susceptibility to Durach's mental attacks. Reeta and myself, we happen to be the highest, now that Mal and Glora have gone back into Third Stage existence."

IT WAS strange, hearing him say these things with hatred in his voice. Yet, I knew he hated this menace... "Durach and the other freaks have feelings of inferiority. They want to compensate, they have developed paranoid delusions. They were persecuted on Earth, naturally as freaks. Regarded as insane, imprisoned, mistreated. They have strong revenge motives; they want to destroy Earth.

"Also, Durach has a theory that Third Stage Earth is holding back the development of Mohln. He thinks that if Earth's plane was destroyed, Mohln could expand into complete Fourth Stage reality.

"Durach made a Merging machine to open a channel between the two coexisting planes. What it really does is regress consciousness molecules to lower and lower stages of development until it becomes again bounded by Third Stage blindness. Durach made the Merger to help him and his freaks destroy Earth's plane. What they don't realize is that the two planes are the same, part of the same reality field, except that one is the result of more complex powers of awareness."

I thought about what Carleth had been telling me. It all started to fit together. I told him what had happened on Earth—about Durach getting control of the minds of the ten Chiefs who ran the Uranium Piles.

Carleth nodded. "You ran Durach back here into Fourth Stage reality. Since then he's been using various kinds of gadgets to destroy us, one by one. A kind of electron force feeler, you might call it. We've caught flashes of his purpose, though they keep their diseased minds locked up pretty well. It's almost impossible, and sometimes destructive, to try to contact them mentally.

"He intends to return to Earth through the Merger. This time he'll take the secret of the electronic feeler with him. He'll be able to kill Mal and Glora with it. He'll be more powerful there than they are, because in returning to Third Stage reality, they've sacrificed most of their Fourth Plane capacities.

"In other words, the next time Durach goes through the Barrier, he'll achieve his purpose. He'll have killed all of us by the electronic feeler. It disassociates electron structure of the nervous system so that it can't reform."

"And I'm the only one who can stop him," I whispered.

Carleth said that was right.

I said, "Why doesn't Durach use the Merger then, right now, and go back and get the job done?"

He explained that to me also. "As soon as he came back this time, we knew what he had tried to do, what he was planning. We got conscious control of the Merger machinery, or part of it anyway. We've maintained that control because we have greater numbers, and the combined mind-energy has been too much for Durach. That is why he's been killing us one by one. Our power over the Merger has been going down. The danger point is reached now."

"And what about Mal and Glora?"

"They followed Durach into Third Plane reality to try to stop him. By so doing, they sacrificed most of their higher abilities. Durach, being a freak, an abnormal Fourth Stage man, came back through. But Glora and Mal cannot; they can never attain Fourth Stage life again."

Carleth paused, then said. "You can destroy, Berton; we cannot. Therefore, you're the last chance of defeating Durach."

I thought about everything, as much as I could. About how bitter it would be to know the feeling of being a part of this higher world of Mohln, then finding yourself once again in the blind and groping world of the Third Plane where no one had any idea of what greater reality was so near.

REETA CAME in. I caught a stray thought from her that sent pain and sickness and futility through me. A thought of sadness and pity for me as she looked at me.

I backed toward the wall. I thought hard, hard, and the wall opened for me. A second of joyous power gave way to despair. I didn't belong here; I didn't belong anywhere now. What if I should kill Durach? And then what if I went back to the Third Plane?

What then? I wouldn't fit there either. I'd still keep some of the power, I knew that. I'd be an ESP freak then, probably working in some televised vaudishow. And I couldn't stay here, I thought, because I hadn't developed normally. I'd been artificially developed so that I could go through the Barrier hadn't I?

I was nobody; I was nowhere. I didn't have a name anymore, not really. These supermen weren't my kind either.

Carleth pointed toward the City. "Durach's there," I heard him whisper. And Reeta's eyes were wet with sorrow as she came toward me.

I didn't want to see her anymore, or feel her hands on me; I didn't wait for anything else. One thing I knew as I went through the wall and started down the beautiful still street:

*I would kill Durach, and then I'd be finished.* I tried to ignore the screams in the village, tried not to see the people dying around me.

I still carried that neutron gun Malcolm Mergon had given me. It had come through the Barrier too.

Carleth's and Reeta's thoughts drifted after me: "We can give you some protection. A constant stream of mind-energy shielding. We'll stay with you, as closely as possible.

"Durach is there, in the tallest building in the City."

I looked back. Reeta stood in the center of the village by the fountain, waving. I didn't wave back. I knew that my smile was bitter. And then I concentrated as much as I could on the flat metal disc that came out at me from the wall of the bubble with a humming of delicate electronic power. I sat on it. I thought: "I'd like to be on my way to the City. To the City."

I was outside the bubble. I was high above the surface of Mohln, with the quickness of thought. And I was—high!

It was like a splash of white light under me, the moon shining on that wonderful world. I looked ahead toward those giant spires of that colossal city. Built for ten men, ten freaks. A city of thought.

That one tower stuck up half again as high as the rest of the City. A blue dangerous looking light shone from its top. There wasn't any use drawing this appointment out, I thought. And a fast appearance might give me an advantage of surprise, if I had any advantage at all, and I doubted that.

"There," I thought, "is where I want to be next. On top of that building, facing Durach. *Now!*"

And I was there.

## CHAPTER FIVE
### *Remember Me?*

DURACH was waiting for me. Not LeStrang; nothing that looked like LeStrang. This was the real Durach, and he was not something you would want to see a second time, nor anything you would care to remember, if you could help it.

He wasn't human; he was a monster, a freak. Yet, he looked much like anyone else. It was the inside of him that was so different.

Durach wasn't alone as I found myself standing there before him. Two women and several men were in the big arched room with him. None of them were any more pleasant on the inside than Durach. Jelahn's dive on the North Canal seemed like the memory of an anti-room to paradise compared with the feeling in this room of Durach's.

It was filthy and obscene, and it made me mad; it made me shaking mad to think that a chance thing like these freaks had been sent into the Fourth Stage world of Mohln where they didn't belong, to contaminate it, and bring hate and destruction and death to a world that had put a few men at least on the edge of marvelous super life.

Durach was bigger than he had been in the personality of LeStrang, a personality he had given to people by suggestion. He was on a couch of bright red that seemed to writhe under him. Durach was a fat white man with white hair, his fat wrapped up in a tight-fitting shiny stuff like resensilk. His face was soft and his eyes wide and bland and blue. Pale jowls hung over his collar on either side, and under his beaked nose was a small, pursed, red button of a mouth.

Silly little mouth, I thought. I wanted to laugh at it, but I didn't; I couldn't laugh. I couldn't do much of anything except stand there and try to figure out what I was really doing here—wherever I was.

The women and men around the room looked at me, very silently, terribly curious, and far away. Durach's little red mouth smiled at me. No one said anything. They just thought—about the ways I could look dead—and about the many ways it was possible for me to become dead—ways that can take so long.

And there were other thoughts pounding at my skull. They were laughing at me; they were feeling sorry for me, and they were thinking I was an idiot, at least.

I felt like a silly little mortal suddenly brought before a bunch of wicked gods. And then it hit me—

*That's just about what I was!*

I was scared. My mind seemed covered with a cold twisted shadow. Winds I couldn't see seemed to sweep and cry and thunder through that giant room. And I could feel power, great stores of controlled power, churning and boiling and ready to explode around me.

No one moved. I saw the great rotary converters spinning away beside banks and banks of transformers, and grid oscillators. Machinery, and it was running and developing power, but it seemed unreal, foggy, as though I was seeing it through a curtain of fog.

Well, I knew that this great room contained the Merger that Durach had built. Durach was a freak, both Third and Fourth Stage. He was utilizing both fields in a mad kind of fusion. He was mad, beyond the mental reach of sane Fourth Stage minds. That was understandable.

Fourth Stage minds, combined, could control some part of the Merger by mental energy, so that Durach couldn't use it. But Fourth Stage minds were being killed off by another gadget Durach and his freaks had made.

The Merger—a big gadget channeling unknown electronic force partly by mind-energy. This Merger could hit hard at a man's entire nervous system and his mind, and force it back to Third Stage awareness, or step it up so that Third Stage reality faded away, and the Fourth became reality.

But I knew this was phony. It was like the old methods of shock treatment for the insane. The methods were wrong, and the results might be harmful, and unpredictable.

Then Durach laughed, and he was laughing at me; his laughter burned and roared inside my skull.

I blinked and gasped out something as I jerked the neutron gun from my pocket and pointed it for the second time at his belly.

I KNEW I was talking, but my voice didn't sound like mine; it didn't sound like anybody's voice. "This time I do it, Durach. You can't go through the Barrier to get away from me now. The Merger machinery, you can't use it. Carleth's people have you blocked, Durach."

Durach's little red mouth stretched at me. He purred. "What do you want to kill *me* for?"

A woman in the corner laughed. It was like somebody had sprayed dry ice through the room.

I said, "I'm not wasting time talking, Durach. I'm killing you because—because—"

Durach laughed again. "Because you've been told to by a bunch of humanitarian perfectionists obsessed with their own vague destinies! Because you think you want to save the Third Plane—a dismal unreal blind world where people shamble like cattle and peer into continuous fog like moles! Is that why you want to kill me?"

I knew I'd have to do it now, fast, or I'd never be able to. I tried to press the trigger back. I knew that Durach couldn't stop me, not by any physical means. They had no weapons; they didn't need any, to deal with the Fourth Stage people in their own plane. They had mental-shattering gadgets, but none of them could work on me. I wasn't built like the other Fourth Stage people. I wasn't built like anyone now. I was a special job, made to get Durach, and that was all.

"You know the reasons you've been told and made to follow," Durach smiled. "You're the big sucker, as you think you are, Berton. You're beginning to see the truth now; you're beginning to realize why they can't touch me—why they had to get *you* to do it."

I tried to fire the gun. The air seemed to get hot and smoky around me with conflicting thoughts. I knew there was a battle going on—a fight of mind-energy. But I wasn't a part of it. It was between Durach and his freaks, and Carleth and Reeta and whoever was left of their kind. A fight for control of the Merger.

I tried to fire, but I couldn't; I wanted to hear what Durach had to say. I knew it was something that might mean a lot to me. I shouldn't want to listen; I had my job. I—

I felt like knives were stabbing me. I was shivering and sweating. I could feel my face growing wet and gray and lips quivering. I was about finished and I knew it. And I knew that if I did anything, I'd have to do it quick.

No physical weapons. What trap would they use against me, what unknown forces?

I felt my lips move, and heard my own tortured, sobbing cries.

"I'll tell you, Berton," Durach laughed. "They can't kill me. But you can. Why? Because you're like us, Berton! They have no more real respect for you than for the rest of us here in this room. You're just a tool they're using, and when they're through, you'll go back into the garbage dumps of Third Plane sickness.

*"Berton—you're just another freak, like us."*

I felt blinded. I forced my eyes to hold him in sight as I tried to fire. I moved toward him; the room was large, and I kept walking, listening to him.

"But we're bigger than they are, because we're freaks, Berton. We're natural freaks, you might say. Mal and Glora created a freak out of you so you would come through the Barrier. But we're all freaks, neither Third or Fourth Stage—*but the strongest talents of both planes are in us!*

"They can't move back from Fourth to Third Plane after having once left the Fourth. They can't destroy anything with their paraphysical power, Berton. That's their weakness. But we can. They call us insane. But use your own intelligence! What do you think?"

I kept walking toward his voice, toward that shifting smoky outline. Sweat made a stream down my throat. I was sick and blinded.

"They're asking you to give it all up just for their fanatical belief in some sort of abstract destiny for all humanity. *Immortality!* Think of it, Berton! And then you can go on and on, through higher and higher stages of reality. Reach heights of experience the greatest dreamers have never touched.

"We'll be gods, Berton! They want to do it by slow and ponderous evolution, and play at chance to become gods. They call us freaks—because we've found the short cut to eternal greatness.

"Mutation, that's one way. You got it another way, thanks to them. But from now on, it can be our show, Berton.

"They want to hold us back, using Third Stage people as pacers. They want to destroy us, because we're superior. They want Third Stage reality, with its disease, its blindness and its million incurable sicknesses to go on being a burden to the realization of Fourth Stage greatness, holding it back, drawing its entropic rate down to zero.

"Listen, Berton! If we destroy the Third Plane, the energy release will speed up the entropic rate of Fourth Plane development a billion fold. You can be one of us. A part of it. And why not? We're mutations. You got through the Barrier because they changed your nervous system and consciousness by synthetic methods. But you're like us. You're a freak too, Berton.

*"You're fighting on the wrong side. You're destroying—yourself!"*

TIME, MOVEMENT, sight, everything seemed to freeze as I stood there. There was Durach and the others, like pale statues in a dream. Then I felt other minds and other eyes around me. Reeta! Carleth!

I saw them. It was like a dream look at a forgotten room, and people almost forgotten; their voices, like stillness beyond a threshold I had once crossed.

She said, her eyes sad and wet, "The decision must be yours, Ray Berton. We can give you the support of what paraphysical energy we have left within us. But we can't destroy directly; you must do that. In that way, you're different from us, but you're not a freak like Durach and these others. You have temporary Fourth Stage awareness. At a given time, that awareness will fade, and you'll go back to Third Stage reality, and be as you were before, with no memory of this world. Destroy him, Berton. *Now! Now!*"

My eyes were shut. I felt like I was falling. "You're gods," I sobbed at them. "I'm still human. You're asking too much. How can I decide? I could be like them—greater than you. And you want me to give it up, go back to—" I thought of it. The stinking disease of Jelahn's tavern, and the girl—

I laughed a little then, and in that laugh was a crazy climbing note of fear and madness and not-knowing. Go back to that, when—

"There are only five of us left now," Reeta said. "Durach's feelers have killed the rest of us. We can't hold the Merger against him but a few seconds longer, Berton."

I thought of the outer planets where I'd always lived. The disease and the cold, the sadistic cops, the taverns with rotten women, minds eaten away with *krin-krin*.

"You picked me wrong," I yelled wildly. "You don't get heroes from where I came from. Like Durach said—he's more my kind. We could be like gods. Immortal—how can I—"

I felt mind-energy, paraphysical power, flow into me from Reeta and Carleth. They told me something, a word—extratemporal—new perception that could let me see things that would happen! Space factors disappeared, for one terrible second. The factor of future time faded—*and I could see!*

I felt it. Hot and horrible and final. A flash of future knowledge. I saw Earth disappear into a great white flame. And where it had been was a white-hot nova in black space.

Horror rose like a volcano of madness, and a sheet of pain seemed to split my head wide open.

"No," I felt Durach's roaring thought. "No, Berton! They're giving you a false impression. That's a probability variant of Earth's future. They've let you see the Earth destroyed—but it's a different variant than what will happen if you join us. By destroying the Third Plane my way, we can save Fourth Stage reality from destruction—but their way—all will be destroyed!"

"It's your choice," Reeta said. "We have only a few flashes of time left, and then it won't matter anymore."

Maybe I didn't make any decision, not consciously. The pressure was too much for me. I had to do something, anything. I heard myself screaming as I pressed the trigger of the gun.

Durach fell beneath its power beam. It sprayed and burned and roared in the great room. He came around the desk as I turned; his white face had turned gray with a coat of wet over it. I felt the sudden complete effort within all of them as they tried to get me.

Freaks. But there wasn't much physical difference between these people and the average looking group. It was the inside of them that was different. Differences in metabolism, neural structure, conscious awareness…a lot more…

Durach and the others were surging in toward me. Walls of mind-energy throbbed around me. Their faces were twisted with hate and fear.

"Berton! You can know immortality, perfection, omnipotence! Don't sacrifice your life for a cause already lost according to that vision you had of the future! You know the conditions on the Third Plane! They have conquered a part of atomic power, but their Third Stage mentalities will never develop fast enough to keep that power from destroying them. Them and us too! That's the probability variant of a future that will happen anyway—unless we destroy the Third Stage now, in a way that will let this higher reality go on, unburdened!

*"EARTH WILL destroy itself anyway, Berton. Let us save ourselves!"* My legs wouldn't hold me anymore. I was on my knees. I tried to lift the gun again.

"It's your choice, Berton," Reeta said. Now her thought and her voice was weaker, faraway, dying. "Remember—Durach's insane."

Insane? Insane by what judgment? It was relative. Who—?

Durach's final argument was the most convincing; nobody wants to die. "It means death for you, Berton, if you kill me. This city, this tower we're on top of—it exists because I will it to exist! This tower is two miles high, Berton! Kill me, and the tower will crumble from under you. You'll fall—fall, Berton! Remember, your Fourth Stage capacity is only temporary. When you kill me, your work for them will be done. You'll automatically start to return to Third Plane existence.

"You could control your fall here, with Fourth Stage energy. But kill me, and you'll find yourself back in Third Stage reality—two miles above the Earth! And nothing under you but death—that'll be your reward for saving Earth for a little while longer, Berton! You want to live!"

Far, far away, I felt Reeta and Carleth, still trying to help me. Sure, a man wants to live. That Marty in Jelahn's tavern, he wanted to live. Millions of people on Earth, they wanted to live, wanted to try to make it work. No man wants to die.

There are some ways no man cares to live.

I fired the gun, fired it point blank into Durach's chest, then moved it around over the others.

There was blinding white light. And Durach and his kind stopped living. They went back to some other energy form, a kind that would never cause anyone any more trouble.

I knew then that Durach had been right, in one respect anyway; when he died, the tower died. I felt it melting away around me as the mind-energy that had created it started to fade away. I felt that awful emptiness opening under me. And—this is funny—I felt like a little boy who's done something he thinks is pretty good and pretty big. But no one knows he's done anything, and he feels hurt, and he wants people to know.

I wanted people to know. I didn't want what I'd done, and everything that had happened and might happen, to be lost to people. It wouldn't be fair. Reeta and Carleth knew what I was thinking. I felt their thoughts coming back again, stronger, and stronger and growing, and joyous.

Reeta—Carleth—help me.

I don't want to be forgotten.

SOMEHOW, they were holding me with them, but I knew they couldn't do it very much longer. Around me was a gray billowing fog, and I was starting to fall through it—

Reeta and Carleth will stay here with Fourth Stage power; they are all right now. Durach's finished, and they have the merger back in their power completely now, and can use it for constructive purposes, or not at all. It doesn't matter. I've done my job. The danger's gone.

But I want people to know.

They're telling me to concentrate. They'll help me, but I must hurry, hurry. I've still some of the power, and they'll help me. Mind-energy. Matter changed from one form to another by thought. MY thought and theirs, together. *Telurgy.* Everything's made from the same stuff, only the electronic patterns are different. So we're willing patterns to change. We change some of the patterns of elements around me to another arrangement—into a metal scroll, my story to you, my thoughts of all that has happened, and what I've done. So you'll remember.

And they'll send it through the Barrier by the Merger.

What I'm thinking now as this tower and this city fades around me, it will all be on that metal for you to read. Maybe they could still save me, someway, but they can't because I guess I don't really want to go back to being a Third Stage guy.

I'm not like Glora and Malcolm, willing to give up so much, for a cause. After playing god, I can't go back to drinking *krin-krin* in Je-lahn's tavern on the North Canal of Mars.

I'd rather die this way.

Durach said you'd blow up Earth and this higher reality too, with atomic power, because you wouldn't be able to learn to think enough to control it. Reeta and Carleth said Durach was insane, that he was wrong.

I don't know; I hope they were right. Because it's all waiting for you. I've seen it and I know. Beauty and greatness you can't imagine now. I don't know when, or how, but it can be yours someday. If you can hang on. And it'll be yours not just for a little while, like it was for me, but forever.

I guess it's up to you to prove whether Durach was insane or not.

I wonder if my thoughts are being recorded now by Carleth and Reeta for you to read? I can't tell. I've lost them. Things around me are blurred, and I seem to be falling down through a gray, slow rain...

\*     \*     \*

From a midnight tele-audocast by International Information Service. New York City. September 9, 1983:

143

Reporter: *The preceding has been teleod as a special interest feature, and is not intended as a factual report, naturally. The body of the man who appeared so mysteriously, according to reports, from the atmosphere two miles above Manhattan, and crashed into the city, cannot be satisfactorily identified. The metal scroll, which fell after him, and was just narrated for your interest; is obviously the work of a quack looking for notoriety, and a possible niche in Fortean records.*

*However, the Atomic Energy Commission has ordered a complete scanning of Uranium Pile personnel. This move is reported to be motivated by the discovery that during the afternoon, Ronal LeStrang, President of the Atomic Energy Commission, disappeared, and no trace of him has been found, up to this time.*

*Teleflashes will be brought to you directly from the scanning room, as soon as further reports come in regarding President LeStrang. Security Police say the that perhaps foreign agents are again trying to bore from within...though they insist that there is no proof up to this time that any foreign State is responsible for LeStrang's disappearance.*

*And now there will be an interlude of music, brought to you by special permission of Interplanetary Cultural Foundation, through the facilities of I. I. S's new Teleospan System. The first number features the Martian folk dance cycle...*

# Dreadful Therapy

*When madness fills a world—madness rationalized by terrible logic—how can the therapists hope to escape corruption, after awhile?*

## CHAPTER ONE

AFTER purchasing a wickedly-brief, costume for the United Powers annual United Ball which, as the widow of the late Foreign Minister to Eurlania, Alan Morris, she was socially obligated to attend, Dania Morris found herself in a somewhat unusual situation. She wasn't accustomed to being annoyed by uninteresting men.

The little, plainly dressed hydroponic peasant who was standing in the entrance to her copter did seem uninteresting—until, in her extremely outraged dignity, she looked into his small gleaming eyes. They were like two black seeds that expanded to larger dimensions out of all proportion to reality…

And the next thing she knew, Dania Morris was in her copter flying to her penthouse apartment in East Washington, and thinking about—of all things!  –George Greg!  There was no reason to connect the unexplainable meeting with the hydroponic peasant with him, so she forgot the peasant and kept on thinking about George Greg—simultaneously trying to comprehend why she should be thinking about such a drab personality.

In fact, Dania Morris was wondering how and why any memory of George Greg should remain in her pleasure-loving mind at all. Greg, now the world's leading nuclear-physicist, had invited her to N'American University's graduation prom—that had been fifteen years ago.  She recalled dimly now that he had asked for that date with a timidity bordering on pathology, and on top of that, had never appeared to keep the date!

It hadn't made much difference to her at the time, because there had been plenty of other more promising males interested in her and markedly lacking in timidity.

George Greg had subsequently risen to an exalted scientific pinnacle approaching legendary.  He ruled N'America's Lunarian Base, together with a minimal staff of scientific and military people.

A strange costume was standing near, only the brilliant eyes discernible . . . a mummy . . .

She remembered him as a tall, gaunt, shaggy man with somewhat dull eyes and a thoroughly grey personality.

All of which made the enigmatic resolve suddenly and inexplicably born in her mind an almost frightening thing.

"Why on earth," she giggled as the copter dropped down on her apartment roof landing, "have I suddenly decided to invite George Greg to the United Powers Ball?"

There was no logical reason; what memory she had of him was as unpleasant as it was brief. Also, George Greg was noted for being a recluse who had not left the Lunarian base for fourteen years. He certainly wouldn't accept her invitation and break such an extraordinary hermitage to attend the farce of the ages labeled The United Powers Unity Ball!

Which only made the fact that she did send him the invitation that much more astonishing and increased the vague fear of such an impulse to the point where it was no longer vague.


THE HYDROPONIC peasant entered suite fifteen-seventy of the Tourist's Hotel. He stood there, shivering and mumbling uncomfortably, until the automatic thermos adjusted to his temperature as he sat down in the big foam-rubber cushions and looked thoughtfully at Darrel.

"Holy Mars," he said to his superior, "but this is a lousy world." He reflected on the irrefutable logic of this generality, then said, "Well, Darrel, I've got George Greg hooked. I finally managed to put Dania Morris under, and plant the suggestion in her sensual little brain."

Darrel, a big blond man—also dressed as a nutriculturist from the hydroponic farms down-river—smiled (a little wearily, thought Anson). "You don't seem overly elated with your achievement, Anson."

Anson frowned; the synthetic stuff that had distorted his alien features to the point where they would pass for the face of the real Anson, who now languished in stasis aboard the *Vordel* (the Headquarters ship), wrinkled heavily. He blinked his two visible eyes that had such a remarkable influence over Dania Morris.

"What are you worried about now, Anson?"

Anson didn't answer. He didn't know; he was a fieldman, an

activist. Darrel and the higher-ups did the worrying; Anson was the boy who did the legwork. But still he worried, worried because he was forced to deal directly with this miasmic, deluded world directly; and it was extremely discomforting. He wanted to go back to Mars to his wife and kids and he admitted it.

He added: "Our plan of therapy looks good. We've got men planted in key positions. Greg's the only immediate threat, and we'll soon have him down here off the Moon where we can get at him with the Shocker. But—"

Anson blinked, *"But all the time I'm running around out there I keep wondering if it all just isn't a screwy dream."*

Darrel laughed, a fair imitation of the way the genuine Darrel might have laughed, before his body had been duplicated and the real Darrel placed in stasis along with all the others whose bodies had been duplicated.

"We're adjusted, Anson. We don't dream; these people dream to escape. But the fact that you're homesick is normal. Just be patient, and we'll soon have our year's time served out; replacements will arrive soon, and we can go back."

"I'm tired," said Anson. "I've been trailing that Dania Morris assignment for three days, trying to get close enough to plant that suggestion."

"Then relax; you don't have another important assignment until the night of this United Powers Unity Ball fiasco."

Anson paused a long time before he said hoarsely, "We should have brought along an entire unit of our own culture, Darrel— something we could go back into, when we want to get our feet on the ground. There's so much we don't know about this mass-therapy. We're pragmatic, and we're supposed to meet these emergencies as they arise; but all the time we're being influenced by this insane culture. We've got to maintain objectivity; and I don't see how we can do it unless we have a big slice of our own culture here to straighten us out. Either that, or we should cut our service-periods here to about a quarter of what they are now."

Darrel nodded. "That sounds reasonable; I'll recommend your proposal to the *Vordel* H. Q. Meanwhile, reports have been coming in from our agents everywhere; we're still safe for at least a year if we can get Greg and cure him. Only Greg is within days of perfecting this radioelement—so powerful and unstable that the chain-reaction could vaporize this world if and when it's employed. Our detectors on Mars only hinted at the potentiality of Greg's discovery. Thank Lumphoor we got here in time."

"We barely made it," pointed out Anson, sourly. "It's taken us a year to get established, and find the psychological factor that would get Greg down off that blasted satellite. The girl, Morris, is the key to Greg's psychosis. It took us a year to find her, and what if it had taken us—say—a month longer?" He spread his synthetic hands in a gesture signifying, *poof.*

"I know," said Darrel. "I realize that we're dealing with a completely illogical and alien culture, and that there are variables—unforeseeable situations that might defeat us. We knew that from the beginning; we're prepared for failure as well as victory."

Anson stared. "I'm still optimistic, too," he said. "But on this world, optimism doesn't last long. We also have allowed for the possibility that the therapists may become influenced by the patients and by the insane environment created by our patients. What I want to know is this—*how can we know when and how our objectivity is failing?*"

"Maybe we won't know," said Darrel softly. "We can only hope for success. Things are clear so far; Greg's the only one close to perfecting this 'Cosmobomb' horror.

"Our first job is to get Greg."

COLD, VAST, and deadly still, the barren frigidity of the moon encompassed him as he stood in his vaulted study atop his laboratory. He stood there, a lean bearded shadow looking through the observation-dome onto an expanse of weird volcanic lava, spread in glassy sheets, emphasizing a silence and a brittle emptiness that would drive most men raving mad. Yet he had been here fourteen years with his small staff of ascetic assistants, and he was not—

Or at least he hadn't considered himself particularly mad, until he had suddenly decided to accept Dania Morris' invitation to attend the United Powers Ball in three days.

It was insane; it was utterly and sickeningly silly. But he was going to do it, and he decided not to castigate his mind unduly by introspection in an effort to understand the motivation. It would probably demand a week in the psycho-wards, and the probing fingers of a psychiatrist to find out; and George Greg had avoided psychiatrists with fanatical thoroughness.

It had occurred to him with subtle shyness that having spent fourteen years in isolation from the normal existence of earth was not a subject about which to introspect too deeply; consequently, a sudden determination to break that isolation was equally taboo as a subject for exploration.

He tossed the radagram onto the dully-shining mesh of his laboratory floor and peered unconsciously into the periscopic screen. He saw in the screen a direct view of Earth, shining twenty times brighter than moonlight from his position here on the moon's dark side—where the expanse of N'America's radioactive metal mines lay hidden from any chance bombardment from earth.

And round there on the moon's earthside, hidden deeply in the bottom of Albategnius' two hundred-mile bowl, were the rocketbombs. He had reached a point in his development of that radioelement—colorfully and typically labeled 'cosmobomb' by the sensationalistic press—where a couple of days technical labor could convert those rocketbombs into what, as far as Greg's limited mentality was concerned, would be man's final contribution to lethality. Frankly, even he, its creator, had but a vague conception of its potential for destruction. One thing alone was important: when it was perfected as a weapon, N'America could—in a matter of seconds—annihilate the civilizations threatening it and each other; and the fear of atomic destruction that had haunted the world since World War III would cease. And with it the psychosis, which had reduced humanity to the level of pleasure-loving robots would cease.

Greg had wondered, sometimes, what had happened in the mental evolutionary process that had enabled him to look upon such destruction with equanimity—an equanimity that had seemed just as barbarious and unethical when manifested during the bombing of civilians and use of gas, flame-throwers, and subsequently the atomic bombs during that abortive, retaliative World War III.

Ethics and morality were variables, of course. But also there was this point: what other answer was there? Apparently none. Man's ethical and moral codes were adaptive; and there was a certain satisfaction in knowing that this particular adaptation had occurred in time, and had been made by N'America instead of one of the other powers. And specifically by one George Greg.

OSTENSIBLY, Albategnius was a weather station, with an observatory to forecast earth's weather; with other laboratories, all theoretically functioning only for world benefit.

But everyone on earth knew, down to the commonest workers. In Pleasure Palaces, and Dream Wards, and Sensory Shows they dreamed and subconsciously awaited the destruction, which their conscious minds denied as a threat.

But he, George Greg, could save N'America at least. "Who controls Luna rules Earth," was an axiom admitted unofficially. Composed almost entirely of earth's crustal materials, the moon was incredibly rich in uranium and other radioactive metals. From the moon, N'America's deadly rockets could plunge to earth, annihilating vast vulnerable targets. Conversely, due to strong gravity, small targets and vital areas hidden on Luna's dark side, the moon was comparatively free from attack.

But now N'America's intelligence had reported new experiments in Eurlania with an isotope approaching the potentiality of Greg's development. It was a long way behind Greg's attainment, but not far enough behind to gamble any more with time.

A retaliative atomic war was out of the question; World War III had cured that delusion. This time it would be one decisive blow—one and one only. Beneath the sensory facade of world 'unity' this first and final strike was being planned.

And behind all this realization a little fragmentary question bounced around forlornly in Greg's cortex. *Why the devil am I leaving all this for seven days to attend a masked ball?*

Greg the lonely pariah, estranged and alone, slumped a little and turned tired eyes from the periscopic screen. He had enjoyed his distaste for society, and the moon had been a perfect escape from it. Living-conditions here on the moon were desirable enough. Atomic piles furnished heat, light, air and also extracted oxygen, hydrogen and nitrogen from the Lunarian metals to create water supply and adequate atmosphere.

Vaguely, with an old buried pain that brought sweat to his bony forehead and long white hands, he remembered Dania Morris and that foolish, infantile prom. It had mattered to him then, awfully. He had been shy and uncomfortable, but he had tried so hard to be acceptable. He had wanted to like people, and he had wanted people to like him; he had wanted more than anything else in the world to take Dania Morris to that dance!

How could such a ridiculous thing have mattered so much to him then? He had tried so hard to learn the fantastic patterns in which one was supposed to move one's feet around, to the mad rhythms of garrish pipings and beatings. But he hadn't had the nerve, and he had never shown up to take her to that prom.

Greg wondered what would have happened had he done so. Would he have isolated himself here for fourteen years? Would he have been finishing the 'cosmobomb'—?

But now if he so strongly considered accepting her invitation to attend this 'unity' ball, perhaps he should. A warning maybe of a psychic need for change. The affair would involve only eight days...

When he radagrammed the Military in Washington of his dramatic intentions, he encountered no outright objections; Greg was much too important a person for that. There was tactful argument, but George Greg won. An armada escorted him. Defense-A shields were thrown around Washington. Guards swarmed around him like so many gnats.

And George Greg, one of the greatest nuclear-physicists, attended the United Powers Ball costumed as a clown.

## CHAPTER TWO

ANSON GLARED self-consciously at his superior. Anson was swathed very realistically and uncomfortably as a mummy, a mummy of very ancient vintage.

Anson pointed at his costume. "Madness," he said. "Rank madness. I contacted the Europan; put him to sleep by suggestion; gave him a posthypnotic hangover and a memory of a masked ball he will never attend. I changed into his costume before leaving his apartment. May I add that I feel extremely ridiculous?"

"You got his identification and his pass, too, of course," asked Darrel absently.

Anson scowled, "Naturally. Now everything's set for the big moment: our first major therapeutic act of benevolence. Greg is here. Both Greg and Dania Morris are filled with subconscious longings for each other, which they've kept buried for too long. I'll tag around after Greg all evening at the ball with the Shocker on him, and he'll be cured; he won't finish the 'cosmobomb'; the earth and Mars will be saved from vaporization, and we'll have a long time to start curing all the other insane leaders who are trying to annihilate themselves and humanity. Everything's just wonderful, Darrel, except for one little thing—"

Anson's small brilliant eyes glowed darkly. "—we're all going crazy!"

It wasn't a facetious remark; certainly, Darrel never accepted it in a light vein. From behind his desk, Darrel just sat and stared morosely out the huge plastilene window over the towering metropolis with its skyways and highways, and monorails, and crystalline towers piercing great soft cumulus clouds.

"Don't bother to elaborate, Anson," he said nervously. "I know what you're driving at. Reports have been coming in here, from Commander Weym on the *Vordel*."

Darrel shuffled some reports. He raised one and said, "Listen to these briefs from some of our fieldmen. Here's one from Howard who took over the identity of the librarian in the philosophy section of World Synthesis:

'Everything here is perfectly rationalized insanity. It's insidious. It's so rationalized that most of it really has no logical counter-argument, because it deals in a kind of ultimate futility that allows these people to accept inevitable and meaningless death. I want to be released from this post, Darrel; and fast. Sometimes I begin to regard myself as human, and I begin to find myself employing human rationalization. One of the most popular philosophers these people read—when they read—is a guy named Schopenhauer. Read Schopenhauer if you want to understand fully what my situation here is. All this philosophy I'm studying is just rationalization of an insane social evolution. And it's getting me. No. Don't read Schopenhauer!' "

DARREL looked up from the brief. Anson said, "He doesn't have to warn me; I've been out there absorbing it first-hand. I don't have to read their rationalizations. I listen to them all day."

"Here," said Darrel, "is a report from Jensen in Eurlania. He's in the Psychological Presidum there, you know:

'In every psycho-chart on file here, the functional death wish exercises a strong influence on all activity and attitudes. In every case such thought impulses as these predominate: *Life itself is evil. The greatest crime of man is that he was born.* Or. *The happiest moment of a happy man is the moment of his falling asleep.* Or. *We have never experienced reality but only our interpretation of a facet of reality.* Listen, Darrel, this job is driving me into a first class neurosis with which I have no means of dealing. This is a different culture, and their rationalization for their particular insanity is so well-adapted that I—' "

Anson interrupted. "It all boils down to what I've been saying: we've got to cut our service periods here down to about three or four months at the most. Either that, or move a big chunk of our own culture down here so we can wash ourselves off in it periodically."

"Maybe you're right," said Darrel. "But we couldn't do that under Plan-A; that'd fall under plan-B. And you know what it means if we start thinking about dropping our first and best plan now, before we even get started: it means we're losing confidence. It may mean that we're beginning to be influenced by non-objective impulses that we're not aware of."

Anson brooded. Behind his calm exterior pulsed a growing fear, a quickening beat of despair.

"Here's another report from James in the psycho-history section in Europa," said Darrel, then added wryly, "if you want to be entertained further."

Anson nodded, "I'll listen; I can still take a little more."

"James says this about this mass historical psychosis, for which we're trying so audaciously to begin the cure:

'I've found the point where this psychosis caused by imbalance really got started, Darrel. It began with an obsession called Western Culture, which got started, really, in a place called Miletus on the Aegean Sea. The so-called 'Eastern' thought had been on the right track approaching mental science first; Western Culture destroyed that approach, establishing the basics for objective science. From it grew what developed into Comte's positivistic historical evolutionary process of advancing from the simplest science, mathematics, through successive stages to more complex forms, physics and chemistry. Consequently we have mastery of nuclear physics and its utilization by mentalities having no concept of its own function.

'This could not have occurred unless certain abnormally developed mentalities had carried on this exclusive and cultistic program. The mass as a whole would prefer to function within its mental limitations. We've got to stamp out all technical science at the level attained by ancient Eastern philosophy, and start these monkeys over again, or we'll end up as part of a new nova—an honor that wasn't intriguing at all to me until I started this research. Now these damnable philosophies are so rationally worked out that I almost don't care whether I kick off or not!' "

DARREL dropped the briefs and sat there stiffly and uneasily. Anson watched him narrowly and wondered if those replacements would ever get here.

"The *Vordel* sent out a special field-research team to Library of Oriental Culture in Canton," said Darrel. "They had an idea of reviving Oriental religious-philosophy to replace modern technical science. We have to have a replacement. But it's no good; it's dead, buried, extinct. There's no chance of reviving it…"

Anson got up, started for the door. "Just so the *Vordel* crew drops this idea about abandoning Plan-A, that's all I'm worried about. As soon as we get Greg taken care of, we'll have plenty of time to work out procedures as we go along. That talk about dropping Plan-A is symptomatic of our own fear and nothing else, Darrel. I hope we can remember that."

Darrel nodded. Anson was smart for a fieldman.

Anson hesitated, turned, pressed a wall switch. A section slid out containing a cage with white rats in it. From a pouch under his mummy wrapping, Anson withdrew his small cube-shaped Shocker. He tested it on one of the rats who changed abruptly from manic to marked depressant traits.

"What's troubling you now, Anson," said Darrel, irritably. "You just tested the Shocker last night."

"Tonight's when it has to work," said Anson pointedly. "If I miss Greg tonight, he might be able to slip away from us and back to Luna. If he does—that finishes our little program of therapy."

Darrel inclined his human-shaped head. "We might be able to find a way to get at Greg, even on the moon; but it would take more time than his research might allow. The latest report from the psycho-ward here says Greg's possibly within a week or ten days of finishing his work."

Anson opened the door. He shut it again, turned.

"Darrel," he said. "After Greg's cured, I'll have to stay with him during his reconditioning process. It's just as important that his readjustment patterns are sane as it is to rid him of his insanity. I suggest that there be several alternate therapists assigned to take over that job in case—in case something should happen to me."

He went out and left Darrel staring at the shifting harmonics of the wall, soft soothing coloration that had somehow taken on a monotone grey without pattern, or warmth.

WEYM, THE *Vordel* Commander, had remained on the *Vordel*. He had retained his own outward appearance instead of utilizing the appearance of someone among these earth-people. And he had never left the *Vordel* where it lay concealed in the vast unplumbed depths of the great rain forest on the upper Matta Grosso in South America. The gigantic ship, protected by force shields, had pierced the protective blankets of various layers of defense, and was now doubly protected by a partial invisibility.

And Weym was beginning to wonder if it were all worth while.

Added to that, was a growing sensation that he was somehow— *vulnerable.*

His position was beginning to appear much more vulnerable than that of any of the others on this therapeutic expedition. And the aim of his remaining on the *Vordel* was to have retained more invulnerability. The trouble was that he was in a central position, that his brain was a clearinghouse for every reaction of every sub--commander in the field.

Each of his field-men and sub-commanders experienced only certain specific and limited facets of this insane culture according to their specialized type of research. But as Chief Commander and Coordinator, he received them all, absorbed them all and...being unduly affected by the constant repetition of attitudes that kept piling up and sloping over in the limited bowl of his mind.

Weym brooded. He had even learned what brooding was from a species that had brooded in one form or another for twenty thousand years. Maybe a species could brood too long. Was there any justification for the germ of thought growing in his aching brain that perhaps a world civilization could have grown beyond therapy? Especially when the insanity was so old, and so specialized and so firmly entrenched in the minds, the mores, the general psychological adjustment-patterns of the species as to almost have become an inherent characteristic?

Weym batted his five eyes, writhed his tenuous boneless body with impatient unease. The infectiousness of this environment had been anticipated. But anticipation wasn't necessarily an adequate defense, nor did it even imply comprehension.

He had felt the miasmic melancholia of their general philosophy of defeatism, pessimism and escape for some time; that was anticipated, too. But there had been no anticipation of that sly, vague *acceptance*! That almost joyful abandonment to grey and dusty despair!

It had seemed so utterly simple in theory; it still was: simply cure the leaders, especially the scientists. Ninety-nine and ninety-nine one hundredths percent of these earthpeople knew no more about abstract science than did their ancestors of generations before. So if the precocious abnormality of their leaders was expunged, then the subsequent procedure was simple enough. In theory.

From then on, always under complete control by therapists, humanity developed only on a scale equal to the capacity of the average intelligence. It would take incomputably longer to get back to this stage of technical development, but the new attainment would be—sane.

But a therapist could never really evaluate his own position in relationship to himself and his patient. Coupled with that was the fact that they were dealing with a completely alien culture in which psychology, to the Martians a science equal to the degree of reliability of all associative sciences, was not a science at all! And in which sociology, the final step in scientific evolution, was as yet not even a stable dream in the mass mind.

WEYM'S FOCAL eye glanced at the layers upon layers of reports on rolls and rolls of microtape. He was getting the basic essence of all his workers' reactions to this culture. Direct reports—*and with those damnable quotes!*—from every field center. From Howard, James, Jahk, Jensen, and five hundred others.

Weym gazed through the *Vordel's* observation dome into the vaporous green of the stifling forest. Beyond this forest wall a world thickly populated with a morbid intelligence that declared it was doomed, and which had created such rational logic for this doom that their arguments were dialectically irrefutable!

There was a world death-wish backed by an accumulation of historical philosophy which seemed the essence of reason—within the environs of this culture…

\*      \*      \*

Weym lay full length on the floor of the *Vordel*. He was ill. His focal eyes burned. Over and over a tape was saying:

*We pursue our life with great interest and much solicitude as long as possible; so we blowout a soap bubble as long and as large as possible, although we know perfectly well that it will burst…*

Weym moved painfully. A peculiar lassitude had settled over him, a dull cloud of indifference. And the tape droned on:

*It is this blind pressure, without goal or motive, which drives us on, and not anything we can rationally justify.*

Weym lifted his hand toward the switch that would stop the

sound. His hand drifted back slowly to his side like a vagrant wind…the tape droned on…

*       *       *

Weym's boneless body writhed across the floor, his appendages digging into the mesh of the grid.

The tape droned on. It filled his brain with a wild ecstatic fire of bitterness and despair.

Why am I here? What hope is there? Infinite complexity.

*Fool! Your reward is neither here nor there!*
*I came like water, and like wind I go.*
*One moment in annihilation's waste…*
*Life is but a dream…*

*       *       *

Weym's mind burned with the thought, the sudden shocking realization. They were here to cure an entire world; but their own social evolution had developed in a balanced harmonious manner, purely by chance! Not by any intent or reason on their own part. Not through any free agency. But here—to bring about such a balanced social harmony of reason and reality, the cure would demand that the therapists apply *reason*—

There! There was the impossibility, the key to the realization of the futility. Apply reason, therefore—

Weym leaned his throbbing head against cool metal. In so far as the mind is free, it knows the truth; in so far as it has a real insight into truth, it is free. Insight.

He managed to lift his appendage. The message reached home base on Mars by electromagnum: *Unforeseen complexity. Must abandon Plan-A. Stand ready to receive further orders on immediate establishing of alternate emergency Plan-B!*

And Weym wanted to turn off that tape, which kept on droning its futile song; he wanted to, yet he didn't. He needed help, but he was alone.

TWISTING senses into hysterical heights, hypnolights and neuro-scents sprayed the vast synthetic gardens where the five thousand dancers moved. Black light on fluorescent dyes gave off fantastic, shifting colors of sense-drunkening suggestion.

Greg felt helplessly trapped. He had finally been talked into drinking a potent glass of *ecstaso* but he only felt clumsier, sweated more, felt infinitely more ridiculous. And he knew he was boring Dania Morris to extinction. Most of his alleged dancing he was spending on her feet. She was nice and easy to look at, too, in a brief ballerina's costume. Vaguely, mistily, he remembered bits of painful conversation:

"Well, you finally kept that date, George—*Mr. Greg!*"

"Yes. Some nucleons detained me." Stuff like that. Her voice was strained, or it appeared so to him. And he thought. *A laboratory detained me.* A snarled conduit from which would burst unleashed hell and destruction of indeterminable measurement.

Beneath her glistening red-and-white mask, Dania Morris' teeth shown painfully white as full red lips smiled widely. Fifteen years ago she had accepted his invitation to a dance, preferring him then to more attractive males. And he had fizzled out. Fear.

Desperately he attempted a kind of whirling step. She exclaimed: "Why you're not at all the cloistered mahatma that scientists are supposed to be, are you, George?"

No—he wasn't—not right now; but he had been. Grimly he whirled her around and squarely into a fat man costumed as some Paleolithic pirate who was jigging around a maypole disguised as a blonde.

*A mummy walked past.*

And George admitted then that he had been growing ill for some time he, didn't belong here. He thought it might be that vile *ecstaso*. Queer tinglings skittered down his back. Hazes and tendrils of memory became entangled with the present unreality. He was a child hunched over a book; outside he heard kids playing; the print of the book blurred, and he knew that the blur was his tears falling on the paper…

The M. C. blared over the audio. "Our guest of honor tonight is, of course, a visitor from the Moon. *George Greg!*"

No one recognized him for he was disguised as a clown.

Everyone was masked here, that was the rule. Ironic—but at the *Unity* Ball, it was dangerous to be unmasked. A drone of appreciative sound exploded. Horns screeched; rains of phosphorescent confetti changed color in misty rainbows of drifting motes. Fluorescently dyed balloons floating...

Dania's hand gripping his arm. Her voice saying, "I'm the only one who recognizes you; I have you all to myself."

The scene was grotesque horror pounding at Greg's heart. The masked faces opening and shutting, and false laughter. The five powers! But it shouldn't be plural; there couldn't be five united *powers*. Only one power. When more than one power danced, they danced a waltz into darkness.

Fourteen years buried in frozen lava on the moon.

He shook his head, tried to clear it. And later he found the girl locked tightly in his arms, her body soft and yielding. Her breath was gasping warmly against his face. "Oh, George! Who would have thought it of *you*? A *scientist!*"

Something broke with a sharp twang. That was it. He, a *scientist!* For anyone else, such an act would certainly have been normal enough under the circumstances at least. But for him—Lord—wasn't a scientist human? Wasn't he—

A strange costume was standing by his sleeve gazing at him. A mummy.

GREG HEARD a dry dusty laugh. It was his own. Wouldn't people ever get over that medieval myth about scientists being wicked shamans, or longhaired crackpots who had to be fed through a tube to survive and—

Glittering clouds of confetti smothered him. Streamers of orange and blue and gold and red trailed from the five-hundred foot ceiling. A crimson Mephisto hopped past, singing wildly. Greg stared; for an instant he seemed to be dancing with someone else, or rather with a woman named Dania, only her last name wasn't Morris. It was Greg. Greg. And it was fifteen years ago. Dania in an evening gown...

He closed his eyes. Mechanically he felt himself moving around, shambling his awkward jig. A horn squawked in his ear. He jumped and violent shocks shivered through him. He blinked burning eyes; he was blinded by glaring lights. The orchestra sounds swelled, faded, swelled, and trembled. A lumbering donkey brayed past. A Don Juan feinted with a real sword, and a woman screamed. Another woman swirled past in the arms of a dancing skeleton whose death's head stared in mock glee.

*A mummy adjusted its mask.*

Greg heard his voice mumbling. "I don't—feel well—do you mind if—?"

Things were whirling. And out of a spinning chaotic mass out of holes in a puckered parchment mask, the mummy's eyes glowed. *Odd*, thought some part of Greg, *those eyes hardly seem human. More like evil little jewels. The mummy seems genuine, and yet—*

Hands were gripping his arms. A laugh, "He's had too much."

"Handle him with ease, senor. Perhaps it is the Prime Minister."

"Ach! Do not remove the mask, even to give him air!"

Greg must have fallen, but he was on his feet now. He was pushing, pushing against walls of sweating, laughing faces. Would he never, never, never get outside, away from these people? Back to—

But he had no place to go. He couldn't go back to the laboratory. For with a burst of agonizing flame he had begun to *know*. Terror flowed from him, leaving him weak and with a feeling of only dim consciousness. Sounds faded. Lights dimmed.

*Insight.*

He knew that someone was helping him toward the towering plastoid doors where Blue Guardsmen stood with neutro-guns crossed over chests as unmoving as armor plating. A trumpet blared like something rather felt than heard. A nasal voice said close against his ear, "Take it easy, friend; I'll help you out to some fresh air."

Greg stumbled. He turned to see who was assisting him; it was the mummy.

He looked oddly at the mummy's gleaming eyes. In a drunken, doped whisper, Greg said to the mummy, "Listen, you. All my life I've been insane. Insane, you understand that. All people who are playing a leading role in this show are crazy. But I've been the craziest of the lot!"

The mummy shrugged frayed shoulders, "You can tell me all about it when you're home. I'll help you."

## CHAPTER THREE

GREG REMEMBERED how several Blue Guardsmen tried to stop them from entering the gyrotaxi. Sure, he was an important person and Guards swarmed around him like gnats. But this fellow dressed like a mummy seemed to have a potent argument, because the Guards walked away and left them. Maybe the mummy was the N'American President. The gyrotaxi lifted with a soft whir into the artificial moonlight.

Greg laughed foolishly. Was it really day or night? Distortion within distortion. His kind had done that, too. Invisible beams of radiant energy shot upward, converted the thin atmospheric gases into gigantic neon-like light almost bright as day. The majority of people had never seen real nighttime. But in spite of a distorted reality created by scientific whims, the mass still clung to a sane custom. Within artificial day, were created artificial areas of night and moonlight, on occasions when such areas were required for romantic atmospheric effects, such as a dance.

Adaptation, the mass adjusted even to the most nonsensical doodads foisted upon them. But the adjustment wasn't a manifestation of the basic insanity. That was represented by the innovators.

But the mass mind could still laugh at its tragicomic cul de sac. They sang songs ridiculing their own plight. Out of Greg's subconscious swam the words of a popular song he would never have admitted he was familiar with before tonight:

*When it's day it's night,*
*And when it's night it's day.*
*And when it's moonlight where's the sunlight?*
*But if you don't find it, don't mind it.*
*I'll love you in the night that isn't.*

*I'll love you in the night that's day.*
*I'll love you in the night that's you, darling.*

*Love you in the same old way.*
*In the same old way.*

Greg remembered mumbling his address, the whirring of the gyrotaxi, stumbling into his apartment. He didn't remember passing out.

\*     \*     \*

In the semidark of Greg's sleeping chamber, Anson climbed out of his mummy wrappings with relief, and reshaped his melting face. He dialed the VHF disk on his wrist.

"Darrel—it worked, terrifically; he'll be completely sane when he wakes up. I'll have to stick by him like a leech to watch his compensatory adjustments. There's so many forms of readjustment he can take, as we've figured. The obvious one will be some religious mysticism. That's where these scientific minds usually end up if they blow their top. Also—"

The small speaker interrupted him with its whining code.

"Never mind all that now," said Darrel's message. "Plenty's been happening tonight. I don't know exactly how much, but Weym on the *Vordel*'s just announced the abandonment of Plan-A. Plan-B is now in effect. That doesn't change your present duty of course, but I thought you'd want to know."

Anson slumped. The darkness about him seemed to thicken and shrink. *They're giving up too easily*, he thought frantically. *Abandoning the first plan when we've barely started; losing confidence; weakening.* Now what if they abandoned Plan-B dropped to the final and open admission of defeat, Plan-C? Plan-B changed the five-hundred-year program to ten thousand. Time didn't matter so much just so they succeeded; but it involved mass exodus, a highly complex and gigantic movement from planet to planet. Logically, it could only signify the beginning of the disintegration down into Plan-C. Plan-C was an abandonment of all peaceful therapy—an open return to insane violence—it called for open invasion of Earth. That was only the final admission of defeat, because the whole purpose behind this program of therapy was to prevent an interplanetary war!

But Headquarters undoubtedly knew what it was doing. The trend of Anson's sudden thought then, had a dreadful familiarity. Defeat. Confusion. Cynicism. Horror tinged with pleasant relief from responsibility. This thing was too big for Plan-A. Too complex, and Anson was beginning to believe it could never be done, even under Plan-B with its scheduled millions of therapists, mass exodus from Mars, ten thousand years—

"Anson! Anson!" The code-signal pounded desperately. "Listen and act quickly; the report just came in. Something's happening to Howard! Get over there to World Knowledge Synthesis right now. Stop him if you can, if you can get to him in time. His mind is full of destruction! If you don't get there in time, be certain his remains are destroyed. Remember the one prime directive—*to avoid discovery!*"

Yes. He remembered. The moment they were discovered, war would break.

"But I can't leave Greg," signaled Anson. "If he should get back to the Moon—some other adjustment motivation—"

"You're the nearest fieldman to Howard. Greg will be sleeping for several hours. I'll try to get another man over there to Greg. Maybe Summers in the biochemistry wards can make it. Soon as you take care of Howard, report back to Greg, just in case Summers can't make it! Hurry, Anson, for the love of Mars!"

Anson hurried. He ran. He signaled a gyrotaxi down, and stubbornly fought off panic as it took him through the artificial day.

DIM TWILIGHT brooded heavily in that room. Anson stood there, breathing hoarsely, his eyes probing shadows. Slowly he shut the door behind him labeled: *Philosophy—Middle-Age Transition.*

This department was apparently used but little. No projection machines were on. He crossed this room quickly, and into another bearing the directive: *Since Hegel—Empiricism And Enlightenment.* Schopenhaur—Comte and Positivism—Evolution Spenser.

Here was only heavy stillness, and suffocating twilight; the autoluminescence had been dimmed. The walls were lined with file cases containing microfilm. There were a number of small booths with screens and projectors. A figure swayed back and forth. A dark shadow gyrating and swinging with a gentle silent rhythm.

"Howard!" Anson whispered, his throat constricted as though that length of plasticord was around his own neck instead of Howard's. "Howard—for the love of Mars!" But that wasn't Howard dangling there so horribly still. No one in the history of Martian society had ever taken his own life. This was something else, something that Howard had become under alien environmental conditions too monstrous to name.

Anson stumbled back, shut the door. There was no one else in the room. He groped his way to Howard's hanging body, as though through thickening vapor.

The synthetic plastiflesh with which his fellow Martian had coated himself—so that he might resemble a man named Howard, who had worked here for a long time and had stayed sane—was cut harshly by the plasticord, stretched and torn away so that the boneless, translucence body beneath showed clearly, clearly and dead.

Anson's fingers shivered as he untied the limp body. Clutched in its synthetic hand was a note scrawled rapidly. Anson looked at the note and as he did so, the environment, which he hated and feared shifted more tightly, squeezed inward, stifling and dense and dusty.

He thought desperately. He might be able to get the body to the *Vordel.* He might block out suspicion in a few chance observers by his limited telepathic powers. But there was too great a chance of his running into a mob. There was another and surer way, though unpleasant. And there had been hope of never employing the catalyst.

Anson stripped away the folds of synthetic flesh, rolled it in a tight ball and stuffed it inside his cloak. He withdrew the phial of catalyst liquid and poured it over the body—

He left the place quickly; he didn't care to see his friend's body vaporize. The friend he had known as Mohlak, but who had become a man named Howard. And that was the dreadful part— he actually *had* become Howard! And Mohlak had escaped from a futile world—much as Howard might have escaped, eventually. For the note he had left said: *The only positive end for man is death. Man's greatest sin is the prolongation of the inevitable.*

*Howard*

WHEN ANSON got back to George Greg's apartment, there was no Greg. Anson had been gone three hours; but that had been plenty of time for Greg to have awakened, aware of his new attitudes, and to have taken some new readjustment pattern.

Anson teetered uncertainly. Where would Greg go? What would he do? What was he now? He had been an abnormality, a mind so far beyond the norm as to justify that label. But only his personality had changed, not his mental potential. What form would that potentiality assume now?

Anson was only a fieldman. Sociology and psychology were one on his world, an instinctively balanced function, emperical. Here, at best, it was an unknown factor even to Weym and his sub-commanders. Anson had no idea, except criteria based on past research of human acts, about what Greg would do now. He could become a religious mystic. That was common. He could rechannel his scientific training into some other field—or—he might even continue his former course, but with different motivation!

And if he did that, he might even desire to return to the Lunarian Labs! Anson headed toward the Moonport in North Washington. Sitting in the passenger compartment of the gyrotaxi he contacted Darrel. He explained developments, then asked: "What happened to Summers?"

Darrel said. "The same thing, fundamentally, that happened to Mohlak. His last report was jumbled, morbid, and said that he was going into one of the Pleasure Palaces for an indefinite period. Those chambers in the Pleasure Palaces are impregnable, Anson! How can we get him out of there?"

"I don't know," said Anson.

"I'm sending Phillips over to see what he can do," Darrel's signal explained hurriedly. "Meanwhile, you've got to find Greg. Guard the Moonport area and I'll send out others to find him."

There was a long blank from the VHF disk on Anson's wrist. Then, slowly. "Prepare for the worst, Anson; I think Commander Weym is also being influenced negatively. Fear has been manifest in almost every summary I've received from H.Q. during the past hour. I have contacted a number of sub-commanders. We have agreed not to attempt to contact the *Vordel* personally, as our interpretation of Weym's releases may be nonobjective. We must realize that the *Vordel* is suddenly swamped with emergency requirements…"

As the gyrotaxi rose higher, the rising sun splashed in Anson's face like a liquid flame. He closed his eyes against it; he was unutterably tired and the horizon held no beauty for him.

BENEATH his cloak, Greg now carried a small neutrogun. All citizenry were granted permission to own weapons, in case of infiltration by an enemy that officially didn't exist; this was especially true with important national figures.

His watch told him that it was noon. And the noon of this day seemed real to Greg. The sun and the light were real. But this was reality, which brought himself and his relationship to it into a horrid focus. He was hunted, and he was alone. He had heard the telenews-broadcasts from Military. They didn't know where he was nor what had happened to him; they thought that he might have been kidnapped by representatives of one or more of the other Powers. A councilman from Europa was under arrest for probable implication in the supposed kidnapping.

This Councilman claimed that he had attended the masked ball as a mummy, but he couldn't remember having left the ball with anyone costumed as a clown. In fact, he remembered very little about the United Powers Ball. He claimed that his costume was gone, as well as his identification papers; he was being analyzed in the psycho-wards.

But he, George Greg, was sane now—no longer deluded by conditioned social attitudes. It was Greg and a neutrogun against the world.

He sat in a small refreshment booth just off a five-speed walkway. He could look across the ten walkways that rolled silently past him and see the apartment building in which Dania Morris lived.

He wanted to see her; he had to see her. But Blue Guardsmen patrolled the area, they were even on the roof landing. They knew about Greg's relationships with Dania Morris.

His plan was simple, but hampered by somewhat colossal

barriers. He wanted to return to the moon, but he had to have Dania Morris with him; she had been part of the inexplicable traumatic shock that had shaken him out of that warped perspective, that abyss of isolation. She, and the dance—the dance he had neglected to attend for fifteen years.

Until Eurlania perfected their version of Greg's 'cosmobomb' he was the most powerful figure on earth. How could he operate? How could he utilize that power for good? Unless he could get back to the moon, he couldn't utilize it at all. But unless he had Dania Morris with him, Greg was psychologically incapable of returning to his Lunarian labs with any expectation of continued efficiency. His plan was a long-ranged one, and he knew that he could no longer live in his former, isolated fashion.

Greg couldn't get past those Blue Guards to see her; he would wait until she came out. By following her then he might possibly get an opportunity to contact her without the Blue Guards knowing.

Sensorays from the lamps in the refreshment booth soothed and relaxed his frayed nerves as he waited. A telenews audio spoke softly from a hidden source.

*"The psycho-ward reveals that electroenephal checks on Richard Galatere, the Europan Councilman, suspect in the sensation Greg kidnapping, has proven positive and that he is being heard before the Military Tribunal at this time. Meanwhile the 'incident' is something more than that. A special meeting of the United Powers Council is being called at which Europan representatives are expected to defend a direct charge by N'America.*

*"The importance of George Greg in this suddenly precipitated crisis cannot be underestimated. Although not official, it has been known for some time that in his Lunarian Laboratories, Greg was developing a new isotope, a radioelement far beyond the destructive capacity of any yet known—"*

Greg stiffened as he listened. He would have to act quickly. Another war with atomic weapons such as those used during World War III was looming because of that mummy business. A business which Greg remembered only vaguely. Certainly he hadn't been kidnapped; anyway, it only meant that he had to get back to the moon, now. Once that was accomplished, there would be no war!

For once he got back to the moon, he, George Greg, would be something only a little less, perhaps, than the Almighty.

169

# CHAPTER FOUR

IT WAS LATE afternoon when she walked out of the front entrance of the apartment building. Greg's eyes softened at the sight of her. A tall, lithe woman in her early forties. Her hair was that vibrant brunette shade with little glints of blue in it. Her eyes, he remembered, were pale green, slightly slanted at the corners. She was beautiful, and he would be inefficient in his new role if he couldn't have her.

She had seemed interested in him last night, and she had invited him to the ball. If he could only talk with her, alone, unhampered, for five minutes, he could explain.

He moved out onto the five-speed walkway and stood behind another group of joy-hunters heading for some sensory experience or other. He kept pace with Dania Morris who was standing on the south speed-five run, gazing up absently at the sky. Only one Blue Guard had left his post and was standing on the walkway behind her. If she noticed that she was being followed by a Guardsman, she didn't evince any such sign.

As he followed her, he thought. *I've got to talk with her.* He couldn't talk with any political or scientific hierarchy; they were insane. He couldn't appeal to vague acquaintances in the psychology departments; for although psychology wasn't even faintly scientific except in the broadest sense, it aped the stricter sciences and considered itself scientific—which made it also dangerously insane and unreceptive to such thinking as his new insight had provided him with.

There was Professor Throckman for example. He had occupied fifty years studying the reflex of the human tendon. An artifact that, separated from the whole organism, lost all relationship to what Throckman thought he was scientifically studying—the human body.

Fifty years of insane obsession with an artifact when the world was rushing to destruction. A hermit in a chrome cave. Objectively, was there any doubt of such a man's insanity? But Greg had been even more abnormal, for he had spent fifteen years in isolation developing the basic means to drown man's thirst for self-destruction!

Dania Morris continued straight down the thoroughfare and stepped off onto a tangent walkway. This walkway was crowded, and then Greg knew where she was heading. Pleasure Palace Number Three! She must have spent a great deal of time there to be ready for the third threshold adventure sequences.

This was a very fortunate break for him. The third threshold adventures lasted seven days, and could not be broken. Consequently the Blue Guard, after determining that she was entering there, stepped onto another walkway that took him back toward the thoroughfare.

Greg went inside and caught Dania Morris before she was assigned her adjustment chamber.

He touched her shoulder and she turned with a slow poise. Her eyes were a lighter green now, they widened. He led her to a couch in the shifting harmonic glow of the lobby: it was in a corner, and they were unnoticed there.

Her eyes studied him speculatively, with candid appraisal. She lighted a paraette and all the time he was looking at her, wondering where and how to begin. It was easy and simple enough the way she did it. "Your tactics with women are unorthodox, *Mr.* Greg. You either never show up for a date at all, or leave them standing in the middle of a big dance floor all alone."

GEORGE GREG felt foolish. He sensed the expanding fires inside him; the new longings; the social consciousness and the love for this woman who had been buried and whom he had dug up again like a forbidden dream. "I think you will understand what I'm going to say," he managed.

Her thin brows lifted. "Really? You mean you'll express yourself in simple terms that even the layman can—"

He flushed with embarrassment like an adolescent. "Ah—no—not that. I only meant that my feelings are such that technical language is no longer adequate. I—I was ill both times you spoke of."

"Ill!" she said quickly, then. "Yes, you were last night. I thought perhaps it might have been the *ecstaso*. You looked very bad."

"It wasn't; it was psychosomatic. Something happened to me. I don't know what it was. It was somewhat like the old mystical enlightenment perhaps. This may seem hyperbolic but—" he paused—"but all my life I've been a victim of a psychosis, a kind of insanity."

"You!" She tried to smile. "The famous—"

"Famous," he frowned. "The masses have learned to fear and exalt us. Maybe insanity is too harsh a term; it's a social-legal term. From the social angle a man can be legally sane, yet obviously abnormal. And—Dania, are you interested? I—I'm in love with you. I want to marry you. I—"

He pressed his eyes. When he opened them again, she was looking deeply into his face. Their eyes clashed, and there was an understanding, an affinity. It was ineffable, but it was there.

His eyes looked away. "To the mass-mind, scientists—whether they were called shamans, priests, seers, or nuclear-physicists—have always been objects of fear and suspicion. Perhaps the mass-mind, through the ages, has known instinctively that, sooner or later, the abnormally-developed intellect of precocious individuals and their esoteric cults of knowledge would lead man to his own destruction."

Greg took her hand. "Maybe the term 'insanity' applied to a mere straying from the intelligent norm of the mass would have been too strong a term—but when we gave atomic power to a world that wasn't ready for it, we became insane by definition. We rationalized; we said that it wasn't our fault if humanity was insane and misused our discoveries. But in reality, the mass has made incredible adjustments to our premature gadgets. But this adaptation, in its present final form, has meant the sacrifice of their will-to-live."

Dania Morris frowned. "I don't know," she said. "This is all so confusing; and I don't understand anything that's happening, either to the world or to you and me."

"You can only understand one thing," said Greg. "That this is the point at which man survives or ceases to survive. That's all."

"Yes, I've known that; everyone knows that. But that affair last night. I felt so strange. And you acted so peculiarly. And then today—I—I had a simple pattern of adjustment. Threshold after threshold in the Pleasure Palace. Lethe, and then sudden and painless death. But you've broken that pattern, and I wonder if I'm glad, or sorry."

"I wonder, too," George said.

"And I don't know what you're purpose is now," she said. "Whatever it is, you actually sound optimistic, afire; and that seems so odd. I haven't any argument against your contentions. As you say, in a social-legal sense, social leaders and scientists can be classified as—too abnormal perhaps. But you also imply hope, George. And—there can't be any hope now. We got off on the wrong road, and we stayed on it too long."

His hand tightened on hers. A vague and wonderful perfume came from her hair.

He said evenly, "This will really seem incredible to you I'm sure. But—if I can get back to the moon, as a free operative, in my former capacity, I can dictate the policies of the world!"

PORCELAIN transparency of her lean face might have grown more transparent; he didn't know. There was no tangible emotion in her eyes. She said nothing.

"Does that sound more insane to you," he asked, "than if I went on carrying out my other destiny, finished the 'cosmobomb' with a chain reaction of incomputable extent? Does it suggest even a chance at survival, or does it seem just another last futile squirming as the curtain falls?"

"I don't know," she whispered.

"Frankly, neither do I know," he said. "I only say that it seems the one last chance, and that it might be worth a try. You were right; man did get off on the wrong road. Human evolution got off-balance. It should have begun with the most complex sciences first—psychology, biology, sociology. Instead we developed the simple abstract sciences of chemistry and physics and mathematics first, and advanced nowhere at all in the science of our own make-up. The result is a colossal imbalance that's pathological."

"I don't see what can be done now."

"We can stop, then force a regression in the fields of physical-chemical-mathematical sciences. We can force development of biological and psychological research until it is ready to deal with reality. The assumption that research would bring the sciences of psychology and biology down to a physical-chemical base has been pretty well exploited. It's a separate science, a closed 'system', and there's no reason why it can't be developed to a level equal to our present mastery of physics and chemistry."

"And you believe that you, one man, could command all the complexity of this world?"

"I might," he said. "On the moon, I would be invulnerable from any attack now capable of being thrown against me. I have a weapon more powerful than even I, its creator, can understand. I could become a dictator in the ultimate sense of the term. If necessary, I could force the destruction of all present scientific attainments in the fields of chemistry and physics. Force a return to a dark age if necessary. By force; by fear."

Her heavy lashes rose up and down as though someone behind were raising and lowering velvet drapes. And he saw it then. A growing spark kindling in the green pools of her eyes. "You might," she said. "But that isn't nearly so important, George, as the fact that you want to try."

His hands slid up her arms, gripped her shoulders. "My claim to sanity now—as contrasted to other scientists and politicians—is rather simple. I'm free from obsession with local divinities such as 'nation' or 'state.' If I can get back to the moon now, it won't be as an N'American, or as an enemy of Eurlania or Europa or of Asiana. It will be as a man of the family of man." And after a long half minute, Greg added.

"Or rather we. I want you to go with me, back to the Lunarian Base. Will you?"

Her voice was heavy. "It would be something important wouldn't it? Something worthwhile, that really mattered."

"Maybe it would," he answered. "Do you want to help me give it a try?"

"You at least have had the distinction of being abnormal," she whispered. "I've been a doll on a shelf; a mistress to a little man who was seldom there. It still doesn't seem real that I should be playing the role you've offered me."

"You can play it," he said. "And you'll play it well. The idea has every chance of failing, of being unfeasible. But will you help me try?"

And she said, "Yes."

THEY STARTED for the exit. Then she stopped him, "George, why haven't you given yourself up to the military? Why should you fear them?"

"I'm afraid of being given a psycho-check," he said. "They'll ask me why I wasn't at the Moonport this morning on schedule, I haven't a logical reason. I can't tell them the truth; I can't say I was kidnapped, either. For even if I were—or could make them think so—that would only precipitate the atomic war that might go off any minute. As it is, the blowup might be stalled until we can get to the moon."

"But what else can you do?"

"We might steal a Moonship. That sounds ridiculous, and it probably is; maybe it's so ridiculous that we can get away with it."

"Wait, George! How do you know you *weren't* kidnapped?"

"What?"

"This Councilman. They say he was there as a mummy and that he left the hall with you—I saw you leave, George. Have you forgotten I was there? And you *did* leave with a mummy!"

He blinked. He remembered it vaguely, unreally.

"Did it ever occur to you," she asked, "that you might have been kidnapped by a foreign power, and put under some hypnotic influence. That all your present attitudes and resolves could have been put in your mind by deliberate intent. If that were true, then their idea has worked very well so far. You've refused to return to the Moon legally. If you should try to steal a Moonship and get blasted—then one of the other powers would soon be in a position to rule by the accepted method of annihilating everyone else even as—we plan to do."

"I never thought of it," he was looking at her strangely. People brushed past to take their various thresholds of dream and forgetfulness. He didn't notice. "You—you invited me down here," he said tightly.

She shook her head. "Yes. But I'm no spy, George. Do you believe that?"

Without hesitation, he said, "Yes."

"I don't remember anything about the mummy, Dania, except his eyes. I remember that once I got the peculiar impression that they weren't—human. They were a solid color, coal black, and glittering like polished beads—"

He heard her breath sharply. "Yes! Yes, the hydroponic peasant. I remember, too, now—the little man who blocked my entrance into my copter. His eyes were the same and—"

She explained further, that vague episode, the moment of staring into those strange eyes, and then the sudden obsession with Greg.

"You think it was the same, your peasant and the mummy?" he asked.

"I don't know, George. But even if it were, what would it mean to us? Would it change your plans?"

"Your ideas have already changed my plans. If this unknown hypnotist—or whoever he is—was responsible for you and I getting together, he has my gratitude. But from there on, I don't like being victimized by suggestion—especially when the motive is so intangible. If his suggestions were for us to steal a Moonship, and thereby get blasted off the map, then we won't steal a Moonship. We'll take a chance on getting back to the moon legally."

"Then what will be your reason for not appearing?"

He grinned almost boyishly. "The simplest possible reason and one they might even fall for: a hangover."

\*     \*     \*

They did, too. It had never occurred to Greg just how important he was, nor to what an extent the N'American Military depended on him—until that ineffable flash of insight in which he saw himself and his world with such lucid and large-scale perspective. He had been serving in his cloistered role with no regard for the whole play. But now he realized that he was everything as far as N'American defense was concerned.

Greg identified Galatere as the man who had helped him home from the masked ball; but he denied that he had been kidnapped in any way. Galatere was released and N'America exuded warm apologies to Eurlania. As for Greg's hangover, they believed it— that Greg had wakened too late to report to Moonport as scheduled, and that he had gone to a Sensory Show for relaxation. The military didn't like it, but their distaste for his vagaries certainly wasn't apparent in their actions toward him.

His determination to marry Dania Morris and take her to the moon on his return was headline news, and the Military were in no position to argue about that, either.

TWENTY-FOUR hours later as Greg and Dania sat waiting for the audio to announce the readiness of the preparing Moonship's flight to Luna. Greg expressed the one confusing, somewhat uncomfortable mystery. "But it wasn't Galatere."

"No," she answered; "it wasn't Galatere."

"Then who was it and why? I'd recognize those eyes anywhere, anytime, and they weren't Galatere's eyes."

She didn't answer. She was looking to his left across the long shining floor toward the further entrance. Beyond the glass-domed walls could be seen the big rocket ramp, and the ship being readied for flight. But Dania wasn't looking at the scenery; the audio called them.

But Greg's eyes followed hers. A little man dressed as a hydroponic laborer was arguing with the guards at the gate. And even as they were seeming to be on the verge of ejecting the little man with physical force from the place, they reacted instead in a conversely peculiar fashion. They turned stiffly, began moving backward. They both turned at once away from the little man and proceeded, as though deliberately, to ignore him. The audio called again, summoning them to the ship.

And then the little man was coming toward them.

"That's him," she whispered tensely; "that's the man I was telling you about who stopped me from entering my copter that day. The man with the eyes like the mummy."

The little nutriculturist was walking faster and faster toward them across the marble mosaiced floor. He was leaning at a desperate kind of angle, and now he was close enough that they could see the first gleaming familiarity of his eyes.

"I'm afraid," said Dania. "I don't know why, but—"

So was Greg. He said so as he rose to his feet. "Let's get out of here; I have an idea that he can't influence us if we are surrounded by a lot of other people." Even as Greg spoke they were walking rapidly away from their pursuer, heading for the exit into the walkway tunnel leading out to the ship.

Then the little man started running. Greg and Dania also began running. "This is silly," panted Greg, though somehow he felt that it wasn't silly at all; he could not for the life of him have said why it wasn't silly. To be running away from a drably clothed nutriculturist.

Greg and Dania stopped at the end of the walkway tube. Looking back, they saw that their pursuer had stopped about a hundred feet away and was waving, then he yelled in a desperate high cry: "Wait! Don't do it, Greg! Just listen to me for one minute before you do anything!"

"I'm afraid not," muttered Greg as they hurried on, and through the automatic doors. They closed, shut out the little man. They stood there a moment staring at the Moonship that was waiting for them with such utter lack of emotion.

"Whoever he was he was desperate," she said finally. "The desperation in his voice was—well it sounded closer to terror."

Greg nodded as they walked toward the ship. He wondered why the man had seemed desperate. If he were an agent of Eurlania, then why hadn't he killed Greg while he had the chance? Or if his idea was subtle impregnation of some posthypnotic action why the paradoxical display of so much efficiency contrasted with rank failure?

Both of them soon forgot the strange little man with the powerful eyes completely.

## CHAPTER FIVE

DARREL'S body sagged behind his desk as he sat there looking at Anson. Anson, after stating his failure to stop Greg's and Dania's flight to the moon, had remained silent, slumping deeply in the thermostatic cushions.

Darrel's head turned. He looked out into the soft gentleness of the sky, so blue and unbelligerent-appearing, over Washington's mile-high buildings.

"We couldn't have anticipated the actions of these people as a whole or as individuals except within certain very confining limits. They have no science of psychology. A fool, turned loose in a chemical laboratory with no knowledge of the material he was using, would soon destroy himself. Coupled with that, our own psychology and sociology is scientific, predictable. That is, within our own culture it was so. Here it has become variable. Our philosophy is pragmatic—the sum and quest of our knowledge had always been: *"How does the outside world work in a given context? Approximately?"* In our own culture, we did well with that search. It gave us as much power over our own environment as we were competent to handle. But this isn't *our* environment, Anson."

Anson gazed bitterly at his superior. "No, it isn't. We took their outward shape; their language; their colloquial expressions. Why couldn't we have predicted that subtly and inevitably we would be influenced by their philosophy?"

Darrel turned slowly. "Is our philosophy really enough, Anson? Maybe this ineffable mysticism of these homo sapiens is superior to our own approach?"

Anson muttered hopelessly. "Maybe. I won't argue now. You've been influenced, too? Whether your rationalization is applicable is beside the point. The point being—has our plan failed or not?"

But Darrel didn't seem so concerned now about the plan. He said. "These people are obsessed with finding some ultimate answer. Think of philosophy based on such a quest, Anson! Think of the exhilaration of being able to assume some ultimate truth! Of launching on such a search, and believing it! Anson, I wonder—is it really fair to ourselves to assume that we'll go on forever just cutting into the margins of the unknown? Just dabbling—feeling blind surfaces?"

Anson felt the little dust-motes of despair choking his mind. Darrel was unintegrated, his mind becoming more wrapped up in meaningless rationalization of the growing fact that Plan-B, too, might be impossible. He appealed frantically to some hoped-for spark of objectivity remaining in Darrel.

"First we abandoned Plan-A; I still insist that we might have made it work. Then we adopted Plan-B, and already we play with the idea that it can't work, either. Greg's gone back to the moon. We cured his obsessions with nationalism, but he returned to the moon because an unexpected incident threw off our pattern so that we failed to provide conditioning measures for Greg's cleared mind. He has a reason for going back. Must we assume that it has any relationship to his former attitudes. No! We've got to give ourselves time under Plan-B. Plan-B is big, vast. It involves ten thousand years, mass-exodus, and therapy. It—"

Darrel interrupted. He didn't seem concerned with whether or not he was being rational, objective. And that was easily explained, too, thought Anson; he had lost insight.

Darrel said. "Plan-B might work, though it would demand the presence here of ninety percent of our population, practicing secretively. We'd need therapists even to guide the therapists. It's too variable; the chances of success are too slim to gamble with."

"There has to be a way under PlanB," said Anson hoarsely; "we *must* make it work!"

Anson's voice cracked off. He stared at the growing whine from Darrel's VHF disk.

It was Weym's voice. It hardly sounded the same now. *"There will be immediate procedure in anticipation of Plan-C!* All fieldmen return to *Vordel* for transfer to Home Base. Therapeutic replacements now enroute will await in space the arrival of first Invasion Fleet under the command of Joyh-vek. Naturally, all former plans based on peaceful therapy abandoned because of limitless complexity. Return to *Vordel*. Return to—"

"No!" yelled Anson wildly as he somehow got on his feet and staggered toward Darrel. "He's mad, too; Weym's insane, too!"

Darrel shrugged, "No, I don't think so, Anson. Plan-C is the only way left. Destruction of earth and the moon and every living thing on them. That's the only way we can survive."

ANSON GRIPPED Darrel's hand. Beneath the synthetic plastiflesh, the real flesh of the Martian was trembling.

"Darrel!" Anson urged with frantic growing terror. Then he changed to the Martian's real name, because it seemed psychologically sound. "Ankhor! Listen to me! You've been conditioned for this job. Conditioned to think, to evolve pragmatic ways to meet emergencies. You've also been conditioned to rationalize. You've used these people's schizoid escape fantasies, and so has Weym! Ankhor, we have one last chance to save these people and our own world, too. We can go to the *Vordel*, overpower Weym and send the true report of what's happening here back to Home Base.

"Given the facts about what's happened here, they can revise Plan-B, make it work. They're still objective. They—"

"And you," interrupted Darrel, "assume your own objectivity and sanity. What could be more insane under the critical circumstances than the proposal of mutiny?"

Anson's hands fumbled beneath his cloak. His hands twisted at the phial hidden there. His mind was a choked confused labyrinth of conflicting emotion. But he knew what he had to do; what little grim chance remained for the success, of this expedition depended somehow on him.

He was an activist. Conditioned in him over a long period of time was the prime desire to carry out specific orders. He had been trained not to think as leaders like Darrel thought, but to carry out commands. Darrel or Ankhor stood in his way. His friend—Ankhor—

He threw the entire phial of catalystic fluid in Darrel's peculiarly-glaring eyes. The chemical began its rapid disintegrative work immediately. Darrel was screaming and falling, as Anson stumbled, blinded and dazed, about the room destroying all evidence of their work.

Then he found himself in the hall. He hesitated only a moment, then headed for the elevator that would take him to the roof landing where he could rent a gyrocar. At a hidden station they had set up on the Hudson in a deep forest, was the equipment that would make the gyrocar resistant to the various electronic detection devises of the Military and the means to make the gyro partially invisible.

Anson moved with a fast yet dogged efficiency and purpose. He had but little time, he knew. Already Weym might have sent his recommendations to Home Base, and already the invasion-fleet might have been launched.

THE ROCKETS, now equipped with his 'cosmobomb' warheads, crouched on leveling legs in the valley of Albategnius. Greg sat looking at them framed in the periscopic screen. Dania stood by the great glass dome looking out across the lakes of frozen lava.

Her voice was a hushed sacrilege to the silence. "We're supreme rulers," she said. "How does it feel, George?"

Greg's gaunt body unlimbered itself. He got up, and when he walked over to her and placed a hand against her warm side and felt the vibrant pulse of her, he was awed at the transformation that occurred in his mind, in his life, in the life of the world. "I don't know exactly what it's like," he said. "I was as surprised as you were at the fear and the subservience of the earth when they received our ultimatum."

He stood there beside her, both of them gazing out over the alien frigid cold and the sheen of the sun on the glassy lakes of lava. They had sent the radagram to all the five governmental powers. N'American Military, aware of the authenticity of Greg's threat, and its true capability, had been the first to back up his declaration of the 'cosmobomb's' unthinkable power.

They had teetered on a mental springboard of uncertainty for a brief breathless moment, then had agreed to any demands Greg might make. Already his rather simple plan had been started. Dismantling of all atomic power plants was first, and the destruction of all atomic power-facilities. The cessation of all scientific research in the fields of chemistry, physics, and allied fields.

Until the human swarms below him developed psychology to a point where they could sanely utilize these fields and their products, these sciences were in stasis.

There would be children, Greg hoped, and they would be trained to carry on the plan which he and Dania would develop thoroughly—a positive plan for the development of biology, psychology and subsequent sociology.

Time would bring either victory or total destruction. Meanwhile, there was a breathing spell, and a time to think, and plan.

One man, one woman; and beneath them an entire world

turned helplessly, waiting, wondering. Greg was showing no favoritism of any sort. To him now it was humanity, the world, a unanimity that must persist. He was free of the remote abstraction of 'nation' and 'state', those grisly shibboleths that had almost brought the final destruction to their worshipers.

"Dania," he said. "We've got to help each other. The position we've made for ourselves is a limitless, complex thing; we can't allow our positions to warp any objectivity. Paranoia is a constant threat to our attitude. A god-complex would be a natural development of a frail human being in such circumstance as ours; we've got to help each other retain our present insight until—"

WEYM HAD cut off all contact with the outside world. Within the confines of the *Vordel* he had tried to return to that sanity that he had maintained for so long and against overpowering odds.

He looked absently at the copy of the report he had sent to Home Base justifying his recommendation for abandoning peaceful therapy and the use of violence and invasion under the conditions of Plan-C.

"We thought we could solve the problem here by applying *reason* to it. We see now that such confidence was wholly unjustified. The sociological problem here cannot be solved even by the keenest reasoning. Reasoning can only work from secure premises; and the necessary premises to sociology—which are psychological—do not exist here. Nor do the premises to psychology, which are biological, exist here; biology is still only in the observational stage.

"Operating on a positivistic historical basis of successive scientific evolution, man has developed his sciences in the order of intrinsic obscurity—and not, as they have mostly assumed, in the order of their amenability of exploitation. Mathematics was their simplest science, wherefore easiest, wherefore it came first. Physics followed because it was the next in complexity. Chemistry came next, then biology—which, as stated, still remains in the observational stage because of its great complexity."

As Weym wearily reviewed that message to his superiors on Mars, he thought of that tape droning the philosophies of Le

Corbeiller and Comte and Spencer. And he wondered how objectively he had evaluated those ideas and how justified he had been in applying them in order to arrive at his dread decision.

There had been other theories concerning this great barrier to the uncovering of psychological science. One of them, by a man named Wylie, had another theory: that the branches of science had emerged in the order in which they had done least damage to man's illusions concerning himself. Mathematics first, because it didn't hurt human vanity at all. Physics next, because—although it diminished human illusions of terrestrial grandeur—it left "miraculous man" unimpaired. Biology is still only in an observational stage because it involves an examination of man as an 'animal'—when he insists on remaining a god. And psychology is aeons away, theoretically, because with its acceptance, a thousand prideful institutions would vanish, even sacred tenets of science would dissolve.

Weym stared at the black jungle steaming outside the *Vordel*.

It was too late, now, regardless of what reasons had blocked the development of psychology and biology.

Psychology would have developed *before* physics and chemistry, perhaps, thought Weym—or even simultaneously and proportionately with it, as had been done on his world. But it hadn't, and now it is too late.

In the ancient Orient, psychology had evolved partly along with objective sciences such as astronomy and mathematics. But it had died, and had never been reborn.

Already a Martian invasion-fleet was enroute to Earth. He had given out a command for all fieldmen to return to the *Vordel* but none of them had ever appeared. They had been defeated by an alien, unpredictable, insane society.

Weym had done his duty as he saw it; but he had decided not to wait for the end. He didn't want to see it.

His head dropped down against the hard surface of the chair arm. Johrl's last report with its inevitable quote ran through his mind.

"Mecanomorphism, a universal ultimate—the mecanomorphic cosmology both of scientific, and mystical thinking—the Universe is just a machine grinding its way toward stagnation and death. Men are only insignificant parts of this machine running down to their own private death—"

He raised his appendage and looked with detached interest at the colorless catalystic liquid in the phial. It would have been inconceivable by those who had manufactured it or even those to whom it had been distributed, that it would ever be deliberately and almost joyfully self-inflected...

*   *   *

IN THE COOL shade made by towering stone and steel that had fallen into ruin, the cowled man lectured to rows of sycophants dressed in the skins of animals.

"The Black Days burst over the world," droned the cowled man, "and in its flaming ruins died the secrets of our past.

"But there were many songs. The most complete were those of Jelwohn the Singer, and the descendents of Jelwohn.

"You have learned many of the verses which were recorded on stone by the wandering Tribes of Shawn. And the most vivid and meaningful of these is that of the flaming chariots that came down from the Sun and partially destroyed the Earth. That song assures us that our Moon God defeated these mighty chariots of war and that the Moon God still reigns over all living things.

"Doubt this not.

"There was much myth and fanciful legend in these old songs. For in those days there was no writing, and knowledge was preserved by wandering minstrels who sang of the Black Days; of the great battle between the Sun Gods and the Moon God; and of the Laws of the Moon which must be observed until the Day of Enlightenment which is to come.

"Doubt not the benevolence and the wisdom and the eternal power of the Moon God, nor the importance of His laws. And do not harbor thoughts of unrest or of change, for His hand and His eye is with each of always. And no thought or wish we might have is not also His thought and wish, to punish or to deny, or praise.

"Doubt not if you would remain on the Sacred Path that will lead us to Salvation.

"Repeat after me the Laws of the Moon:

*"The Mind is all!"*

THE MIND IS ALL.

"Reality is only a reflection of the mind.  To understand reality one only need understand himself."

"Meditation and non-attachment are the ways to enlightenment."

"AUM!  AUM!  AUM!"

# Last Call

*A soldier of the Disciplinary Corps hadn't cracked up in all the years of Captain Morrow's service. Bronson was the first... Bronson who reckoned he was one of the rare beings who had heard THE CALL from Mars.*

THE small cargo rocket was halfway to Venus when Bronson decided it was time to take it over. He took care of Orlan first. While Orlan slept in his bunk, Bronson hit him behind the ear with an alloy bar and killed him instantly. He then dragged him down to the cargo bins. The robot was down there, waiting to be sent out into the highly radioactive areas of Venus where the valuable stuff was, but where no human could go. He dumped Orlan in there. It might be construed as an accident, but it probably wouldn't matter to Bronson one way or the other.

Bronson then went up the narrow ladder to the control room where Captain Morrow sat with his broad back to Bronson, bent over tile charts. He felt slightly nervous now, looking at Morrow's back. He brushed the black hair out of his eyes. His long, rather hard face tightened a little.

He eased the neurogun free and said, "Morrow, get up and turn around. I'm taking this ship to Mars instead of Venus."

Morrow did what he was told. The Disciplinary Corps were conditioned to be amoral and fairly unemotional. But Morrow's gray eyebrows raised. His smooth tanned face twisted. "How unexpected can anything be, Bronson?"

"Get over there," Bronson said. He had figured out the new course already, and it took him only a minute to change the present one.

"A Corpsman hasn't cracked up as long as I've been in the Service and that's a long time, Bronson. What hit you?"

"I don't know. I'm going to Mars that's all."

"Why?"

"Because there's a death penalty for going there. Maybe because something's there no one's supposed to know about. I found out something very interesting, Morrow. *The Call comes from there!*"

Morrow's eyes widened a little more. But he didn't ask any more questions. Bronson tied him in his bunk with plastic cord so he wouldn't interfere for a while. He rather liked Morrow, said sentiment being unusual for a Corpsman. But that was another of Bronson's deviant characteristics that had perplexed him for some time.

# Last Call
## By BRYCE WALTON

By the time the rocket approached Deimos, Morrow expressed something that had seemingly been bothering him. He called Bronson in there and it wasn't an act. He was interested. He wasn't mad, or particularly disturbed. Just curious and interested.

"What are your plans, Bronson?"

"Land on Deimos and take the auxiliary sled to Mars. I'll have something in reserve and can approach Mars with less chance of being spotted. If there's anything there to spot me. I'll find out."

Morrow nodded. "That's the way I'd have done it. Will you see me again before you finish this unbelievable incident?"

"Sure. I'll have to. I wouldn't want to come back to Deimos and find you'd taken the rocket, loneliness doesn't appeal to me. I'll be back to kill you. Maybe not the way I did Orlan. Probably in an easier way."

"Thanks," Morrow said.

Bronson felt nothing about having killed Orlan. Why should he? Such feeling was reserved for the illiterate masses. And yet; somehow he felt differently. Orlan had served in the Elimination details and had been responsible for the killing of a few thousand people. Orlan couldn't have any kick coming even if he could kick.

Bronson got the rocket down and looked out over the airless cold of the rock called Deimos, at the stark contrast of shadows, dark as death and splashes of light brilliant as flame. But no movement. Nothing but an eternal lifeless cold.

He went in for his last scene with Morrow. Bronson's stomach went hollow as he stared at Morrow's empty bunk. He started to twist suddenly, grabbing for the neurogun. His arm froze.

Morrow was over in the corner a gun in his hand. "That plastic is stronger than any alloy cable," he said, gesturing toward the bunk. "It's odd though—but a flame, say from one's cigarette lighter, will burn this particular kind of plastic like paper. You know why I waited?"

"No," Bronson whispered hoarsely.

"I was waiting for you to bring the rocket down. I had a lighter worked to the point where a pull in the right direction would slide it into my hand. Sit down, Bronson, and talk to me. Throw that gun into corner."

Bronson threw the gun, then sat down stiffly, clenched his big hands together, feeling the sweat slippery between them.

"Tell me about it, Bronson, I'm a little curious. So curious I might do something unexpected myself."

Bronson felt numb and sick. And then he started talking and as he talked he forgot about Morrow, and the last few months on Earth were vivid during re-call.

HE REMEMBERED mostly the long agonizing nights in his dark apartment alone in Central City, suffering the intense agony of increasing anxiety and fear.

He had thought from the start that it was only a matter of time until someone found out that he had gotten THE CALL.

Incredible that a Corpsman should get THE CALL. To the illiterate masses, sure. But that didn't matter. They didn't know what THE CALL was, nor what happened when they got it.

But Bronson knew, only too well, what happened. It wasn't what they thought. To them it was the culmination of an intensely religious experience, an ecstasy of realization. THE CALL entitled them to leave their routine, mindless work and play, and follow THE CALL to some Earthly paradise or other. None of them had seen it, or rather no one had ever returned to tell of it.

Bronson had seen it. A little white room. A chair in the middle. You sat there. You were strapped down. A little gas pellet dropped from the ceiling. You didn't know what hit you, but you never worried anymore. From there a conveyor belt carried you into an incinerator.

They didn't know what hit them, so it didn't matter. But Bronson knew! That made all the difference. He had been lucky to have gotten THE CALL alone in his apartment. When he had looked at Mars, that's when it had hit him. An indescribable experience bordering on dope dreaming, but not the same. An odd tingling, a feeling of marvelous detachment from anything Earthly, and after a while it seemed there were voices in his mind, and the touch of an alien thought pattern, perhaps. He didn't know.

The association of THE CALL with Mars grew until there was nothing else, except his fear of discovery. He didn't want to die. Living wasn't so bad for a Corpsman. One lived pretty high above the menial masses with their happy idiot faces. There were many privileges, and though a Corpsman couldn't marry, one was allowed to develop interesting friendships with the women Corps members.

That was another thing. Marie Thurston. What if, as a result of long intimacy, she should suspect?

He paced in his apartment, perspiration streaming down his throat, his muscles tense. He didn't want the little white room. Sometime THE CALL would strike him out there where people were, and he'd act like any of the others. Raise his arms. Raise them to sky, walk blindly, oblivious to anything else, his head raised, his mouth gaping, his eyes closed, feet slogging, stumbling. Mumbling—

But it seemed that Bronson was wrong about that. The masses wanted it and they didn't know what THE CALL was, so no inhibitory factors. But Bronson knew, and as a result, he found he didn't get THE CALL unless he asked for it.

He could look at Mars from his darkened quarters at night alone, and get THE CALL, and no one knew. And what surprised Bronson was that he did ask for it. THE CALL became an obsession, with even the Pleasure Marts, and Marie, sliding into unimportance.

He had to deal with an enigma. He had two choices. Assume he was insane, the most logical, perhaps. Or that he wasn't insane, in which case THE CALL was a phenomenon with some material basis in fact outside of himself.

He decided on the latter as a working hypothesis. He tried to find out what might really be back of THE CALL. There were the files in the Corps headquarters at Central City. He questioned some sources subtly. Studied people who got THE CALL. He even managed to talk with Jacson, one of the higher echelon Psychologists. The Psychologists had taken over, established the New System, above them was a small Elite Ruling class no one ever contacted. They lived apart with very very special privileges. The Psychologists kept things as they were. They were the Pavlovians, the reflex boys. Something to do with dogs and ringing bells.

Jacson gave the usual answer. "Regression. But only a few get THE CALL each year. It can never cause social disorganization or dissociation. The last symptom of the old escape drive away from unpleasant reality, inherent in the germ cells no doubt. But now there's no escape. Everybody has fun. No troubles. No conflicts. Someday there'll be no one getting THE CALL."

Who was he kidding, Bronson thought? More got the call each year. That was hush-hush. Jacson said other things, too. He talked a little about the pre-New System era. It was schizophrenic, reality and fantasy all mixed up, and everyone wanting to escape. But the Pavlovians fixed that. There were bells everywhere in the world. And everyone was happy, and having fun all the time. Why should I be skeptical, Bronson thought?

He found out a few bits of information in the files, but nothing that meant anything to him. The stuff about Mars, and the penalty for going there. No reasons. It was Marie who gave him the idea, a solid course of action. They were taking a small private monorail car to the ocean for an undersea trip. Bronson admired Marie's beauty for a while, but then he began thinking about THE CALL. Marie had a good build where it counted. The big brown eyes and the face a little on the pert side, and always so sweet and smiling. And always full of fun. One seldom saw a face that wasn't full of fun.

But he didn't react much to her beauty tonight. He stared down through the falling dusk at the ruins of old cities like bones piled in the moonlight. Monoliths, leaning and cracked, to a former age no one remembered. And about which all records had been destroyed.

Bronson said softly. "Sure, there was a big war. Because everybody was crazy, it's said. But what happened? Who fought who for what and why and how? The New System is supposed to be sane. But if we don't really know what the other was like, what's the basis for comparison?"

"You think too much," Marie said, and grinned and kissed the lobe of his ear. "The idea is to have fun. What's really troubling you, darling? You can tell me."

If I want to go into the little white room, I can.

"And anyway," she said, "what better proof of insanity do you need than the fact that they almost blew themselves and the whole world into an asteroid belt?"

"They?" he whispered. "Who were *they*? Everybody didn't do it. I know all the stock answers. They weren't sane, socialized, didn't know how to live together. Big weapons ahead of social science. Imbalance blew up the world. The war came off in 2037. Economic problems were solved. Production-consumption balance figured out. Industry producing more than enough for all, no wants. *Who fought who, for what?*"

SHE frowned. He irritated her these days. He interfered with her love of living and that was a Number One Sin. Having fun was a twenty-four hour a day job. And unless you thought about proscribed subjects, even thinking wasn't considered fun.

"Darling," she said. "If you don't snap out of it, we'll have to find other companions. Life's too short to bother with questions that have no important answers."

He shrugged. Until the situation between himself and THE CALL cleared up, there wouldn't be any room for any other problems, Marie included. He said, "I wonder what's really behind those poor devils who get THE CALL?"

She gasped, "Why should you be bothered about—oh, well, they regress that's all. The psychologists let them believe they're, having visions of paradise and that makes it easier for them. But it's regressive aberration and they have to be eliminated to prevent social disorganization." She sounded like a parrot, he thought. "What's so mysterious about it?"

"I don't know," Bronson said. "But the past's dead, buried, the tomb markings burned. The psychologists are the ones who're really supposed to know. They're not talking. We're the disciplinary boys who keep things turning their way. But I'd sure like to know some things."

"You'd better snap out of it. I'd hate to think of you getting that pellet in your lap."

Bronson laughed. "I wonder if it would make any difference to you at all? The sea is full of fish, all about the same general shape and efficiency as I am. I have curiosity. An interest in what no one seems to know. A dissatisfaction, and those are my only unique qualities— those you reject me for. Otherwise I'd be like everyone else. Drop me for those few unique qualities and you'd find millions of others equally satisfying to your basic demands for male companionship."

She frowned harder. The moonlight streaming through the

duralex windows into the lonely, hurtling car gave her blonde hair an eerie shine. "Darling, I've liked you because you're a 'man'. I didn't know you were secretly the un-fun type. Here it is then, straight. Either climb down to my level and act like a Good Joe, or I'll be selecting one of those other few million."

Bronson didn't care much now. He didn't say it to her especially. He murmured it to—the stars maybe—but he was afraid to look up there. This would be a very bad time to get THE CALL!

"All those who get THE CALL," he said, "are always looking at the Stars."

She didn't say anything.

He said, "I wonder if there's something connecting THE CALL with the stars? Something out of Space. Maybe there's something real about THE CALL."

She jumped up, leaned over him. Her eyes seemed hard now and distant. "Darling. Why the devil don't you go up there among the Stars and find out for yourself?"

He sat there staring at her, scarcely seeing her. At the moment, he didn't think about it logically. But the suggestion hit him hard and deep and he knew then, though he didn't think about it anymore that night that that was exactly what he would try to do.

He didn't see Marie again, but once. At that time she was hanging on the crooked elbow of one of the other few million. It didn't really matter who. A big blond lad with a constant glittering smile. A Good Joe who would always be having a good time, and who never never would ask any questions.

There was a slight tinge of jealousy for a moment, and when that passed he didn't seem to care much at all. It was the System that made everybody seem so much like everyone else so that it became so difficult to see anything special in a lover. Everything was for convenience, strictly, and any irritation was an unnecessary unpleasantness that seldom occurred.

Curiosity was irritating in the New System. A person who got THE CALL was so irritating he was eliminated. They would find out sooner or later about him, and then they would kill him. So he volunteered for duty on an Earth-Venus cargo three-man rocket.

He had nothing to lose but his life in attempting to grab the rocket and take it to Mars. And almost any other imaginable way of losing it would be preferable to being taken into the little white room—knowing what to expect instead of Paradise.

BRONSON stopped talking. Morrow leaned forward. "What do you expect to find on Mars?"

"What? But—you mean you'll let me—?"

Morrow nodded slowly. "Maybe. I've been curious too at times. We have that much in common. Maybe the new blood has been conditioned more thoroughly than I have, but I've been in a long time, and I get bored with routine. Now here's a situation that is stimulating, and I say to myself, why not exploit it? However, I've never gotten THE CALL and that puts up a wall between us. Otherwise, I feel a certain rapport."

"Well, are you making a deal or something?"

"Yes, you might say, a kind of deal. Curious, this idea of yours that THE CALL comes from Mars, added to the fact that it's forbidden to go to Mars. In the period immediately following the beginning of the New System, I understand a few rockets went to Mars. None of them ever came back. No one ever heard of them again."

Morrow sat there, apparently thinking. "So I'm curious, Bronson. You've already flaunted the law by taking this ship, killing Orlan. You've admitted you have THE CALL. Certainly you'd be no worse off if you went to Mars. You might find out something interesting. So there could be a chance for you. Go on to Mars if you like. I'll wait here five days. I'll fix the log and the reports, and arrange it so it will appear that there was an accident on Venus. If you're not back in five days, I'll stop off at Venus, load a cargo, return to Earth."

Bronson stared, then said, "And if I do come back, what then?"

"I'll rig up a story about Orlan. Too much radiation on Venus. That's happened a few times before. Officially you'll not be responsible for Orlan's death. And if you get away from Mars, you can do as you like. Stay if you want to. Or return to Earth with the rocket, and take a chance on it being discovered that you have THE CALL, or being able to conceal it. That's your business. All I ask of you, Bronson, is your word that you'll come back here in five days if you can. And satisfy my curiosity."

Later Morrow said, "Good luck, Bronson. Whatever good luck will mean to you."

Bronson thought about that as he dropped the small grav-sled toward Mars' surface. Anticipation became anxiety, fear mixed with excitement, as the sled circled the planet a number of times for purposes of observation.

*What will good luck mean to me?*

The memory of his experience during THE CALL came back after he spotted the big metal dome in the deep valley and landed behind a low rise of red hills. He lay there bottled up inside the narrow, gunlike barrel of the sled, his helmeted head tight up against the instrument panel.

A metal dome, like the monstrous baldhead of a giant buried to the eyebrows. He had seen no other sign of habitation, no structures of anything, only barren seabottoms and high naked crags. The dome might be all that was left of what the traders had built here before the Blowup.

Funny, he didn't feel anything like THE CALL now. He felt nothing but fear.

Red dust sprayed up around as he crawled out of the sled. He readjusted his oxygen mask, threw the electronic rifle over his shoulder, and finally reached the top of the ridge and looked down at the dome. It had a gray quiet quality. His throat was tense and his chest ached as he got down on his stomach to watch.

No movement. No sound. A kind of panic hit him, and impulsively, he started to twist around, not wanting to return to the sled particularly, but just wanting to see it, feel a comfort with it.

The sled was gone.

Sweat dotted his face. It loosened a nervous flush along his back, which prickled painfully. No sled. He blinked several times, still no sled. There had been no sound. He would have heard it take off.

He jerked himself back toward the dome. He felt the thought fingers, then, like tendrils of outside force subtly probing. Something, something greater than before stirred incredibly through his body. The old feeling of change, of unutterable new-ness, of an unguessed sense, opened within him like nothing before. Then…nothing.

He crawled down. The dome was still. No openings in it. The red dust drifting was the only movement anywhere except his own. He glanced back, hoping to see the sled. He didn't and then when he turned back toward the—

The dome wasn't there.

His fingers dug into the red dust at his sides. Sweat turned it to reddish mud on his fingers. He felt as though an immense cyst of suppuration and purulence had burst inside him. All the water in his body seemed to rush to the surface. Sweat dripped steadily, automatically from the top of his nose, over his mask. His heart pounded like a fist beating against a wall.

Just dust down there. No dome. He dropped his forehead on his arms, closed his eyes. Surely he was being influenced by outside force. Negative hallucination.

He raised his head, opened his eyes. Around him was a small island of red dust, a small oasis large enough to support him. Nothing more. Nothing else at all.

The painful tension in his chest grew until he could scarcely breath. His jowls darkened, his mouth pressed thin by the powerful clamp of his jaw.

No—not nothing at all. Grayness, though no form, or sound or movement. Meaninglessness within nothingness surrounded by a terrible infinitude of quiet. He felt a kind of final helplessness, an utter isolation.

He glanced down then at himself as the small red oasis around him drifted as though to merge with grayness. He was going too. Even I, I, I, am going too. His feet, his legs. He brought his arms around before his face and as he did that his arms went away. He didn't feel anything.

He closed his eyes as he began, seemingly, to fall. Sensations washed through him, through fibers of seeming delirium. A vortex of nausea then, resolving in his stomach.

Somewhere, somehow, there seemed to be the promise of some kind of solidity. Of being. Bright light from within, the bright splinters of brain light lancing outward through the tender flesh of his eyeballs, dancing back and around the base of his brain in reddened choleric circles. He had a brain, a mind, yet, somewhere.

Desperately he felt his mind scurrying about inside his body?

Or perhaps a retentive memory of that body, like a rodent in a maze, concentrating frantically on first the nothingness that had been a limb, then on the tingling aftermath of where his fingers had once moved.

He fought. He fought to grasp something, to see, to feel, to comprehend. He fought wildly against nothing so that it all circled around and round and exploded inside, bursting, bathing him with fire as though he were inside an air-tight container boiling himself in his own accumulating heat.

He gave up. He gave in to an overpowering drawing force. Immediately there was no fear. It was as though he had stopped struggling against a strong current in a vast ocean, and was now floating serenely away, buoyed without effort, drifting forever.

He seemed to glimpse the cloudy, shapeless motion of shadows, like storm clouds boiling and driven before a gale. Familiarity grew, impressions, inchoate mental patterns. Shadows and shapes appeared in the cloudy whiteness, ghostly and strange, and wavering outlines darkened and altered.

And then he became a part of IT, of something else. And he knew. He had been tested, and there had been the madness of shock as he was being investigated, and finally accepted and absorbed. None of it was incredible to Bronson after he had been taken in. The truth came through then—clear and bright.

IT was far greater than Bronson, but he was part of IT, and IT was part of him. And he knew.

Morrow was waiting for him. As Bronson came into the control room, Morrow's face paled and he slowly licked his lips then plunged his hand toward the neurogun. His hand froze, then crept back guiltily. He tried to speak, but his lips moved wordlessly. Sweat began pocking his face.

Bronson sat down facing Morrow. He could see Morrow now for what he was. A disease. Rather a symptom of long forgotten sickness. Maybe he could be cured.

BRONSON said, "You were curious, but you would never have gotten THE CALL. You were curious and you helped me and the world, Morrow, so I'm going to explain it to you. You want to hear about it?"

"What?" Morrow said hoarsely. His eyes were sharp with fear. "Three hours—back in three hours. You look—different, so different—your eyes and—"

"I found out things, Morrow. About the War, about the Plan. Some scientists calling themselves Freedom Unlimited, bio-chemists, physicists and geneticists, organized and said they were going to bring about the realization of man's unlimited potentialities. Create a Paradise on Earth. An old dream. Those who get THE CALL haven't been so far wrong, basically. But the Psychologists reconditioned them so the real nature of THE CALL was distorted."

Morrow shook his head.

"No, and you probably won't understand after I tell you," Bronson said. "But so what? I promised to tell you. Freedom Unlimited took hold, wiped out national barriers, started to sweep the world. They had found the secret of the human mind and nervous system, adopting the methods of atomic physicists. X-rays tear an electron from an atom. They did the same thing with genes, with the cells of the nervous system. Genes and cells, the roots of life. The rock-bottom of life. The problem of the gene and that of the atom were the same. Anyway, they learned the secret of the human brain, that it was a perfect calculating machine."

Morrow was struggling with himself, not moving.

Bronson went on, "I'm controlling you some now, Morrow. You can't move. We're in a hurry so I'll make it brief; there's a job to do. A perfect calculating machine, maybe the most perfect one in the Universe, limitless, inexhaustible. Secretly, Freedom Unlimited started releasing people, clearing them of aberrations, clearing their nervous systems of sludge, fusing emotion with analytical power, so the perfect calculating machine could operate. The movement spread so fast, it threatened various governments, including those in power. The status quo would rather maintain power and be ignorant and blind than to give up their power to the final step of progress. There was a pogrom. The real reason couldn't be revealed of course, so the big powers cooked up a war to cover up the purge. It got out of hand. The result was that civilization was about wiped out. The world burned. Freedom Unlimited had learned the power of the human brain, but they were too few, and the Psychologists managed to fight them long enough to carry through the war. Freedom Unlimited fled to Mars. They couldn't engage in wholesale slaughter. But they had to survive."

It was so clear now in Bronson's mind, as though he were experiencing it.

"Many of the scientists had been killed, only a few reached Mars. But they had launched a Plan. They planted basic undying commands, responses, in the reactive primitive cells of individuals whom they knew would reproduce in kind. They knew how to treat genes like chemical formulae. They knew the genes and cells would carry these commands from generation to generation. The commands led to THE CALL. A call to come to Mars, that's all. Once they got to Mars, they would be free."

Bronson leaned forward, "But Freedom Unlimited didn't anticipate the utter nihilism, the complete inhuman attitude of those who had defeated them. There were variables. Freedom Unlimited couldn't anticipate the utter power and suppression put into effect by the Psychologists, the reflex boys. That they would condition every bit of imaginative, creative, original thought and action out of everyone but a small elite who, because of their own destructive nihilistic attitudes, were never human in the first place, but only aberrated monsters. And all the rest of humanity became little more than robots, zombies, mechanicals, their analytical power chopped off, short-circuited completely. They can only have fun like well-trained moronic children. With bells ringing everywhere, the Pavlovians turned humans into dogs."

Morrow didn't say anything. His face was pinched and afraid, confused and helpless.

"The Psychologists suspected the basis of the Plan. They converted it by conditioning into a kind of religion. Then it wasn't dangerous anymore. Meanwhile, they had also learned they could never reach Mars. There's a final step to releasing the pure analytical power of the human mind. Synthesis. Similarization. There's a dome down there shaped like the skull of a giant. Inside that metal skull is a synthesis of human intellect and machinery, pure analytical power. The brain, at its optimum, is a perfect thinking machine. No five perfect thinking machines would solve a problem differently. The result is synthesis. With synthesis came an ultimate thinking machine because it gives off energy, electrical let us say for convenience, in the form of thought.

"And that master brain down there has the will to radiate and control this great energy. It's a kind of final perfection of the unguessed power of the brain. It goes beyond the human, for them at least. They can send out beams, or rather it, sends beams of sheer power, solid thought, by dipping into nine million brain cells plus a hundred. That brain can stop any enemy's approach to Mars, but it couldn't reach Earth. Yet.

"You follow me, Morrow?"

Morrow nodded slowly. He slumped a little. His face was shabby now and old. "Some of it," he whispered. "I don't understand. But I believe. I have to believe. You—power—"

"I HAVE a lot of power," Bronson said. "I'll have more of it. You see, the Plan really did work in a sense. Variables work both ways. Over a period of time, circumstances meshed in such a way that a Disciplinary Corpsman named Bronson got THE CALL. The sight of the planet Mars was the key-in stimulant. I happened to be alone in my apartment so that no one knew I'd been hit. I happened to be a Corpsman, which meant I knew what happened to those who got THE CALL. I couldn't accept that, so I had to look for other reasons. I also happened to never have undergone brain surgery, any prefrontal lobotomies for example. Those things destroy the analytical mind so even Freedom Unlimited is not certain of a cure. I couldn't doubt my own sanity. So I came to Mars, I answered THE CALL. It happened to me by accident, but I had the command in my cells ready for re-stimulation."

"What now?" Morrow said. "What do you do now? What about me—and—"

"I'll go back to Earth and start to work. With each clearing of a human being from his Pavlovian prison, I'll gain greater strength, allies. No one will know. This time there'll be no disaster because the destructive elements of war aren't there. The Psychologists are too sure of themselves. We'll win the world and free men's minds."

"And what about me?"

Bronson looked at Morrow's face. A thoroughly conditioned face really. Hardly human at all if one knew what a human face could really express. Strange, that spark of curiosity in a man whose brain had obviously undergone deadly probing with steel picks under the eyeballs, tearing apart the cells of the greatest thinking device ever developed.

"You're going to Mars," Bronson said softly. "Maybe they can clear you. I had THE CALL planted in an ancestor. You didn't. It missed you, Morrow. With the command carried forward always in the cells went also resistance to conditioning. You didn't have it, Morrow. It may be too bad and it may not. They've learned a lot in a hundred years."

Bronson got up and put a hand gently on Morrow's shoulder. "I don't know," he said. "I'm sorry. Maybe you'll be with me later. If you're not back here in a short time, that'll mean good-bye. I'll wait for you…"

Morrow got up. He nodded once to Bronson, and went out. Bronson heard the sled blast out of the rocket.

Morrow didn't come back.

Bronson took the, rocket up, headed toward Venus. He would pick up the cargo; the story Morrow had arranged about an accident on Venus could work just as well to explain Bronson's single return as Morrow's.

He had some advantage in his command of the human mind. But it wasn't omnipotent by any means. He would be operating alone against murderers who had turned human beings into cattle. He would have to play it slow and with the utmost care.

And though he might fail, there would be others. He could forget about Morrow and Orlan. So much of them had been destroyed by surgery that in a comparative sense they hadn't been really human anymore.

He wasn't troubled by the tremendous challenge ahead of him. It exalted him.

Some day, we'll win, he thought. Freedom Unlimited. The freedom of the free human mind. He might fail. But THE CALL would go on. There would always be deviants from the norm. He could fail. The Plan could not.

Bronson smiled at the twilight expanse before the rocket wide and frosty and marvelously dear.

As long as there were people, there would always be a few who would get THE CALL.

# The Last Hero

*Hendricks didn't care why he wanted to go out to the stars, didn't care what this desire revealed in him. He just wanted to go, and no one was going to stop him...*

THEY DIDN'T want to go to the stars. None of the old crowd, none of his friends. No one anywhere seemed to understand it. Even Maria didn't want him to go. And that was the least understandable; Maria had always taken so much pride in his achievements.

With anything involving the conquest of the last frontiers of space, Major Hendricks had been first; and he would be the first man to the stars.

There they were though, all not wanting him to go, working at it, all against him, using every wile short of abducting him and hiding him somewhere to keep him from man's final and greatest adventure.

Tonight Maria was even wearing practically nothing, as a distastefully-obvious way of persuading him to stay on Earth, where anyone but an idiot belonged.

"You're pushing your luck," Lieutenant Jake said. He had said the same things so many ways so many times before.

"The big hero," Michelson said. "The big blowoff!" That was lousily-obvious the way Capt. Michelson always was.

Colonel Comden at least had dignity, with his size and lean face, and greying hair, and the fact that sometimes he had a nasty logical persuasiveness. "Look here, Major," he said to Hendricks. "Space? What in hell for?"

Major Hendricks found his laugh seeming slightly uneasy as he sipped his scotch and took two long easy strides to the wall-window that opened out over Washington. Maria slipped near and put her arm around his lean waist, and her glinting brunette hair nestled cozily as ever under his arm.

"Like the man said who finally climbed Everest," Hendricks said. "Because it's there."

Comden's laugh wasn't uneasy. "A mountain *is* there. It has a top to reach, even a view. But where's there when you're heading into space, Major? You find one sun, there's always a million more. A billion more after that. They never end, space never ends. Once you start, Major, when are you *there?*"

# THE LAST HERO
## by Bryce Walton

The uneasiness increased and Hendricks felt the rage of cornered emotion seeking release. Only Comden could do it to him. *"Because it's there."* Really, what kind of answer was it, after all? It was full of philosophical evasions, but Comden cut through that stuff.

Comden moved toward Hendricks—a big, impressive uniformed figure of conviction, beneficent and a little condescending. His face was slightly flushed with Hendricks' bourbon, Maria, sensing a strong ally who needed the complete stage, moved away and into the shadows. Lord, she was beautiful, Hendricks thought. Why hadn't he ever convinced himself he ought to marry her? She didn't want him to go, but she'd said she would go along if he didn't give up the idea. No spirit, nothing but frightened martyrdom. But later, she might feel what he felt about the stars.

"See here, Major!" Comden almost growled. "What's the real reason? Don't be a damn fool! They've sent up monkeys. Rats. There's no challenge of the unknown up there; we know what it's like. The telemeters and servometers have already been there. They've mined, explored, covered it. We know Mars and Venus, and the rest of those balls of clay, as well as we know our own earth—without ever having set a foot up there!"

"We've found out everything," Hendricks said, "except how it feels to be out there." He looked up at the stars. "The rats can't tell, and the monkeys won't."

Michelson laughed. "Some guys never grow up. Even a fifty-year-old Major, who's pushed rockets faster than any other man. Even a distinguished Major with greying hair can still be obsessed with what's behind the looking-glass. Now you're a sucker for the never-never land of zero gravity." He sat down in drunken heaviness and continued studying Maria with desire. "And anyway, Major, maybe Maria doesn't want to go through the looking-glass, into a subzero wonderland."

Hendricks turned. "That's her business, some of mine, and none of yours!"

"Whoa—whoa there," yelled Lt. Jake and slopped cognac all over his girl friend Lara—who was also against Hendricks going to the stars—but who never said anything, even now. "Hey, wait, you guys! Cut that kind of stuff. Listen, Major, you can trust me, believe in me. And I'm telling you, you're crazy as hell!"

"Thanks, buddy," Hendricks said.

"But it's a fact! What about the psyche tests?" The immediate silence was more painfully accusing and condemnatory than all the yelling that had gone before.

"I've been through that testing-mill already, years ago," Hendricks said. He turned his back to them and poured another double-shot of scotch on the rocks. The glass was shaking slightly. He didn't turn around.

"But you'll be out there for years, that is—if you ever can get started back," Michelson said. "I must admit a deep respect for Maria. But even with her, what's going to happen to you—years bottled up in a metal capsule?"

"In the eternal high noon," whispered Comden, "where nothing ever changes, except some needles on some dials." Hendricks could hear Comden's long military strides behind him. Comden whispered, "The reason you don't take the psyche screening, Major, is because you know that no human being could pass it. No human being can stand it for one year out there, let alone more. You'll be a raving psycho in no time!"

"Sure," Jake said. "And as long as you know that's inevitable, maybe that's what you're looking for."

HENDRICKS felt what he had called rage, long-suppressed, at the negative attitudes, the ridicule, the arguments, the red tape that had kept him from his dream so long.

What was happening, or had already happened to everybody? No more wars, no more excitement, no frontiers in easy reach. Everybody scared, pretending they'd reached a balance and that it wasn't fear, but happiness. Everything locked in stasis, a mechanical malaise. Like rotting Rome—only with no frontiers left, no barbarians waiting on the fringe of decay. Endless rounds of parties and drinking, and easy safe adventures in childish games!

No more frontiers to call men's spirit out of frightened bounds. That was their excuse.

"You're all a bunch of cowards," he shouted all at once. He wanted to smash Michelson's thin face in. "That's it! The big frontier, the big adventure—it's too much for you. You've quit, all of you; everybody's quit!"

"We're scared!" grinned Michelson. He winked at Maria, "Why should a brave hero go out there for nothing, when nobody cares?"

"You running away from something, Major," James mumbled.

"The Russians still might attack, give you some excitement," Comden said.

"Sure," Hendricks said. He still hadn't turned around. "With telemeters and electronic eyes. You guys anxious to prove your bravery in the great button-pushing contest?"

"Let's drop this ridiculous wrangling and get down to cases," Comden said. "Nobody thinks much about space anymore. That's old-hat escape stuff. The motivation's gone; nobody wants to run away anymore. There's still plenty to do right here—"

"As long as the liquor holds out," Hendricks said.

"And the pretty girls don't," Michelson said. And he looked at Maria in a distorted, veiled obviousness.

"Anyway," Comden said. "You alone have persisted, Major, overcome every obstacle; and now they're going to send you out there only because you've earned damn near anything you ask for from the service. You've done it. But why? Good Lord, why? Why haven't you married Maria and settled down to a pleasant and sane life, like everybody else? *Why*, Henry? That's the question—"

The rage, which Hendricks had never thought about as possibly fear, exploded up through the length of his body. He was aware that it was more than rage—something unpleasant, to say the least—buried just below the threshold of consciousness. Why not marry Maria? Why not take one of those nice glass service mansions, more fabulous than the hanging gardens of Babylon, and raise kids in the quiet contented atmosphere of the new era? Why not? Why not indeed why not?

Always conscious of Michelson's libidinous attitude toward Maria, still at this moment Hendricks' tolerance dissolved in pink acid; he heard the faint, far thud, felt the pain in his arm, and Michelson was lying on the floor, still grinning cynically as he dabbled at his split lip.

Hendricks felt his eyes fixed on the blood strangely, then he was sick.

His voice choked. "All of you get the hell out! The party's over!"

So they moved from him slowly, not veiling sadness that was even a kind of pity.

"Get out!" Hendricks yelled hoarsely. "The party's over! Stay here in this sick green paradise of Earth and rot. Stay here in your great big global nursery, kiddies, and play with one another!"

"Wait—" Comden said and raised his hand.

"Get out!" Hendricks yelled, louder and louder. "Make this the farewell party. Goodbye! Farewell, old comrades in each other's arms!"

They filtered like dimming light into the hall, and the heliocars started purring on the gravhook landing that encircled the apartment building. Guidebeams hummed as the automatic pilots prepared themselves.

SHE WAS dragging at Hendricks and he pushed her violently to the wall. "You too, baby," he said softly. "You're not in this either. Thanks for trying."

"But, honey—but Henry—let me—"

"You'd keep on saying I was crazy for wanting to do this thing. And then at the last minute, you'd be a martyr and go it with me. But then what? You don't belong out there any more than any of the rest of these soft-bellied dogs!"

How thin her face was suddenly, and shadowed with the dark worry of lonely and frustrated and humiliating years. She touched his hand. "I don't care how wrong you've gotten all the other things, honey. I only care about how you're wrong about me."

She moved back then and he almost moved toward her—as he had almost done many times before. He didn't; he never had. He started closing the door panel. Then suddenly, shockingly to Hendricks, she kicked savagely at the door and screamed at him.

"You've been lucky, you think," she said bitterly. "You've had everything. Handsome, a hero. You've had me the way you wanted me, any time. That would have been all right; I'd have been happy, never marrying you, knowing you were afraid, a scared kid. I would have been happy, honey. You made me feel like somebody. But it's over, and you did it, so thanks."

"Don't mention it, baby," he whispered. "Especially, don't scream it."

"You've had everything you wanted, honey, except yourself."

He slammed the door, turned the lights off, and stood in the star-shine that flooded silver over the glass-paned wall. He could see the giant silver heliocar bugs of the night, whirling across the moon.

And then he saw Maria's small red sports job, and that was last to go.

"Goodbye, baby," he said. And for a moment he felt sad. But other things of thought that might afflict him frightened him and he stopped thinking. Why, he had almost thought, was it so nice suddenly—now that everyone was gone and the door was closed so tight against them? He almost thought about how it could be that—all during the years, in spite of the ritualistic acts—he'd never really been with Maria. But these, and so many other things he had almost thought about so many times before, he again did not think about now.

He liked being here alone. He didn't have to drink when he was alone.

At the window, he looked up.

But would it be so up there in the last great silence? In those interstellar silences that the psyche boys said could only, for a human mind, be wastelands of pain and loneliness and inevitable crackup?

He went to bed knowing he had seen the last of them, his buddies, relatives, friends, mild acquaintances. No more Maria; no more longing unfulfilled.

In the morning it was his day and he walked along the walk-ramps toward Central Headquarters in Washington.

Monkeys had been up there and returned; rats had survived. Men never had been able to take it, and finally they didn't care anymore and stopped dying for it. Meteors. Tempests of radiations; extremes of heat and cold; acceleration and deceleration tearing the weak inner organs from their feeble moorings.

And then, anyway, the enthusiasm waned. Men, who could adapt to anything, solve anything, go anywhere, do anything, no longer cared about the stars.

Only Hendricks cared.

Only one man left who cared about the stars.

Maybe there were others scattered through the apathy. But for him, the conditions were fortunate. He had authority, prestige, seniority, high rank; he'd been able to push himself through against terrific odds.

Well, this was the day. Even for him, the man who was going out there, the man who had pushed it against every conceivable obstacle, the way of his going was still a mystery.

Why, he thought as he walked over the city of the land of the world he would probably never see again, was so much withheld from him?

COMMANDER BURTON, Chief of Biological Research, and several other allied branches, looked at Hendricks for at least two minutes before he got up and went to the window. He was thin and delicate and meditative, but so cold, detached. "Take a good look, Major," Burton said. "You won't be seeing it again."

"I could come back."

"You could."

"Anyway, I've seen it all."

Burton shrugged. He didn't look sad or remonstrative, or anything like that; he didn't care. Hendricks had always liked him because he never seemed to care.

Burton said casually, "It'll take some time to prepare you, Major. Quite a while—"

Hendricks jumped up. "What's that? Some time? I've been waiting for some time. This was supposed to be the day!"

"It is," Burton said. "But a flight into space doesn't start with the ship blasting hydrogen flames. It starts—" he hesitated and pressed at his stomach and his heart and his head—"in here."

Hendricks felt a slight tremor in his knees. And in his stomach where Burton said a space flight really started, a pool of ice-water seemed to form. "All right," he whispered. "What do you mean, Burton? I pushed this thing through impossible channels and I got an okay. I signed away myself and gladly. Who has anything to lose? Why in hell don't we get started?"

"We *are* getting started."

"I've had to do everything from beginning to end. Nobody was interested—"

"Not entirely true," Burton said. "Purely from an experimental point of view, we've always wanted to send a man out into space. Not that it's necessary, but the results would be of some clinical interest. We had to know for certain of someone who really wanted to go, whose psychological reasons were sound—even though hidden from himself. And the better reasons for that. It's a funny thing, Major, but you're the only one."

"I know that!" Hendricks shouted. "And here I am. This is the day, and I'm ready! I've been ready for a year, waiting, waiting. A lot longer than that! Now you give me a song and dance about getting ready! I am ready—"

"Psychologically," Burton nodded. "Physically, you have to be prepared."

"No one can take more G's than I can! You know that! If any man can take a blast-off, I can—"

"That's just it," Burton said. His eyes weren't looking at Hendricks, but at the wall. "Monkeys, rats, yes. But men can't take it, that's for sure."

Hendricks took a deep breath. "All right," he finally said. "What do you mean? And whatever you mean, why haven't I been in on it before this?"

"The process wasn't perfected, now it is. So now, Major, you'll be in on it."

Burton came back to his desk and picked up the phone. "Martin, is the lab ready for Major Hendricks?"

He nodded and dropped the receiver. "Let's go over to the lab now, Major, and you can be in on it."

Hendricks turned Burton around, "I don't care what it is. All I want to know is—how long will it take?"

Burton hesitated. He had never obviously hesitated before. "A year."

Burton's face began to blur slightly like something seen distorted through watered glass. Hendricks felt the man's hand on his shoulder.

"But it won't matter, Major, believe me. Time won't have any meaning like that to you. There's too much anesthetizing necessary; time will resemble a dream."

Hendricks didn't say anything then. He wondered what it was he was feeling somewhere deep that stirred his heart and swelled his throat.

"Have you settled up everything thoroughly, Major? Said goodbye to your friends, and so forth?"

"Yes."

"Then why not just consider your flight as beginning today?" Burton opened the door. "A year, more or less, won't matter to you." He turned, holding the door open for Hendricks. "Will it, Major?"

Hendricks had to admit that it wouldn't. Or that it shouldn't. He thought about it on the way down in the elevator to the big labs, trying to figure how it ever could.

And it never did.

It was like a quick nap that somehow seems long but you know it isn't, and you dream complex, involved dreams that makes the false duration bearable, and often times pleasant.

Only when Hendricks woke up, and knew he was awake, it was still a dream, and the pleasantest dream of all.

He wasn't really one of men anymore. Perhaps in a purely symbolic sense he represented the spirit of *Man*. He was something that could stand to get alive into space, and once there stay alive indefinitely.

Oh—he would die there too if he stayed long enough perhaps, but it would take longer for him to die than if he had been still one of men.

He had known what was coming. And now that he no longer really was capable of knowing in his former capacity, he was happy.

COMMANDER BURTON was there when the spaceship blasted off, and was no longer distinguishable from the stars of night that received it without question. He stood by the big window and watched it disappear.

"No one will follow you, Hendricks. You're the last of your kind. And where's the heroic concepts of this moment they used to dream about, Major? Your motive is fear, the old fears that most have lost."

Burton smiled thinly to show that he didn't really care. "Fear, Major. Fear of too much complexity, of no identity, fear of obligations, and—" Again for the second time that he could remember, he noticeably hesitated. "And what else, Hendricks? Fear of the awful challenge of a bounded life that no longer offers neurotic frontiers into which to flee?"

He sat down at his desk and straightened some papers, which he scarcely saw. "Running away, Major. The last escapist, and the final escape."

He switched off the light and sat there in the star-shine filtering through the panes. And if he really cared, now only the moon could see.

And somewhere beyond the orbit of Saturn, beyond the Black Planet, the ship was a speck in the immensity that has no end, and after a while Hendricks remembered no beginning.

His eyes were closed in that basic kind of sleep from which there is no compulsion to awake. His body was curled up, foetus-like, in its shock-proof liquid tank. This indeed was no wasteland of pain, loneliness, complexity, or regrets. The challenge of frightening unknowns was over for him—over for good.

Ten, a hundred, a thousand years, aeons. What did it matter to Hendricks? Nothing mattered to Hendricks anymore. He floated in his liquid, his body reconditioned to breath-liquid instead of air, to absorb nourishment from self-perpetuating liquid, an amniotic fluid, oxygen-bearing. It filled his loose, vulnerable bodycavities against the shaking shocks, and he was warm in it and safe.

Fifty years before, Hendricks had floated in such a liquid, warm, protected from shock, fed, curled up in the soft dark fluid of gentle unawareness.

And as the ship headed on out toward interstellar silence, Hendricks turned lazily in his protective liquid, knowing nothing of future's fears, or yesterday's pains.

Without beginning or end, in an eternal moment of contentment, Hendricks headed outward carrying the spirit of *Man* to the stars.

# Doomsday 257 A. G.!

*Prince Cadmus slew the Dragon and sowed its teeth. Could this latter-day Cadmus smash Akal-jor's atomic monster? Could he halt the devouring Gray God before—*

## CHAPTER ONE

CADMUS trembled now as he waited. He had been waiting too long. Sweat was heavy on his clean-muscled body. A bright eagerness blazed from his gray eyes. And beyond the small pressure dome of the combination lab and living quarters, the frigid night pounded at the translucent teflonite—gnawed hungrily at that small dot of life and warmth on the barren asteroid.

Now that he was almost ready to step into the matter transmitter, each moment had become an eternity as he waited to be transported almost instantly to Mars. To the city of Akal-jor. To his final destiny.

He cursed softly at the cloud of amnesia aching in his skull. Johlan the Venusian scientist had had him in various states of hypnosis for some time, educating him for this task, and had placed a protective veneering of amnesia across his mind to protect his purpose from the Silver Guard's mental probers in case he were captured.

Since birth, Johlan had raised Zaleel and Cadmus on the asteroid. The three of them were unconditionally dedicated to the great "plan." Because of his fogged memory, Cadmus now knew but little concerning the details of the plan. He only knew that he would die to carry it through. That if he failed, Tri-Planet civilization would go on down to final decay and ruin.

The three of them, three frail motes of intelligent life, must save the vast System. Old Johlan the Venusian. Zaleel of the golden hair and generous red lips. And Cadmus the fighter. To fight the Silver Guards, and the gigantic mechanical intelligence of the Great Gray God, Cadmus had only the sword at his side and the crude energy gun Johlan had made. The energy gun was too small for efficiency but it had to be small in order to be carried unnoticed beneath his tunic.

Zaleel was gone. She had stepped into the transmat months before to carry out her part of the plan. Cadmus remembered only the shiny richness of her hair, the warm promise of her lips.

A signal light blinked. A glow crackled round the electronic power rim of the transmat. Cadmus shot one last glance through the pressure dome where he had spent most of his lifetime in preparation.

A thin hard smile parted his space-burned face as he stepped into the transmat and melted into a blurred vortex of coloration.

Pain beyond thought shattered his consciousness to shreds. The blackness was absolute. The cold was ineffable.

IT WAS the year of the Gray God, 257 A. G.

Tomorrow was the day of Worship at the Gray God's shrine. Beyond the city of Akal-jor was the vast valley where the Gray God was born, and where it lived on, eternally, beneath its impregnable gray metal dome, five miles in diameter, and a mile high. Shielded by half a mile of deadly radioactive field, a teeming moat of gamma rays through which no living thing could pass.

On three worlds, hopeless, futile, static beings of a dying civilization prepared for the big exodus to Mars and to the Gray God's altars. Then they would return to their dull cycle of meaningless existence to dream in some drugged escapeasy, or to die horribly in one of Consar III's atomic power plants, mineshafts, or his isotope factories.

Consar III had arrived in Akal-jor for the worship. With him were five thousand slaves. Bathing in countless hedonistic luxuries, he awaited the worship to begin at tomorrow's dawn. Meanwhile he looked for new and interesting female slaves.

Next to sensual pleasure, Consar enjoyed most the contemplation of his great power over the masses of three worlds. He could never lose that power. Unless the Gray God died, and that was impossible of course. Or unless he died. He would die certainly, sometime. Then he wouldn't worry about pleasures or power.

From the windows of his Martian mansion, the Palace of Pearl, he looked to the east into the valley of the Gray God. It towered, a massive gray metal skull. Consar III laughed. The Gray God was a machine. Therefore it's position as governmental dictator of the System remained absolutely stable. Nothing could ever change again. His position as sole exploiter of the resources of the System, under the title of Consar Exploitations Interplanetary, was to remain unchanged forever. It was a perfect setup.

Prince Cadmus slew the Dragon and sowed its teeth. Could this latter-day Cadmus smash Akal-jor's atomic monster? Could he halt the devouring Gray God before—

# DOOMSDAY 257 A.G.!

## Novelet by BRYCE WALTON

The System was Consar's really, despite the fact that the Gray God ruled through mechanical dictates. All the dictates favored Consar. Consar and his hedonistic rituals, sycophants, courtiers and concubines.

There was always the rumor of an underground seeking to overthrow the status quo. The Cadmeans, who had tried once before to destroy the Great Machine, had been wiped out of existence. Or at least most of them. If any did remain alive, they were ineffectual. They would be discovered and killed or enslaved by the Silver Guards. The Guards didn't really work for Consar, not directly. They were conditioned in the council tower to obey the dictates of the Great Machine. But those dictates all favored Consar's position of royalty, so it amounted to the same thing.

He moved the animated throne across the room to the edge of his roseate pleasure pool that shimmered in the middle of the jeweled floor. Above him, joylamps spun their songs of colored sensuality. His three hundred pounds of white flabby flesh settled into depths of luxuriance.

A small spidery man entered and bowed, "There is a girl here in Akal-jor, Illustrious Consar."

"Ah. Go on, Gaston," Consar's voice bubbled with soft power like lava. "You have acted rapidly and with customary clarity."

"She is a dancer in an escapeasy called the Maenad on the Street of Shadows. She is alive and vital and desirable as no woman among your women, My Ruler. She—"

"Bring her, Gaston, before dawn. After the worship, I'll take her back to Terra. Is she Martian?"

"Terra. Her name is Zaleel."

"Good. You can obtain the services of Silver Guards, as usual, under the Gray God's labor conscription edict fifty-seven."

The spidery little man bowed out. Consar III pressed a button. Soft durolite arms lowered him into the swirling waters of his pleasure pool. He sank slowly as the crystalline waters washed him gently in its bath of a thousand dreams.

SPIRALING patterns fused, disassociated atomic rejoined. Cadmus stumbled from the transmat receiver. As he lurched through dusty damp shadows, a familiar, non-terrestrial voice called. The Venusian padded toward him on webbed feet, green scales shining in the cold luciferin light of a trunjbug lamp.

Cadmus' voice was still shaky, rattling through the subterranean gloom somewhere below Akal-jor. He couldn't remember where. He could remember very little. "I've got to know more about the plan," he said quickly. "More about myself. This fog is driving me crazy!"

The ancient Venusian said, "You'll know more, a lot more, if you succeed in destroying the Great Machine. It wouldn't be safe to know very much—at least until just before you're ready to strike. And you must strike the final blow at dawn."

"Was it necessary to wipe practically everything out of my mind," growled Cadmus. "I seem to be desperately groping for some memory, some facts that I should remember now! Do you—?"

"Forget everything but the immediate task before you," said Johlan tensely. "You strike just as dawn strikes. Just as millions of worshippers emerge from those transmats in the valley, the Great Gray God, which they worship will die—before their eyes. They must see it die so they can carry eyewitness accounts back to their own worlds. We must, succeed this time. Another solar year and the System will be too sunken in the disease of unchange and futility and defeat ever to change."

Cadmus breathed hoarsely, "Let me get on with it. Give me the necessary information!"

"Very well," sighed Johlan. "You have only one advantage. You realize what it is. Having been born in the asteroids, you don't have the disciplinary band in your head. The Guards, by using their coercion rays, can slay or paralyze any living inhabitant of the three worlds through the disciplinary band. That will allow you great advantage. Now—first you go to the Maenad on the Street of Shadows. Zaleel is a dancing girl there. She'll give you the equipment to destroy the Machine."

Cadmus gripped Johlan's boneless cold fingers. "I'll get the job done," said Cadmus with a certainty he was far from feeling.

Johlan nodded, "Straight ahead and up the first stairway. It will lead you directly onto the Street of Shadows."

Later, Cadmus gripped the sword hilt as he hugged the mouldy green wall of aged dhroon-stone. His eyes shifted up and down the crooked alley through filthy pools of splashing light from Phobos. Down its scrofulous length were a number of nameless dens and dives where defeated hopeless beings found solace in deadly drugs and deadlier dreams. He sucked in his breath. Yes—he had heard the jackboots on the stone street. Coming toward him from the direction of the Maenad, cutting off his advance. Part of a labor recruiting drive no doubt. Phobos' pale light glowed on silver uniforms and an array of deadly weapons. They were fine looking soldiers though they were nothing really but slaves.

He slid the sword free. The energy weapon beneath his tunic must be saved for an extreme emergency. Swords had been in use when the Machine had been constructed. Anyone could still carry one. Few bothered. Few cared. They were past the hope of fighting.

Cadmus turned. He had to run away, away from the Maenad as well as the Guards. He might not get back and time was getting too precious. The city swarmed everywhere with Guards because of the great worship at dawn.

He snarled like a trapped animal as hunched shapes spilled from the dark before him. Huge shaggy Bluemarts from the desert caves. Anthropoid mutations of a savage intelligence at the end of an evolutionary blind alley. They mimicked the Guards, killed for them, captured labor conscripts for them. Sometimes they died, too, thought Cadmus as he ran among them, striking desperately in an attempt to cut his way through to escape the Guards.

Blood ran black. Bluemarts bellowed pain. Two sprawled out to writhe and die on the ancient stones. Long heavy leather whips studded with brass spikes crashed around Cadmus as he dodged and fought and danced away.

He saw the Guards, close now. They were confused. Their coercion rays were being used, Cadmus knew, but he had no disciplinary band. A policejet came down and hovered overhead. A brilliant search beam slithered over the walls. A whiplash crashed against his shoulder, stunning him. Another scraped cloth and flesh from his side.

Dazed, he reached for his energy gun. But that whiplash had ripped away his harness, holster, gun and all. He staggered along the wall. A dull roaring pounded in his temples. Then he heard the unreal, whining voice of the old woman from the thick shadows of the wall. He heard but he could see nothing of her.

There was a dismal creaking of stone on stone.

"This way, my dear boy. Quickly, or you're a dead one!"

# CHAPTER TWO

HER hand was hard and dry, running down his torn arm like a deadly scorpion. The aperture in the wall opened further and a hot, stinking wind belched out. He dropped as paws gripped his booted ankles from behind. He twisted, thrust his sword into a shaggy throat. His hand felt the harness he had lost. He dragged it inside with him, into a black, forgotten hole.

The opening closed. There was an invisible stench of stale bodies and drug vapor. He could hear the old woman's hoarse breathing. He hooked the broken harness about his waist.

"Light," he gasped. "What's this, a tomb?"

"It will be, dear boy," she said. "We must move quickly down into the catacombs. I wear the receiver band. I feel them groping, but it's you they want. They don't know I'm helping you, and they don't want an old bag of bones like me. But hurry. They'll blast in the wall."

Flame glowed. She lighted a smoky taper. He saw a bent ragged packet of animated bones, a mop of gray hair and a narrow hawked beak. In niches along the winding cavern, shapes stirred. Moisture dripped. Turgid Lethean vapors from escapist drugs curled sluggishly. Skeletal faces stared, glazed and unseeing, dying.

Cadmus swore. Three worlds were dying like this. A vast social system that had stopped moving, evolving, so it was dying. Fast! A yellow Martian girl's luminous eyes stared vacantly into shadows, buried in some dream far from the hopeless, meaningless reality.

Cadmus studied the old woman with growing suspicion. The amnesia was a throbbing ache of unknowing. If he only knew more. There was so much he felt he had to know, right now, but he couldn't remember! Who was this sudden benefactress? Not from the Asteroids, for she wore the disciplinary band. Yet she had saved him, preserved him a little longer to carry out an impossible task.

She turned, anticipating his suspicion. "Zaleel sent me. You can trust me, Cadmus. I know these catacombs. I'm old Pirri who sells her Lethean drugs along the forgotten places of Akal-jor. You Cadmeans have a few sympathizers. Some still have hope. The Cadmean society is that hope."

221

A wave of fear blew through Cadmus' fogged brain, "Cadmeans. My—memory! Johlan erased almost everything, I remember nothing—yet—there's something—something I've got to remember!"

She didn't answer. They walked on. A Martian half-breed ogled them from a niche in the stone, jaws chewing the mind-shattering pulp of the Venusian thiln-flower. Wrecks of three worlds. They believed in nothing but their dreams—and the Gray God in the valley. The former they believed in as an only escape from a hopeless reality. The latter, because they had been conditioned to regard it as a god, as omnipotent.

You may fear a god, and hate a god, Cadmus mused, but you cannot desert a faith with impunity.

"You know a lot of Cadmus and the Cadmeans," he said as they walked deeper into the gloom. "I know nothing. Nothing! Listen, who is Cadmus?" He frowned. A ridiculous question.

"You are he," said Old Pirri. "Gods and heroes will never die."

"Who am I?"

"Cadmus."

He swore. His head ached more with doubts and hidden fears. A desperate yearning to *know* clawed frantically in his skull.

Old Pirri said, "There is a myth, centuries old, dear boy." Her voice softened. "But myths repeat themselves. They're rooted in the soul. In this myth, that was born on Terra when it was young and fresh and when blood was hot with early flames, there was a prince. He was tall and strong, and his skin was gold over muscles of steel."

She peered over her shoulder. "His name was Cadmus."

"Yes."

"Prince Cadmus slew a dragon and sowed its teeth. From these sprang armed men who fought and founded a great city—"

"Teeth—dragon—armed men, what are the symbols here?" A strange thrill trembled in him as the words took hold.

"You are the son of a much more recent Cadmus who was named from that ancient myth. Only he knew why he called himself Cadmus. He kept that secret to himself. But you are his son. If anyone knows your father's great secret of why he called himself Cadmus, it is you. You are Cadmus, now."

"But Johlan—he stifled my brain so the Guards couldn't probe my secrets—"

Old Pirri's eyes glowed, became red pools. "Zaleel told me. She, too, is ignorant of many things other than her assigned duties. Beware, lovely boy. Beware of friends and patriots who are out to achieve selfish ends. Beware even Zaleel, and Johlan, and Old Pirri. Remember history, and recall that when the Great Machine God was spawned and stopped all progress, wars were brewing between the worlds. Remember that was the reason the Machine was made—to halt progress and social evolution that might lead to another atom war. If the Machine is destroyed, remember that the old hates will return. For the ancient hates between peoples and planets and ideas still smolder."

Cadmus shivered. The sword hilt was ice in his grasp.

THEY turned. Several corridors branched into black mouths. Bats darted from hollows. Nothing must deter him from his objective. Yet—Old Pirri spoke wisdom. When the Machine quit, the three worlds would be plunged into chaotic anarchy. No government would exist until some kind of governmental agency was established. Who, then, or what group, would aspire to power? Consar III of course, if he lived. Others if there were others who still knew how to think.

They came into a subterranean street illuminated with cold luciferin light. Escapeasies lined its length. A forgotten river flowing from ennui to forgetfulness, and death. Archways crumbled overhead. Purple spider webs shimmered.

"We're directly under the Street of Shadows," said Old Pirri. Sense-drunkening music floated from dark maws. "Just inside that escapeasy, Cadmus. A door just inside leads up into the Street of Shadows, and into the Maenad." She gripped his arm. Tears shone in her eyes.

She took a chain from about her neck. A square of metal dangled heavily from the chain as she put it over Cadmus' head.

"Dear boy," she said, "this is a small force-shield device. I got it from a Cadmean who was killed in the last revolt. Press this small lever." She demonstrated. The unit hummed with power. It glowed with a strong effulgence. "This will nullify the vibroguns of the Guards, for a while anyway."

Footsteps pounded. Old Pirri screeched, horribly, then went down on her knees. "Run—dear boy. Guards—" her voice shattered with pain. Her flesh jerked with the agony of a vibro-beam.

But he was safe, thought Cadmus quickly, while a sad rage wrenched his heart. She had sacrificed herself for him. She had given him the little force-shield unit.

He dropped down behind a crumbling column near the old woman as three Guards edged along the street. "Back—into the wall—find Maenad." Red froth specked her lips. "Beware all who might get power—when you slay—the Gray God—dear boy—"

She died. A blind rage burned up, flamed in Cadmus' brain. He yelled wildly as he raked the energy gun from his tunic and fired point blank at the approaching Guards.

Part of the street, with the Guards in it, erupted in a sheet of white flame. Shattered bodies, bits of uniform spread out through blazing columns like an unfolding flower. He dropped the burned-out gun and leaped backward, into the wall.

He ran blindly. Many-legged rats spilled out into the dark, ran with glowing eyes beside him. Pink, fleshy scorpions scurried before the vibrations of the blast. Later he found a wandering Venusian drug-peddler who guided him to the trap door leading up into the Maenad. It was only a few minutes now, until dawn.

There were no Guards in the escapeasy. Dancing girls from three worlds danced with a bored lifelessness. All except one. Zaleel. A flood of red-gold hair, flashing rust-flecked eyes, and smooth agile limbs. Her vitality failed to stir the sluggish futility clouding the Maenad. Her eyes flashed recognition as Cadmus edged along the wall and sat down in a shadowed booth. As the climax of her dance ended she walked to his booth and sat across from him. There was no applause. Apathetic eyes failed to follow the lithe swing of her gleaming body.

He held her hands, felt the animal warmth sparkle and tingle in his arms. "You made it, Cadmus," she breathed, eyes glowing. "I knew you would, I've got the microtape here. It's all you need to destroy the Machine—if you can reach it."

She handed him a small role of microtape. "Listen, Zaleel," he said. "I'm going crazy because of this amnesia Johlan threw over my brain. I tell you there's something vital to the plan I should know."

"You've got to keep blind faith. We can't hesitate now."

He told her about Old Pirri. She blinked at tears.

"Poor Old Pirri. She was in the first revolt. She was captured, had a disciplinary band put in her head, and slaved five years in one of

Consar's mines. She lived only to see the Machine's end."

"She died too soon," said Cadmus.

"Your memory will return if you succeed, Cadmus. Johlan planted a threshold-response word in your subconscious mind. When you hear that word your full memory will come back. I heard him make the posthypnotic suggestion. But I can't tell you what it is. If you were captured—"

"I know. How and when will I receive this word?"

"It will be on millions of lips—if you succeed."

CADMUS said quickly. "All right. Give me the details, and let me get at it! Now what's the microtape for?"

She leaned forward. The fragrance of her hair was a promise.

"You know how the Machine's mechanical brain works. But because of your amnesia, maybe I'd better refresh your memory. Now—any question, social, economic, individual, is submitted to the supreme council in the council tower. On the top of the tower is the question submission chamber. There are big digital panel-boards with facilities to receive the questions and problems, which are submitted on microtapes.

"These microtapes are placed before the photoelectric analyzing eyes of the digital panels. From there, the problems or questions are carried by electron beam tubes directly into the Machine for solving. The Machine's answer comes back through the electron beam tubes and is recorded on answer tapes. Audio tapes are recorded and broadcast from the tower. Also the broadcast is received in every Martian city and is conveyed to Venus and Earth by ethero-magnum. You remember all this?"

"Some of it," said Cadmus, frowning. "Go on."

"The Machine's doom is in that microtape I've given you, Cadmus. It contains a highly complex problem which Johlan has worked out during all these years of isolation on our asteroid. You have only to get inside that question submission chamber in the council tower. Get that tape in front of those analyzing eyes. That's all. Get the problem on that tape into the brain of the Machine."

He looked at her steadily. "And then—is that the end of the plan?"

Her hand trembled. "There's you and I, after that."

"I remember that, Zaleel. If I succeed, it's you and me together, in a new System of progress and change and hope. If I fail—"

"If we fail, Cadmus, there'll be nothing for you and me. Nothing for anyone, ever again."

He got to his feet quickly. "Zaleel, what's your part in it? Why are you dancing here?"

Red flushed her face. "I knew that one of Consar's scouts would find me during the worship. One has already found me. They'll be here to pick me up before dawn."

He gripped her shoulders, hard. His face worked with unvoiced emotion.

"I've got to do it, Cadmus. My father died in one of Consar's Lunarian mines. He died—horribly. I'll settle with Consar myself. I have an explosive lithium capsule which…" It would be easier to do it than to talk about it.

She finished. "Everything will be dead then that threatens our System. The Machine, Consar, the Guards—they'll die when the Machine goes. The council tower will be the next center of governmental operations, no matter who handles it. The people have grown accustomed to receiving all their commands from the Tower."

"I'll see you then," said Cadmus. "If we succeed." He went quickly out into the Street of Shadows.

He flattened against the wall as the five Guards came past and turned into the Maenad. A civilian was among them, a grotesque little man, like a spider. His garments were studded with jewels and precious stones, which could only signify that he was one of Consar III's personal slaves.

Which, in turn, signified that they had come for Zaleel.

A bitter hate burned in Cadmus as he edged past the Maenad's entrance toward the policejet the Guards and the civilian had parked in the street. He unsheathed his sword. He turned the little force field unit to full power. This was it. Dawn was about to break.

He had the advantage of surprise and here was a way. He knew he could never get into that council tower from the ground levels. It was too heavily guarded. He might manage it from the air.

He ran straight out of the shadows, taking advantage of the surprise that froze the two Guards standing outside the entrance panel of the policejet. Deimos blinked as Cadmus' sword struck. Its light was red. The slain Guard sank wordlessly in a fresh warm pool that was redder still on the worn stones.

Cadmus laughed tonelessly as he struck again.

# CHAPTER THREE

THE second Guard's face lost its sharply disciplined mask for an instant, then he, too, died in the shadow of his glistening plane. Cadmus was retrieving their weapons as two more Guards ran out of the Maenad toward him, evidently called by one of the two slain Guards before they died.

Cadmus shot the policejet straight up beneath a blast of fire. Through the predawn chill, he angled it toward the council tower. He had only minutes now to get inside the Tower and get that microtape before the Machine's analyzing eyes.

Below him sprawled the spires and sharp minarets of the ancient capital city. To the east beyond the fifth cut-off from the Low Canal, was the newer modernistic plastic council tower, rearing up into the sky for a mile, directly in the valley's mouth.

Beyond the council tower was the gigantic rounded dome of the Great Machine, gleaming dully in the mists. To the right was Consar III's pleasure palace, glittering like a monstrous and evil jewel.

Zaleel would be there soon, groveling among his slaves.

Now, from various roofports all over the city, silver policejets began to dot the sky. Cadmus unhooked an antigrav belt from beneath the seat. He pressed a stud and the cowling above him slid open. He belted the antigrav belt about his waist and stood up.

The council tower was a mile distant. A parabola would allow him to reach it, if he could avoid being spotted by the Guards while falling.

About twenty policejets, in formation as usual, were coming in from his right. He raised both neutron guns, fired, simultaneously. He used both weapons full charge.

An incredible blast ripped out, leaving paths of condensation in its wake. Radiant energy spread forth in its basest and most deadly form, heating intolerably by sudden kinetic interchange. There was a devastating fire, a supernal electronic flash. Radiant energy blinded and burned.

The pre-dawn grayness became searing light. For an instant the area was bombarded with fragments of molten metal. But Cadmus had sent his plane in a sudden leap high above the disaster even as he fired. His plane trembled, then began to burn. Its metal hull became unbearable.

227

Cadmus leaped out into the darkness and began floating down, utilizing the antigrav belt's angle facets to control the direction of his fall. He looked about him. A mile behind, a hundred or so policejets were converging on that spot where he had created the sudden holocaust. By lifting his own plane and bailing out, he had put himself half a mile away, a small dark speck, falling in a slow curve directly at the top of the council tower.

The policejets were swinging away in large, ever-increasing circles, searching. Far away, he saw his own jetplane burst suddenly into white flame and crash into the sluggish red waters of the canal. Most of the policejets headed for it. Apparently there was no suspicion that he had been able to escape the ship.

Cadmus struck the top of the Tower. The mile-high dome was cold and smooth as ice as he slid down its side onto a narrow ramp. He lay flat for a moment in order to get back his strength. The city was moving from its somnolence. Beings shuffling from drugged states to worship the Gray God of stability. It was eternal slavery or death to neglect the worship.

Far below he could see a balcony opening into what would be the question submission chamber. Utilizing the antigrav belt, Cadmus slid from the ramp, down the shadowed side of the Tower. He attained the balcony and crouched behind the colonnade. The sun peered over the mountains. It reached into the valley, lapping the Machine's towering skull with crimson tongues.

Streaming from the city's main avenues, a solid river of Akal-jor's inhabitants were marching to worship at the shrine of the Gray God.

Cadmus stared at the fantastic and horrible scene. Worshipping a machine that had chained them to its unchanging pattern and was killing them. A thunderous chorus of wailing and chanting rose in a moan of suppliancy.

From every city on Mars, via transmat, other rivers of worshippers were debouching into the valley. For a brief time they would gaze with trembling awe at the monstrous metal dome that ruled them inexorably, then return to their hopeless patterns.

Via huge transmats on Terra and Venus, other rivers of worshippers numbering millions were flowing across the void. They, too, would gaze upon the Gray God's face, then return by transmat sender to their own worlds. Cadmus stared in sudden shocked fear. One abruptly obvious and terrible fact left him stunned.

The great transmats on the right side of the valley were not disgorging any worshippers. Nothing was emerging from the Venusian transmats.

## NO VENUSIANS WERE COMING TO WORSHIP THE GRAY GOD.

BEWILDERED, stunned, Cadmus ran through the panels into the vaulted height of the question submission chamber. He would worry about this other fearful emergency once he got the microtape installed.

Across the chamber were panels containing many eyes of the photoelectric analyzers—lenses that must focus his microtape. Receptacles in front of the eyes waited for the microtape to be inserted. A red light indicated that none of the eyes were being used at that moment to analyze a problem for the Machine.

A problem scanned by these eyes was carried into the Machine by electron beam tube. The Machine, a colossal mechanical brain, was the result of the final achievements of the finest scientific minds in the System.

It could think. It could think, but its answers could never vary. The Gray God.

Cadmus ran across the chamber, inserted the microtape on its spindle shaft and moved a small switch. The eyes glowed. The red light dimmed into green, signifying that the Machine was now handling a problem.

Cadmus stumbled back toward the windows. There was no feeling of triumphant release for having fulfilled his destiny. Now that the problem Johlan had devised was submitted to the Machine's vast mechanical mind, the Machine was supposed to destroy itself.

But the big problem now was why weren't those transmats bringing Venusians to worship the Gray God? Why should only streams of screaming psychopaths from Terra and Mars march out of transmats to their pathetic worship?

What had Old Pirri said?

"Beware of friends and patriots who are such only to achieve selfish ends. Remember history, and recall that when the Great Machine God was spawned and stopped all progress, wars were brewing between the worlds. Remember that was the reason the Machine was made—to halt progress and social evolution that might lead to another atom war. If the Machine is destroyed, remember that the old old hates will return..."

Cadmus shivered as he hesitated before the panels leading onto the balcony. The sun was higher now. The area about the valley was a sea of surging humanity marching out of transmat receivers.

And the Machine lay there in its vaulted silence. That mass of thinking apparatus was preparing now to solve the problem which Johlan had prepared and which Cadmus had succeeded in injecting into its mechanical brain. It would take a few minutes at least before any results appeared.

But Cadmus knew something was terribly wrong. No Venusians were yet emerging from those transmats!

A number of policejets were circling the areas about the non-functioning Venusian transmats. A greater number had landed and Cadmus could see Guards running in and out of the powerhouses.

He turned quickly as he heard the panels of the doors opening behind him. He dropped to his side, dragged frantically at the neutron gun in his belt. He caught a smearing glimpse of many faces and acted too late to save himself.

He tried to activate the force shield unit Old Pirri had given him. But paralysis beams reached out like the fingers of a hand, gripped him, held him rigid in a slowly fading consciousness. He thought of Zaleel. He tried to understand how their plan had seemed to succeed, but had failed.

## CHAPTER FOUR

THE voice penetrated through layers of pain. Cadmus lay outstretched, his eyes remained closed.

"The probers won't find anything more. I know his name. I know a little about him. But very little. He is Cadmus, the son of the first Cadmus who started the first revolt against our great System. The revolt failed of course."

A whining voice answered. "I've revived him, my ruler. He feigns unconsciousness."

"Open your eyes, Cadmus," said the heavy thick voice ironically. "Open them and look at the destruction you have brought upon our nice stable order."

Cadmus sat up, blinked back nauseous fog. An unbelievably fat man sat before him on a golden throne, studded with precious stones. A cloud of metallic birds piped a strange subdued song. Cadmus' eyes shifted to the spidery little man standing beside the throne. But Consar III gestured, and the spidery little man bowed out.

The room was bare except for several mind-probing machines, and wire mesh cages with graph screens. There was little on the screens. Johlan's amnesia injection had been very effective, thought Cadmus. Too effective. He was helpless now unless he got his memory back. He knew part of the answer. His father was the first Cadmus. And there had been a reason for calling himself that. It was of vast importance. But that threshold response word. The key word—it might never be heard now.

He was fully clothed but he was without weapons. The force field generator was gone. His antigrav belt had been taken from him.

Cadmus said, "I never expected to meet you alive, Consar."

Consar's mountain of flesh trembled in a rumbling laugh. "So many unpredictable games the jester Chance plays, eh. It doesn't matter now what you did or didn't expect."

Cadmus started. He knew that Consar was mad with power. He knew nothing else about Consar III, except that Zaleel was to have killed him with a lithium capsule, and that she had failed.

"We tapped your mind, Cadmus. I know a great deal about you, but so little, too. You submitted a problem to the Machine—we shall refer to it as a Machine as neither of us are quite convinced that it's a god—and your purpose was that the Machine was to have destroyed itself."

Consar laughed. "It was a ridiculous purpose. You rebels with your high ideals of progress and change! Progress and change are the great errors of entropy, Cadmus. But it's too late to discuss that now. You submitted the problem but the Machine still functions."

Consar smiled. "You have driven the Machine, insane!"

Cadmus' throat was dry, thick. He didn't understand.

"Come, I'll show you," Consar III pressed a button. The throne carried his bulk across the marble floor to the wide windows overlooking the council tower and the valley of the Machine.

"You see, Cadmus. The Machine is insane. You submitted a problem to it. I don't know what the nature of the problem was, its details, but it was planned to be unsolvable to the Machine. Although the Machine isn't organic, it functions much like an organic brain.

Faced with an unsolvable problem that nevertheless must be solved, a human mind goes insane. Our Machine did the same thing. Insanity is a decision of a sort. Sometimes it's the only logical answer to a dilemma. That seems to be the case this time."

Cadmus stared, but he still found it difficult to grasp the scene below. What he saw and heard through the opened windows was horrible beyond the maddest nightmare. The Venusian transmats were still dead. No Venusians were emerging into the valley. But vast rivers of humans from Terra, and Martians from all the cities, were spilling in great masses into the valley—

And to their death!

Wailing, crying in sobbing ecstasy, these rivers were pouring directly into that half-mile deep area of deadly radioactivity surrounding the Machine.

Cadmus murmured in sheer horror. Millions were dying. Millions more would die. The valley was a gigantic pit of carnage. Unless it were stopped every living person on Terra would march out of those transmats and die. So would every living Martian.

"Like the lemmings," said Consar III absently. "A suicide drive. See what you Cadmeans have done with your foolish revolt. Listen to the voice from the council tower."

Cadmus was listening. A decision from the Machine was automatically transcribed and broadcast from the Tower.

"Listen to what the Tower is saying. The voice of the god. It couldn't solve the answer it was forced to answer in any other way except by this extreme and apparently insane way. Yet if this is the only way it could answer the question, then it's logical isn't it? Logical that its answer should be one of defeat, futility, abandonment of all hope."

From the Tower the public address system thundered out over the wailing shambles of destruction in the valley. Its waves of sound bludgeoned the helpless, milling hordes into an ecstatic suicidal rush.

*"Life has no meaning. All is futility. There is no hope. The only way out of this problem is death. Death is the final and complete escape."*

CONSAR said, "Few are ignoring the Machine's voice. That's natural. They have long since abandoned hope. Without progress, with no goal, the Machine's answer is logical to them. It's very interesting, this end of System life, isn't it, Cadmus? Look at the rabble. Look at the bawling cattle you dedicated your life to save. What have you done but pushed them on down into the slime where they belong?"

Cadmus hardly heard Consar's cynical humor. His head throbbed. Blood rushed his temples as he tried to break that web of amnesia. It was there, the answer, the solution.

Johlan! He was Venusian. And no Venusians were dying in the valley. The sudden clarity of the monstrous truth hit him like an explosion. Johlan had formulated a problem to submit to the Machine. True. But not to destroy it. Only to cause its reaction to be analogous to those of an insane brain.

Now it was directing the suicide of its worshippers. But not of Venusians. The old hates still smoldering...

A few inhabitants of Terra and Mars might remain alive when this ghastly massacre ended. But Venus would be untouched. Johlan had brought about a monstrous suicidal drive that would decimate the Terran and Martian population. And leave Venus the unchallenged ruler of the System.

And Consar III laughed. Cadmus lunged at his throat. His hands struck an invisible barrier. From behind the shield surrounding his throne, Consar smiled.

"You're helpless now, Cadmus. I see you've noticed that the Venusian transmats are dead. The Guards have investigated. The power generators have been destroyed so they won't work anymore without being repaired. You've taken the rule of the System from the unchanging Machine, and have given it back to the people. Therefore you've destroyed the System. Already the Venusians are trying to wipe out Terra and Mars.

Cadmus pounded against the invisible barrier.

"You can't touch me, Cadmus. And what would it gain for you if you did? We probed your girl comrade's brain, too. She came here to kill me, but she had hidden the explosion somewhere and the Guards couldn't locate it. She's gone now. She was taken to the slave quarters. But none of the slaves are in their quarters now. They have all gone into the valley to march into the Machine.

"You see, Cadmus, everyone is conditioned to carry out the Machine's dictates. Those who do not follow the commands of the Machine will be driven into the valley and to death anyway by the Guards. The Guards, too, will walk into the Machine to their deaths when everyone else is dead. Including me. The Guards will force me to my death, too, Cadmus. I have utilized the Guards only within the limitations of the Machine's laws, you understand. Everyone will die except the Venusians. Let them have it! I've enjoyed myself, I'm ready to make my exit."

Cadmus ran back to the window.

POLICEJETS were circling above the marching hordes of suicidals, raying those who fell out of the surging river. Thousands of Guards were circulating at the edges of the human tide, keeping the lines solid, threatening stragglers with neutron charges. There were few stragglers. In that hopeless, un-evolving system, the majority had wanted to die. The Machine was sanctioning their psychotic desires.

And somewhere, perhaps in that horde, Zaleel was trapped. Or she might already be dead.

Regardless of the amnesia, his hopeless position, Cadmus saw one thing he could do if he could escape. Try to destroy as many of those transmats as possible and stop the flow of doomed Terrans and Martians. Johlan had stopped the Venusian transmats by destroying the generators. He could do the same.

From the Tower the thunderous voice of the mad Machine still called:

*Life has no meaning. All is futility. There is no hope.*

Cadmus tried to shut out the sound. He knew that if he had to listen to it very long, its suggestion would overpower him.

His own voice buried the voice of the mad Machine momentarily.

"It isn't over yet, Consar. You're a victim of unchange like every other poor suicidal out there. The blood of millions who have died in your enslavement is on your hands. Your only excuse is that there never was hope for humanity anyway. But there is, Consar. And I'll prove it to you. You'll die, but I'll prove the truth to you before I kill you."

Consar laughingly waved a flabby white hand. "The magic shadow show still goes on. Join it. I'm not holding you here. See—the doors are opening for you. Without the rigid discipline of the Machine, System life will destroy itself. Every institution contains the seeds of its own destruction. Even the Machine. Blind tropisms, rabble, robots, cattle. Those are the stupid dolts you Cadmeans dedicated your lives to save, to set free. Freedom! Hah!" Consar broke into a rumbling laugh. But Cadmus didn't hear it.

Freedom.

FREEDOM!

Cadmus leaned against the coruscating wall. A thrill of returning memory flooded him.

Freedom! That was the key word. Zaleel had said that if the Machine were destroyed the word would be on millions of lips.

Ironic that Consar should have spoken the word unwittingly and set Cadmus' mental fountain of memory free. Behind closed eyes, in a brief flash of recollection, Cadmus' memory, his destiny, his potentiality, returned.

He knew why he was called Cadmus.

HIS father, the first Cadmus of the newer myth. The greatest hero of the System. For years, since the Machine had been placed in power, his father had worked toward its destruction. A shadow, a mystery in the starways. He had gotten scientists and had constructed secret arsenals. He had constructed small matter transmatters and installed a secret transmat underground between the three worlds and the asteroids.

In the asteroid belt had been thousands of free men who hadn't had the disciplinary bands installed in their skulls because they had been born there in the belt, away from all legislative control, of mucker parents. Men and women and children who were inaccessible in the thousands of uncharted little worlds between Terra and Mars.

Led by his father, they had attacked through the transmats and had marched on the council tower and the Machine. But they had been defeated, slain and taken into slavery. Only a few escaped. Only three. Two children, Cadmus and Zaleel. And Johlan. They returned to the asteroids to plan the second revolt.

But they had marched on the Machine, knowing it was surrounded by half a mile of deadly radioactivity. And now Cadmus knew how his father had expected to overthrow the Machine in spite of this barrier. His father had planned the direct assault on the Machine—alone. His father had trusted no one. He had lain the groundwork, had accomplished the whole preparation himself. He had been intending to launch the direct attack on the Machine by releasing the armed men.

...*slew a dragon and sowed its teeth. From these sprang armed men...*

Young as he had been then, Cadmus still remembered starkly. His father had given him the information and directions. No one else knew, Johlan had suspected. That was why he had blanked out Cadmus' mind until his own terrible plan had been achieved.

Cadmus could hear his father's words now, plainly, after the many years. As his father lay dying in a hidden cavern after having failed to reach the other great cave on the side of the valley facing the Machine.

"I've worked it for almost a century, son—the armed men—transported them one by one from Terra by transmat...an underground filled with armed men...ready to march into the Machine...ready to blast its accursed heart...the lever is under the roots of the komble-plant at the mouth of the cavern...when the doors are opened..."

His father had given him the directions, how to reach that secret cavern where the armed men wafted. Then he had died. The three survivors had been waiting for Cadmus, and they escaped, returned to the asteroids via transmat. Johlan, the leading scientist, had raised and educated Zaleel and Cadmus.

Cadmus was running across the room. He heard Consar's laughter fading behind him as he ran into the hall. But the pattern was clear in Cadmus' mind.

## CHAPTER FIVE

CADMUS dodged into a doorway as Guards came down the hall pursuing three Martians. Behind him he caught a glimpse of a huge pleasure pool in a lethean garden. Vacant now, its hedonistic lovers caught up in a grisly destiny.

The two Guards were chasing three Martians who hadn't digested the idea of suicide, evidently. As the Guards raised vibro-guns, Cadmus hurled himself through the doorway. His leap carried one of the Guards to the floor. One desperate blow knocked that Guard senseless. Cadmus raised the Guard's vibro-gun and brought the other man to the floor in a paralyzed sprawl.

The Machine's voice still thundered from the Tower as Cadmus ran from the palace, into the street toward the valley's mouth. The city was almost deserted now, except for a few Guards and policejets circling, hunting out deserters from the suicidal march.

Cadmus ran frantically, straining, along the street, keeping next to the shadowed wall. But no Guards bothered him now. To them he was another suicidal lemming who had gotten the call belatedly.

His breath came harshly, burning fire. His muscles groaned as he forced himself up the steep rocky slope leading up and along the valley's rim.

His father's directions were vivid in his mind now as he staggered along the wind whipped trail. Higher and higher until the mid-afternoon winds were a thousand icy lances driving through his sweating body.

He finally dropped in a gasping heap at the base of the flowering komble-plant. To his right was the high flat wall of granite. Huge doors were behind the red clay and dust, waiting to open. A high wide door.

His hands clawed at the red clay. His fingers bled as the hard cracked stuff came away in reluctant layers. His fingers grated on metal. Frantically he tore at the clay binding the small lever.

Below him in the vast valley, the carnage continued. The radioactive field was piled with uncountable bodies. Only deep within the radioactive field did the gamma rays have the intensity to kill quickly. But much further out, thousands were dying as the radioactivity spread through the bodies of comrades. Masses behind kept moving, surging, pressing forward, hurling walls of humanity into the deadly field.

Cadmus shoved the lever. The massive doors broke through the years of clay camouflage behind him. A grinding roar shattered the thin air. Startled, Cadmus cried out, and leaped away. He was running desperately out of the field of the armed men who came darting in deadly ferocity from the silence of their ancient crypt.

Huge, glistening, streamlined metal monsters. They shot from the dark opening. A line of twenty, they glowed with a deadly field of gamma radiation and death spray. And Cadmus kept running away from them. His heart pounded with a deathly fear and awe as he hurled himself down the steep trail. He glanced back a few times. That was enough.

Those great metal tanks were deadly to any living thing near them. They sped from the cavern, headed in a grim straight line directly for the Machine. Once set as his father had set their automatic robot controls long ago, nothing could divert them from their objective. Straight down the slope they plunged in silent, ferocious intent.

Cadmus remembered other things now. Of how his father had installed secretly a transmat sender in a Terran museum where such curious mementos as giant robot tanks were no longer of interest to Terrans. One by one, via transmat, the tanks had been transported to this hidden cavern on the edge of the valley.

In that last ghastly war, robot tanks and drone planes had been employed almost entirely in place of human beings. Atomic engines were built and used to drive these drone planes, tanks, ships. But no living thing could pilot them, nor come within a quarter of a mile of them, and survive.

They were robot controlled. Man's final contribution to annihilative warfare. Equipped with raw, unshielded atomic engines, the tanks were deadly beyond imagination, with atomic bombs as warheads, and giving off a sheet of robot death-spray. They were impervious to any kind of atomic weapons for they were the ultimate in robot-controlled atomic weapons. Silent, implacable, they rushed down the slope, over rock and through brush, and finally over mounds of dead and dying. The human lemmings rushing to their death didn't notice the tanks. They did not notice anything.

Up and up over mounds of clawing bodies and hills of dead the terrible robot weapons climbed. Over heaps of human lemmings, red and yellow and black Terrans, and yellow Martians. And then they struck the smooth gleaming side of the Machine.

The machine exploded!

The valley was suddenly a seething boiling cloud of chaos. Bits of Gray God rained for miles over the desert, mountains and ruins of Akal-jor. Boiling dust clouds rose blackly, flung by a tremendous flash like a ball of fire the size of the setting sun. Churning debris climbed thousands of feet in the air, while smoke climbed higher. The dying day was relighted by a searing light, golden, purple, violet, gray and blue. Then came the first of a series of air-blasts, to be followed almost immediately by the sustained and awesome roar.

Cadmus stumbled to his knees. He crawled, managed to regain his feet, lurched blindly through clouds of choking dust. His clothing hung in strips. Blood seeped from his ears and nose. Somehow he managed to deactivate the rest of the transmats. For although the Machine was now utterly destroyed the great crater that remained was even more deadly in its neutron and gamma radiation than before.

The last of the matter transmatters stopped working. The rivers of desperate beings were dammed. On Terra and in the Martian cities, waiting worshippers were wondering what had happened as their own transmat senders stopped functioning.

They waited for a long time. They waited until it finally occurred to them that the transmats might never function again. They wondered, and kept on waiting. But three quarters of the Terran and Martian population had been saved from suicide.

CADMUS dragged himself up the sweeping steps of the council tower. It was dark now. And silent. On three worlds, people waited, not yet aware of the full significance of what had happened.

Phobos was a hurtling curse in the sky. Deimos was edging up into the night like an after thought. Cadmus stumbled. He staggered to the elevator and inside. He watched the lights blinking as he climbed to the Tower's top. He went into a hall leading to the large audi-chamber.

A massive bulk lay sprawled in the shadows. Consar III. His flesh was charred. Even the brilliant jewels that had bedecked him seemed exhausted of their luster.

Cadmus paused. Consar hadn't wanted to die, not really. He, too, had come to the Tower. He hadn't given up his position of power and wealth easily. He had come to the Tower to attempt to assume the direct power that the Machine had once controlled. Someone had prevented him. Johlan?

He peered through the opening into a large, gloomy chamber. It contained the transcription and audiocasting facilities of the council tower. Somewhere, the ten council members, aged children conditioned to voice the dictates of the Machine, were crouched in blank fear.

A large audiocasting set was humming in the far corner of the room, a strip of tape running beneath its electronic needle.

Cadmus stopped in the shadows. He had made his way to the Tower fast. He had heard that voice from the Tower, and it had changed. He knew whose voice had replaced the voice of the Machine. Johlan.

Cadmus' eyes adjusted to the gloom. The Venusians preferred gloom. Then, beside a recorder across the large chamber, Cadmus saw the greenly iridescent body of the Venusian crouched over a microphone, recording more tape for the audiocaster.

Cadmus listened to Johlan's voice coming from the loudspeaker atop the Tower.

"The Great Gray God of stability was only a Machine. It has been destroyed. The Venusians destroyed it to save the System from disaster through the Machine's static pattern of unchange. But a tri-planetary government of organic agency must replace the Machine. There cannot be a return of old inter-world antagonisms. There must be a united System. A tri-planetary government will be established here on Mars. Directives will soon follow from the council tower that once voiced the machine-dictates of the Gray God. The Ven—"

Cadmus fired. Not at Johlan. The Venusian's recorded message stopped as the blast from Cadmus' gun melted the audio unit. The thundering voice from the Tower's summit died. Johlan turned quickly.

"That was enough of that speech," said Cadmus. "So far, you spoke very well. There'll be a new tri-planetary government, but the Venusians aren't dictating terms from this Tower. No one world will dictate any terms from anywhere."

"Wait," interrupted Johlan. "Don't fire, Cadmus. We can rule together."

Cadmus' voice was brittle as steel. "You're worse than Consar, worse than the Machine. Millions have died today because of you. Because of old greeds and ambitions you couldn't bury—dreams of Venusian imperialism."

"The Venusians never got fair representation from the System," cried Johlan. "They never will. Fishmen! That's what you call us!"

His lidless eyes gleamed as his hand flashed. Cadmus yelled once, then fell to his knees as a ray of neuron-shattering force from a paralysis gun swept across his knees. His legs crumbled him to his side. Another stream soaked into his arm. His neutron gun toppled from nerveless fingers.

The fingers of his other hand crawled toward it. That arm went dead. Only his torso was still capable of sensation. Cadmus turned fevered eyes on Johlan. He waited, his heart pounding. The little Venusian's scales glinted with triumph as he padded forward on webbed feet.

"You did a fine job, Cadmus," he said, looking down. "No one else but you could have accomplished it. No one else had the will, the courage, or the strength and audacity. Nor the human gullibility. That's why I used you."

Johlan paused. He looked away from the window. A splash of white moonlight flooded down, rippled over the mosaic floor. It glinted from Johlan's scales and danced in his lidless eyes. His voice was dreamy with power. "My question to the Machine was simple. I merely devised a series of opposed questions, requiring one answer for all of them. In other words, the Machine was forced to make a compromise. But the Machine was fixed. It couldn't make a compromise. It had to go insane."

He looked back down at Cadmus. "That was a magnificent idea of your father's—those ancient tanks from the atom war. He was a great man. Maybe the greatest Terran who ever lived. But I'm a Venusian. I am greater, because I used him. And I used you, his son. So Cadmus slew the dragon and sewed its teeth, and from these sprang armed men!"

Johlan smiled gently, "But the dragon was never really slain, Cadmus. I was the dragon."

Cadmus heard the door open. He heard her voice, sharp and clear. It was beautiful, he thought, like music. Though music could never be so deadly.

"But dragons always die, Johlan."

The Venusian gasped as he turned. He started to die as he faced her. The death ray glowed on his green-scaled chest for a while, then faded as the Venusian stumbled across the room, the neutron gun hanging limply and forgotten in his webbed hand. He finished dying with his face pressed hard against the window.

Far away, Venus shimmered brightly in the sky.

She knelt beside Cadmus. Her kisses were wet on his face. He could feel her hands and her lips.

"You'll be all right, Cadmus," she said as her hands caressed his face. "As long as it didn't get your heart."

Cadmus looked at her hungrily.

"I managed to hide for a while," she said, "when we fled from Consar's palace. I heard that terrible explosion. Later I heard Johlan's voice from the Tower and I came here. I didn't know, until I overheard him talking to you, what had really happened." Her voice broke. "How could he have been—so fiendish—so—"

"Forget it," he murmured. "Or try to anyway. We did it. The

Machine's gone."

"Yes." A glitter of faith shone in her eyes. "The System's free again. Free to evolve and grow, and reach greatness or ruin. But at least to be free."

"Zaleel—Where do we go—from here?"

"We're going again, and that's what really matters," she said. "It's us now, Cadmus. It'll be just you and me now for a while. Remember?"

Cadmus remembered.

# To Each His Star

*"Nothing around those other suns but ashes and dried blood," old Dunbar told the space-wrecked, desperate men. "Only one way to go, where we can float down through the clouds to Paradise. That's straight ahead to the sun with the red rim around it."*

*But Dunbar's eyes were old and uncertain. How could they believe in his choice when every star in this forsaken section of space was surrounded by a beckoning red rim?*

THERE was just blackness, frosty glimmering terrible blackness, going out and out forever in all directions. Russell didn't think they could remain sane in all this blackness much longer. Bitterly he thought of how they would die—not knowing within maybe thousands of light years where they were, or where they were going.

After the wreck, the four of them had floated a while, floated and drifted together, four men in bulbous pressure suits like small individual rockets, held together by an awful pressing need for each other and by the "gravity-rope" beam.

Dunbar, the oldest of the four, an old space-buster with a face wrinkled like a dried prune, burned by cosmic rays and the suns of worlds so far away they were scarcely credible had taken command. Suddenly, Old Dunbar had known where they were. Suddenly, Dunbar knew where they were going.

They could talk to one another through the etheric transmitters inside their helmets. They could live…if this was living…a long time, if only a man's brain would hold up, Russell thought. The suits were complete units. 700 pounds each, all enclosing shelters, with atmosphere pressure, temperature control, mobility in space, and electric power. Each suit had its own power-plant, reprocessing continuously the precious air breathed by the occupants, putting it back into circulation again after enriching it. Packed with food concentrates. Each suit a rocket, each human being part of a rocket, and the special "life-gun" that went with each suit each blast of which sent a man a few hundred thousand miles further on toward wherever he was going.

Four men, thought Russell, held together by an invisible string of gravity, plunging through a lost pocket of hell's dark where there had never been any sound or life, with old Dunbar the first in line, taking

# TO EACH HIS STAR

## *by* BRYCE WALTON

the lead because he was older and knew where he was and where he was going. Maybe Johnson, second in line, and Alvar who was third knew too, but were afraid to admit it.

But Russell knew it and he'd admitted it from the first—that old Dunbar was as crazy as a Jovian juke-bird.

A lot of time had rushed past into darkness. Russell had no idea now how long the four of them had been plunging toward the red-rimmed sun that never seemed to get any nearer. When the ultra-drive had gone crazy the four of them had blanked out and nobody could say now how long an interim that had been. Nobody knew what happened to a man who suffered a space-time warping like that. When they had regained consciousness, the ship was pretty banged up, and the meteor-repellor shields cracked. A meteor ripped the ship down the center like an old breakfast cannister.

How long ago that had been, Russell didn't know. All Russell knew was that they were millions of light years from any place he had ever heard about, where the galactic space lanterns had absolutely no recognizable pattern. But Dunbar knew. And Russell was looking at Dunbar's suit up ahead, watching it more and more intently, thinking about how Dunbar looked inside that suit—and hating Dunbar more

and more for claiming he knew when he didn't, for his drooling optimism—because he was taking them on into deeper darkness and calling their destination Paradise.

Russell wanted to laugh, but the last time he'd given way to this impulse, the results inside his helmet had been too unpleasant to repeat.

Sometimes Russell thought of other things besides his growing hatred of the old man. Sometimes he thought about the ship, lost back there in the void, and he wondered if wrecked space ships were ever found. Compared with the universe in which one of them drifted, a wrecked ship was a lot smaller than a grain of sand on a nice warm beach back on Earth, or one of those specks of silver dust that floated like strange seeds down the night winds of Venus.

And a human was smaller still, thought Russell when he was not hating Dunbar. Out here, a human being is the smallest thing of all. He thought then of what Dunbar would say to such a thought, how Dunbar would laugh that high piping squawking laugh of his and say that the human being was bigger than the Universe itself.

Dunbar had a big answer for every little thing.

When the four of them had escaped from that prison colony on a sizzling hot asteroid rock in the Ronlwhyn system, that wasn't enough for Dunbar. Hell no—Dunbar had to start talking about a place they could go where they'd never be apprehended, in a system no one else had ever heard of, where they could live like gods on a green soft world like the Earth had been a long time back.

And Dunbar had spouted endlessly about a world of treasure they would find, if they would just follow old Dunbar. That's what all four of them had been trying to find all their lives in the big cold grab-bag of eternity—a rich star, a rich far fertile star where no one else had ever been, loaded with treasure that had no name, that no one had ever heard of before. And was, because of that, the richest treasure of all.

We all look alike out here in these big rocket pressure suits, Russell thought. No one for God only knew how many of millions of light years away could see or care. Still—we might have a chance to live, even now Russell thought—if it weren't for old crazy Dunbar.

They might have a chance if Alvar and Johnson weren't so damn lacking in self-confidence as to put all their trust in that crazed old rum-dum. Russell had known now for some time that they were going in the wrong direction. No reason for knowing. Just a hunch. And Russell was sure his hunch was right.

Russell said. "Look—look to your left and to your right and behind us. Four suns. You guys see those other three suns all around you, don't you?"

"Sure," someone said.

"Well, if you'll notice," Russell said, "the one on the left also now has a red rim around it. Can't you guys see that?"

"Yeah, I see it," Alvar said.

"So now," Johnson said, "there's two suns with red rims around them."

"We're about in the middle of those four suns aren't we, Dunbar?" Russell said.

"That's right, boys!" yelled old Dunbar in that sickeningly optimistic voice. Like a hysterical old woman's. "Just about in the sweet dark old middle."

"You're still sure it's the sun up ahead...that's the only one with life on it, Dunbar...the only one we can live on?" Russell asked.

"That's right!" Dunbar yelled. "That's the only one—and it's a real paradise. Not just a place to live, boys—but a place you'll have trouble believing in because it's like a dream!"

"And none of these other three suns have worlds we could live on, Dunbar?" Russell asked. Keep the old duck talking like this and maybe Alvar and Johnson would see that he was cracked.

"Yeah," said Alvar. "You still say that, Dunbar?"

"No life, boys, nothing," Dunbar laughed. "Nothing on these other worlds but ashes...just ashes and iron and dried blood, dried a million years or more."

"When in hell were you ever here?" Johnson said. "You say you were here before. You never said when, or why or anything!"

"It was a long time back boys. Don't remember too well, but it was when we had an old ship called the DOG STAR that I was here. A pirate ship and I was second in command, and we came through this sector. That was—hell, it musta' been fifty years ago. I been too many places nobody's ever bothered to name or chart, to remember where it is, but I been here. I remember those four suns all spotted to form a perfect circle from this point, with us squarely in the middle. We explored all these suns and the worlds that go round 'em. Trust me, boys, and we'll reach the right one. And that one's just like Paradise."

"Paradise is it," Russell whispered hoarsely.

"Paradise and there we'll be like gods, like Mercuries with wings flying on nights of sweet song. These other suns, don't let them bother you. They're jezebels of stars. All painted up in the darkness and pretty and waiting and calling and lying! They make you think of nice green worlds all running waters and dews and forests thick as fleas on a wet dog. But it ain't there, boys. I know this place, I been here, long time back."

Russell said tightly, "It'll take us a long time won't it? If it's got air we can breathe, and water we can drink and shade we can rest in— that'll be paradise enough for us. But it'll take a long time won't it? And what if it isn't there—what if after all the time we spend hoping and getting there—there won't be nothing but ashes and cracked clay?"

"I know we're going right," Dunbar said cheerfully. "I can tell. Like I said—you can tell it because of the red rim around it."

"But the sun on our left, you can see—it's got a red rim too now," Russell said.

"Yeah, that's right," said Alvar. "Sometimes I see a red rim around the one we're going for, sometimes a red rim around that one on the left. Now, sometimes I'm not sure either of them's got a red rim. You said that one had a red rim, Dunbar, and I wanted to believe it. So now maybe we're all seeing a red rim that was never there."

Old Dunbar laughed. The sound brought blood hotly to Russell's face. "We're heading to the right one, boys. Don't doubt me...I been here. We explored all these sun systems. And I remember it all. The second planet from that red-rimmed sun. You come down through a soft atmosphere, floating like in a dream. You see the green lakes coming up through the clouds and the women dancing and the music playing. I remember seeing a ship there that brought those women there, a long long time before ever I got there. A land like heaven and women like angels singing and dancing and laughing with red lips and arms white as milk, and soft silky hair floating in the winds."

Russell was very sick of the old man's voice. He was at least glad he didn't have to look at the old man now. His bald head, his skinny bobbing neck, his simpering watery blue eyes. But he still had to suffer that immutable babbling, that idiotic cheerfulness...and knowing all the time the old man was crazy, that he was leading them wrong.

I'd break away, go it alone to the right sun, Russell thought—but I'd never make it alone. A little while out here alone and I'd be nuttier than old Dunbar will ever be, even if he keeps on getting nuttier all the time.

Somewhere, sometime then…Russell got the idea that the only way was to get rid of Dunbar.

"You mean to tell us there are people living by that red-rimmed sun," Russell said.

"Lost people…lost…who knows how long," Dunbar said, as the four of them hurtled along. "You never know where you'll find people on a world somewhere nobody's ever named or knows about. Places where a lost ship's landed and never got up again, or wrecked itself so far off the lanes they'll never be found except by accident for millions of years. That's what this world is, boys. Must have been a shipload of beautiful people, maybe actresses and people like that being hauled to some outpost to entertain. They're like angels now, living in a land all free from care. Every place you see green forests and fields and blue lakes, and at nights there's three moons that come around the sky in a thousand different colors. And it never gets cold…it's always spring, always spring, boys, and the music plays all night, every night of a long long year…"

Russell suddenly shouted, "Keep quiet, Dunbar. Shut up, will you?"

Johnson said. "Dunbar—how long'll it take us?"

"Six months to a year, I'd say," Dunbar yelled happily. "That is— of our hereditary time."

"What?" croaked Alvar.

Johnson didn't say anything at all.

Russell screamed at Dunbar, then quieted down. He whispered. "Six months to a year—out here—cooped up in these damn suits. You're crazy as hell, Dunbar. Crazy…crazy! Nobody could stand it. We'll all be crazier than you are—"

"We'll make it, boys. Trust ole' Dunbar. What's a year when we know we're getting to Paradise at the end of it? What's a year out here…it's paradise ain't it, compared with that prison hole we were rotting in? We can make it. We have the food concentrates, and all the rest. All we need's the will, boys, and we got that. The whole damn Universe isn't big enough to kill the will of a human being, boys. I been over a whole lot of it, and I know. In the old days—"

"The hell with the old days," screamed Russell.

"Now quiet down, Russ," Dunbar said in a kind of dreadful crooning whisper. "You calm down now. You younger fellows—you don't look at things the way we used to. Thing is, we got to go straight. People trapped like this liable to start meandering. Liable to start losing the old will-power."

He chuckled.

"Yeah," said Alvar. "Someone says maybe we ought to go left, and someone says to go right, and someone else says to go in another direction. And then someone says maybe they'd better go back the old way. An' pretty soon something breaks, or the food runs out, and you're a million million miles from someplace you don't care about any more because you're dead. All frozen up in space...preserved like a piece of meat in a cold storage locker. And then maybe in a million years or so some lousy insect man from Jupiter comes along and finds you and takes you way to a museum..."

"Shut up!" Johnson yelled.

Dunbar laughed. "Boys, boys, don't get panicky. Keep your heads. Just stick to old Dunbar and he'll see you through. I'm always lucky. Only one way to go...an' that's straight ahead to the sun with the red-rim around it...and then we tune in the gravity repellors, and coast down, floating and singing down through the clouds to paradise."

After that they traveled on for what seemed months to Russell, but it couldn't have been over a day or two of the kind of time-sense he had inherited from Earth.

Then he saw how the other two stars also were beginning to develop red rims. He yelled this fact out to the others. And Alvar said, "Russ's right. That sun to the right, and the one behind us...now they ALL have red rims around them. Dunbar—" A pause and no awareness of motion.

Dunbar laughed, "Sure, they all maybe have a touch of red, but it isn't the same, boys. I can tell the difference. Trust me—"

Russell half choked on his words. "You old goat! With those old eyes of yours, you couldn't see your way into a fire!"

"Don't get panicky now. Keep your heads. In another year, we'll be there—"

"God, you gotta' be sure," Alvar said. "I don't mind dyin' out here. But after a year of this; and then to get to a world that was only ashes, and not able to go any further—"

"I always come through, boys. I'm lucky. Angel women will take us to their houses on the edges of cool lakes, little houses that sit there in the sun like fancy jewels. And we'll walk under colored fountains, pretty colored fountains just splashing and splashing like pretty rain on our hungry hides. That's worth waiting for."

Russell did it before he hardly realized he was killing the old man. It was something he had had to do for a long time and that made it easy. There was a flash of burning oxygen from inside the suit of Dunbar. If he'd aimed right, Russell knew the fire-bullet should have pierced Dunbar's back. Now the fire was gone, extinguished automatically by units inside the suit. The suit was still inflated, self-sealing. Nothing appeared to have changed. The four of them hurtling on together, but inside that first suit up there on the front of the gravity rope, Dunbar was dead.

He was dead and his mouth was shut for good.

Dunbar's last faint cry from inside his suit still rang in Russell's ears, and he knew Alvar and Johnson had heard it too. Alvar and Johnson both called Dunbar's name a few times. There was no answer.

"Russ—you shouldn't have done that," Johnson whispered. "You shouldn't have done that to the old man!"

"No," Alvar said, so low he could barely be heard. "You shouldn't have done it."

"I did it for the three of us," Russell said. "It was either him or us. Lies…lies that was all he had left in his crazy head. Paradise…don't tell me you guys don't see the red rims around all four suns, all four suns all around us. Don't tell me you guys didn't know he was batty, that you really believed all that stuff he was spouting all the time!"

"Maybe he was lying, maybe not," Johnson said. "Now he's dead anyway."

"Maybe he was wrong, crazy, full of lies," Alvar said. "But now he's dead."

"How could he see any difference in those four stars?" Russell said, louder.

"He thought he was right," Alvar said. "He wanted to take us to paradise. He was happy, nothing could stop the old man—but he's dead now."

He sighed.

"He was taking us wrong…wrong!" Russell screamed, "Angels—music all night—houses like jewels—and women like angels—"

"*Shhhh*," said Alvar. It was quiet. How could it be so quiet,

Russell thought? And up ahead the old man's pressure suit with a corpse inside went on ahead, leading the other three at the front of the gravity-rope.

"Maybe he was wrong," Alvar said. "But now do we know which way is right?"

SOMETIME later, Johnson said, "We got to decide now. Let's forget the old man. Let's forget him and all that's gone and let's start now and decide what to do."

And Alvar said, "Guess he was crazy all right, and I guess we trusted him because we didn't have the strength to make up our own minds. Why does a crazy man's laugh sound so good when you're desperate and don't know what to do?"

"I always had a feeling we were going wrong," Johnson said. "Anyway, it's forgotten, Russ. It's swallowed up in the darkness all around. It's never been."

Russell said, "I've had a hunch all along that maybe the old man was here before, and that he was right about there being a star here with a world we can live on. But I've known we was heading wrong. I've had a hunch all along that the right star was the one to the left."

"I don't know," Johnson sighed. "I been feeling partial toward that one on the right. What about you, Alvar?"

"I always thought we were going straight in the opposite direction from what we should, I guess. I always wanted to turn around and go back. It won't make over maybe a month's difference. And what does a month matter anyway out here—hell there never was any time out here until we came along. We make our own time here, and a month don't matter to me."

Sweat ran down Russell's face. His voice trembled. "No—that's wrong. You're both wrong." He could see himself going it alone. Going crazy because he was alone. He'd have broken away, gone his own direction, long ago but for that fear.

"How can we tell which of us is right?" Alvar said. "It's like everything was changing all the time out here. Sometimes I'd swear none of those suns had red rims, and at other times—like the old man said, they're all pretty and lying and saying nothing, just changing all the time. Jezebel stars, the old man said."

"I know I'm right," Russell pleaded, "My hunches always been right. My hunch got us out of that prison didn't it? Listen—I tell you it's that star to the left—"

"The one to the right," said Johnson.

"We been going away from the right one all the time," said Alvar.

"We got to stay together," said Russell. "Nobody could spend a year out here…alone…"

"Ah…in another month or so we'd be lousy company anyway," Alvar said. "Maybe a guy could get to the point where he'd sleep most of the time…just wake up enough times to give himself another boost with the old life-gun."

"We got to face it," Johnson said finally. "We three don't go on together any more."

"That's it," said Alvar. "There's three suns that look like they might be right seeing as how we all agree the old man was wrong. But we believe there is one we can live by, because we all seem to agree that the old man might have been right about that. If we stick together, the chance is three to one against us. But if each of us makes for one star, one of us has a chance to live. Maybe not in paradise like the old man said, but a place where we can live. And maybe there'll be intelligent life, maybe even a ship, and whoever gets the right star can come and help the other two…"

"No…God no…" Russell whispered over and over. "None of us can ever make it alone…"

Alvar said, "We each take the star he likes best. I'll go back the other way. Russ, you take the left. And you, Johnson, go to, the right."

Johnson started to laugh. Russell was yelling wildly at them, and above his own yelling he could hear Johnson's rising laughter. "Every guy's got a star of his own," Johnson said when he stopped laughing. "And we got ours. A nice red-rimmed sun for each of us to call his very own."

"Okay," Alvar said. "We cut off the gravity rope, and each to his own sun."

Now Russell wasn't saying anything.

"And the old man," Alvar said, "can keep right on going toward what he thought was right. And he'll keep on going. Course he won't be able to give himself another boost with the life-gun, but he'll keep going. Someday he'll get to that red-rimmed star of his. Out here in space, once you're going, you never stop…and I guess there isn't any other body to pull him off his course. And what will time matter to old Dunbar? Even less than to us, I guess. He's dead and he won't care."

"Ready," Johnson said. "I'll cut off the gravity rope."

"I'm ready," Alvar said. "To go back toward whatever it was I started from."

"Ready, Russ?"

Russell couldn't say anything. He stared at the endless void which now he would share with no one. Not even crazy old Dunbar.

"All right," Johnson said. "Good-bye."

Russell felt the release, felt the sudden inexplicable isolation and aloneness even before Alvar and Johnson used their life-guns and shot out of sight, Johnson toward the left and Alvar back toward that other red-rimmed sun behind them.

And old Dunbar shooting right on ahead. And all three of them dwindling and dwindling and blinking out like little lights.

Fading, he could hear their voices. "Each to his own star," Johnson said. "On a bee line."

"On a bee line," Alvar said.

Russell used his own life-gun and in a little while he didn't hear Alvar or Johnson's voices, nor could he see them. They were thousands of miles away, and going further all the time.

Russell's head fell forward against the front of his helmet, and he closed his eyes. "Maybe," he thought, "I shouldn't have killed the old man. Maybe one sun's as good as another..."

Then he raised his body and looked out into the year of blackness that waited for him, stretching away to the red-rimmed sun. Even if he were right—he was sure now he'd never make it alone.

THE body inside the pressure suit drifted into a low-level orbit around the second planet from the sun of its choice, and drifted there a long time. A strato-cruiser detected it by chance because of the strong concentration of radioactivity that came from it.

They took the body down to one of the small, quiet towns on the edge of one of the many blue lakes where the domed houses were like bright joyful jewels. They got the leathery, well-preserved body from the pressure suit.

"An old man," one of them mused. "A very old man. From one of the lost sectors. I wonder how and why he came so very far from his home?"

"Wrecked a ship out there, probably," one of the others said. "But he managed to get this far. It looks as though a small meteor fragment pierced his body. Here. You see?"

"Yes," another of them said. "But what amazes me is that this old man picked this planet out of all the others. The only one in this entire sector that would sustain life."

"Maybe he was just a very lucky old man. Yes...a man who attains such an age was usually lucky. Or at least that is what they say about the lost sectors."

"Maybe he knew the way here. Maybe he was here before—sometime."

The other shook his head. "I don't think so. They say some humans from that far sector did land here—but that's probably only a myth. And if they did, it was well over a thousand years ago."

Another said. "He has a fine face, this old man. A noble face. Whoever he is...wherever he came from, he died bravely and he knew the way, though he never reached this haven of the lost alive."

"Nor is it irony that he reached here dead," said the Lake Chieftain. He had been listening and he stepped forward and raised his arm. "He was old. It is obvious that he fought bravely, that he had great courage, and that he knew the way. He will be given a burial suitable to his stature, and he will rest here among the brave.

"Let the women dance and the music play for this old man. Let the trumpets speak, and the rockets fly up. And let flowers be strewn over the path above which the women will carry him to rest."

# They Will Destroy

*"Don't you see, you idiots? We're in section 80-epicenter-57. That little light right there happens to the Sol!"... But they shouldn't have been back home; they should have been in M-32 in Andromeda!*

## CHAPTER ONE

CONRAD'S stirring consciousness told him that the fantastic journey had ended. The automatic equipments beside their beds were geared to waken them as they approached that far, far constellation. M-32 in Andromeda.

Andromeda! He didn't feel the injectors punching new life into his limbs; he didn't feel anything except growing fear. He heard the voiceless susurration of the ship as it thrust itself on through the cold and lifeless night. Something was horribly wrong!

While relays and photoelectric circuits assured his steady rise from the still dust of suspended animation. Conrad's wide-set brown eyes stared wildly at the chronometer. His big body trembled in his bed.

Surely the chronometer was wrong. But the ship was no stronger than anyone of its many intricate parts, and everything else was working properly. Suspended animation, the only possible way a human could manage the vast journey, was scheduled to be broken as the ship reached one point five light years distance from the fringe of the star system of M-32 in Andromeda. At that instant of awaking, allowing for errors involving such great sweeps of space-time, the chronometer should register approximately three hundred years.

It didn't, though. The dial pointed an unshaking finger at—six hundred years.

Six hundred years, four months, twenty-two days, five hours, eighteen minutes, and—

But what did the seconds matter? The four of them had slept on in their suspended animation at least twice as long as they were scheduled to. Nine hundred thousand light years too long.

★     *Moving swiftly, Conrad and Kaye subdued Krisha.*     ★

Surrounded by that infinite darkness expanding forever beyond the thin shell of the spaceship, Conrad was suddenly bathed in cold sweat. Blinking, he peered across the small sleeping cubicle at the other three. None of their shadowy bodies moved in the dim auto luminescence. His eyes passed over the big clumsy body of Karl Koehler the astrophysicist and galacticist: over the slim delicate body of Frank Hudson, astrogator and electro-engineer. He looked at his wife.

Tears stung his eyes as he looked at Kaye. She was so beautiful with her head pillowed in a deep cushion of violet-black hair. And she was alive, the dials showed their vague spark of life. That was the almost-frightening reality—all alive after so long.

Alive, and lost, somewhere, somehow—

Trembling impatiently to find out what had happened, and with fear of finding out, Conrad waited. Other injectors kept his nerves anesthetized against the intense pain of returning sensation.

Finally, after almost two hours, he was able to get up and move about. The others should be awaking too; something else was wrong. Hurriedly he set their awakening equipment to working, then ran to the forward control chamber, groping his way fearfully through the strangely alien-feeling cylindrical body of the hundred-metre spaceship.

But he didn't open the door. Not just then. No use going in until the others were conscious. He wouldn't understand the full significance of the astrocharts without Koehler. Nor could he know whether or not 'Kilroy', the automatic pilot, had gotten out of commission without Hudson.

He wandered back to the sleeping cubicle. What colossal blind faith they had put in the ship, especially in 'Kilroy.' They had trusted completely in the ability of that mass of free electrons, magnetic fields in a hard vacuum; and it had lost them unmercifully in a timeless immensity somewhere at least 90,000 light beyond M-32 in Andromeda.

Nothing could be done toward finding what had happened, or easing their circumstance except as a group. The others were specialists; he the 'coordinator', a graduate of the Synthesis Academy. He was a 'non-specialist acting as informal 'Captain' of the experimental fight, man's first beyond his own galaxy in which had been found only faint hints of intelligent life. His job was to correlate the work of the specialists.

Conrad slid nervously back along the bulkhead. Through the appalling thinness between him and that black abyss beyond the ship he could feel the infinite whispering night rushing, rushing—

The others were beginning to stir painfully. While he waited, he relieved some of the tension by opening and eating a can of concentrates; but after that he felt no better.

He sat there broodingly, his head in moist hands. There was something in his brain, something psychosomatic that ached because it shouldn't be there and wanted to get out. The ache symbolized something else, suppressed, he was sure; it was a hidden fear—perhaps something deeper than fear—imprisoned there.

LATER THEY sat looking at each, other, aware of the mutual fear growing among them. Kaye's hand rested in his. Her peculiarly opaque eyes studied all of the others with the discerning eyes of psychiatry. The giant Koehler stretched, his big jaws yawning widely. "Well, Hudson, you ready?"

Koehler's dislike for Hudson was ill concealed. Conrad understood that, though he had tried to control his own distaste for Hudson's particular psychological type. Cynical, egomaniacal— incipient paranoia, Kaye had said. His motivation for volunteering for this flight was a symptom; he had said he wanted to be the pioneer of man's eventual conquest of the Universe. Unpleasant obsession, Conrad had thought. Yet many men at the time they had left earth had probably had somewhat similar ideas.

But those men were gone now, dead a long time. What men moved now in their patterns? What ideas prevailed now? Little chance of their ever finding out.

Hudson was smiling thinly. "Sure. Let's take a look at 'Kilroy.' Not that it makes any difference now; we're through. A delicate mechanism like this either works right, or very, very wrongly. And it caught us asleep. But we're only the first; not important. Men are tired of a barren Utopia. We need a Universe to conquer, to bend to our will. There'll be plenty of other ships."

Kaye smiled at him. "We each have our individual motivations for volunteering for this journey, Hudson. Koehler simply loved the stars. Alan—" her eyes found Conrad's—"wanted a chance to lead men under new conditions, test his power of adaptation as a coordinator. As a psychiatrist, my reason is primarily an interest in human reaction to such inhuman conditions as this, and possibly to help in case of maladjustments. But yours, Hudson, seems to be compensatory. Don't you get any *personal* satisfaction? Is a dream of some future vast conquest your whole motivation?"

"Is it?" Hudson was on his feet. His eyes were narrow. "I rather think it's my own affair; I'm not concerned with your psuedo-scientific prying."

Conrad intervened. "Break it up! I hope we can all realize how important unity is going to be from here on out. Come on and let's see what the control chamber has to say."

"It won't make any difference," said Hudson as he started up the tubular corridor.

"He's probably right," growled Koehler in his deep monotonous basso. "We're lost. I could have plotted our return from M-32; that was all arranged. But from wherever we are now—" He shrugged his huge shoulders.

INSIDE the control chamber, Koehler voiced one booming roar of astonishment, stood staring at the observation screen over the control panel. He stood there with his mouth hanging open, then whispered, "It can't be—it can't."

Conrad and Kaye saw no meaning in the screen, saw only dead blackness spread across with countless billions of lifeless frigid white dots. Hudson wasn't interested in the screen. His slender hands ran lovingly over the smooth gleaming surface of Kilroy, a big case of hard vacuum, aswirl with electrons and dynamic magnetic fields.

Hudson checked dials, gauges, graphs. "Kilroy's okay. Nothing wrong with the controls." That's what his voice said, noticed Conrad, but his eyes shifted, swirled with little specks of hidden fear. "Yes, I'm sure Kilroy has operated perfectly. But that chronometer—you, Koehler, lover of the stars. What do the stars say?"

"Ahhhh—" groaned Koehler. "Take a good long look at this chart; check it with what you see there on the screen. I'll have a padded cell rigged up."

They kept on looking.

Koehler cried. "Don't you see, you idiots? We're in section 80-epicenter- 57! That little light right there happens to be *Sol*! We're inside Pluto's orbit now. That's *Earth*."

Conrad managed a harsh aspirate. "It would appear that we have been to M-32 in Andromeda—and back again!"

"But we were in suspended animation," said Hudson with sudden violence. "You're crazy; it's an illusion."

"I think the evidence is obvious," said Conrad.

"But someone," said Hudson nervously, "someone among us had to have wakened to compute the return, reset the controls, replenish the anesthesia capsules, chart our course. And it's no coincidence, you know; that of all the infinitude of places we might have ended up, we've returned directly to Earth."

He looked at Koehler. "You're the only one who could have charted our return with such precision, Koehler; let's have an explanation."

Koehler's face reddened. "Okay, Hudson, what about you? You're the only one who could have worked over Kilroy for the return flight! I didn't plot any course back to Earth, but even if I had, you're the only one who could have gotten it back here."

Hudson lunged at Koehler who dodged the blow, grabbed at Hudson's jacket. Conrad stepped between them. "Relax," he said.

Kaye's voice was not too well controlled. "One among us, someone, must have awakened and accomplished the initial work necessary to return this ship. And he must have had a good reason. Doesn't anyone remember anything? "

No one did.

"Six hundred years—thrown away, lost," said Koehler oddly. "You'd think we would be glad it turned out this way. But we're not, are we? We're scared silly; we're scared because we know that something happened—something happened in Andromeda."

## CHAPTER TWO

KOEHLER was in the observation 'blister' working over a report. "For whom, or why, I wouldn't know," he had said. Hudson was stretched out on his bed reading from a volume he had brought along entitled: *Conquest—A History of Man's Evolutionary Motivation*, by Anschull Myers. A monistic, dogmatic work that would appeal only to paranoid thinking like Hudson's.

Conrad talked with Kaye. Her hand trembled as he held it and looked into her eyes; he always found a great deal of strength there.

"Well," she said. "I can't find out anything. We've all been subjected to both pentathol and hypno-rays, and our unconscious minds seem to be completely blank."

"But there must have been some processes even after we went into suspended animation," insisted Conrad.

"What kind of censor would block off both pentathol and hypno-rays, Alan? It's impossible; they'll dig out anything. Yet, I agree that there must be impressions there. Six-hundred years— nothingness—one might almost think that life and death and time as we've known it is just an illusion like the old mystics were trying to convince everyone of when we left Earth."

"Come off that," said Conrad with not all-mock concern. Then doggedly, "Space-warp, whatever that might be—well, there must be *something* to explain what happened. We could have been influenced unpredictably by displacement due to intense gravitational pull, or—"

Hudson threw the book aside, jumped to his feet. "But not in six hundred years. That would hardly have allowed us to circumvent a space-warp."

"I sit corrected," said Conrad wryly.

"You two console each other," Hudson snapped; "I'm going into the control chamber and take another look at Kilroy."

Kaye stared at the panel that closed automatically behind Hudson.

Conrad said, "Don't you sense that something's happened that is—well—forbidden? Sounds ridiculous doesn't it? Anyway, I feel like the answer's in my head, in spite of your pentathol and hypno-rays. But I can't dig it out."

Her answer was low; he scarcely heard her. "It must have been so alien there, so far from earth. What was it really like? Where were we, really?" Her voice rose, sharpened.

"Alan—we've got to find out where we were. And if we even

reached M-32 in Andromeda. What happened there? *Why, Alan?*"

The panel opened again. Koehler lurched into the room. He stood there, white face staring, his hair a bushy mass. His heavy mouth worked incoherently, then words spilled out. "Something's happened to Hudson! In the—control chamber!"

Conrad ran past him, Kaye followed, then Koehler. He heard the big man muttering, "I heard him go in. Then in a little while he—screamed; it sounded very bad."

Conrad found Hudson sitting on the mesh grid. His eyes bulged with a mad vacant kind of light. His hands pawed around in front of his greenish-white face. He slid back away from Conrad, moaning and crying softly.

"Hysteriform siezure," said Kaye quickly. "Maybe it's only temporary—I don't know. Meanwhile he's dangerous. I'll bring a hypo, and while he's unconscious we can lock him up in the spacesuit locker."

She returned quickly, efficiently injected Hudson while Conrad and Koehler held him with great effort. After he was locked up, inside the small room aft, Conrad asked Kaye to warm up some concentrates for them to eat before they hit Earth's atmosphere. Only a matter of a few minutes. He didn't want her to go with him then into the control chamber.

Koehler walked with Conrad as far as the door into the 'blister' where Koehler spent most of his time.

"I checked our course," he said. "We're hitting Earth dead center; a bull's eye. If I didn't know better I'd say I *did* chart this return from Andromeda; it was perfect." He closed the panel between them. Conrad went into the control chamber.

HE SAT THERE on the deep foam-rubber mats staring at the observation screen and at the smoothly clicking controls. That odd psychosomatic ache in his head was stronger now; a dull, nameless cold blew through his mind.

He shook it away partly, stared at the screen. Earth loomed strongly. The ship was still on automatic control, thought Conrad grimly. All in the hands of Kilroy now, just a lot of free electrons; but it was still more reliable than he would be. He could change the ship to manual and try bringing it in himself. He wasn't a specialist, though; he knew the principle but not the practical applicational experience. Only Hudson had that, and he was a raving madman.

Conrad gripped the edge of the control panel. He said into the intership audio. "Strap yourselves in your shock chairs as directed. It may be a pretty awkward landing."

Awkward was hardly the word. Kilroy was constructed to handle everything about the ship, including blastoffs and landings. But Kilroy didn't have free agency; it couldn't abstract. They'd probably smash into a charred lump.

Conrad stared awed, at looming Earth, shining twenty times brighter than the reflection from the moon. Black shadows and bright splashes of earthlight contrasted. Behind it the Sun was setting, surrounded by its corona and zodiacal light. The Moon, slightly blue with a white rim, shown behind.

Then the earth grew completely dark except where the Sun splattered down on its far half, a pool of light bright white in its center and radiating outward into dissipating orange and browns.

Conrad said into the intercom. "We're landing. We're back—home—" His voice choked off.

After six hundred years. But Earth had grown much older, though they on the ship had not. Evolutionary metabolism had an accumulative speed. After a slow start, it had moved with frightful rapidity. So much could have happened—

Conrad froze. They were low; he could see land looming that he had never really expected to see again. A splotched expanse of faded colors with tendrils of rivers and splashes of lakes faded strange blue. Along the far horizon stretched a blue and yellow mist.

He said with difficulty now into intercom. "This is it, Kaye. I'm leery about sending an advance notice. We've been away a long time. How the devil do we know what it's like now? What kind of a reception we'll get?"

A gigantic mass of green surged across the screen, sullenly flooding it. The automatic controls clicked frantically. The scene in the screen whirled, blurred in a senseless vortex. Nausea gripped Conrad, and he knew there had been a sudden mechanical let-up in acceleration. He felt the ripping bursts of repulsion rocket fire.

Dimly like a sound in a bad dream, he heard the grinding roar. It exploded in his brain. He found himself staggering blindly out of the control chamber. Thick blackness pulled at him as he staggered down the tilted corridor. He fought desperately against the insistent darkness wooing his mind, called for Kaye, many times.

Then he felt her hand, but he saw only a frightened blur that must have been her face. He heard Kohler yell. "Hudson—in the locker! I'll get him!"

Cold air. He knew they must have gotten out of the ship. Then a blast of heat seared his face as he stumbled over rough ground. Cool air struck his face again, "Kaye," he said. "Kaye!"

But neither her voice or hand were strong enough. He drifted away, dropped on down into a dense dark; it was soft and nice there. He would stay a while.

"Alan!" Conrad would know Kaye's voice anywhere, even in a displaced nebulae, in some closed Universe, even in Andromeda. If there was such a constellation, such a thing as 'time' at all in which you could lose six hundred years, and have it haunt you with some monstrous secret that you had to name, but feared to name—

"Alan, are you hurt badly? Say something!"

He tried to say something. He felt her wet face against his, her soft breath crying over him. He wanted to say something but couldn't.

"Alan—some men—they've taken us prisoner, I couldn't leave you. They have us in some kind of aircraft; they're taking us somewhere. They won't say anything, I'm afraid—Alan, please open your eyes!"

He managed it then with great effort. Things went round in a colored mist. Two men over controls...a 'blister' with clouds rushing past...a spherical flying craft...wingless...moving with silent speed...Kaye's face...tears...

"Shut up, Kaye. I hate girls who cry."

He heard her hysterical voice fading away. Her face whirled, got smaller, exploded in a rain of yellow lights. Soft slumber pulled, clung. Numbness crept in. He was drifting gently on clouds of sun-yellow beauty, through splashing craters of color, symphonies of soaring song.

*Andromeda*, a small voice said.

M-32 in Andromeda.

## CHAPTER THREE

OR HE HAD found Paradise. Men used to believe in Paradise, celestial spheres...

There was no familiar sky; it was golden liquid flowing down over a panorama of strange trees with foliage of topaz and sun amber that glistened and shimmered; and splashed with great seas of gigantic flowers of flaming scarlet; immense valleys of curtained mists, trembling rainbows of aureate lights, harlequined with cratered colors.

There was a lovely 'oneness', a fusion of form, of colors and music and more material reality in an ecstatic, endless chord, ringing, caroling, calling...

Gigantic birds soared through rainbow veils on wings of gleaming emerald, and pale tenuous figures swam in pearly flowing waters and showers of amethystine floods.

Sound, voices, tendrils, pale lovely faces, not human. They traveled with him, down an endless hall of silver light. He could move; he followed their beckoning call. Gentle, sweet voices fondling him with fingers of gentle curiosity.

He felt Kaye near him—but only as a shifting tremulous cloud of freed existence. He knew she was laughing with the sheer joy of unleashed care, and the sound bubbled and tinkled and echoed through the vaulted splendor of the place like the crashing of a million tiny crystalline bells. Where her teeth might have shown he saw only glittering shafts of ivory light.

A delicate petaled face peered wonderingly into his. A small red mouth opened. A little cry of tinkling horror shattered the beauty.

"*They will destroy*," the tiny voice said.

The cry rippled away, shimmered and shattered like exploding prisms. "*They will destroy!*"

*Evil.*

*Destruction. Destruction, forever.*

The luminous, webbed mist suddenly darkened in wavering black veins like spilled ink, running out in darting ragged rivers of despair. The flooding symphonies of carillon song shivered, dimmed into faint dissonances and grating dischords.

A chorus of those alien frightened petal faces cried. *Evil. Destruction forever and ever. Until nothing remains.*

*But only the one is evil. The other three carry the vital seeds that can grow to glory.*

*But the evil one must die.*

The sound and the glitter fused in discordant crescendos of horror. *They must die, the evil ones, though they have never learned to live.*

It vanished. The great color-splashed forests with its crimson flowers; the jeweled birds; the petal faces and the symphonies of song. A grey suffocation closed over him and choked him in acrid vileness. He smothered and cried out. And then there was only memory that died beneath grey depthless cold.

\*     \*     \*

AS HE OPENED his eyes, Conrad wondered if it were a dream. It seemed too alien and too utterly lovely, even for a dream; and it seemed to have no meaning, no possible significance. It wasn't' complete. He blinked his eyes. A big bronzed figure in transparent plastic clothing of a strange design stood there.

Conrad was sitting in a low metallic chair. A heavy helmet was on his head from which thin wire tentacles led away to large gauged units. The man handed him a glass of colorless liquid and said in a barely comprehensible English vernacular. "Drink this; you will feel better."

Having no reason to doubt him, Conrad complied; meanwhile he studied the big man. His skin was dark, his face angular—not cruel—worse than cruel. It was a completely amoral face. The big man's two feet added up to only eight toes.

Conrad saw part of the big room. It was gleaming with metal, naked and harsh with no warmth. No warmth anywhere. Everything metal, benches, the machines covered with dials and gauges; there were two large tri-dimensional screens waiting lifelessly on the auto-luminescent wall.

The stuff he had drank was potent; the throbbing was gone. The burning fled from his eyes, left them clear and bright. The big bronzed man's pale, emotionless eyes looked at him without any reaction at all that Conrad could see, unless it were vague distant curiosity.

"Just call me guinea pig," said Conrad. The man stared, Conrad heard a nervous laugh to his right and behind him. "Kaye!" he turned.

She was in the same predicament as he. In a low metallic chair with a silver helmet covering her violet-black hair. "Thank Mars you're conscious, Alan! I'd about given up hope."

"I'm all right, Kaye. And you're looking swell, too."

The big man mused. "Curious types. It's odd; your minds resist our probers. But you'll give in to us eventually. There are many ways remaining."

Conrad still looked at Kaye. Like him, she was bruised, cut, her clothing tattered ribbons. "Kaye, how long have we been here?"

"Just a little while. They've been trying to probe our brains. Evidently they've found nothing at all. He thinks all that pre-suspended animation content of our minds is only fantasy thinking, that we've been intentionally conditioned with meaningless thought to mislead them. He thinks we're enemies, of course, I—I haven't told him anything." Her eyes finished a meaningful message. *Don't talk, Alan. Don't tell them a thing.*

The big man brushed his thin nose with a slender hand. His voice was terse, without color. "You submen—it's hard to believe you're descendants of human stock. Living like animals in the forest, ignorant, stupid mystics! Come—what were you doing near *Shiva?*"

Conrad shrugged. Kaye said. "Shiva, that's the name of this city."

"Please," the questioner said. "Enough pretense." He turned back to Conrad. "Now. What were you doing out there? We know that you *Upinshads* are childishly plotting against Shiva. Even though you mystics claim to have nothing to do with material things such as machines, we know you had some kind of weapon out there in the forest. Children can start fires. What were you doing there?"

"I don't know; really I don't."

"You must know. The forest burned for half a mile. What kind of a weapon were you trying to use?"

"I don't know of any weapon."

"Where did you get this odd kind of cloth? When did you animals stop wearing the skins of animals?"

Conrad shook his head, studying the man. His questions didn't hold any real urgency. He wanted to know, but it didn't really matter. Evidently the Upinshads were far indeed beneath the frigid dignity of the people of Shiva.

The man stepped back. "This sort of secretive activity has forced the inevitable upon you *Upsinshads*. I can tell you because you will soon be rendered either mindless or dead, and won't be able to communicate the knowledge. The time is here; you've known it was coming. We, the Destroyers, are ready to strike outward, boundlessly outward as is our destiny. As part of it, we're going to exterminate you Upinshads. All of you. In fact, we're going to exterminate all of you within a day; we are only waiting for the decree from the Grand Shamdhi."


THE BIG man pressed a minute stud on a small round crystal on his wrist. A somewhat feminine voice, whiny and distorted, came out of it. "Yes, Lingan."

The man, Lingan, said tersely. "Come up here, Krisha. The subman's conscious now."

Conrad thought rapidly. The loneliness and shock were gone, drowned by desperate urgency.

Well, this was Earth; but it didn't mean much. He had not expected it to be much the same anyway; he had never expected to get back to Earth at all. But with his background of general knowledge and basics from the Synthesis Schools, he did recall the significance of the names.

Shiva—which was ancient Indian or Hindustan, and it meant Destroyer. City of the Destroyers. And Upinshad, too, was ancient Eastern in origin. The Upinshads were devoted to discussions of philosophy and 'intellectual mysticism'—whatever that was, or had been.

Maybe the ancient philosophies of the East had fused with

Western culture. The trend had been under way long ago when they had left for Andromeda. A rebound from the futile walls of positive science into mystical worlds of Bhrama, Yoga, and the other philosophies that had arisen, supposedly, in Pamir sixty thousand years before Western Culture had started on its materialistic pathway of machine worship.

But the Upinshads had been considered a rather exalted order among the ancients. Here they were considered submen. Kaye and he were also considered as submen. "You two," he had said inclusively. Then what had happened to Hudson and Koehler? For evidently these men of Shiva knew nothing about either of them nor—

Evidently they hadn't found the ship either.

*What had happened to the spaceship?*

A figure that had every qualification of femininity in theory, but appearing to have very little, if any, in practice, entered with machine-like precision. She gazed coldly at Conrad. "He won't confess either, Lingan?"

"Nothing. Pretends complete ignorance."

"Maybe they are mindless. The Upinshads do have peculiar mental ability, Lingan; they have some sort of control. Remember that Yogin we captured and put through Ward Six? I still insist that he willed his heart to stop; there was no physical reason for him to die."

"Krisha, let's not discuss it here. I'll admit it. A subman is liable to do anything: they're unpredictable, like animals."

"Look here," she said to Conrad. "What were you two doing out there? Did you have some kind of machine?"

"I don't remember," said Conrad. "My head aches."

"Well," she said carelessly. "We'll have to use the electrodes. The electrode needles should find something besides these meaningless fantasies about a pre-war spaceflight, and such nonsense. You realize what will happen, of course, if we use them. The mind is almost completely destroyed; only thalamic levels remain. We've sent more than one subman back into the forests as an example, with no mind. If you cooperate, we won't have to use electrode needles. You'll be permitted quick and painless extermination, and that's more than the rest of you Upinshads will get. We're going to spray that valley with atomic dust, you know, among other things."

It would be better, thought Conrad with an inward shudder, if they gloated, or looked even a little sadistic. But there was no visible emotion at all. He bluffed, for time, for knowledge. "I would tell you, but I can't remember. There was some sort of machine, then an explosion. Now there's just a dull ache in my head."

"There was a machine," she said, turning to Lingan. "It's possible he's telling the truth about the rest of it, but it isn't worth our time. Soon they'll all be exterminated. Send him to Ward Seven." She started for the door. "Peculiar dialect, sounds like an animal."

She paused by the door. "See you later, Lingan."

"Yes. Thanks, Krisha."

He turned back toward Conrad. "Well, that's it—the best way for you, too. You'll escape the very painful death the other Upinshads will know. Extermination in Ward Seven is utterly painless. You two are very fortunate Upinshads."

"I'm not quite convinced," said Conrad, and tried to think of a way out. He wasn't manacled at all, except by the metal helmet. Evidently these Shivans considered the Upinshads too inferior even to bother with on that score.

*I don't want to die,* he thought. *Kaye either. We've been too close to it, and we know what it is.*


## CHAPTER FOUR

LINGAN removed the metal helmet from Kaye's head, laid it on one of the metal benches. He turned to repeat the process with Conrad. Conrad tensed. Behind Lingan, Kaye was creeping forward, the heavy helmet raised high; a fierce determination drowned the fear in her black eyes.

The helmet made a pleasant, hollow thud against Lingan's skull. His eyes rolled up, and his body sagged down into Conrad's arms. "Magnificent," said Conrad, sincerely. "That was quick thinking; you're a real subwoman."

He told her his quickly conceived idea even as he started

271

stripping the torn cloth from his body, substituting the sleek, skin-tight transparent stuff wrapped around the inert Lingan. Looking down at the results of the completely transparent stuff, he said wryly, "This is almost indecent."

"An amoral society," elaborated Kaye in a small weak voice. Then, stirred by professional enthusiasm, her voice strengthened. "Eastern and Western thought merged during our little absence, Alan. Now neither of them has but vague resemblance to the old. The caste system has merged with Western love of militarism and power. Shiva, the Destroyer, rules. And philosophers, intellectuals; are now living like animals, considered as subhuman."

"Interesting, but we've got to get out of here. The forest would look wonderful to me right now, even as an animal. We've got to find Koehler and Hudson and," he hesitated, "—and the ship."

"Yes," Kaye said it with an uneasy flicker of her long lashes. "The ship. When I led you away from there, the ship was still visible."

Conrad moved the stud on Lingan's wrist radio as he had watched Lingan do. That familiar, pseudo-feminine voice whined distortedly. "Yes, Lingan."

Conrad was no actor, but he made a good try. The small receiver distorted his voice; that helped. Also he was terse. "Come here." Rather peremptory, but effective.

Conrad moved over quickly to the smoothly paneled metal door. Krisha walked in mechanically, with certainty. She stumbled, her eyes widened, her mouth opened. Conrad covered it with his hand. Her body was suddenly twisting, wiry cords; but he held her.

"Sorry," he panted, "but somehow this doesn't seem an affront to chivalry." He didn't hit her hard; but she collapsed soundlessly. "If she had any doubts about my being a subman, I'm sure her doubts have vanished."

He dragged her over to the metal chair. Together they stripped her clothing off, and Kaye put the filmy material on. It looked good on her. Or rather Kaye looked good; they studied each other.

"Fantastic," he said, then they went out through the door and down a long straight metal hall.

"No warmth here anywhere," said Conrad.

"It's natural enough," whispered Kaye. "Take every dominant trend of Earth when we left it, carry it out six hundred years along logical lines of development and where does it lead?"

"Extermination."

"You get here, inevitably. There's a synthesis of Western and ancient Eastern philosophy, which were always diametrically opposed. Western mechanical positivism has been developed by the warrior class of the East. The thinkers, philosophers, idealists, relegated to barbarism. The ruling class are the militarists and materialists, worshiping machines, gadgets, science-power, here in Shiva—amorality, statism, individual unimportance. Racial-group superiority. Subservience to state or council. It's all here; only a miracle could have made it any different."

"A bigger miracle will have to get us out of the City of Shiva," muttered Conrad as they walked with slow caution down the long cold hall.

Kaye didn't comment. The hall branched into several corridors. They walked to the left. Around a smooth curve, they found a great oval opening looking over a magnificent city—all metal. A blinding glare like molten steel struck their eyes. Mighty buildings rose to awesome heights, many blocks square at their base, cut through with skyways, and highways. Tubes of metal wound between the buildings.

Conrad leaned against the edge of the high opening, staring with rising hopelessness. That seemed an insurmountable barrier with no weapons, knowledge.

One of those spherical flying craft settled in the opening, clicking against a runway at the opening's base. The panel slid back; a thin slightly grey man started to step out.

"Let's grab the other horn," suggested Conrad, and hit the man in the face. As the figure stumbled back into the flying craft, Conrad and Kaye leaped in after him; they heard someone behind them yelling in sudden alarm.

CONRAD cast one wild glance at the control board, around the rest of the aircraft. Wingless, atomic-powered, he remembered its silent flight. The few levers on the control board were meaningless.

"Try to operate the thing," he urged as he turned, faced the men running toward them. "I'll try to keep these warriors out of here."

Kaye's voice trembled. She' had been through a lot, thought Conrad grimly as he kicked one of the dark men in the groin, parried a peculiar flat-handed punch of the other.

Dimly, he heard Kaye's voice. "I was conscious—I remember this—"

"Try to get this door shut," yelled Conrad, as the heel of the man's hand smashed hard across his nose. Tears blinded him; he dodged. The sharp ridge of hand chopped across his back. An intense pain hitched through his stomach. This man's face was a grinning mask of emotionless purpose.

Dazedly, he heard the clicking sound. The panel shot across, blocked out the face. Conrad staggered back, turned to stand beside Kaye.

Odd that these warriors carried no weapons, at least here in their City of metal. He watched her fumbling at the control levers. But maybe there was only one city of Shiva, one warrior class, so there were no opponents, no need for weapons ordinarily.

Then what did they destroy? Surely there was more to destroy than merely the Upinshads. That had sounded merely an incidental part of a vaster plan for destruction. The Universe—that must be an analogy of some sort.

The craft heaved outward. He heard a tearing grind beneath them, then a sudden, sickening acceleration hurled them skyward. "Good girl," he gasped; "get everything out of this crate you can!"

He staggered over to the cowling, looked out and down. They were suddenly very high. Conrad could see all of the City, miles of surrounding country. And the left half of the City... Conrad gazed at the spectacle, awed, overwhelmed. A gigantic bowl and in it were at least half a thousand gigantic spaceships. They were balanced with noses skyward on four wide spread-leveling legs. They were huge, formidable; and they were waiting.

He mentioned them to Kaye. She kept on jerking the levers, but Conrad continued verbalizing thought, and his thought had sheered away from the ships. Something horrible about their gigantic silence. Something—unthinkable.

"This City isn't so large, Kaye. Looks like Southern California country. The ocean and peninsula—but that tremendous forest is new. And the City is many times smaller than it used to be. Florida is different, too; must be a lot lower average temperature now. The forest is all pines, conifers. I don't see any other towns or villages anywhere…"

He turned, swore softly, Kaye had passed out, was sprawled limply across the control panel.

He eased her down on the soft rubber-like synthetic of the floor. Shadows passed over the ship, darkened the cowling. Pursuers, small deadly skycraft, circling, darting. He saw long narrow snouts snap out of the crafts. Guns, power weapons of some kind. He saw no explosion but felt the effects. The craft buckled, sheered wildly in boiling air. Smoke curled delicately from the control panel. The interior was suddenly a dense choking mass of acrid gas.

He jiggled the control levers with desperate indiscrimination, he punched buttons. He felt the sudden rapid drop of their fall diminish, start again, then plunge in a plummeting path straight down. The cowling burst open. An icy wind roared through, almost sucking him out of the craft.

He saw a mass of high pointed pine peaks rushing up into his face. The skycraft spun into the topmost branches. A sweet pungent scent of pine clouded him. He heard the crash of limbs, the soft brushing of foliage. The craft groaned, bounded high in the air, crashed again, this time striking thick solid branches, and trunks, and plunging to earth.

Conrad, buffeted around, managed to protect his head with his arms. The skycraft dropped quickly, struck a large branch, rolled over and thudded heavily and with finality against solid earth.

HE DRAGGED Kaye out of the wrecked craft onto a cool, shadowed expanse of brown pine needles. The air was crisp, cool, moving softly through the scented boughs. He carried Kaye a while until she was conscious again, and insisted on walking. Then they ran weakly through the sun-dappled quiet of the great forest.

Sometimes when they could see the solid expanse of blue sky through the high small openings between the trees, they also saw their pursuers circling doggedly.

Once they hid themselves in thick brush while two warriors of Shiva edged past with guns poised, eyes searching. They did have weapons now, elaborately coiled mechanisms suggesting basic energy. They were available when needed.

The effects of the stimulant Lingan had given them wore off soon. Old, prolonged weariness seeped into their blood, slowed them; it began to grow noticeably colder as evening slipped in through the great silent trees. And finally they dropped down, unable to force themselves another step.

Kaye was shivering. They crawled beneath the low hanging boughs of a small spruce that formed a kind of shelter from the cold wind and searching eyes. They lay there in each other's arms, fighting off the invading cold, "Babes in the darkling woods," said Conrad softly.

But Kaye was already sleeping.

Conrad remembered the nursery rhymes he had studied as a part of a course on pre-atomic psychological expression. Part of a study of inherent death impulses expressed in children during the old systems. It had a kind of terrifying nostalgia as those children's songs usually had.

*"Do you remember, a long time ago, two poor little babes whose names I don't know—went out to play one bright summer's day, and were lost in the woods I've heard people say—"*

The warmth from Kaye's body seeped through him slowly; a warm blanket of lassitude settled over him. Above him a night bird sang mournfully. Some large shadowy form padded by.

*Went out to play one bright summer's day—*

Eighteen hundred thousand light years—*and were lost in the woods I've heard people say.*

*And when they were dead the robins so red brought strawberry leaves and over them spread—*

M-32 in Andromeda—the petal faces and horror that shattered that beautiful land? Was that a memory of Andromeda?

Extermination. Philosophers in caves sprayed with atomic dust.

*And sang sweet songs the whole day long.*

Poor babes in the woods.

# CHAPTER FIVE

A SHAFT of liquid, gold moonlight shone strangely on the man who had parted the low hanging boughs and was awaking him. A white-headed elderly man, with a sun-leathered face of what seemed to be infinite wisdom and kindness.

He smiled gently at Conrad, stopped shaking him, and stood up. He was clothed in animal skins; his cap was silver and black fur. Strong white teeth gleamed warmly. "Hiyah," he said. "You two had better come with me. It isn't exactly safe here. Bears and big cats get pretty hungry after dark."

Conrad said, "How did you know about us?"

"Saw you crash and followed you. Had to be careful though; the Kshatya were thick as flies around here for a while."

Kaye stirred, sat bolt upright, stared, then relaxed when she got a good view of the stranger.

*Kshatya*, mused Conrad; a slight alteration of another Eastern word for warrior class. *Kshatriya*. The men of Shiva.

The older man held out a gnarled hand, helped Kaye to her feet. "We'd better hurry. You'll be safe with us—that is, as long as we're safe from attack. I guess that won't be for very long. But meanwhile the Rigeda fire burns brightly tonight, and you're welcome to join our great *Aum*, even if it's for the last time."

"Sure," said Conrad. They followed him along a moonlighted path through the towering trees. The wind sang a gentle night song that had undertones of sorrow, and old, old pain.

Kaye hadn't said anything. She walked pensively, staring at the elderly man leading them.

The Rigeda Fire. Conrad dug into his memory. He didn't get the fire part, but the Rig-veda was a collection of hymns which the Aryans brought with them to India—thousands of years before Christ brought his Eastern beliefs to the West. Eastern philosophy had been the big movement throughout the world, when the four had left on their escapist flight to another constellation. And the theory then had been that soon Eastern thought as developed in Asia was to come again out of the incomputable past to rescue Western culture from suicidal materialism.

Even in his time, materialists, positivists, scientists, had been succumbing to 'intellectual mysticism' by the millions. But somehow the fusing of the two philosophies had resulted in a terrifying final form of materialism due to Western culture's obsession with machines, power, with metals and lust for conquest.

And *Aum*. A part of the mystical processes of Yoga. A great sound symbol which was supposed to set up certain rhythms and vibrations to enforce one's fusion with the allness, the oneness, of Karma.

Well, Conrad was no mystic; he wasn't a positivist either. He had always enjoyed the freedom of abstract theory. But he wasn't anything now; he was lost. It looked as though everyone was lost, caught at the end of a blind alley.

The Eastern cults had said materialism was the wrong course, an illusion. And the development of atomic weapons had made such a philosophy most attractive. But during their absence, in suspended animation, while cities rose and fell and ideas with them, what had really happened?

"Ah—hold it a minute will you?" called Conrad.

The man turned. "Call me Risha. What's on your mind, Conrad?"

"But how did you know," Conrad began, then dropped it. "This is Kaye."

Risha nodded, "I know. There are few secrets among true *Upinshads*."

*Risha*, Conrad knew, had meant sage or teacher. He said, "Risha, we're strangers in our own house, or our own world, I'll explain to you about us before we go on any further, if you have the time."

"Go ahead. Talk," said Risha. "I'd appreciate it if you would hurry though. I'd like to get to the Rigeda Fire before the attack."

The attack. Conrad had almost forgotten about Lingan's statement about the extermination of the Upinshads. But he went on, explained everything about themselves. He was brief. You could be brief with words. With one word, one could say— eternity.

AFTER HEARING their story, Risha looked up at the sky. His long leathery face shone oddly in the pale light.

"You believe me, Risha?"

"Of course. Our Rigeda includes your journey from earth. Few records survived the war except in song."

"There was war after we left?" said Kaye in a hushed whisper.

"Yes." Risha moved away. "Only a few survived." His voice lightened. "We'll sing about your flight tonight at the Rigeda Fire."

His gaunt figure passed into dense shadow, back into a splash of moonlight. A large dark shape crashed away through the undergrowth. Fireflies wavered among the leaves. Somewhere below them an invisible stream churned down over worn stones.

"It's beautiful, this kind of life," said Kaye. "And they are going to destroy it—"

Conrad called to Risha. "Why are the *Kshatriya* going to attack you? What have they to gain?"

Risha's voice floated back to them, seeming a part of the wind through the pines, the soft voice of the night. "Because we spurn the use of machines and all the mores of their kind of culture, they think we're inferior beings. And it is part of their belief that 'inferior' peoples should be exterminated. Then, in spite of their thinking us inferior, they fear us a little; they know we've developed mental abilities they don't understand. There are three castes of us Upinshads living in isolated Leagues in this valley. The *Kshatriya* will finish us this time; there's nothing we can do. There's really nothing we want to do."

"Don't you want to go on living?" asked Kaye.

"Yes. It would be more interesting to know what part of reality the surface called 'death' is before meeting it, but it doesn't make any difference. In *Samyama* we have learned much. Still we've found only a small part of reality. Given more time, we might know Karma. But we haven't the time; perhaps in some other plane we will go on with the search."

"We know nothing about what happened during our absence," said Kaye.

"Much has happened. Much destruction, regression, near extinction. The ancients knew the road to Karma, the road through three-dimensional illusion into fourth-dimensional reality; they knew many centuries even before your time, before any records of the Western world began. But the Destroyers came and distorted it, and materialism hid reality. Remember—through history there have always been these people who sought only to destroy and conquer and destroy. There have been others, the thinkers and philosophers; but the Destroyers have won because they forced the thinkers to accept their illusory philosophy. Now it's too late to fight back; we would have to fight them on their own materialistic plane, which would be futile. Violence only creates more violence; means must justify the ends."

"The war must have been a horrible thing," said Kaye. "When we left for Andromeda, there seemed little chance for a war—not with atomic power."

"People feared an atomic war," said Risha sadly. "But trapped by unreal material philosophies they seemed helpless. Eastern philosophy swept the world, urging non-attachment to the 'things of this visible world'. Even scientists flocked into the various cults by the thousands. For it was science, really—cosmology that was aware of many other realities underlying the narrow concepts of the phenomenal world. This ancient Eastern philosophy spread like a great fire. But it came too late. War. It was almost final. Only a few left..."

RISHA WALKED silently for a while. The night seemed to echo an unfinished thought, a voiceless whisper of horror.

"It left few people on the Earth. Most of the heavily inhabited places became radioactive seas of poison. Certain parts of the world remained untouched. This was the one most attractive to those wretched people who still lived. And the City of Shiva rose. The others, the *Upinshads* who sought true reality, were driven into the forests and scorned as idiots. For we retained the old teachings, and we knew that the 'reality' of the materialists was illusion, and that it led only to final destruction.

"Now the *Kshatya* are through with Earth. It offers no roads to conquest; they're abandoning it in ruins and death."

"I saw the spaceships," said Conrad. "They're *all* leaving?"

"Most of them; the others will be killed. There are only a few thousand of them."

Risha paused and looked to the West. "They never intend to come back to Earth. They're going to burn their conquered worlds behind them. Conquered worlds, conquered galaxies. For them, there's no end."

Conrad felt Kaye's hand, suddenly damp and cold. "It seems too fantastic and ridiculous, yet it isn't really," she said. "It was bound to end this way. If the pattern is conquest, it must find expression. What man imagines, he creates. What he imagines, he destroys."

"And the attack will be soon," said Conrad.

"We know it will be within a day. We've studied, spent many years and generations in the halls of *Samyama*. But Karma's still a very distant concept for us. We've caught moments of reality through the three dimensional veils. But we haven't even started yet. If we only had more time; relaxing time—"

"But surely there's some way to fight or resist them," insisted Conrad.

"Violence?" Risha laughed softly. "That's only part of the old, old fallacy. The means determine the nature of the ends produced. Violence can never end in anything but more violence; that's only part of the illusion of a restricted illusory three dimensional world."

"*Babes in the woods,*" said Conrad, and caught himself smiling grimly, without humor.

Kaye said. "Remember, Alan, how positivistic methods were breaking down? People were dissatisfied."

"Naturally," said Risha. "Everyone was afraid. Five senses, three dimensions. And the rulers held people within that restricted area like herded animals, wouldn't let them escape. But these five organs of sense are in reality just feelers by which we feel the world around us. The three-dimensional man lives groping about. *He's never seen anything!*"

"Scared of the dark," said Conrad.

Her hand tightened. Far away toward the West they heard a rumble of what might have been thunder. "They're getting ready," said Risha.

The three walked on, coming to a sheer cliff looming up blackly, and Risha led them inside, around a black corridor and after a while into a large subterranean cavern. There were people, people in animal skins sitting around a fire. Philosophers in caves.

The Rigeda Fire. The people were singing. Hymns out of a lost

Hindu history sixty thousand years old, interwoven with many sagas of the Intervening centuries.

THE PEOPLE greeted them, acknowledged their presence, their history, with gentle tolerant smiles, then returned to their singing, dark eyes reflecting the flames of the Regeda Fire.

Risha stood silhouetted against the flames.

"*Manu*," he said ringingly. The singing died. "*Samyama*."

There was wisdom here, thought Conrad. He saw it in the twisting shadows in the cave, in the faces staring into the flames. Wisdom of many ages. Mysticism had fused with science; science's primary concern, ultimately, had always been with the invisible. Twentieth century mysticism had been the beginning of a newer science of the fourth dimension, of non-Aristotelianism, the same as alchemy and astrology had led the way into 'sciences' of a more acceptable kind.

They had *felt* the fourth dimension.

"*When we reach the fourth dimension, we'll see that the world of three dimensions doesn't really exist, and has never existed! That it was the creation of our own fantasy, a phantom host, an optical illusion—anything one pleases excepting only reality.*"

But Ouspensky had talked only to the stars. A few people heard. Too late. *Shiva* ruled.

"*Infinity isn't an hypothesis, but a fact, and such a fact is the multi-dimensionality of space and all it implies, mainly the unreality of everything three dimensional.*

"*A restriction of only two dimensions is inconceivable to a man. A restriction of three dimensions is equally inconceivable to a fourth-dimensional consciousness. And the fourth dimension...*"

The Hindus had called it Karma: "*Everything will exist in it always.*" It was the eternal now of the Hindus. But whatever one labeled it, perhaps these Upinshads, hindered by ancient forest mysticism, were again on the right track. They needed time.

People had broken faith with 'science' and had sought a higher reality, which they called Karma. The dissatisfaction with science had been well grounded, and the complaints about its insolvency entirely just, because science had really entered a cul de sac out of which there had seemed no escape; and the official recognition of the fact that the direction it had taken had been wrong had been realized—too late!

These philosophers living in caves practicing ancient Hindu rituals of non-attachment, were on a saner road. But the Men of Shiva were destroying them. Because the Men of Shiva had been made for destruction.

*Aum. Aum. Aum.*

The chant rose stronger and vibrantly from those around the fire. Conrad gazed into the hypnotic flames.

And suddenly, without any physical motivation, the flames burst, lifted up and up, roaring and sighing. But no one had put any fuel in the fire!

He remembered. The power to identify oneself with any object! Samyama!

The brilliant body of the Rigeda Fire lifted higher and higher, ate out the high cold shadows of the cavern's roof.

And died.

## CHAPTER SIX

THE DISTANT thunder sounds continued, rolling nearer and nearer from the City of Shiva. The ceremony of Samyama, of identification, continued also, oblivious to their approaching destruction.

*Aum. Aum. Aum. Aum—*

Kaye whispered. "The psychologists had words for this sort of thing. Autosuggestion was one. That was a good word, then; what does it mean now? Alan—look!"

The pile of wood fuel beside the fire seemed to shimmer, shift. The top piece shivered, trembled as though some invisible nervous hand were grasping it. Abruptly it rolled down from the top of the heap, scuttled across the stone floor like a live thing; it slowed, slowed, did not quite reach the flames.

The chanting of the sound-symbol *Aum* died in a sigh of resigned failure; then the Rigeda hymns began again.

Risha sat down beside them. "You see. We only touch the barest fringe of the higher plane of reality in which all is one. We need so much more time. But Shiva wins."

He sat staring into the flames, his lean face like rough brown stone in the light. "Karma," he whispered. "The unbroken oneness—only the invisible, the hidden, preserve for us the illusion of time."

'You believe that everything is—is one," said Kaye. "So death is only a part, a facet of a larger perspective?"

Risha nodded, his eyes bright with inner fire. "We know nothing of reality. Only glimpses, touches. Death isn't an end, any more than birth is a beginning. It's all part of the 'eternal now'. Our three dimensional world we see is only surface, part of the fourth dimensional plane. Death's only a part of a part of a surface. We have no fear of it."

Conrad was on his feet. "I wish I had your faith, Risha, my friend. To me, the invisible remains invisible. Death has a horrible finality for me." He lifted Kaye by the hand. "Let's get out of here—as far from this valley as we can."

She nodded. "I guess I'm still with you in the third dimension; I think I'd prefer almost any dimension to the third right now. Let's go."

"You can't escape the Men of Shiva," said Risha. "Or even if you could, why prolong the inevitable?"

"We've got to live," said Conrad. "I don't know why; maybe with you Upinshads, working long enough, we could find out why."

Risha smiled with sad tolerance, "You still think in positivistic terms, but you're a real Upinshad, anyway. You're not evil; you have little of the Kshatya's blood. Just remember, Conrad that your three-dimensional world is narrow, only a concept involving small sections and surfaces of reality. Remember that the cause of the visible is the invisible."

Conrad smiled tightly. "You coming with us, Risha?"

"Where? The Ship of Shiva will turn this whole continent into a radioactive hell. They'll leave no intelligent life on this world when they go!"

But he followed them out of the cavern into the clear cool night, and a soft-voiced grey-haired woman held his hand and walked with him.

OUTSIDE they stood for a moment listening to the distant thunder.

"Have you no machines, no weapons at all?" persisted Conrad.

Risha shrugged. "The mind is its own reality—it contains the stuff from which we create our illusory machines. The mind needs no shiny symbols, no machines to grind it to destruction. Wha—"

Interrupting Risha's 'truth', a shape stumbled toward them from the line of darkly ingrown trees. "Koehler!" yelled Conrad.

The big man stumbled to his knees. Conrad dropped beside him, supported him there. Koehler's face was scratched and bloody; he gazed blindly at Conrad and the others, then groaned sudden recognition. "Hello, Conrad. How's the coordinating business?" He coughed, gasped for breath.

Conrad felt his big frame shiver. "Where've you been, Koehler? What's happened? Where's the ship?"

Koehler licked his heavy lips. "I guess I'm insane. I can't figure anything; I feel like I've been walking in a fog; I can't see anything!"

"How'd you get here?"

"The Ship brought me. It landed over there about a hundred yards. I heard your voices, I guess, I don't know. I saw a light. Something chased me, something big that roared. If it had caught me—"

"What happened after we landed? You were going to unlock Hudson—"

"Yes, well—I stayed in the ship, tried to get to the locker and get Hudson out. I didn't make it; the ship knocked me out. Hudson was still in that locker when I came to. He was yelling. He kept saying, *'Stop the Ship! Damn them! Stop the ship!' "*

Koehler lifted a big raw hand to his eyes. "You won't believe this—but about then I began to realize that the ship was in the air, coasting along on stratospheric power. I ran into the control chamber. There wasn't anyone there, never had been. Listen now—I know that the ship blasted off alone!"

"What?"

"Sure, I'm crazy; I can't help it. It landed again, too—and no one was at the controls. The ship went out to sea, landed out there in the water, just off shore in a fog, and sat there. It was waiting for something. I could hear Hudson screaming, but I knew I shouldn't let him out."

Koehler raised his tortured eyes. "Conrad! The ship's alive!"

Koehler threw off Conrad's hands, staggered to his feet, weaved. He stared at Risha, at the woman standing beside him gazing serenely at the sky. A flash of white fire curved upward exploding in pyrotechnic pillars far away above the mountains. "You say the ship brought you here, Koehler?"

Koehler's mouth twitched, "You don't believe me, and I don't care."

"I believe you," said Conrad. "The ship brought you here, right?"

"Right or wrong, it did," said Koehler. His hands trembled as he pushed them through his thickly entangled hair. "Look, I don't know what really happened. I know Hudson wasn't piloting the ship, nor I. I kept Hudson locked up and as far as I know he still is. I wouldn't let him out; he's a screaming maniac. *Stop the ship!* he keeps yelling over and over. *Destroy the ship!* I don't know why he keeps yelling that, do you?"

"Not yet," said Conrad half to himself. "The ship landed on the sea, you say—then what?"

"Well, it just sat there on the water; it was waiting. I don't know what for. It was so still there, so quiet in the fog. I tried to get out of the ship, but the doors wouldn't open. When I tried to work the lever, I couldn't. I couldn't touch it. I tried—"

Koehler sucked in his breath. "I wondered about the ship. I couldn't stop moving. I was afraid; I admit it. Every time I started to think, I got scared. 'Eighteen hundred thousand light years,' I'd say to myself, 'and no one remembers anything. Six hundred years all shot to hell.' And all the time I could feel the ship around me. It's alive, I know it's alive!"

Koehler's shaggy head twisted. "Who's this?"

Conrad explained; he told about the City of Shiva, and about the Upinshads, the philosophers who had been driven into the caves; about the Kshatriya.

"It's time now; they're going to strike," the woman beside Risha said in her calm serene way. And Risha answered. "Yes. This is the Time of Shiva."

Koehler started to speak, stood silently gazing skyward. There was a tremendous streaming blue fire, then a wave of wind. Far down the valley was audible the repercussions of great explosions. A blast of boiling air swept them. The great pines bent low, snapped back, quivering.

"This is madness," yelled Koehler. He shook his fists at the rising mushrooms of fire. "They're planning to conquer the Universe?" He threw back his head and laughed wildly. "The Universe! A few hundred ships manned by a bunch of crackpots who—" He stopped laughing, stared at Conrad. His voice dropped to a whisper.

"But they can, can't they? They're human; they can go on and on once they get started. What can stop them? *What?* I hate myself because I'm human too. They'll go on destroying, tearing everything out of their way until—" his voice died.

A buried ache in Conrad's head shot out burning sparks. A small musical voice, trembling like shattered glass, said: *"They will destroy."*

*"Destruction. Destruction, forever."*

Risha put an arm about the woman.

Conrad heard him say. "If we'd only a little more time, Madge. We're at the gate."

Another tremendous explosion shook the world. A gigantic flash shone like a new sun across the sky; the whole country was lighted by a searing brilliance, like the strange glowing of a new and deadly aurora borealis, golden, purple, violet, gray, and blue, rising through intensities of heat into the X-ray part of the spectrum, into invisibility. The darkness of the forest became pits of flashing light; every distant peak and crevasse and ridge assumed a horrible clarity and beauty.

A few seconds later came the air blasts pressing hard, followed by howling roaring sound. A wind of hurricane proportion hurled them along the ground. There was doomed finality in the awesome roar and supernal fire.

# CHAPTER SEVEN

CONRAD crawled against the howling winds to Kaye's side. He heard the blundering frantic flight of animals crashing wildly through the glimmering hell; saw wild eyes blazing madly as they bounded down the valley toward the sea. He gripped Kaye's arm. "The ship," he gasped. "It's our only chance." He turned, yelled at Koehler a few feet away. Fine debris rained on them in clouds of minute spray.

Koehler stood facing into the wind, shaking his fists, swearing.

"Snap out of it, Koehler. Lead us to the ship! Know where it is?"

"I guess so. I can try to find it. But I'll not board her, not that ship, it's alive!"

"Maybe *we* can stay alive if we find it."

Clutching each other's hands they fought their way into the moaning wind. Conrad turned, yelled at Risha who stood with his arm about the woman. They were looking quietly toward the distant fires. Conrad turned away from them. They didn't care; nothing mattered. They had known a part of Karma, a touch of 'reality'. Maybe these Upinshads were insane. What was reality? Karma. Fourth-dimension. Words. But no one had ever answered the enigma poised by Kant. "*What was the thing-in-itself?*"

*Babes in the woods.*

Conrad yelled hoarsely. Koehler had broken away, was running ahead through the mad, distorted shadows between tortured trees. Conrad and Kaye stumbled after him. "You sure this is the way?"

Koehler's lurching form weaved faster through the toppling forest. Weird lights played across the sky; tides of fear-crazed animals, whining and shrieking, surged blindly down the disintegrating valley.

Ahead of Conrad, Koehler's body was ripping through brush, tearing branches aside. Conrad heard him swearing and crying by turns. Kaye struggled silently, her face a white blob, drained by the glaring whiteness of the distant heat.

"It's right here somewhere," shouted Koehler. "Somewhere—"

A trembling roar rolled over them in a colossal sea. Conrad screamed as the pain of high velocity compression waves tore through him; he went down. He crawled, and he saw Kaye dragging toward him, edging slowly over the buckling ground.

Debris, fine and large, pelted him with bullet-like force. Trees crashed in long, splintering cracks. He felt Kaye's hand in his. They were managing to regain their feet, fight out through a barrier of imprisoning branches. The sky was a seething tide of cloud-boiling smoke and flame. A blast of furnace air sucked into his lungs; he coughed, staggered, cried out.

Conrad felt his foot on something soft. He dropped down. He tugged Koehler's body partly from beneath a shattered tree trunk. Splinters of wood had pierced his stomach; he lay motionless. Koehler looked calm, sane for the first time since they had awakened on the ship; he was dead.

Kaye moaned, staggered as though blind. Swimming through only dim reality himself, Conrad pulled her after him in the direction Koehler had been leading them. Fires burst up around him, seared his face. An antelope sprang past, aflame, shrieking with its graceful neck twisted in an arc of pain.

Red rage, redder than the sky, rose in Conrad. There had seemed to be no possibility of war when they had left in the ship long ago. But man had always rationalized that way. After each orgy, he brushed away the vile film of its touch, and said, *"No more. We've outgrown it. We're too civilized now."*

Six hundred years ago they had said that, eighteen hundred thousand light years. But there were still men who could only destroy, forever; they knew nothing else. The extent of inherent characteristics had never been known. Perhaps the will-to-power, and destruction, was hereditary, and only death would cure it.

And it had evolved to form the City of Shiva with a few thousand star-vikings in galleys shaped like spaceships. Planets, solar systems, galaxies would be ravaged, pillaged, burned.

*Evil,* the little dreamed faces sang.

*Destruction. Destruction, forever.*

*The evil ones must die.*

But those voices were only dreams.

Dreams were naive, wishful thinking. The *Kshatriya* of Shiva,

289

under whatever label one chose, had conquered; Earth was going down into final destruction. Earth was only the beginning. *"The end of the beginning,"* someone had said long before, prophetic beyond his wildest nightmares.

CONRAD picked up Kaye, staggered forward; he slipped down a sharp incline. He felt the fire licking him; it was hungry. He dropped Kaye with sharp whines of horror, began beating at the flames around him. He knew agony, knew it in every screaming fiber of himself as he strained, half-blinded, choking, blinded, by smoke.

And then a curtain of smoke swirled aside and he saw the gleaming silver and black hull. It sat there, immobile, implacable, in the chaos of flames and crashing forest.

He sobbed. He dragged Kaye after him toward the smooth outline of the outer lock. Almost to it, he staggered, went down on his face. He crawled, dragging her along, though he wondered where the strength was, where the will. Visible effect, invisible because—

He was sinking down, giving up, and the door opened for him. Somehow he dragged Kaye inside, through the air-lock chamber, and through the inner door.

The ship trembled around him, and he knew it was blasting off. He tried to turn his head, but he couldn't. He was sprawled out on his back, stirring weakly. A voice, a thought, in his fevered mind ripped with fiery urgency.

*Remember, Conrad, the voice said. Remember. Fight, before it's too late! Remember us, Conrad, and the City of Light.*

And of course he did remember; because *they* wanted him to. Because there was something depending on the memory that he had to do—now; something of fearful urgency.

*      *      *

IT WAS a lonely-looking, isolated sun on the distant rim of the galaxy. They wakened, Kaye and he, and saw the small elfin petal faces swimming through high layers of air that glowed with soft pearly luminescence.

The ship's automatic pilot had thrown them into an orbit around a small world that crowded against a tiny red sun for warmth. Koehler and Hudson kept on sleeping; the alien things out there had awakened Kaye and Conrad only.

Their small petal faces beckoned, hovering in shimmering clouds on membranes as fluttering and delicate as tendrils of rainbow.

The great jeweled birds he remembered from that other dream returned, winging across an opaline sky. And the petal-faced people looked in at Conrad out of huge golden eyes flecked with iridescent colors that changed.

Conrad didn't know whether their bodies or their minds followed the petal-people down to their City of Light. Conrad felt no fear, only ecstasy; hand in hand with Kaye he floated down through warm cloud layers into that crystalline jewel city of light and song and jade pools.

Communication was mental, or perhaps something even more incomprehensible. It was thought-communication that was partly music, partly movement of color: but there was utter understanding.

And at that moment of mutual understanding—that was when the beauty shattered, became darkened as with stains of wretched ink; the music broke into dissonances and dischords.

For these were alien people who had forgotten ugliness; they lived, breathed, drank, floated in beauty; they swam in a vast sea of it. They were alien to all ugliness and fear and hate. And they found all that was alien to their beauty in the minds of their visitors.

Conrad felt their reactions, saw their round tiny mouths wide with silent fear. Wide golden eyes that seemed to cry.

*"They come from a diseased place; they will carry plagues of violence and death wherever they go."*

*"They are blind; they are lost in a nightmare of illusion."*

*"But there is hope for them!"*

*"Yes. There is hope."*

*"Their minds show that all of them are not evil; they are not all the same. They think they are the same, obsessed with the delusion of similarity. They are of many kinds; some are driven by thirsts that make them destroy and rule; others seek only truths, and these desire to build. There are others who have no positive impulses at all, but float ill a strange, unreal land of grey shadows."*

*"Yes, These two are not evil; they have come here to escape evil."*

*"But the two who did not awaken—one is evil and would destroy; the other knows only grey despair."*

Conrad could see Hudson, his eyes bright with dreams of conquest and the grandeur of power. He could see Koehler the lost, battling indecision, uncertainty, dreaming his futile dreams.

*"Their world trembles with the rule of evil beneath which the builders and seekers are helpless. The evil ones must be destroyed; their dark dreams are limitless as the stars are numbered in all the galaxies."*

*"These minds carry the ultimate plans of the evil ones. Read the plans of the evil ones here, the plans to destroy and conquer."*

*"Death!"*

*"Evil!"*

*"Destruction. Destruction, forever."*

*"We must send them back. Place the spark in their machine, for their machine is built for the spark. Erase our memory from their minds; they must not know until it is done. They must not be moved to act against our purpose. When the evil ones are destroyed, then these two may know; they may return to us then, should they desire."*

*"Yes. They may return to us."*

Conrad groaned as the far sounds died, vague murmurings, rippling, falling away in far sweet tinklings. He had remembered now because *they* had willed that he should remember. Voices from far Andromeda. M-32 in Andromeda.

And as Conrad struggled to his knees, he knew why this moment had been chosen for him to remember.

Silently, with deadly purpose, Hudson was creeping toward him across the small compartment. He had managed to break out of the suit locker. His intentions were obvious as he raised the alloy bar above his bloody head. He was going to kill; and he was going to wreck the ship.

That was why Conrad had remembered, so he would know what to do. He had to prevent Hudson's madness from wrecking the ship. It didn't want to be wrecked yet. It still had its assigned job to do.

## CHAPTER EIGHT

THERE WAS little about the murderer coming toward him that Conrad remembered. He clutched the bar in one hand. His eyes glared with fanatical purpose; his hands and face were bloody and bruised from crashing against the walls of his prison.

Hudson hesitated, face twitching, eyes roving with fear and hate. "You're in with the ship, Conrad. You're going to help the ship. Help *them* against your own species! That's what you'd like to do, but you won't. Unless I destroy this ship, it'll wipe out the human race. I don't want that, Conrad."

Kaye stirred, moaned gently, lifted an arm. Hudson swore at her. Conrad got one foot under him, managed to stand. Around him he could feel the steady throbbing of the ship's powerful motors. "You can't touch this ship, Hudson. It's too big for you."

"Traitor! Idiot!" snarled Hudson. "*They've* blinded you! I've known about them and their purpose; I've felt them. *They* drove me out of my mind, and had you lock me up. But I've won out. I'm stronger than *they* are. But you're insane, Conrad. Fighting with aliens against your own species! Insane!"

"Only against a part of humanity, Hudson—a part that should have been wiped out a long time ago. Men like you."

Hudson's eyes shifted; the ship throbbed, pulsed under them like a great heart.

He yelled suddenly, harshly. His muscles strained as against some invisible power, then he hurled himself at Conrad. The bar fell. Weakly Conrad managed to duck his head aside, but the heavy metal smashed into his shoulder. Numbness stiffened that arm, left it lifeless. He rolled aside on the grid mesh as the bar swung hungrily at his head. The bar sung past his ear, bounded from the bulkhead, Hudson swore, dropped the bar from hands momentarily paralyzed by the shock of metal on metal. Conrad pushed the bar with his good hand, sent it spinning across the mesh and under a low shelf.

Conrad got to his knees in time to meet Hudson's attack. They strained. Conrad felt dark waves of blind nausea billowing about him. He tried to pull those sweating bloody hands from his throat; but they were clamped there with a terrible kind of purpose.

Dimly he saw Kaye weaving toward them; then he heard a scream as Hudson kicked her savagely, sent her smashing back against the bulkhead. She sagged down slowly; and kept on sitting there.

RAGE GAVE Conrad enough strength to kick upward with his

knee. Hudson groaned, bent back, and his hands slipped away, returned as knotty madly beating clubs. Dull, jolting pain exploded in Conrad's head. He was falling back; he was lying there looking up at Hudson's heaving body leaning over him. It was a strange-looking body. It shimmered and wavered back and forth, got small, then large.

Conrad thought dully. *I can't move, I want to, but I can't.*

He thought of the ship, the ship that lived. It had intelligence; but it could only operate within the limitations of its bodily structure, and it was only a machine. It couldn't help him now. Could it even defend itself from an enemy who was *inside* of it? Conrad wondered. He realized that he knew nothing at all about the ship now that *they* had altered it. *They* had given it the 'spark'. What specialized function it had now, he couldn't know. Besides, he couldn't move to anything about it if he did know.

He watched Hudson's blurred figure dig the bar out from under the shelf, stand clutching it a moment hesitantly. Then he strode resolutely toward the panel leading into the corridor to the control chamber.

The man's intentions were inevitable. He would smash that automatic pilot. 'Kilroy's' hard vacuum brain case.

The panel slid open, Hudson started through, gripping the bar in his two hands.

The panel darted shut with quick determination; it closed on Hudson's neck. With a kind of triumphant horror Conrad heard the dying cries, saw the body jerking and kicking futilely in the vise of the door. The panel kept on closing. Conrad shuddered, managed to let his eyes fall shut. The panel had closed tight, closed completely.

The ship's acceleration fell off suddenly. He heard the air sighing against the ship's stressed skin. Wherever it had been going, it had gotten there.

Kaye disappeared from his restricted vision, returned. He felt the needle sink smoothly into his arm. He felt the sudden artificial fire brighten his blood, clarify his vision, shoot energy into his depleted system.

They avoided the horror blocking the floor by the panel, hurried into the control chamber.

Below them, through the observation screen, they saw the City of Shiva. But Conrad's first impression of the city had altered; through what had seemed before an indestructible fortress, chaos ran screaming through many layered tiers of crumbling grandeur.

The ship trembled around them. They saw the dropping rain spilling from beneath them onto the city. Gigantic mushrooming clouds of boiling dust and churning debris shot toward them. A white cloud plumed upward through the center of the blackness. Seconds later came a sustained awesome roar.

As the gigantic column of smoke writhed away, Conrad saw the half a thousand Ships of Shiva again; most of them remained untouched. More explosions leaped skyward, edging toward the ships.

The rows of great ships was the vortex of milling swarms of small dark specks. Then suddenly in a drowning cushion of blasting flame, one of the ships began a slow acceleration. From it, Conrad saw rockets emerge, small, dark and deadly. They plunged straight for their attacking ship.

"Five hundred to one," muttered Conrad.

"Come on, Kilroy!" Kaye said.

One by one the rocket bombs exploded harmlessly in the air. They felt their own ship bend away in an abrupt curve of tremendous speed. Conrad watched the rising ship of the *Kshatriya* arching toward them supported by a surging column of blue flame.

Their own ship bucked, recoiled, strained. Conrad fought dizziness that threatened blackness. His vision blurred, cleared with great effort of will. The rising spaceship ceased to exist in any visible form. It flamed in the sky like a miniature sun, then became nothing, nothing at all except shattered energy.

Their ship climbed up and up until the entire City and the grounded Ships of Shiva were all part of a small confused pocket in a bowl. They saw the gigantic cloud of falling bombs, dropping like metal rain. Then there was nothing below them but an incredible rising blossom of seething black, billowing gas. An awesome final roaring encompassed them, buffeted the ship.

They circled far over the Sierras, returned when the gas had partly cleared. Kaye gripped Conrad's arm. There was nothing down there now but a colossal blackened crater. It was huge, and of great depths with tendrils of aimless smoke curling out of it through clouds of fine debris. There was nothing else down there; not even small rubble. There was nothing to preserve even a memory of Shiva.

"It was a bad memory," said Conrad wearily. "It took a long time to get rid of it."

*       *       *

THE SHIP later set them down in a forest clearing, opened its doors for them. They walked away from it in the warm early-morning sunlight, turned looked at it. It wasn't moving. It wasn't saying anything. But it was alive. As they looked at it, the air-lock doors slid noiselessly open once more, and remained open—a question. The ship waited their answer.

Kaye's voice was thick. "Well—shall we? They invited us."

He didn't answer for a while. He remembered the City of Light. A City of incomparable wonder across nine hundred thousand light years. He shook his head. It wasn't that he didn't want to go. Yes, it was beautiful there, but it wasn't human. It wasn't for them; he felt the truth of that; and he knew that if they went to that City of Light again they would never come back to Earth. And Conrad knew that Earth would be a lot different now, a lot better. It had gotten rid of an old disease.

The ship knew; its doors closed. For protection they covered their eyes, stumbled back into the forest. When they opened their eyes and looked, the ship was gone.

They started walking down the valley slowly, along a small wild stream. Warmth from the water made a faint fog in the morning chill. They walked through areas that were blackened, burned; into others that were green and fresh.

"You were right, Alan. We belong with the Upinshads, mystical or not. No matter what the name is, they're on a right road."

Conrad shrugged. "I wouldn't know. I don't think we're quite so lost now, anyway. We're out of the woods."

"It would have been nice there, though, in the City of Light," said Kaye. "They saved us, and the Upinshads. But their main motive was self-preservation." She paused. "So much space and time, yet there was unity in it all, Alan!"

"I know." Conrad looked at the cloudless blue sky. "*They* knew human psychology, and they knew about the two basically different kinds of human pathology—both fanatical, both abnormal, but one good, the other destructive. They planned well, caught the forces of Shiva unawares with a terrifically weaponed ship the Kshatriya didn't even know existed. They would have found out about the ship too, if those people in Andromeda hadn't blanked out our minds so thoroughly."

"*They* looked in our minds, and they read the whole future of men. They saw what had to be done, and they did it, with terrible efficiency. And they made a genius and a hero out of 'Kilroy.' That's where they put the 'spark.' "

Conrad kicked a stone into the water. "Kilroy was close to being able to think anyway."

"Let's rest," suggested Kaye. "We've got lots of time from here on." She stopped, repeated the word. "Time."

Conrad stretched out on the bank of the stream with a long sigh. Kaye rested her head on his arm. They looked at the sky until their eyes closed.

"Time," he repeated sleepily. "Positive science and the concepts of Karma agree on that anyway. The unbroken consecutiveness of phenomena. Events most distant from one another, touch one another in—well—the fourth dimension? The unity, the 'oneness' of Karma, becomes a 'timeless fourth-dimension' of theoretical physics. This whole episode of ours—involving over six hundred years of so-called 'time' and 'space'—eighteen hundred thousands light years and generations of men. Yet for us it was a unity of consecutive consciousness."

Her voice stirred, half sleeping, "I'll bet poor Kilroy's lonesome. I wonder if he's—?"

Her voice trailed away. He looked at her worn face, relaxed now, soft and childlike in its cushion of brilliant hair.

He closed his eyes. Vaguely he heard birds calling. The splashing of fish in the stream. The soft droning of insects.

*"Babes in the woods—"*

# The Passion of Orpheus

*He was the last man...*
*and only he could make the music to bring life again.*

BROTHER HAMMOND pointed to the far horizon. "The City's in that direction, but I can't say how far, my boy. I've forgotten. But a long way. You'll take some cheese and pemmican biscuit, but you'll have to forage along the trail. It'll be dangerous—strange beasts and who knows what kind of men?"

A hawk dropped through the clouds and fell like a black stone past the high promontory on which Jonathan Scott stood.

Brother Scott said, "I've prayed all day, since you told me I was chosen to carry the Song, that the Divine Ultimate Reality behind appearances would guide me in safety."

"You were chosen, my boy, because you play the Song with greater passion than any of us." Brother Hammond's harsh brown robe flattened in the high wind against his bent, bony frame. He took the ritual cylinder from the cloth bag suspended from his neck. He turned a dial to refresh his mind with the Temple Voice. He was old, and sometimes he forgot the older words, "You hear the words, Jonathan, my boy? Even the Voices of the Temple are fading, growing old." The words were scratchy and distant.

Brother Hammond blinked and whispered. "It was so long ago when we Elders were sent from the Temple with the Song. Four hundred years— Longevity is a hard burden, my boy. Maybe you should be grateful you don't have to carry it."

Jonathan's shoulder-length blond hair glittered as he threw his head back to the sun. His eyes were bright with the ecstasy of anticipation. *He would carry the Song!*

The cylinder spoke in a kind of fading whisper:

*"The Word is the Song!"*

The two on the height repeated it, chanting softly:

"The Word is the Song."

*"The Song is the Word."*

"The Song is the Word."

*"The Song is the Key to salvation, for all hope and realization..."*

Jonathan's eyes were glassy and hot, and his throat felt dry.

"Sanctus...Sanctus...Spokesman of the Divine, Revealer of the Reality behind Appearances...the Integrating Principle of the Universe..."

So they listened and repeated the old, old instructions from the Temple...

Jonathan said goodbye to the people who lived in the Valley of the Preservers of the Song. A hundred and thirty in all—men, women and children—the workers coming in from the fields to their stone huts, the women preparing the evening meal in open stone furnaces to be served on flat stone plates.

At dusk he went to the small stone chapel at the end of the village street and played the Song. Only two articles were left of all the things the Elders had fled with from the Temple: the cylinder, and the small pipe organ with a thirty-two-note AGO pedal keyboard. Jonathan did not know what thirty-two notes meant, nor AGO. But he knew the Song.

Outside the chapel the other Brothers, neophytes, acolytes and workers, stood and sang while Jonathan played the vesper song. His head was angled back, his eyes closed. Sanctus...from the Divine Mass in D, as it was called—though what these symbols meant, no one knew any more. The Song had been recorded on the cylinder, and Jonathan had been able to play it as long as he could remember. Sanctus...composed from the substance of the Source, the stuff of true physical reality that underlies the world's diversity. Also, it was written by a very ancient hand of the Source, a Brother called Batoven.

And the next morning at dawn, Jonathan went through the pass and down out of the Valley toward the plains and the sea that would take him toward the City. It was in this direction, even if there was no City left now, that he would find the people waiting to be delivered by the Song. It was a long way, but Jonathan's strides were long and sure. His body seemed fired with a strength beyond that of anyone man, and he knew he was approaching the City and the Temple, the Key to the Source. He kept on walking and walking, but there was no City. He would find people though—somewhere, people and the Temple. Knowing this, he kept on walking.

He ate fruit from the forests and clean white flesh from the seashells along the shore by the warm-winded sea. At night, he sheltered behind rocks and built small intimate fires and lay dreaming

# The PASSION of

### MUSIC TO BRING LIFE AGAIN.

### HE WAS THE LAST MAN, AND ONLY HE COULD MAKE THE

### by Bryce Walton

to the stars, gentle warm south winds of promise whispering and calling him to the west.

Sometimes the white clouds drifting with him seemed like full-bodied women beckoning with white angel's arms and calling lips that faded into mist, and he would awake, sweating, wondering why he should be tempted so at this time. Sometimes in the moonlight when the sea foam curled to the white sand, little wisps of fog danced in slow motion round and round like mist-clothed girls, laughing and calling in most gentle voices. They too melted toward the west, leaving a trail for Jonathan of whispered urgencies and hints of choral voices singing his destiny to the Sun.

They are images of the Song, he thought. No one can understand the Song. It's something one only feels, and so he had to put it into pictures that he could understand.

He saw beasts he'd never seen before. The Valley was a locked land, except to men there who knew the way in and out of the Pass. It had been three hundred years since anyone had left the Valley. And maybe much longer than that since any kind of land-bound creature other than man had been in there.

None of these beasts bothered Jonathan. They seemed afraid of him. Maybe they had never seen a human before. The thought lowered some of the soaring flame that burned so strongly in him to an uneasy flickering.

Where were the people?

He sat down on the side of a hill where the grass waved in long rolling swells. It looked like a green ocean with blue shadows. He gazed in all directions and, although he could see a long way, he saw no signs anywhere that there were, or had ever been, human beings.

Digging the staff into the ground, he raised himself and began to walk again. His sandals had worn through and his feet were blistered. He was very tired. His muscles, even his bones, ached.

The Brothers had talked about what might have happened out here after that last Great War. Two things could have come to pass: the end of human life; or a return to some kind of primitive life, barbarism, resulting from a terrible lessening of humanity.

The first one didn't hold true. There was still human life in the Valley. But only a few could procreate, and the Elders' longevity was almost ended. To renew the great civilization of the past from that small group in the Valley seemed impossible. They were only there to preserve the Song that would purify and renew, would inspire whatever people remained to the celestial, heights of their true destiny. There would still be a future, for he had the Song and mankind could start afresh, free of the old curses of materialism, as the evil thought was called, and the demons of science that destroyed the values of the Soul.

He walked faster. He went along the sea and passed the black whispering weeds of the ebb, and he went inland where the oak trees thrust elbows at the wind, and bigger, blacker trees, smoldering with foliage, were dense with singing life.

His pulses rose with the Pacific surge, heavy with summer. Time and land flowed under his determined struggle. Sun and night met him and were friendly and he left them behind, while the east wind ran like glass under the peeping stars, and the south wind ploughed in the shadows of the trees.

And as he reached the further slope of a foothill at the base of high mountains, he found the City.

He stood there a long time, scarcely breathing, his crooked staff pressed sharply into the earth. It was the right City. There had been only one after the first Great War, one City for everyone in the Democritan half of the world. One City for the Asians in the other half of the world. That was the way the Brothers had told it to Jonathan, back long ago when he was younger and the Elders remembered things better. Two Cities were all that had been left.

And then the second Great War, though few knew much about that. Anyway, only the Democritan City would be left. If any people still lived, they would live here. So it was said. The Asians could not have survived the second and last Great War. The Brothers had said that only the democratic side could win the ultimate victory.

Jonathan felt weak in spite of the ecstasy that had flamed up inside of him at the sight of the City. His face felt flushed and hot. He couldn't eat anything.

He sat up there on the hill a long time and watched. There seemed to be no life below him in that vast fifty-square-mile area. Finally, Jonathan stumbled on down the hill, then stopped and sank to his knees. All the weariness of that journey seemed to settle around him. The sun's light on the City had distorted his vision. Now that he was closer he could see he had filled in terrifying vacancies and gaps and holes with his own dreams, his preconceived dreams of what the City would be like.

Actually now he could see that there wasn't much of a City left. A burning sensation of fear was growing in his chest. A kind of dark and terrifying vacancy threatened to open before him, and he seemed to cling to little rays of light like a man about to fall through a glowing net into an abyss.

Bones, he thought. Shiny, brilliantly shiny metal bones, polished and still. Shiny metal joints like giant elbows twisting up from cratered ground, twisted brokenly as far as Jonathan could see, into the narrowing valley that wound back with the river from the sea into the mountains. Across the river a few strands of glistening cable hung motionless like dried tendons. And here and there, the ragged ends of fused and melted metals protruded from the water and the further shore.

*"And the priest will be fire,"* the Asians were reported to have said. *"And blood the witness."*

Grass grows where the flame flowered. Metal, the burned-out chemicals of the demons' tools, lay in the shattered crucible of the devil science...

No life at all, Jonathan whispered, except small furry animals with tails, and the birds.

The landscape seemed to turn like a wheel under Jonathan and the sun dimmed. Sweat was damp and sticky under the coarsely woven cloth of his robe. His heart thundered in his temples and he longed to lie down in the cool grass and sleep—here within sight of the greatest sleep of all.

Peace...peace, the heir of dead desire...

He lay there feeling the insolent quietness of steel and stone. Above him, the clouds raced northward as the river raced below. Every fiber of his body trembled with faintness. The people he could have saved had all bubbled up in the violence of fire and become ash in evil metal...

"Hello. Why do you wear such funny clothes?"

He did not look up at once. He hardly trusted his senses now, but he'd heard no one approach. Yet it was a real voice, for now he saw a shadow bend softly before him. A young woman's voice, gently sweet but with an undertone of deep feeling and sympathy. It was almost as though her voice reflected his own momentary despair.

"Are you resting? Can you hear me?"

"Yes." He saw her, and he got up quickly. He forgot his weakness as he stared. He saw a nobly formed woman, erect and browned and strong as a new tower of stone. Her features were sculptured into a strong dark face: straight nose with a high bridge, firm wide eyes, that gazed down with open and steady curiosity into his.

She was too much like those mist-draped, forbidden women of his dreams. She wore a slightly concealing, brightly-colored cloth around high breasts and flat, almost boyish hips. The thin cloth fluttered in the hushing and creaking of the wind.

An inward pressure grew in his throat and he could not speak for a while, even in a whisper. Then he realized in a tide of emotion what this really meant, to him, to the old, old plan of the Temple.

He grabbed her shoulders. "There are more of you—! I mean more women, men, children—."

"There are many of us around here. Children—?"

He said "children" again, and she shook her head. Maybe they had some other term—.

She put her hands on his arms, ran them softly up toward his shoulders and down again, and smiled. Her teeth shone and her eyes were brighter now as though reflecting his own growing excitement.

"But there doesn't seem to be anyone living there." He pointed at the City.

"No. Maybe no one ever has lived there. Who would want to?"

"Where do you live?"

"I'll show you. You need rest and sleep and food." She took his hand. Her warmth and softness reached out to him in his weakness and his loneliness. The longing that ached in him at the same time made his hands tremble with guilt. Nothing should interfere with a Brother's devotion to the Song and the Temple and the Work.

"I like you," she said lightly. "I could love you. You're very appealing. You're bigger and your hair is brighter and your shoulders broader than any man among us."

His face reddened. No woman among those in the Valley would ever speak to him, to any Brother, this way. Tingling excitement he couldn't control ran up his arm like a chill, and the sound of the ocean was like blood in his ears.

They walked slowly down the sloping hill and moved under the shadows of the mountains in the sunny afternoon. They went through sweet high grass filled with the scents of summer. They stepped among red, purple and golden blossoms that wavered in the warm winds.

"Who are you?" she asked again.

He tried to tell her, but he stumbled and would have fallen had she not held him up.

"You're too tired and ill now to talk," she said. "You must have walked such a long while. We'll talk about it later. After you've rested. You will rest and sleep a long time and grow strong again."

But he kept on trying to explain. She didn't seem interested, not really. She seemed only to be trying to be interested. But she just didn't understand. Few of the significant words he used were even familiar to her. This he realized as he whispered to her.

She just looked at him and her eyes had nothing in them that he could recognize, except a kind of passionate sympathy which had nothing to do with what he said, but seemed only her attempt to share with him feeling and hope and longing and need.

"I just don't know about these things," she said again. "It only seems to me that you aren't happy. Everyone should be happy. There's nothing else."

His toes dragged a little as he staggered beside her. They went much nearer to the City, past the edge of vast piles of shiny rubble, circling back again toward another sector of the foothills. Birds floated from girder to stone and sang strange prolonged and varied patterns of song.

The Song, Jonathan thought, as the world blurred and seemed to shift crazily under his feet. Words aren't adequate. The Song is the Key. The Word is the Song. He would find the Temple, which was indestructible. When he played the Song, Syndra and the others who heard it would understand. She had said her name was Syndra. That was an odd name.

He rested and slept, drifting through a timeless land. The people had seemed to be numerous enough, if he remembered correctly, and they lived in caves in the side of the hills under the big granite overhang, deep cool caves with open fires in the front.

Sometimes he awoke slightly in the easeful darkness of the cave and always he heard the bright, starry laughter outside. He couldn't remember hearing anything else our there except that free, abandoned laughter, like birds' voices. And he remembered also the soft, careful whispers when they came into the cave where he lay.

Syndra seemed to stay there beside him all the time. Whenever he awoke slightly, she was there looking at him, her eyes always under-standing, always reflecting whatever he felt. Joy, lethargy, half-sleep, dream, those moments of forbidden desires, brief looping instances of sadness and shame, times of exhilaration—whatever fleeting mood was his, he saw it reflected in her face and eyes, in the posture of her body, in the soft, caressing movements of her hands.

And once, when he had dreamed of something he couldn't remember, and awoke startled by his own fear that was there too, in her face and eyes. Fear—and he shut his eyes at once.

In daytime there was sun, muted and streaked with dust that gave a cozy, lazy warmth to the cave. And sometimes at night when he awoke for a while, still half-dreaming, her body was etched in moonlight, moving a little, sighing gently. And beyond her, through the cave's mouth, he could see the enormous films of moonlight trailing down from the mountain heights. Space, vastness, and the distant shining ocean lay light like a haze. Little vapors gleamed and little darknesses marked wood and valley, bur the air was always warm and soft and contenting—and there was always Syndra in the moonlight.

Sometimes at night the wind raved in the dark, and the fire-shad-ows flapped, and the ocean battered against the rock. And once thunder walked down the canyons over the cave mouths and he saw her still there, sitting, looking into his face and eyes.

They were beautiful people, Jonathan discovered later, when he was well and strong again. But of course it was all wrong. He walked with Syndra among the caves, up and down the hills above the City. It seemed blasphemous somehow. But he felt a peace, a contentment, he had never felt before. And he knew it was wrong. It was a kind of paganism, and it wasn't right.

There were no machines—that part of it was good—none of the gadgets of the devil, no evil tools of the destructive demons of science. Not even a wheel. These people had intelligence enough and the potentiality to learn. But they had no drive in that direction. They were just happy, thoroughly satisfied, and of this Jonathan approved and was very glad.

He explained to Syndra as best he could why this pleased him, and he kept hoping that she or someone among these people would understand. Science, materialism, had destroyed civilization in that First Great War. It had been misused, it was evil, because people had worshiped it and almost destroyed themselves. After that war, the City State of Democritas had gotten on the right road, away from the worship of materialism. They had put philosophy, religion, psychology, as it was called then, ahead of materialism. Now these words were almost meaningless. But the spirit, the understanding was there, even if he couldn't put it into words. It was all in the Song that put truth and final understanding into the human heart.

The Democritans had combined science and religion into one governing force. The scientists and priests became one. Religion and philosophy were the motivating forces for science. Science was only a method in the development of the soul, never an end in itself. All this the Brothers knew who had fled from the Temple to preserve the Song. So now Jonathan knew.

The Asians had been on the wrong road. They had not learned. They had been strictly material, coldly scientific, believing in any means to justify the end. They had hated the Democritans and prepared to destroy them for purely cold and, to them, scientific reasons.

So the Democritans had had to stay prepared for a long time to meet the Asian threat. And then the second and last Great War...

What had really happened? These people of Syndra's had no idea, seemed to have no cultural memory. Some kind of mass shock, Jonathan thought. They stand still. They're afraid to move back, and afraid to move forward. But I have the Song, and that will show them the way.

He had to find the Temple. There, science and religion had been combined. From the Temple came all directions, guidance, inspiration, from the scientist-priests. Science alone wasn't enough. Religion alone wasn't enough. The Democritans had been on the right road, and now he, Jonathan Scott, could preserve that road, see it widen out and out into a glorious future...

But he had to find the Temple. He asked about the Temple and tried to explain what it meant. No one knew. He was frightened and he didn't know why. He was glad because they had not gone along the suicidal pathway of strict materialism. But they had no religion either. No religion at all. And this made him afraid.

He saw no children anywhere, and this frightened him, too. But no one knew what he was talking about when he tried to ask them about children. They had never seen humans smaller than themselves. Love, sex, these things they understood thoroughly—up to the point of procreation. That they could not comprehend.

Everyone seemed about the same age. He saw no old people. No one was ever sick that he could see. No one was ever dissatisfied, or irritated. No quarrels, no violence or hostility. There were just a round of simple duties to keep the small social units, somewhat like a family, functioning. And the rest of the time was for dancing and laughter and drifting leisure. It was like being on a clear and warm-scented river that had started nowhere and was going nowhere, and whose currents were barely determinable.

No science. No religion. Nothing. No awareness of anything beyond the visible and immediate. No yesterdays. No tomorrows.

He was glad he wouldn't have to convert them. He had the Song and he would find the Temple and that would be enough. They had no false beliefs from which to be converted. You couldn't educate them because they had no understanding of his words. But the Song could make them know, the Song went directly to the heart.

He started walking, one midafternoon, down the hill toward the City. Syndra ran after him. He knew he had to find the Temple. A kind of lonely, desperate panic came over him as he stopped on a height and looked downward and Syndra's face reflected how he felt. He could be with all these gentle loving people, and still be more alone than if he were actually physically alone, for they seemed always to share what he felt. If he was sad, someone should be happy. If he was suddenly afraid, someone around should show courage.

He walked faster. The Temple seemed suddenly more important than it ever had before. No children. No old people. No science. No religion. No movement forward. No memory backward... It was meaningless on the surface, but all the answers were in the Temple.

"But we've never been in that City," said Syndra, running behind him. "Why should anyone go in there? It's ugly. There's not much fruit to gather. And no animals worth hunting. I can't really believe people lived in there once..."

"I've explained," said Jonathan, somewhat exasperated. "That's what happened to those buildings. People lived there, then they had a war, a terrible war. And the buildings were destroyed. It wasn't always this way."

"But if they liked living there why did they destroy it?"

Jonathan sighed. "Total war..." How could he explain it? They wouldn't understand mass warfare; they couldn't. Even the faintest hostility between individuals was unknown amongst them.

He turned. He felt embarrassed as she stood up close to him, and he could see the warm, intimate light in her eyes. "Don't go," she said softly. "Stay with us...with me."

"I must find the Temple," he said desperately. "Look here...you go back. I may be gone a long time..."

She shook her head. She seemed in pain, as though torn between some strong desire to do what he asked, and something else—and yet it all seemed only a reflection of how he felt, even the desire for—

So he guessed that she sensed also how much he really wanted her to stay with him. That also made him afraid. He did not trust his own sense of right and wrong any more.

He turned and started walking rapidly, moving away from the caves, following a narrow, winding pathway toward the valley and the ruins of the City. She followed him. She did not say anything, now.

There was so much that the Brothers who had been sent to the Valley with the cylinder, the organ and the Song, had not known—or had forgotten. In four hundred years one could forget. And—maybe it had been longer. Sometimes Jonathan wondered if the Brothers really knew now how long they had lived in the Valley.

The uneasy flickering began again in his stomach. There was something frightening about all this, strange and inexplicable, something invisible and everywhere that crowded down around him. He walked faster.

The Temple had the answers. There, he would play the Song. Somewhere was the Temple. It had all the answers.

It was a long time since they had left the hillside and the caves. Jonathan lay on his side, his hands extended upward along the shattered rubble of stone and steel. Behind him, Syndra sat, her head bowed. In the hot sun's glare, they were burned and glazed, thin and soiled. They looked like two figurines fallen from a shattered height, somehow miraculously preserved.

He whispered through cracked lips. "That's—that's the Temple. See…"

She looked up slowly and nodded, but there was nothing in her eyes except the same weariness that he now felt. Beyond that there was no understanding. It seemed as though she was trying hard to react as fully as he did, to fill her heart and face and eyes with the ecstasy that Jonathan felt.

"It's so big, Jonathan. It's…like a mountain."

Far beyond the inland part of the City they had found it, high, very high up the side of it mountain, so that it dominated the entire valley clear to the sea. It overlooked the entire fifty square miles of ruins, yet itself was untouched by time or violence.

They had seen it the evening before, shining down through the sun's glare, in a far, high splendor of shifting hues. But Jonathan had not believed it then. A mirage, he had thought, an image created by the longing in his heart.

But now he knew the Temple was real. It had loomed larger as they came close, until now its spires and steeples and columns and glistening domes seemed to tower higher than the eye could reach, stretching up beyond the clouds.

The light reflecting from it sent an incredible renewed strength into Jonathan, lifted him to his knees, then his feet. Above him alabaster steps circled up and up. Half a mile wide at the base, they narrowed in graceful spirals, disappearing somewhere above their heads in a blaze of promising color.

The awful weakness of fatigue was gone. Now he could not feel anything. His feet seemed to float as he went up the winding steps. There was no world beyond this world of the Temple, and no sounds except the Song that was stirring for release in his brain and in his eager fingers.

Far away it seemed he could hear Syndra calling, calling, but he couldn't be sure. He climbed faster, up and up. Cloud mists raveled round him and the choir music of all his dreams fevered in his brain.

Syndra had not recognized this towering structure as the Temple. No one had told him. But he knew. He knew as a flower knows and opens to the sun.

He reached dizzy; vertiginous height, up steps worn deep by the climbing of many feet for many hundreds of years. They would climb again. He would play the Song. The Song would lead all to the final glory that had long been man's due—freedom to act without the age-old curse of the devil science and its materialistic demons of destruction. There would be no Asians to express an attitude of destruction and mar the bright highway of human progress. There would be no science, with its blinding values, to race too far ahead of philosophy and life.

He seemed to hear Syndra calling from somewhere that seemed very far away.

"Jonathan— *Jonathan!*"

He did not look back.

"Jonathan—don't leave me! *I'm afraid!*"

He glanced back as he reached the top step, and saw her. She seemed far away and small. He was beyond feeling what he knew he felt for her. He was larger, a part of something far greater than two people and whatever emotions they might have for each other.

He turned back toward the Temple. He couldn't hear her any more. He couldn't see anything but the divine building, looming up like a mountainside across a vastness of sun-splashed mosaic. Fountains stood lifeless between soaring columns and purple shadows. Rising up before him, the Temple seemed to be a mile wide, perhaps wider, Jonathan thought, for it curved away on both sides into the clouds and a haze of distance.

He looked up. He could not see the top of the Temple because of clouds, but steeples and towers and columns climbed higher and higher. They seemed to glitter and shiver and Jonathan felt he was floating on endless radiance as from millions of shards of multicolored glass. He felt an ecstatic suffocation, a blinding joy as though he somehow was becoming a part of the light, a part of ineffable ecstasy of love and adoration and the eternal Passion or the spheres.

He walked toward the giant doors while the red rays of sunset reflected down from the clouds. The doors were fifty feet high. They seemed to expand as he approached, his shadow growing small, seeming to diminish slowly in size until he felt like a small stone in the middle of a vast plain. He was like a man caught up in a far world designed for giants.

The dying sun's rays found new life and rebounded from the metal doors. A deeper inner light seemed to come out of the metal. He kept on walking and his mind and body were pulsing with the rhythm of the Song. He went on through the doors that had not opened. No human hand had ever opened those doors, but he was through—like dissolving oneself in glass, walking through water one could inhale like high fresh air.

From so far away he seemed to hear Syndra's voice in a wild and fading cry. "Jonathan...where are you?"

And then from even further away he heard what might have been a beating of fists against giant doors.

There was a strange inner tingling in him as he walked down the endless aisle, between the rows of worshipers' seats that curved away and out of sight in both directions. Bars of light streamed down from somewhere so high Jonathan could not find it. But he was aware of the distant arch that rose far above him, fusing and meeting somewhere like the archway of the sky.

So long, so long, he thought, since the thousands had come here to receive the light and the Song. And now he alone—no, not alone. He walked with ghosts, invisible shadows of the thousands upon thousands who had once come here. He walked with the memories of centuries. He stopped and sank slowly to his knees.

The golden, shining pipes of the organ rose up and up forever like giant columns. He thought of that tiny instrument in the Valley and compared it with this, and he began to tremble. It was too big, it was vast, it was inconceivable— Yet there was no one else to play. He thought, but I'm not worthy...not worthy...

And yet, the doors had melted for him. That was the sign. And there was no one else. He went up the carpeted walkway past the dais, past the giant console and shining instrument board, and sat down. He seemed surrounded by pedals and keys and pipes.

He lifted his hands. They hung poised. They seemed like the hands of someone else. Or not like any hands, but dissociated instrument of a will greater than one man, or all men. His hands fell.

His eyes were closed. He forgot where he was, or what he had been. The tides of sound carried him away in a surging flood. Starting from somewhere deep down and spreading upward and outward...yet it seemed as though the music were being called inward through his fingers; it was as if he were drawing the music from afar, from the distant star points of time and space.

Muted and slow at first, the symphonic voice mounted thunderously, and he was floating on the mounting tides, breathing it as the swell rose higher, throbbing in great deep-throated sound. Each separate nerve cell of his brain flamed, and the stars fell from their place and left their cry in his mind.

He drifted on the upsurging fountains of the wines of sound, and everywhere shiny lights and walls kept slipping and drifting around and faces were smiling in front of him. And he was aware then of other sounds, under the music, a throbbing and grinding, a clicking and clacking and roaring and thundering, a meshing and crackling and shifting of weight.

He could see his hands looming large and white and pale and wet, but they were no longer playing. The music continued, growing, roaring, racing, rising, thundering, rippling. And then he knew.

Jonathan was on his hands and knees, crawling, until he lay there where the colored light came down in pastel patterns that shifted and glowed on the pallor of carpets. His mind reeled with remembered ecstasy...no, not remembered, for he had never known. But he knew now, as though he was remembering. Voices, voices in the brain; faces, eyes...

Somehow the magnificent music of clear light had suddenly turned into the forgotten corridors of the past. Burning sensations of fear grew in his chest. A coldness too, the coldness of certainty and infinite wisdom, for now he knew.

The Temple knew everything. And now Jonathan knew everything. All at once, all that the Temple knew, he knew.

His eyes felt hot. The vastness of the place was suddenly chokingly hot. Memory rose in him like a volcano bursting with flame. And centuries, with lightning feet, marched suddenly, thoroughly and completely through his brain. No—not HIS memory. The Temple's memory...the Temple's memory. It had known everything, and it had never forgotten.

And now he was part of the Temple, so it was as though he too remembered. He had had a curious inner vision of the mind, and the intoxication of swooping motion through space and time, a kind of ultimate freedom. But that was only briefly; now it was gone, and he was part of the Temple.

He knew how it was. At first you need only know the Song, the complex but meaningful notes and rhythm and sequence of the Song. It was a Key. It made you one with the Temple, you were in harmony with it, the doors dissolved for you, and when the organ sounded, the machinery started.

He screamed—once.

Machinery...

He got to his feet and ran wildly up the endless aisle toward the doors. He had started the Organ and he knew he could not stop it. It would continue forever now. To stop it required another Song—a Song he had never learned.

Maybe it had gotten lost somewhere in time or in the brains of dead men. But the other Song was gone. And the Temple itself didn't know it—for the Temple had not been built to stop itself from functioning. It could repair itself, keep itself going forever, now that the harmonies of sound were established. But it could never stop itself.

He had known only the Song, and now he knew everything the Temple knew—but that wasn't enough.

He went through the doors that dissolved for him like liquescent glass. He ran after Syndra across the plains of mosaic no longer splashed with sunlight, but with lights that seemed more powerful in the night than ever the sun had been by day.

The entire valley blazed with whiteness as though caught in the eternal glare of celestial flame. The fountains murmured and frothed with life. The vines were turning green on the walls.

"Syndra! *Syndra!*"

She did not turn. She did not say anything, and then she disappeared far ahead of him, down the winding steps that led into the City.

He ran on to the edge of that tremendous height and looked down. He fell forward. He put his hands up and felt his tears squeezing through his tightly locked fingers.

"Syndra...Syndra...I can't stop it. I can't put things back again.

It's all too big. Syndra..."

But then he knew that the shape, the shadow, fading, diminishing down the alabaster steps, was not Syndra. Not any more. It was something else, something that reacted as part of the workings of the Temple. And now it would always be that way, forever and ever...

He got up and looked down. He watched the valley begin to move. Everything had been channeled in and out of the Temple. It was more than a place of communion with the Divine Reality behind appearances. It was also a machine of incalculable complexity.

And the vesper Songs of the Organ had kept it functioning until that last terrible day when the Asian bombs had come. But the Temple had been ready for that too. It was a synthesis of all knowledge, and it had been conditioned to handle any and all emergencies. It had the power to protect itself. And it had had enough power, while protecting itself, to destroy the Asians: their ships, their City and every last quivering cell of life they possessed.

It was all so logical, Jonathan thought, as he stood there and watched the valley below throbbing and pulsing and beginning to assume a strange and meaningless pretense of living. Science and religion and philosophy, all thought, combined in the minds of men, channeled outward from one center of final control. Science, religion, philosophy, psychology—all fused. And the scientist-priests who knew the Song were thereby one with the Temple, part of the harmony of its complex structure.

The scientist-priests who had remained here to work with the Temple until the end had sent a few of their numbers away, to preserve the key that would set the Temple to acting again, when the enemy had been destroyed. The Temple had always been alive, only waiting, waiting for someone to activate the sensitive relays...

All around him, Jonathan felt the massive murmuring. Below, under the sun-bright glare of giant floodlights, he could see the valley beginning to grow.

Science, like religion, had always been based on faith—faith in the truth of the mind's logical processes; faith in the ultimate ability to explain the world; faith that the laws of thought would someday become the laws of things. But science came to realize that the scientific picture of the world was only partial—a product of the scientist's special ability in mathematics. They also realized the need for aesthetic and moral values and religious motives, and intuitions of experience.

Science and religion found their goals to be the same. They no longer took separate paths. Everything fused. The Temple, the final synthesis of all FAITH.

Jonathan knew all this. He knew all the Temple knew. He knew a lot more than he even cared to think about now. He stood there, unable to move, a paralysis crowding down around him, and watched the valley, directed by the reactivated intricacies of the Temple, pretend to come alive.

Under the great lights, he saw the giant, sleek machines dart out of suddenly revealed openings in the hills. Giant streamlined cranes, tractors, loading cars, streamed in and down from all directions, everything working according to preconceived plans, electronically intelligent, operating out of the complexity of ten million binary digits of directive brain.

With fantastic speed, the thing grew. The metal frames began to go up, sprays of plastic and metal and steel spun through the air like monstrous cobweb skeins of silver. As though sentient with life of its own, a bridge began projecting itself across the river. Rockets shot skyward and rockets came down. Monorails began growing up and up, looping and curving, and then small silver dots began speeding like specks of quicksilver along the lines of metal.

Tubeways, skyways, tiers upon tiers, sprang outward in all directions, making first a mad meaningless maze that suddenly joined to form a perfect pattern—one that kept growing, gaining speed, expanding outward, shooting higher.

He could see the streams of tiny human figures moving in even, darting lines, like ants to and from a mound. The figures streamed out of the caves, down from the hills, moving in orderly, swift rivers that merged and became one with the lines and curves and loops of the City.

A giant explosion of constructions streamed red fire. Metallic dust sifted across the light-splashed mosaic and settled on Jonathan's robe, on his face, and coated his hair with fine silver spray. He saw the bigger machines streaming out. The smaller machines had been busy building bigger machines. The bigger machines were expanding the City, tearing and chewing at the hills, blasting down the faces of the mountains.

They would build bigger machines. The bigger machines would build bigger machines. There was no way to control it, Jonathan knew. No one knew the Song that could control anything. He had known only the Song that began, that began everything...everything, everything all over again.

Except now it wasn't quite the same. Maybe that part was wrong. That part about the workers. Maybe that part of the Temple's knowledge was wrong, distorted perhaps. He couldn't believe it.

He ran down the steps. He got lost. He found himself caught up in the swirling, growing, grinding pattern. But somehow he kept moving, sometimes up to dizzy heights in tiny, darting, bright capsules, sometimes hurtling along subterranean tubeways.

He looked at every worker he saw. Some of them he partly recognized, but of course they weren't the same. They walked, ran, worked, with a terrible intentness.

The Temple was right. They weren't the same. Maybe not. But if he could find Syndra, talk to her, then he would know for certain.

He found her sitting in front of a machine. Around her were walls of dials, knobs, meters, needles, voltage amplifiers, and pulsing power tubes.

He touched her shoulder. "Syndra," he whispered. It wasn't loud enough. The whisper was drowned by the murmuring, whirring and humming of the valley and the City growing.

"Syndra," he said, louder this time, bending down.

She looked up. Hot pain seared his throat. There was nothing in her eyes now but a glazed and glassy efficiency, like the luster of the metal knobs and dials and amplifiers.

He backed away. He did not call her name again. She would have a number, and he didn't know what it was. And anyway, it wouldn't matter now. Robotics of some kind—he hadn't been able to understand that completely from the Temple. Perhaps he had forgotten because it wasn't quite worth remembering, something no one would care to remember. Whatever their labels were, they were merely imitations of life.

But they had seemed so human, all of them, he thought. And that too had a reason, everything had a reason. They all had certain tasks to do in the rebuilding, in the functioning of the City in peace and war. They were made to serve, to reflect the needs of men.

*But there were no more men here.*

Only the reactivated commands of men long dead. No men to control the key harmonies of sound.

Now Syndra's people only helped rebuild. No power of the Asians had been able to destroy them. Perhaps they were, like the Temple, indestructible. And they had been constructed to live on, even when the Temple stopped, or to lie quiescent on some dim, low stage of activity, appearing like human beings—so much so no one would ever know they were not humans at all.

That too had had a reason, Jonathan knew. To fool the Asians, to disguise the efficacy of the Asian's destructive force, to divert, to have certain psychological effects—it didn't matter now. There were no more Asians. The Temple knew that. No more Asians. No more Democritans. *At least, not here.*

Jonathan managed to escape from the rapidly expanding complexity of the City. He went back up over the hills and down again to the sea, and started on the long road back to the Valley of the Preservers of the Song.

He remembered the laughter of Syndra and the others in the caves, the sunny days and the long dreamy nights. He remembered her face and her eyes, and how human, how real they had been to him. He remembered the compassion, the sympathy, the depths of understanding. But then, they had been made for empathy. Perfect empathy.

Behind him receded the glaring sun-lights of the valley and the growing City. He looked back and saw the entire horizon glowing, a thin, twinkling white line, as if a new and frightful white-hot sun were coming up for a new and incredible dawn.

And then he walked on through the moonlight until the line thinned and finally went out altogether.

*If I had never played the Song to the City*, he wondered. Would Syndra and the rest somehow have become human after all? How human had they been, really? That strange and haunting light he had seen in Syndra's eyes, it had seemed so real, so precious— He shook off the thought, and with it the terrible sickness that threatened to engulf him, the sickness of the machines, of a world filled only with machines in a macabre imitation of life.

He walked faster through the moonlight, back along the sands. Maybe there was a way. He would—he must—make a way! He would find out! The Elders had lived too long, had grown senile, forgotten much and lost the ability to interpret and translate. But on that cylinder they had preserved so long there could very well be the answer. The other Song, some way to stop what he had started. He had to stop it. It would never stop unless he stopped it. The buildings would expand in all directions, keep climbing higher and higher, moving over the world like some looping metallic plague.

And if it was not on the cylinder then it was there in someone's soul. Of the few who remained in the Valley, the few human beings that remained in the world, someone must know—some old man, some child, some woman. Somewhere among them there must remain a spark of memory, of soul. If he could find it, nourish it—his heart leaped with hope. He was still human, after all. And somewhere he would find a fellow-soul to help him start a new human race.

He walked faster. There were a few left in the Valley, and they would find a way to stop the rising, mounting tumult of the Song.

## THE END

*If you've enjoyed this book, you will not want to miss these terrific titles…*

## ARMCHAIR SCI-FI & HORROR DOUBLE NOVELS, $12.95 each

**D-1**   **THE GALAXY RAIDERS** by William P. McGivern
**SPACE STATION #1** by Frank Belknap Long

**D-2**   **THE PROGRAMMED PEOPLE** by Jack Sharkey
**SLAVES OF THE CRYSTAL BRAIN** by William Carter Sawtelle

**D-3**   **YOU'RE ALL ALONE** by Fritz Leiber
**THE LIQUID MAN** by Bernard C. Gilford

**D-4**   **CITADEL OF THE STAR LORDS** by Edmond Hamilton
**VOYAGE TO ETERNITY** by Milton Lesser

**D-5**   **IRON MEN OF VENUS** by Don Wilcox
**THE MAN WITH ABSOLUTE MOTION** by Noel Loomis

**D-6**   **WHO SOWS THE WIND...** by Rog Phillips
**THE PUZZLE PLANET** by Robert A. W. Lowndes

**D-7**   **PLANET OF DREAD** by Murray Leinster
**TWICE UPON A TIME** by Charles L. Fontenay

**D-8**   **THE TERROR OUT OF SPACE** by Dwight V. Swain
**QUEST OF THE GOLDEN APE** by Ivar Jorgensen and Adam Chase

**D-9**   **SECRET OF MARRACOTT DEEP** by Henry Slesar
**PAWN OF THE BLACK FLEET** by Mark Clifton.

**D-10**   **BEYOND THE RINGS OF SATURN** by Robert Moore Williams
**A MAN OBSESSED** by Alan E. Nourse

## ARMCHAIR SCIENCE FICTION CLASSICS, $12.95 each

**C-1**   **THE GREEN MAN**
by Harold M. Sherman

**C-2**   **A TRACE OF MEMORY**
By Keith Laumer

**C-3**   **INTO PLUTONIAN DEPTHS**
by Stanton A. Coblentz

## ARMCHAIR MASTERS OF SCIENCE FICTION SERIES, $16.95 each

**M-1**   **MASTERS OF SCIENCE FICTION, Vol. One**
Bryce Walton: "The Highest Mountain" and other tales

**M-2**   **MASTERS OF SCIENCE FICTION, Vol. Two**
Jerome Bixby: "One Way Street" and other tales

Made in the USA
Las Vegas, NV
24 April 2021